Criti<

MW01611282

"Scorpio Rising does for astrology what *The Da Vinci Code* did for art history. The rapid pace and constant tension will please thriller fans, and if you enjoy a good crime story with a protagonist who gives you a unique glimpse into a specialized field, then this book is for you." ~ *Suite101 Book Reviews*

"Scorpio Rising by Alan Annand, the first of his New Age *Noir* series, is a gripping murder mystery with a Hitchcockian twist. Private investigator Axel Crowe is an appealing and upstanding protagonist who uses astrology, palmistry and other esoteric techniques to solve crimes. With bits of Vedic wisdom sprinkled throughout, this book is an enjoyable read and an engrossing narrative." ~ *The Mountain Astrologer*

"Annand is a terrific mystery writer. *Scorpio Rising* sweeps you along in a cross-fire of interlocking plot-avalanches, with vivid characters, a luminous sense of place, and no shortage of carnage. But to me, Annand's greatest strength is the way he weaves a convincing working knowledge of a metaphysician's world view into each page. Readers of synchronicities and omens will sense, not only a kindred spirit at work here, but a genuine teacher." ~ Steven Forrest (author of *The Inner Sky, Stalking Anubis* & other books)

"Incredible power as a poet in prose – in the style of Hammett and Hemingway – to describe places and people. A page-turner for sure, and a seriously magnificent piece of work." ~ Michael Lutin (astrology columnist for *The Huffington Post*)

"Annand has done a masterful job in creating a whole new type of hero – astrologer as detective – with a believable character who is personable, intelligent, and multi-faceted in his approach to crime solving. It's a 5-star combination!" ~ *North American Jyotish Newsletter*

"Rarely do we find a mystery novel featuring a character who is an astrologer/palmist with an active spiritual life. Axel Crowe, the brilliant investigator of Annand's *Scorpio Rising*, is Agent 007 for the New Age noir set. I was entertained, intrigued and delighted to be along for the cosmic ride."
~ *Astrology Toronto*

"If you like thrillers and detective stories, this one is a terrific read. It's fast-paced and has plenty of twists and turns – as well as enough astrology and palmistry – to keep you flipping the pages. I enjoyed it immensely."
~ *National Council of Geocosmic Research Newsletter*

"*Scorpio Rising* is an engaging mystery with twists and turns that keep you reading all the way to the end. Axel Crowe is a new character on the mystery scene, a quick study when presented with a baffling murder because he combines his own intuitive methods with a thorough understanding of police and crime lab procedures the world over."
~ *Horoscope Guide*

"In *Scorpio Rising*, Alan Annand has written a fascinating murder mystery, with great characters and plot. I can't wait to read about (hero) Axel Crowe's next adventure, and how he solves a crime using astrology, palmistry and other natural oracles. This is a wonderful book for anyone with even a little knowledge of astrology and palmistry to enjoy!"
~ Ray Merriman (author of *Evolutionary Astrology*)

"*Scorpio Rising* by Alan Annand is a step forward in the New Age detective genre. Those interested in astrology will take delight in hero Axel Crowe's analysis and interpretation, and the story line is a welcome entry into twenty-first century fiction. For those with a mystical blend and more than a touch of Scorpio darkness, you're in for a treat." ~ *Dell Horoscope*

SCORPIO RISING
by
Alan Annand

Scorpio Rising
Copyright – Alan Annand 2011

Published by Sextile.com

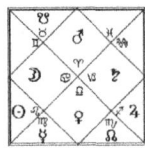

V.18012013

This is a work of fiction. Names, characters, places and incidents are the product of the author's imagination or are used fictitiously. Any resemblance to actual events, locales, or persons living or dead, is entirely coincidental.

ISBN 978-0-9869206-4-6

This book is dedicated to my wife Diane,
whose advice, editing and loving support
made it a reality.

1

Tuesday

New York

After a day of trying to sell herself, Carrie Cassidy felt breathless and empty, like she'd spent the last eight hours blowing up balloons for someone else's birthday party. She wanted a drink but, knowing what lay ahead, it wasn't a good idea. Six hours from now she'd need all her wits about her and it'd be foolish to compromise her plan for the sake of self-indulgence.

She entered a Starbucks near Columbus Circle, bought a coffee and out-maneuvered another client to capture a seat near the window. She eased her shoes off and leaned back, watching the end-of-day crowd surge along the sidewalk toward the nearest subway.

She looked at her feet. She'd worn her most comfortable dress shoes but she'd underestimated the walking she'd had to do today. Both feet were close to blistering. She probably should have returned to the hotel and changed into running shoes but, for what she had to do tonight, high heels were part of the package. Stick with the plan.

She drank the coffee and savored the pleasant jolt to her system. She had a sudden craving for a cigarette. New York, despite its attractions, made her feel nervous. The competition was omnipresent and you could see the stress in everyone's faces. If she lived here she'd end up smoking again and counting the minutes each day until martini hour.

Being a writer was no walk in the park. She felt she had talent but every time she entered a large bookstore she was forced to admit books were just another commodity. When she was at her keyboard she felt like a creator but here she felt like a salesperson and it drove her crazy. Who did she have to kill in order to get noticed?

She'd met five literary agents today – four women in their offices, and a man for lunch. The women had ranged in age from mid-twenties to early-forties – smart, well-dressed, hip to the ways of the publishing world, and with uncanny ability to deconstruct her pitch and find fault with the novel she'd spent three years writing. As for her lunch date, he'd reminded her of a kid with ADHD in a roomful of toys. She'd had to talk fast and loud just to compete with his BlackBerry. And she'd ended up paying for lunch.

It was ironic, she thought. She'd have far preferred killing him than the person she'd actually come to town to murder.

Carrie walked up Broadway past Lincoln Center and into her mother's neighborhood. Her mother had come to New York with her third husband, staying even after he'd died, favoring Manhattan's crowded streets over the back roads of Vermont where she'd grown up. She could afford it. Her third husband had been in the fur business and, aside from keeping Frances warmly dressed for New York's chilly winters, had banked enough to keep her in elegant style in a two-bedroom co-op overlooking Central Park.

Carrie arrived at her mother's building. A doorman in cap and brass-buttoned jacket opened the door. He squinted at her with piggy eyes as he returned to the desk from which he commanded the foyer.

"Carrie Cassidy," she said. "I'm visiting my mother. Frances Faber, apartment nine-oh-six."

"I remember you from yesterday," he said with an European accent, winking with an eye that looked permanently bloodshot. He had white hair and one of those alky noses, like a red golf ball with veins. In his doorman's uniform he looked like a war-weary Russian general. She imagined a flask of vodka hidden in his desk drawer. "I will call to let her know you're coming?"

"No. She's expecting me."

She headed for the elevator. The door was about to close

but someone inside held it open. She skipped aboard and pressed the button for the ninth floor, glancing at the passenger who'd held the door for her.

The sole passenger was a twenty-five year old currency exchange trader named Ron Stiles. Stiles had just returned home from his office on Wall Street, where he'd successfully traded the Canadian and Australian dollars, making a quarter million dollars for his employer and fifteen grand on his own account.

They exchanged looks. She saw a handsome specimen of Generation X in a Hugo Boss suit. Six foot even, she guessed, weighing just over one sixty, a guy who looked like he worked out once a day and had a long shower afterwards. Fit as an athlete and squeaky clean, just the way she liked them. She imagined she could eat sushi off his bare chest and not swallow a hair. He smiled and she saw perfect teeth. She smiled back.

Stiles saw an attractive brunette in her mid-to-late thirties. She had a short haircut whose layered shag loosely framed her face, and a nose reminding him of Nicole Kidman. He glanced at her hands and saw a cluster of rings, silver and turquoise, but no wedding band. Back to her face, whose blue eyes beneath generous eyebrows watched him. She was leaning back in the corner, her elbows on the handrail, taking the weight off her feet like a fighter between rounds. She was slim but with a jacket, hard to tell how she was built on top. Looked like a weekend runner, maybe a cyclist.

The elevator stopped at the fifth. An old man in slippers got on, peered at the control panel and pressed the button for the seventh. Carrie and Stiles exchanged looks again. The door opened at the seventh and the old man shuffled off.

"First time to New York?" Stiles said.

"Not really," she said. "Why do you ask?"

Stiles shrugged. She had some kind of soft Texas accent but it was her eyes that encouraged him. "Just thought, maybe you'd like someone to show you a few of the sights."

She nodded sympathetically as if it wasn't such an

outlandish idea. "And you think you might be the one?"

Stiles flashed her that smile. "Occasionally I get lucky."

She looked at her watch, then at him again. "I'm sure you do." He reminded her of a disposable camera, a perfect medium on which to record a few vacation memories, but no big loss if she forgot him on the way to the airport.

The elevator stopped at the ninth. She looked at the control panel. The light for the twelfth was still illuminated. She looked back at him. He gave her his lucky smile again. She reached out and pushed the button to close the door, then took hold of his tie and reeled him in.

Carrie stood naked at the window looking out at Central Park. She had a clear view of the Tavern-on-the-Green and, further to the south, a few people pitching irons on horseshoe courts. There were probably bird-watchers out there too, occasionally scanning the apartment towers ringing the park, hoping for a view of something like this. She pressed her breasts against the window pane. What the hell did she care? Here today, gone tomorrow. She turned to face the room.

"Nice view, Ron. You are a lucky guy."

Stiles was thinking the same thing as he lay naked with one leg hanging off the bed. She had a great body, a bit on the lean side but buff as hell, and more than his match between the sheets. No sprinter, she had the stamina of a long-distance runner. He ran his hand across the sheet. Still moist, and most of it was from *his* sweat.

She sat on the bed and plucked her underwear from the floor. She looked at him. His hair was all mussed up, his face still flushed.

He ran his fingers down her back and squeezed one of her cheeks. "You're going?"

"I told you I couldn't stay long. I'm visiting my mother."

"Can we hook up again?"

"Afraid not." She fastened her bra and pulled her top over her head. "I'm on a pretty tight schedule."

"Just a quick in and out?"

"Isn't that the way you like it?" She pulled on her slacks, stepped into her shoes.

"I thought maybe we could have dinner, come back later for dessert..."

"That's a lovely thought but I'm on a bit of a diet and I can only allow myself one indulgence per day."

"What about tomorrow?"

"Sorry, I'll be gone." She picked up her bag and jacket, moving toward the door. She gave him a final look, not like she was getting nostalgic or anything, just checking to see she hadn't left anything of hers behind. "But thanks for showing me the sights."

Carrie took the stairs down three flights, stopping halfway to sit on the steps and fix her makeup. On the ninth floor she rang the bell at apartment 906. The door jerked open on a chain heavy enough to restrain a large dog. Her mother's face appeared in the gap, perplexed and peeved at the same time. The chain rattled and the door opened to reveal Frances in a black skirt and low heels, a royal blue sweater and a string of pearls.

"Where've you been?" her mother said. "You're an hour late."

Carrie walked in. "My last meeting of the day ran late. Then I got jammed up in traffic."

Frances bolted the door and hooked the chain. "I told you not to take a cab. The subway's faster."

"I came as fast as I could."

Frances stood with hands on hips, like a marionette that had escaped her control wires and was defying her puppetmaster to string her up again. She was only five foot two and less than a hundred pounds but she radiated an intensity that reminded Carrie of a drill sergeant she used to know in Alamogordo, New Mexico. Little wonder that her last two husbands had died of heart attacks. They'd just wearied of the fight and threw in the towel.

Carrie gave her mother a hug. Woodenly Frances accepted her embrace, then turned and marched down the hall. Carrie followed, dropping her purse on a foyer chair and draping her jacket over its back.

"I made Coquilles Saint-Jacques," Frances said. "It's probably overdone by now but maybe you won't know the difference anyway."

"I told you not to cook. We could have gone to a restaurant."

"There's nothing fit nearby and everything's so darned expensive, I wonder how anyone can afford to eat out any more."

Carrie shook her head. Frances was stingy beyond belief and to watch her part with money was like ripping bandages off raw flesh. Her mother never talked about it so Carrie could only speculate what she was worth, but she assumed several million. Although Carrie was an only child, Frances was still on the shy side of sixty and so healthy that she saw a doctor only once a year for an annual checkup. Somewhere down the road, maybe decades away, a pot of gold awaited Carrie, but so distant it was little more than a mirage briefly glimpsed in a daydream. What could you do? God helps those who help themselves.

Carrie followed Frances into the kitchen. A bottle of white wine stood in an aluminum cooler on the sideboard. What the hell, Carrie thought, I'll never make it through the evening otherwise. She found a corkscrew and pulled the cork with a resounding pop. She poured two glasses. Frances was busy at the stove. Carrie drank most of her glass straight off and topped it up.

2

Los Alamos, New Mexico

In the Jemez Mountains northwest of Santa Fe, New Mexico, a silver grey BMW X5 drove along winding Highway 502. Along this highway were several anonymous installations hidden among the juniper and pine or half-buried inside a rocky hillside. The BMW slowed, signaled a turn and climbed a road up a wooded slope to a security gate.

A sign identified the installation as Los Alamos National Laboratory Site No.27. The driver extended a hand, passing a control card to an officer in the booth. In a moment the card came back, the gate swung open, and the BMW continued up the driveway into a parking lot. As the driver climbed out of his vehicle, he paused a moment to admire the view from one of the higher peaks in the Jemez Mountains range.

Dr. Walter Cassidy was forty-two years and exactly where he wanted to be in life, at least professionally. His personal life was a shambles, with a wife he suspected might be a nymphomaniac, to which some of his acquaintances could attest. But as far as the job went, he was in the zone. He had a Ph.D. in Mathematics from Rutgers University and if he weren't forbidden by the State Secrets Act to publish a fraction of what he knew, he'd likely be acknowledged as the world's greatest expert on order theory, an abstract branch of mathematics that had gained great new currency in the war against terror.

He'd built simulations of *al-Qaeda, Hamas* and *Hezbollah* by dumping newspaper articles and other publicly available information about their organizations into a computer database, supplementing that information with everything the CIA could feed him, from addresses, cell phone numbers and license plates to family relations and business affiliations. He'd guided the development of computer programs that used all that information to find patterns and relationships between individuals, identifying weak and strong figures, power brokers and people with crucial skills.

Order theory was all about hierarchies and, once you knew how to examine the data, you could identify people with critical leverage and govern your strategies accordingly. The CIA was lapping this up and using it to advantage on a weekly basis. His little team of nerds had grown exponentially. He now guided the activities of almost a dozen technical units.

He took a last puff on his cigarette, dropped the butt on the asphalt and tapped it dead beneath his shoe. Never mind that he was in the middle of a parking lot, New Mexico was in the third month of a drought and the surrounding mountains were forested with parched *piñon* that could catch fire and burn in the blink of an eye.

He hitched his belt higher on his hips and strode toward the entrance of the low-slung compound that looked like a giant wedge of concrete and smoked glass driven into the brow of the mountain. He started to sweat just getting from the car to the building and he knew it wasn't just the afternoon heat. He was packing about sixty pounds extra, and it was costing him his marriage.

As he approached the entrance he passed his control card in front of a waist-high steel post and the smoked-glass doors slid open. In the foyer behind a counter sat an officer he'd never seen before. The security staff in these installations constantly rotated, and you could go weeks without seeing a familiar face. All part of making it impossible for anyone to take it for granted that just because they'd let you in yesterday, they were still authorized to do so today.

The officer looked at Cassidy's face, then swiped the card through a reader and stared at a monitor. He slid the card back across the counter. "Have a nice day, Dr. Cassidy."

Cassidy pocketed his card and walked on. Another smoked-glass door slid open and he entered a hallway that curved to the left. He headed straight for the men's washroom where the urinals, toilets and sinks were all brushed steel, and small electronic eyes monitored everything that came and went. He took a leak, tucked his shirt in and tightened his belt a notch. He washed his hands and splashed water on his flushed face.

He sometimes imagined that these electronic eyes might be taking pictures of his privates, and that the drains from the toilets and urinals were routed to hidden labs where his urine and feces could be tested for substance abuse. But that was all just too Orwellian to contemplate. With the responsibilities on his shoulders, he had trouble enough sleeping as it was. He ran a comb through his wet hair, smiled for the hidden cameras behind the mirror and went off to his meeting.

It was a get-together that Dr. Cassidy genuinely relished, sort of an intellectual boys' club. There were just the four of them today and, despite the pressures of their own recognition-desperate egos and the very real demands of national security, it was all very chummy. They sat at the conference table, everyone with colas or spring water from one of their sanctioned suppliers. They had a fridge full of Eagle Spirit, Big Bear Mountain and Crystal Rock mineral waters that some patriotic quartermaster had imposed upon them. Ever since Gulf War II, Evian and Perrier were *verboten*. Hell, the cafeteria didn't even serve *French* fries anymore, and if you wanted potatoes, it was Idaho baked or mashed. But they weren't here for the food and beverages, they were here to outsmart a bunch of Koran-thumping tribesmen half a world away.

His colleagues were all in their thirties, each with advanced degrees in mathematics, physics, computer systems or some combination thereof. Jim Morris was a Stanford man with shoulder length hair who came to work in shorts and sandals half the time, sometimes leather pants and snakeskin boots in colder weather, proving you could take the weirdoes out of California but not vice versa. Bob Kruger from MIT had one of the biggest foreheads you'd ever seen, you'd think it concealed a giant sonar, and his fingers constantly fingered air guitar riffs. Brian Denman was from Georgia Tech, a quiet guy with a thousand-yard stare who meditated in his spare time and performed intellectual heavy lifting on the job.

Idiosyncrasies aside, they were a brilliant team and among them had enough doctorates to paper the smallest room in anyone's house. Cassidy was grateful to have them on his most important project, which involved counter-terrorism in cyberspace. His wasn't the only little skunk-works fighting this war, just another squad of computerized grunts taking on *jihad* one server at a time, eliminating terrorists so the forces of freedom could prevail. But they were producing results acknowledged by his grateful superiors, and were looking at serious bonuses come performance review time, maybe even a letter of thanks from someone high in the Directorate.

So, here they were, late Tuesday afternoon, everyone comfy in their thousand-dollar-plus ergonomic chairs, fluid levels adjusted, notebooks and smart phones at the ready, studying the big flat-screen monitor which displayed the front page of a website with Arabic characters.

Kruger, whose domed forehead possibly concealed a state-of-the-art bullshit detector, was the team's self-appointed cynic. "Do we know for sure it's *al-Qaeda*?"

"Who else would post the formula for sarin gas?" Morris said. "Along with maps of every American embassy in the world, and range coordinates for everything from RPGs to heavy mortar?"

"Well, at last count we have three dozen independent factions operating out of Pakistan, Iran, Yemen… for starters. And just because it's in Arabic doesn't mean they're Islamists. The North Koreans have scholars in foreign languages too, and they're a mischievous bunch of bastards."

"But the site's down now?" Cassidy said.

"Within four hours of going online," Denman said. Driven by a super-computer, they had programs that scanned cyberspace 24/7 looking for telltale character strings correlated with terrorist cell activities. There were a thousand-plus websites associated with global *jihad*, offering everything from recruitment exhortations to training manuals to bomb-making recipes. Staying current with them was a monstrous task. But once their program found a target, it unleashed the cyberspace equivalent of a heat-seeking missile, overwhelming the target with virus-laden worms that burrowed into the host and hollowed it out from the inside.

"Their server's toast for now," Morris said, "but that information was out there for almost four hours."

"We've got to shorten our search-and-destroy cycle," Cassidy said. Aside from setting the agenda by stating the obvious, he now had to roll up his intellectual shirtsleeves and guide them through an intensive brainstorming session lasting almost eight hours.

3

San Francisco

In the Grand Ballroom of the Hyatt Regency Hotel, an audience of highly educated, highly paid and mostly bored banking executives in expensive suits listened to the luckless speaker of the last presentation of the day. Many of the executives, typically AVPs and below from dozens of national and regional banks, were working their smart phones to answer emails, monitor stock quotes or search the web for recommended restaurants or off-beat night life, of which San Francisco had much to offer. Onstage, the speaker stroked his laptop to advance a slide in his colorful but listless PowerPoint presentation being projected onto the big screen for all to ignore. Above the projection screen a big banner read '*America – Banking on the Future*'. All around the stage were logos of banks.

"...And our choice for the future is clear," the speaker was saying. "Nickel-and-dime our clients on services or use better technology in more innovative ways..."

Jeb Stockwell, a 39-year-old vice-president whose handsome features lacked any distinguishing characteristic that could make him GQ material, stared into space, his mind far removed from banking. For the third time in fifteen minutes, he looked at his watch, then at his hands. His nails were manicured and his hands were as smooth and clean as a doctor's. But they were nervous hands and they kept twisting and turning this way and that, locking fingers and pulling apart, reuniting again to rub each other anxiously like forbidden lovers who've been warned to keep their distance but just couldn't stay away from each other.

He looked around him. Most of these third-tier bankers were men but there were a few women among them, maybe ten percent of the attendees. He felt a vague pity for everyone here. Banking was one of the most regimented industries, upon whose moneyed altar all serious aspirants sacrificed their individuality for the higher good. Secretly he prayed he'd soon escape these cloisters of commerce and find his true calling in less restrictive circumstances, like managing his investment portfolio from the terrace of some Caribbean hideaway.

The speaker wound up his presentation and opened the floor to questions, of which there were none. At the end of the day, the only question in anyone's mind was, *Where do we go for dinner*? The speaker acknowledged defeat and, like a teacher on the last day of class, released his restless audience by powering off his laptop. The audience applauded politely before surging toward the exit.

Stockwell, along with a couple of other AVPs he knew from New York, caught an elevator back up to their rooms. Scott Nelson of JP Morgan, a baby-faced guy with the girth of a wrestler, peeled off his jacket and loosened his tie. Eric Stanley of Citibank, who was into personal mergers as much as corporate ones, checked messages on his phone.

"What do you say, guys?" Nelson said. "A drink in the bar before dinner?"

"Let's go out," Stanley said. "There're no eligible women here."

"I've seen a few prospects."

"Bankers," Stanley made a face. "Like sleeping with your cousins. Bad for business. Some day you could find yourself trying to do a deal with one. But if you've kissed her off in a one-night stand, there goes your deal and bonus and God knows what else."

"There's a sports bar just up the block. Even if there're no babes, we can watch a game or something before dinner."

"You guys are on your own," Stockwell said. "I need to take a nap. This time zone's put me way off stride."

"You want to rendezvous for dinner?" Nelson suggested.

"Nah, you guys go on alone. I'm ordering room service and working on tomorrow's presentation." The elevator door opened on the 18th floor and Stockwell got out. The door closed behind him.

"What a putz," Stanley said.

"Married old money," Nelson shrugged. "It's tamed his wild animal spirit."

"Yeah, right," Stanley smirked. "Like he ever had one."

Half an hour later, Jeb Stockwell emerged from the hotel's underground garage, now wearing running shoes, cap and sunglasses. Scanning the sidewalk for familiar faces, ready to cross the street if he saw one, he walked over to Market Street just as a streetcar clattered down the hill. He followed it all the way down to the Embarcadero, the palm-treed avenue that accessed the piers between Fisherman's Wharf and the East Bay Bridge. He entered the Ferry Building, found the ticket booth and paid cash for a two-way fare to Larkspur.

Fifteen minutes later, he was seated in the ferry's forward lounge along with hundreds of other commuters heading home to the North Bay after a day in the city. Off in the distance he saw the Golden Gate Bridge, its orange paint barely discernible in the late-day haze. The guy in the seat across the aisle kept looking his way, maybe a tourist checking out the distant bridge, maybe gay and checking *him* out. Stockwell went out onto the deck. They were passing Alcatraz, the decommissioned prison that was now a tourist attraction. He stood at the rail and stared at the island as the ferry shuddered its way across the bay. He imagined the regrets of so many luckless souls who'd stood at their barred windows with a reverse view, watching a ferry go by, perhaps thinking, there but for a twisted chromosome go I. Again he said a silent prayer that everything would go as planned and he'd never see the inside of a cell.

He remained on deck for the rest of the trip. He felt a little queasy but it wasn't the ride. He enjoyed boats and had done quite a bit of sailing, both during his graduate studies at Berkeley and more recently these last few years out of Southampton. Rather, it was the thought of what he had to do in the next hour that knotted his stomach.

As he looked ahead, he realized that the complex of buildings on the headland off the starboard bow was San Quentin. Two prison views in one trip, he hoped this wasn't an omen. He tightened his hold on the railing. Get a grip, man. Don't let your imagination get carried away.

The ferry maneuvered up to the Larkspur Terminal dock. He remained at the railing, watching passengers gather on the deck as the dock crew lowered the boarding ramp and opened the gate to let passengers disembark. As the last of them straggled off, he brought up the rear. Although his feet moved at a shuffle, his heart was galloping.

He passed through the terminal. Most passengers had dispersed into the parking lot, heading for their cars, while others queued up for buses. He killed time, examining a print media dispenser, flipping through real estate brochures and community newspapers, like a tourist trying to assess the lay of the land.

He scanned the parking lot. The last passengers had found their vehicles and headed home. He walked out along the nearest row of cars, tugging a pair of leather gloves from his jacket. It wasn't the season for gloves but they were a pale tan, almost flesh-colored, and at a quick glance would probably pass for bare hands.

It only took a minute to find something suitable – a 1995 blue Jeep Cherokee. He sidled up to the driver's side door, putting the Cherokee between him and the terminal. He whacked the door with his hand, its lack of response confirming the older vehicle had no alarm. The door was locked but he'd come prepared. He drew a 12-inch aluminum ruler from his jacket sleeve. He'd bought it yesterday from a hardware store, along with a pair of small metal shears with which he'd cut a deep notch in the ruler an inch from the end. He jammed the shim under the rubber window seal, felt for the door mechanism and pulled. The door popped open and he got in.

He bent down to look under the steering column's ignition lock and, using yet another modified hardware tool, started the Jeep. Amazing the things he'd learned on a summer job with the AAA road service crew several years ago. He put the Cherokee into gear and drove away.

4

Toronto, Canada

Axel Crowe sat listening to Margo Riordon, a Police forensics instructor who'd invited him to join her for a luncheon talk at the University of Toronto. Margo was telling the audience in her lively and articulate manner about fingerprint technology.

"Thanks to TV programs like *CSI*, you know that high speed computers can access huge databases to perform print matching in mere minutes. But did you know that police services world-wide now routinely print much more of criminals' hands than just the fingerprints? Other parts of the hand are also being captured. Ultimately these too will be added to databases for matching."

Margo turned on a projector and used a laser pointer to indicate a portion of a fingerprint form – four fingers grouped side by side, their relative heights making obvious which were the index, middle, ring and little fingers.

"For example, Toronto Police Services use Motorola's PrinTrak console to scan fingerprints, but also the panel of four fingers grouped together, what the FPTs – fingerprint technicians – call a flat. One for the right hand, one for the left."

She pointed to another section of the fingerprint form, a vertical swatch of skin. "They also scan the subject's edge-of-palm, what the FPTs call the writer's palm."

Margo indicated another band of the palm just below the fingers. "Finally, they capture the skin ridge patterns at the base of the fingers. FPTs call these the inter-digitals."

As he listened, Crowe used his iPhone to review tomorrow's planetary lineup for the first race of the day at Woodbine racetrack. He had a system for playing the horses, using astrology and numerology. A couple of years ago he'd enjoyed a winning streak that included a trifecta win paying 800 to one on a $20 bet, which had helped him make the down payment on a house in The Beaches. In recent months, however, he'd been on a losing streak. Although he couldn't quite bring himself to quit what he considered a research effort, he'd scaled his bets back to staunch the bleeding from his bank account.

Margo was saying, "Axel Crowe, a graduate of this criminology program, has since become something of an expert in a different field. Axel, care to take it from here?"

Crowe mounted the podium and looked out at the audience. There were about thirty people, equal numbers of men and women. To judge by their apparent ages, most were students but some of the older attendees were almost certainly faculty.

"I graduated fifteen years ago," Crowe began, "but didn't

follow through on my original plan to pursue a career in law enforcement. Shortly after university I met my guru and, next thing I knew, I'd spent fourteen years studying astrology, palmistry and other related subjects like *ayurveda*, the Vedic science of health."

"That's quite a leap," someone in the audience said, "from criminology to astrology."

"Yes," Crowe agreed, "although some would say they're both black arts."

That got a laugh from the audience.

"For several years I've researched all things related to the hands – from the esotericism of palmistry to the forensic science of fingerprinting – which is how I met Margo. A few years ago, she gave me a tour of her office and explained crime scene procedures to me, at least insofar as they relate to fingerprint technology. Since then we've become colleagues of a sort, albeit on different sides of the fence."

"He keeps trying to coax me over to the dark side," Margo said, "but so far I've been strong."

"Close-minded, she means," Crowe said.

Another laugh from the audience.

Crowe held up his hand. "I'd like to talk about the future. As Margo said, police forces now have more data than ever to work with, so if a fingerprint isn't available from the crime scene but a writer's palm is, they can still match a suspect to a crime. Aside from providing identification, these additional points of reference also supply fresh data for profiling – using fingerprints and handprints to extrapolate behavioral characteristics of the perpetrator."

A hand went up in the audience. Crowe nodded to the young man. "But fingerprints aren't currently used in profiling," the student said. "Or did I miss that episode of *CSI*?"

"You're absolutely right, but I predict that within a decade fingerprint technicians will routinely print the entire palm for purposes of both identification and analysis, the latter of which will provide input to the process of offender profiling."

"And you think FPTs will do the profiling as well?"

"Depends on their interest and talent. Patrol officers get promoted to detectives. With training, FPTs could become handprint profilers. Even if the job seems routine, it involves pattern recognition which is interpretive."

A young woman raised her hand. "Could you give us an example of a suspect profile based on the hand?"

Crowe looked at the fingerprint form still projected on the screen. At a glance he saw sufficient detail to make a good example. He turned to Margo who'd taken a seat in the first row. "Margo, do I know the identity of the person whose prints are shown here, or any background regarding crimes they may have committed?"

"No," Margo said.

"I'll start my profile with the structural elements of the hand." Crowe used the laser to point at the form. "In the flat, the index finger is short and the ring finger very long. There's a scientific correlation between testosterone and index-to-ring finger length ratios so I'll play the odds and say this is a man's hand. Based on the same ratio, I'd say this person has low self esteem but takes risks to prove himself. The pinkie is long, delicate, and crooked, so he's a white collar criminal."

He pointed the laser at another feature. "In the right-hand writer's palm, a horizontal line an inch above the wrist suggests substance abuse. Since it also appears in the left hand, a family history of the same."

He targeted another aspect. "Within the inter-digitals, loops flanking the ring finger indicate cleverness and entrepreneurial instincts. A deep vertical crease under the ring finger suggests a risk taker or a gambler."

He pointed to the fingerprints. "Arch patterns occur five times out of ten, which is significant, since arches are less common than loops and whorls. He's a skilled craftsman with an eye for details."

Someone in the audience asked, "Who should the police be looking for?"

"A solitary white collar criminal, maybe someone writing bad checks to support a drug habit." Crowe turned to Margo. "What can you tell us about this subject?"

"Both parents were alcoholics," Margo said. "In high school, he forged birth certificates for underage classmates to get into bars and clubs. After developing a cocaine habit, he wrote bum checks to pay for it. Recently arrested and charged with counterfeiting."

Crowe's correct interpretation earned a flurry of applause.

A professor spoke up. "That was quite a demonstration. But surely you don't suggest palmistry will replace traditional profiling?"

"Of course not. It may become just another element in the profiler's toolkit."

"But profilers would need training. Will police academies give courses in palmistry?"

"Not such a crazy idea. Palmistry has been practiced for thousands of years and is a well-documented science."

"Most people would object to calling it a science," the professor said.

"Times change. Fifty years ago, offender profiling was itself unknown. The FBI enjoyed its first success in 1973. Initially profiling was accused of being too subjective, even *mystical*." Crowe paused to let that sink in. "Ultimately the willingness of profilers to study all facets of the *unsub* – the unknown subject – will include psychological clues from fingerprints and handprints. If we have to borrow interpretations from palmistry until we can build a database of statistical behaviors, so be it."

"Good grief! What's next on your agenda – astrology?"

"Don't write it off. But that's a subject with even more emotional baggage than palmistry. Let's stick to the subject at hand – no pun intended."

The group had several more questions, which Crowe answered with authority, clarity and occasional humor. A faculty member thanked Crowe and Margo for their time and reminded the audience there'd be another pair of lunchtime talks next month, details on the faculty site. Crowe descended from the podium.

Margo gathered her acetates into a briefcase. "That went over pretty well."

"Thanks for inviting me," Crowe said. "It's always nice to speak to the open-minded, even if only because there are so few of them."

"The more they're exposed to different ways of thinking, the more likely they'll embrace new methods of police work. Like you said, things are changing fast..."

Margo trailed off as a member of the audience approached them. She was an attractive redhead with green eyes and freckles, wearing jeans and a tight sweater that made profiling her somewhat more than just an intellectual exercise.

"Hi. My name's Rosalyn." The redhead extended a hand to Crowe. "I found your lecture very relevant to the thesis I'm working on."

"Which is...?"

"Working title, *Deduction versus Induction: Forensic Psychology at a Crossroads*."

"Provocative," Margo said in a tone that made Crowe wonder if she was referring to Rosalyn's thesis or her sweater.

"How can we help you?" Crowe said.

"Are you familiar with Bayesian theory?"

"It's the foundation for artificial intelligence. Bayesian theory says probability is a measure of a state of knowledge. Computers learn to do the things that experience teaches them to be statistically correct."

Rosalyn and Crowe regarded each other with frank and mutual interest. Or was it just his imagination? She was after all several years younger than him.

Margo realized they were talking a language she didn't understand. Or to judge their body language, sharing a message from which she'd been excluded. She checked her watch. "I guess I'll be going. Need a ride, Axel?"

"No, I'm good. Thanks again for inviting me."

"I'm sure you're good." Margo headed for the exit. "See you around."

Crowe turned back to Rosalyn. "I'd love to hear more about your thesis."

"I'd love to tell you about it," she said. "Want to go for coffee?"

5

New York

Shortly after ten, Carrie Cassidy helped her mother load the dishwasher. Frances added detergent and started the machine. Carrie looked at the clock on the wall. It was 10:05.

They returned to the dining room where a cribbage board and a deck of cards lay on the table. Frances shuffled the cards with a brisk flutter of her hands, like a card shark stacking the deck for some unsuspecting pigeon.

"Another game of crib?"

"It's ten o'clock, Mom. I should head back to my hotel. I've got a big day tomorrow."

"It's only eight, Mountain time."

"I have a breakfast meeting tomorrow. I'll be dog tired if I don't get to bed early."

"Why didn't you stay here instead of a hotel? When I think of the money you throw away…"

"The hotel's closer to my meetings. And I need time alone to practice my pitch."

"Didn't you practice on Walt before you left?"

"Walt doesn't give a shit about my work, Mom. He's busy saving the free world."

Carrie remembered a candlelight dinner a long time ago when Walt had waxed poetic after two bottles of wine and told her she was the jewel of his existence, a desert rose that had brought beauty to his barren world. Lately, she found the metaphor ironically apt. This blossom had experienced a lengthy drought and started to wilt alone in the desert.

"You could have practiced on me," her mother said.

"I don't think so." Carrie fetched her jacket from the foyer. "Thanks for dinner. I'll call you tomorrow before I catch the shuttle."

"Do you really have to leave so soon?" Frances looked petulant. "You've only been here two days."

"Please don't act like I'm just springing this on you. We talked about this before I came. Things are really busy for me this month. I just don't have much time to spare."

Her mother started to sniffle. Carrie grimaced. Frances was such a drama queen. She could play the drill sergeant, the dewy-eyed ingénue, and all parts in between. Still, she was her mother and she'd been to hell and back a few times, first with the death of Carrie's father, then again with Carrie as a teenager and all the drama of that shape-shifting age. Carrie gave her mother a fierce hug, like shaking a crying child, just wanting to avoid a scene and get out of here as quickly as possible. She should have been gone by ten. Time was now of the essence.

"Next time, I'll stay a week. Okay?"

"When?" her mother pressed.

"Thanksgiving."

"Is that a promise?"

"Of course. But now I really have to go."

Frances wiped her eyes, snorted back her crocodile tears and followed Carrie to the door. She unhooked the chain and turned the bolt. She stood there expectantly. Carrie gave her a hug again and kissed her on both cheeks. Her mother smiled and this time she looked like she was going to cry for real.

"Good luck tomorrow, Carrie. I bet they love your book. One of these days, we'll see your name on the bestseller lists."

"Thanks, Mom. I'll call you tomorrow before I fly out."

"Oh, wait, I wanted to give you some shortbread to take home to Walt."

But Carrie was already halfway down the hall, running for the elevator.

A different doorman was on duty, watching a basketball game on a small TV behind his desk. Carrie stiff-armed the door open and ran into the street where she put her fingers to her mouth and whistled. A taxi on the other side of the street hit the brakes, crossed lanes and backed up to where she was. She jerked the door open and jumped in.

The cabbie, a tall guy with glasses who looked like an unkempt version of Neil Simon, one of her literary heroes, looked over his shoulder through the Plexiglas divider.

"Broadway and Fifty-First," she said. "And I'm in a big hurry."

"Aren't we all?" he said, but to his credit promptly started the meter and matted the gas. The taxi ran the yellow light at Columbus Avenue and careened around the corner in a turn that pressed her against the door.

"Got an idea how much the fare's going to be?" she said.

"Seven or eight bucks."

She took a ten from her wallet and rapped her knuckles on the Plexiglas. He slid open the little window and she passed the money through. "Keep the change."

"You want a receipt?"

"Not if you have to stop to write it."

He wrote it out anyway when he had to stop for a light. She looked at her watch. Cripes. It was 10:22. She felt sweat popping out all over. If she missed this window of opportunity, God knows if or when she'd ever get a chance to do what was supposed to be done tonight.

6

San Rafael, California

Out on San Pedro Road, just outside San Rafael, Marin County, 52-year-old Bernie Lang was plugged into his iPod and taking his daily run in a canary yellow track suit. Ever since he'd crossed the half-century mark, he'd been in a constructive state of denial. No turning back the years but he was determined to make the best of what God in his infinite wisdom had bequeathed him. Getting a little thin on top, he kept his hair trimmed fashionably short. Although not really an outdoorsy type, regular visits to a tanning salon maintained the illusion. And when his butt had begun to sag, a regimen of jogging and vigorous workouts with a personal trainer of sadistic inclinations had tightened things up so that he wasn't shy about getting naked with men younger than himself.

Life was pretty good for Bernie and its almost predictable regularity now gave him comfort in his golden years. He was wealthy beyond his expectations. Dividends from his investments fell like manna from the heavens on a monthly basis, swelling both his net worth and his ego. And except for the occasional hemorrhoid he enjoyed an almost perfect state of health the like of which, his doctor assured him, should see him into octogenarian status. That was a mixed prospect but so long as he still had an erection to go along with it, he couldn't complain.

He had a live-in boyfriend, a hard-luck case in terms of his own career, but a fun guy in the sack and a good companion most of the time. And for those other times, lately more than once a week, Bernie visited the Castro District where he amused himself trying on different relationships, just like any guy with a sedan in the garage at home but a fascination for sports cars. Yes, life was a bowl of cherries and every now and again he was lucky enough to pop one.

Bernie's daily run, a regimen to which he religiously

adhered, took him from his gated community of Marina Bay Park north on San Pedro Road to the top of the hill. There the road entered China Camp State Park, winding along the bluff of the headland overlooking San Pablo Bay. Bernie's routine was to jog a mile and a half to Buckeye Point and back. The whole run was about three-and-half miles, a good part of it hilly, which took him a little over half an hour.

As Bernie labored up the last hill in the home stretch, he met a blue Jeep Cherokee coming around the corner at a sedate speed, less than the 30 mph posted for this stretch of road. The driver moved into the other lane, allowing Bernie to maintain his pace and not break his stride by stepping off the steep shoulder. Bernie waved in appreciation to a good driver who obeyed the speed limit on this curving road, something local teenagers failed to do.

Jeb Stockwell tapped the brakes as he approached the jogger and got a good look at him. From the yellow track suit alone he suspected this was his man but he needed to be sure. Shaved head, deep tan, diamond stud in his right ear. Just like the picture Dave had provided. Sure enough, that was Bernie Lang.

He drove another half a mile and turned in the parking lot of China Camp Point. There was a picnic ground and a restroom facility but not a soul in sight. He needed to take a leak but forced himself to wait. No telling what kind of investigation might arise from this and he was absolutely paranoid about leaving any DNA trace near the scene. He wheeled the Jeep around and headed back toward San Rafael. Since he'd entered the state park, he hadn't seen a single other vehicle.

As he drove back up the hill towards the turn at the crest, he saw the yellow track suit a good hundred yards ahead, jogging around the corner, briefly hidden behind the trees that lined the road. He glanced at the speedometer. By the time he reached the top of the hill and negotiated the turn, he was doing fifty. On the straight stretch he pushed the gas a little harder, touching sixty as he quickly overtook the jogger.

Lang didn't know what it was, but some animal instinct flashed an alarm. He looked over his shoulder and saw the Jeep coming up behind him way too fast and way over the yellow line. He spun in his tracks to face it, thinking how ridiculous a gesture it was, like a matador trying to deflect a charging bull with a wave of his hand. Before he could pirouette out of the way, hurl himself into the ditch, the Jeep angled all the way over onto his side of the road, its wheel hugging the edge of the highway, and there was nowhere left for him to go.

He threw up his hands to protect his face. Bang! The grill smashed into him, collapsing his arms, driving them into his chest. He flew through the air, one last image etched in his brain, the face of the man behind the wheel, his expression both frightened and fierce.

7

Los Alamos

Dr. Cassidy was wasted. He and his team had mapped out a project agenda measured in weeks, the mere documentation of which had elicited great protests. It had not been an easy eight hours. The two wall-length white boards were covered with flowcharts, system architecture diagrams and to-do lists. The wastepaper baskets overflowed with soda cans and empty cartons of cafeteria pizza. As the day wrapped up, an unofficial census would have recorded one migraine, vague abdominal pain and multiple bruising of egos.

Having drawn short lots, Denman and Kruger were

assigned the first critical steps, requiring code rewrites and several trial runs. They were left behind to survive the night on coffee and cafeteria leftovers, with a mandate to demonstrate something tangible in the morning that would justify their high salaries and perquisites.

Still discussing work, Cassidy and Morris signed out at the security desk, emerging into the crisp New Mexico evening just as the sun sank behind the nearest mountain ridge. Cassidy took a deep breath of mountain air and loosened his belt. What a fucking day. Right now he just wanted to go home, have a Scotch with a beer chaser, and watch some basketball on ESPN.

He took out his cigarettes and lit up. The marathon brainstorming session had felt like an eternity and he'd allowed himself only three smoke breaks in the past eight hours.

As they walked across the parking lot to their respective vehicles Morris said, "Aside from software development, we also need better hardware. You know, Cray's about to release a new model that'll make some of our other stuff look obsolete."

"You write the specs, I'll get the funding," Cassidy said with an air of cockiness, an attitude he was beginning to make his own. After hearing others talk about it, now he actually knew what it felt like to be in the zone, a player on a winning streak. He and his team were scoring so many points with the CIA field officers who directed wet work on the other side of the globe that his superiors had all but granted him *carte blanche*. Even though those were dirty French words, it was music to his ears.

"I'll get right on it tomorrow," Morris said.

"What's the matter with tonight?"

"I've got a date." Rumor was, Morris was enjoying covert ops with the wife of another team leader currently doing top secret work with the F-111 Stealth squadrons down in Alamogordo, which kept him away from his Taos home two weeks at a stretch.

"Your date can wait."

"That's not what she told me on the phone."

"What with all that screwing, maybe you've lost sight of your priorities. So long as the government's paying your inflated salary, national security is job one."

"Right," Morris shrugged.

"So I'll see a spec on my desk by noon tomorrow?" Cassidy knew that even for someone as experienced as Morris, it was a good four hours work.

"*Jawohl, Herr Doktor.*" Morris gave him a Nazi salute. "*Ich vill on der job begetten.*"

They parted, Cassidy going toward his BMW, Morris toward a Ford Mustang. Cassidy took out his car keys and pressed the remote to unlock the doors, start the engine and get the A/C going. He whistled a little tune as he twirled the key ring on his finger. He was so hot these days he could even get away with buying a non-American vehicle, something most peers were loath to do.

From the BMW's stereo system came a cacophonous roar of Arabic music – *bazoukis* and *tablahs* and reed pipes all screaming for attention like a bunch of cats on fire. What the fuck...?

Cassidy jerked open the door. The music assaulted his ears in a near-deafening wave. He heaved himself into the driver's seat and jabbed at the volume control.

Two cars over, the music was so loud that Morris turned abruptly, just in time to see Cassidy's vehicle erupt in a violent fireball. He flattened himself behind his Mustang and narrowly avoided a hailstorm of glass fragments blowing outward from the explosion. When he raised his head a moment later, debris from the BMW was raining down all over the parking lot and what was left of the X5 was burning like an oilcan. Car alarms were going off all around him.

Within minutes, alarms of a different kind went off all over Los Alamos. Some of them were heard as far away as Washington.

8

New York

Carrie Cassidy was at Broadway and Fifty-first by 10:25 PM. As the taxi pulled away, she crossed the street and stationed herself in front of an electronics store. She glanced at a TV on display and was shocked to see herself in a playback from a camcorder on a tripod. She moved away from the camera. That's all she needed, evidence placing her at the scene. She checked her watch again.

Across the intersection just east of Broadway, a theatre marquee lit up the front of its building. The doors suddenly opened and hundreds of theatre-goers spilled into the street. People dispersed in all directions, some spreading out along Broadway to hail taxis, others bunching up at the crosswalk waiting for the light to change.

Carrie felt herself tense up, eyes narrowed as she scanned the unfamiliar faces among the crowd. Relax, she told herself, it's no different from a cowhand cutting an animal from a herd, just a question of one out-maneuvering the other. Piece of cake when only one of them knows what's going on.

The light changed. A group of pedestrians surged onto the crosswalk. Among them were two blondes in their mid-thirties, one in a light beige raincoat, the other in a short red leather jacket. Carrie's focus jumped back and forth between the two. Then a bearded man took the hand of the leather-jacketed blonde and they swung south on Broadway. Carrie saw this was *not* the woman whose photos she'd received in the mail last month. The one she now recognized, the blonde in the raincoat, headed east on Fifty-first walking alone.

Carrie looped her purse strap over her head, thrust her hands in her pockets and followed. She had a golf glove in one pocket which she pulled onto her left hand. Staying on the south side of the street, she paralleled the blonde for most of a block, meanwhile steadily drawing ahead of her.

At the next intersection, Carrie crossed to the north side, getting about twenty feet ahead of the blonde. It was a deserted stretch of block – a long line of parked cars, some obscene graffiti on a plywood wall where a building was under renovation. Only a few pedestrians were in sight, far ahead on the other side of the street and going the same direction. Carrie glanced over her shoulder. The blonde was still behind her and there was no one else on the street as far back as Broadway.

Carrie staggered against a parked car, kicking a shoe off. "Oh, Jesus, my ankle!" she yelped, loud enough for the blonde to hear, as she leaned against the nearest fender for support using her gloved hand.

The blonde began to swing wide of her.

Carrie stepped away from the car, balancing on one foot as she tried to get her other foot back into her shoe. "Frigging sidewalks. I never should have worn these heels."

The blonde paused. "Are you all right?"

"I think I sprained something." Carrie flailed an arm, still balanced on one foot. "Give me a hand, would you?" The blonde hesitated, then approached. Carrie put her right arm over the blonde's shoulder.

She glanced up and down the street. The nearest pedestrian was half a block distant, going the other way. Now or never.

Carrie hooked her forearm across the blonde's neck and clapped her gloved left hand over the woman's mouth. The blonde bit her. Carrie cursed and yanked her hand free. Before the woman could cry out, she slammed the heel of her gloved hand against her victim's chin, snapping her head back. With the blonde's neck still in the crook of her arm, she gave her head a violent twist.

There was a muffled squeal of pain from the blonde and then, to Carrie's surprise and alarm, the woman's right hand came out of her coat pocket with a small red canister. There was a sudden hiss. Carrie caught a bitter whiff of pepper spray as it discharged toward the sidewalk. She seized the blonde's wrist and rotated sharply left with the woman's face pulled tight into her jacket to muffle her cries, trying to snap her neck as she'd intended. They turned in a tight circle, still struggling. The blonde tried to punch Carrie with her free hand but only succeeding in thumping the back of her head. Their breathing grew labored. The pepper spray hissed again into the air above their heads.

Carrie banged the blonde's hand on the nearest fender, dislodging the pepper spray from her grip. With that threat eliminated, she got a fresh purchase on the blonde's neck and gave it a savage twist. She heard a satisfying crunch and a gasp from her victim. As the woman suddenly sagged in her arms, Carrie guided her down between two parked cars. The pepper spray lay a foot from the curb. Carrie grabbed it and forced the blonde's mouth open with her gloved hand.

"Had to make it hard for me, did you?" Carrie hissed, her jaw clenched with anger. She held the pepper spray in place until its pressure was expended, along with her fury, and everything else.

9

Toronto

Axel Crowe whistled a lively blues tune as he approached an apartment building in the Parkdale neighborhood. Lately he'd learned to play *Little Girl* from one of the early John Mayall albums on which Eric 'Slowhand' Clapton had established himself as a guitar god. Now the tune was stuck in his mind day and night.

Crowe entered the lobby and pressed a button on a mailbox. The door buzzed open and he walked inside. He took the elevator to the seventh floor and arrived at a door with a brass OM symbol mounted above the peephole. He knocked lightly, opened the door and entered. He slipped his shoes off and walked into the living room.

The place was an incredible clutter. A take-out pizza carton lay on the coffee table. Newspapers littered the floor; stacks of books covered two-thirds of a sofa. Small brass statues of the elephant-headed god *Ganesha*, Remover of Obstacles, and other Hindu deities stood atop the TV, on window ledges and bookcase shelves. Across the mantle of a fake fireplace, monkey god *Hanuman* and other deities competed for space, reminiscent of battle scenes from the epic *Ramayana*.

Guruji sat in a reclining chair watching the news on TV. He was East Indian, Bengali to be exact, seventy years old but looking ten years younger. His head was shaven and he wore a *kurta*, a long check-patterned shirt that came to his knees.

Crowe bent and touched both hands to Guruji's bare feet, then touched the top of his own head.

Guruji used his remote to mute the TV. He gestured toward the pizza carton. "Are you hungry?"

"No thanks. I ate earlier." Crowe pushed some books aside to make room on the sofa.

"What did you eat?"

Crowe shrugged.

Guruji gave him a canny look. "Something hot and spicy? Something that satisfied your appetite or left you hungry for more?"

Crowe looked at the floor. There was no right answer to these rhetorical questions. Guruji had the uncanny ability to discern virtually anything about anyone. What color underwear were you wearing? What did you dream of last night? How much money in your wallet? These were parlor tricks Crowe had seen Guruji perform so many times that he'd long ago ceased to be astonished. You could hide no secrets from Guruji. If you'd spent a couple of hours with a woman, you might as well have tattooed all the details right there on your forehead for him to read.

"What a program! Constant eating is going on. What the

eyes see, the eyes want, and then the belly cannot digest. Better that you should turn your eyes inward before you devour the world."

"You would make me a blind man, Guruji?"

"If you had ears to hear, I could give you eyes to see."

"I'm listening."

"Listening is not enough. Invite five hundred people to a lecture, only two hundred will come. Of those two hundred, only fifty will listen. Of those fifty, only ten will remember. Of those ten, only one will practice. Where are you?"

Crowe descended from the sofa and sat cross-legged on the floor. "Right here, Guruji."

Guruji sighed. "In the old days, a guru would beat a student with a stick until he wept tears of gratitude. Lucky for you I've become civilized from living in Canada too long."

"I'm sorry to disappoint you, Guruji."

"You are not sorry. You are an omnivore. You just want to eat everything on the table – sound, touch, color, taste and smell."

"I am here to learn."

"You have learned all you can from me. We are finished with this program."

"But there's so much more. You said you would teach me..."

"Stop it. You sound like a little kid whose eyes are bigger than his stomach."

Crowe looked at the floor. Guruji had told him many times that he was an infomaniac, obsessively collecting concepts and techniques. Crowe acknowledged this truth but at the same time excused it because he was fascinated by the rich spectrum of Vedic thought. But Guruji had said it was all too easy to mistake information for knowledge, that long periods of reflection were necessary to let the big mind catch up to the little mind.

"We have spent fourteen years together. In that time you have learned many useful tricks. I trust they serve you well."

Crowe nodded.

"It would take me another seven years just to empty your head so we could start a new program. You would learn nothing new. You would have to deny yourself your usual pleasures. Only by letting go of everything coarse could you make yourself pure enough to let the light shine through. Are you ready for that?"

"I believe I am."

Guruji stared at him. "A man says to his parrot, 'Are you ready to discuss the *Bhagavad Gita*?' And the parrot says, 'I believe I am.' What do you think?"

"That's one smart parrot."

"Just because the bird speaks the language doesn't mean it knows the subject."

"You think I'm a parrot, Guruji?"

"It would be simpler if you were. I'd keep you in a cage away from the female parrots and you'd have eyes and ears only for me."

"What do you want of me, Guruji?"

"Nothing more. We have done our best but now it's time to go our separate ways."

"What do you mean?"

"It's time for you to fly away. You need to be with the other parrots."

"I don't understand."

"Yes, you do. And you know that's why you have to go."

Crowe stared at the floor. He'd always known this day would come but he hadn't known it would come this soon. Perhaps that's just the way it was, you were never quite as ready as you thought you ought to be. It was all part of the endless ebb and flow, the cycle of seeking, getting and letting go. But to be reborn, you first had to die... Crowe cleared the corner of his eyes with a finger.

"Don't cry," Guruji said. "There was a time when that worked on me, but I have no sympathy for you now. You were a man before you met me, you will be a man once again."

"May I have your blessing?"

"You are already blessed. You need nothing more from

me."

Guruji laid his hand on Crowe's head. Crowe sat motionless at Guruji's feet. *Hanuman* looked down from the mantelpiece with a magnificent scowl. Even the gods agreed, it was time for him to move on.

10

San Rafael

Out on San Pedro Road, traffic approaching the suburb of Peacock Gap found a San Rafael Police Department patrol car blocking the road to China Camp State Park. Three hundred yards further uphill was another SRPD patrol car, an ambulance, a white van and a black sedan. Drivers gawked as they were waved through by a pair of cops wielding flashlights made redundant by the lingering California twilight.

At the incident scene a female Field Evidence Technician took pictures from different angles of the victim in the ditch. Moving in a crouch along the road, her male partner bagged fragments of glass and orange plastic left behind by the hit-and-run vehicle. A dozen feet away, two ambulance attendants waited for the technicians to finish up so they could take the body to the coroner's office.

Detective Fred Hutchins leaned on the fender of an unmarked Ford, talking on his cell phone. In his mid-fifties, Hutchins had a huge shock of snow-white hair and enough extra weight to have made him Santa Claus for the SRPD's annual Christmas charity event seven years running. Some guys in the department considered him ready for pasture but Hutchins was still helping a daughter through med school and retirement wasn't in his plans for a few more years.

On the other side of the road, his partner Detective Jim

Starrett, mid-forties, was talking to a guy on a trail bike. Starrett was a rangy six-foot-one with no extra weight on him and had the wind-burned complexion of a weekend sailor. One of Starrett's guiding principles was 'Work hard, play hard', to which either of his two ex-wives might have added 'party hard'. If anyone looked close enough to distinguish hairline traces of broken blood vessels in his nose and cheeks from the more innocent ravages of sun and wind, there was probable cause to believe the ladies.

Starrett had a few final words with the guy on the trail bike and stuck his notepad into his back pocket. He crossed the road to speak to the Field Evidence Technician putting her camera back in its case. She and Starrett had an on-and-off thing that was currently off since she'd hooked up with a plumber from Petaluma with a remarkable talent for laying pipe.

"Finished with my body?" Starrett said.

"That old thing?" she smirked. "Some time ago."

"Time is on my side. You'll come running back."

"Sure, and the South's gonna rise again."

"A lot of things have come back from the dead. Many a time you've been pleasantly surprised. Even grateful, however little you like to admit it."

She shook her head, conceding her inability to keep up with the smartass repartee that had attracted her in the first place. She could keep up with him in every other way, but his mouth was in a league of its own.

"Seriously," she said, looking into the ditch at the crumpled fellow in yellow, "I think we're done here." A glance over her shoulder confirmed her partner was sealing his two bags of roadside vehicle debris, apparently sufficient to the task ahead.

"How soon can we get a vehicle confirmation?"

"If you're lucky, maybe within a few hours. Depends on the lab."

Starrett whistled to the ambulance attendants. "Okay, boys, let's get him out of there."

The attendants went into the ditch and put Lang's body on a stretcher. As Starrett watched, Hutchins finished his call and came over to join him. The attendants carried the body to the ambulance. The victim's face was intact but the jacket of his track suit had turned dark red with blood coughed up in his last minutes of life.

"I've put a bulletin out for a blue Jeep Cherokee with a smashed headlight," Hutchins said. "In case it's already back home inside a garage, I asked DMV for a listing of every Jeep in Marin County. You get anything else from the cyclist? Partial plate numbers, description of the driver?"

"Nope," Starrett said. "He only spotted the body as he came up the hill, and remembered seeing the Jeep go by a minute earlier."

"But he recognized the vic?"

"Both belonged to the Peacock Gap Golf and Country Club." From where Starrett and Hutchins stood, they could see the golf course from here, surrounded by a relatively new subdivision of luxury homes, the like of which honest cops could never call home.

"His face looked familiar," Hutchins said. "I must've seen him around town."

"Maybe in the newspaper. Bernie Lang. High-tech whiz, made a few million in the dot-com heyday. Openly gay but an upstanding member, quote-unquote, of the community, the cyclist said. He lives just down the road apiece in that gated community, Marin Bay Park."

"Check out his digs?" Hutchins twirled the silver keychain he'd removed from Lang's body. They'd found nothing else in his pockets to provide ID. Lucky the cyclist had recognized him, otherwise they'd have faced hours of canvassing door-to-door with a photo of the victim.

"Let me call Dispatch first, get the right address," Starrett said. "They can phone his place, give anybody there a heads-up that we're dropping in for a visit."

* * *

The entrance to Marin Bay Park was only three hundred yards from where Lang's body had been found. The gated community had a Y-shaped driveway at the edge of the highway, one gate in and one gate out. Although the entrance gate was closed, awaiting a resident to buzz a visitor in, ironically, the exit gate was open, so Starrett just drove in the wrong way. They followed a serpentine road through some trees up a hill. Lang's house was right on top of one of Marin County's many little rolling hills.

A yellow Porsche Boxster sat in a driveway whose paving stones were bordered on either side by flowerpots, all of which hosted yellow blossoms. Although Starrett prided himself on being able to identify at a glance the make and model of most guns, cars or sailboats, he'd never applied much of his skills to botanical classification.

"Pretty flowers," Hutchins observed, summing up all that needed to be said about that. "Guess his favorite color was yellow."

They waited in the car until they got a call from Dispatch saying there was no answer on either the land line or the cell phone in Bernard Lang's name. They were cleared to enter the house using the victim's key.

Inside they found Lang's favorite color had been applied here as well. The living room featured a contour sectional sofa in yellow Italian leather. The walls were white, the floor mahogany, but there were splashes of yellow here, there and everywhere, including the drapes, a Mexican scatter rug, two vase lamps, and a larger-than-life painting of a tanned male ass on a bright yellow beach blanket.

"Suppose he's married?" Hutchins joked.

Money was in evidence, literally. Aside from the leather furniture, high-tech entertainment system including 60-inch flat screen TV and Bose speakers, there was a display cabinet of rare coins, a couple of which looked to be gold. Out on the deck, a hot tub overlooked more yellow flowers in a landscaped garden sloping steeply downhill. Over the tree tops, they could see Richmond on the other side of San Pablo

Bay. Starrett figured the place was worth three or four million. While Hutchins checked out the lower half of the house built into the side of the hillcrest, Starrett looked around the main floor. The dining room had a massive teak table and chairs for eight. In the kitchen were brushed steel appliances and a refrigerator the size of a walk-in closet, purring like a contented cat. It was a far cry from his Sausalito bungalow downwind of the tidal flats, where his old fridge gurgled and heaved in the middle of the night like an asthmatic hippo on life support.

He inspected a message pad on the granite kitchen counter, saw a few names and local numbers, nothing that triggered suspicion.

Downstairs, the master bedroom had a king-size bed with yellow sheets and pillowcases. Huge mahogany dresser with a big jewelry box lying open – rings and bracelets and chains in gold and silver, several expensive watches. Mirrored walk-in closet, packed to the scuppers with clothes. Ensuite bathroom done in yellow tile.

At the end of the hall were two more bedrooms, one set up like an office with desk, computer and bookcases. Hutchins was in the other room which had a lived-in, smoked-in feel to it, from the casually-made-up bed to the scatter of magazines on the floor. Two guitars, one acoustic and one electric, flanked a stool in a corner.

Hutchins sat on the bed, flipping through a bunch of brochures and other loose documents he'd found in the night table drawer. Along with a baggie full of weed, to which he silently drew Starrett's attention.

"House guest?" Starrett said.

Hutchins shook his head. "Too much personal stuff. More like a roommate, I think. Some kind of bowling freak by the looks of this. Got a brochure here for a national tournament this week in Albuquerque, New Mexico. Along with flight itinerary via Southwest Airlines..."

"Man got a name?"

"Reservations in the name of Dave Munson."

"Anything with a hotel indicated? In the absence of next-of-kin, he's the logical place to start with notification."

"Not that I can see," Hutchins said.

"Let's go back to the office. I'll call the phone company, see if they've got a cell number in Munson's name."

11

Albuquerque, New Mexico

Roughly in the middle of the Land of Enchantment, where I-25 intersected I-40, Albuquerque sprawled in a westward slope from the Sandia Mountain ridge to the Rio Grande. The old Route 66 that ran right through the city was now little more than a memory preserved by nostalgic route signs and tacky souvenir shops along Central Avenue, the ancient route of passage now subsumed by the I-40 that took people to Arizona or California much faster. South of the Interstates' crossing, several affordable motels catered to budget-minded tourists and working professionals on limited expense accounts.

Visible from the southbound traffic on I-25, a neon sign flashed beneath the desert-clear night sky: *Roughrider Motor Inn*. On the west side of the motel court a black Dodge Ram pickup and a white Chevy Cavalier were parked so close together a coyote couldn't squeeze between them.

Inside Unit 12, a trail of running shoes and combat boots, jeans and shirts, socks and underwear, led to a king-size bed where two naked men in their thirties made out, their sweat-glistened bodies illuminated only by the flickering light of a muted TV. On the bedside table an alarm clock radio displaying a few minutes past eleven thumped out some rockabilly rap music, to which the lovers provided the occasional counter-point of appreciative grunts and expletives. Next to it lay a cell phone that was turned off, thus rendering it unavailable for an incoming call from California or anywhere else.

From atop a dresser a smoky red-and-blue bowling ball peered through the open flap of its tote bag, silent witness to its owner's transient pleasure. Etched in its satin finish were the words *Triple Storm Xpress*, a name that evoked powerful natural forces, coming quickly.

12

Toronto

Axel Crowe rode the streetcar from Queen Street West across the city to The Beaches, almost an hour between his place and Guruji's. Occasionally he drove his car but often used public transit. Aside from minimizing his eco-footprint, the trip gave him time to observe and think. Tonight he had a lot to think about.

Guruji had cut him loose.

Crowe had seen it coming from a distance. Traditional wisdom held that when Jupiter and Rahu, the ascending node in the Moon's orbit, occupied the same sign, rifts developed between teacher and student. The phenomenon was called *Guru-Chandala Yoga*. *Guru* was the teacher, while *Chandala* were people who hunted animals or traded in skin and bones. Although not taken literally, it implied a difference in values that ran the gamut from dietary to intellectual, moral, sexual and spiritual.

Metaphysics aside, there was a mundane element. Crowe had studied with Guruji for fourteen years. For thirteen years he'd rented apartments in the Parkdale neighborhood where a former mental institution had been closed due to budget cuts and many of its inmates set free on the streets. Now it was more of an artist's community, although sometimes it was hard to tell them apart. He'd lived there because Guruji lived there, a matter of convenience since they'd spent so much time together.

During those years, he'd learned many things from Guruji – astrology, palmistry, *ayurveda*, numerology, philosophy, and *vaastu*, the Vedic science of spatial dynamics. He'd also sacrificed many things – eating meat, drinking alcohol, sleep, ego. And there were things he'd been forced to confront – his aggression, ambition and lust...

A year ago he'd bought a house in The Beaches. It was a neighborhood he loved – the small-town ambience of Queen Street East where the big box stores were unable to wedge themselves into the heavily-treed blocks of houses a stroll away from Lake Ontario. There was a park that ran along the shore, a bicycle path and boardwalk, the beach...

Below the surface, a secret motivation had lurked. He'd needed some distance from Guruji. For the last seven years he'd been under a spiritual injunction to minimize his sexual activity. It was all part of the program, Guruji had lectured him. *You cannot let your little head do your thinking. You must show him who is boss. Until you master this on your own, I am the boss. You have a choice to make. If you want to learn subtle things, you must become a subtle person. No meat, no alcohol, no drugs, no sex.*

At first, there'd been slippage – one step back for every three forward. Meat, drugs and alcohol were never a problem but when it came to the opposite sex, it was a struggle. Crowe liked women. He'd always had more female friends than male, been as willing to share his feelings as assert his opinions, more interested in discussing psychology than sports, as intuitive as he was logical...

To forbid himself the pleasure of their intimacy was like denying a part of human experience. But he did so for seven long years. When he moved to The Beaches, however, things changed. Parkdale had been a confinement, a starvation diet. The Beaches had given him a newfound freedom, like a college student moving out of his parents' house to take his first apartment.

But he was never completely out of Guruji's sight. He could run but he couldn't hide. Never mind that his birth chart in Guruji's hands rendered him an open book. Guruji's intuition was so powerful that wherever he turned his attention a glaring spotlight revealed naked truth, warts and all. To associate with Guruji was to give up all disguise and pretense.

Crowe didn't kid himself that moving across town would allow him a secret life. Maybe it was just the remnants of his ego that risked defying a rule laid down years ago. Had lust corrupted their relationship or was it Nature's way of saying, time to move on? His actions had in turn prompted Guruji's response. He would have the rest of his life to digest the ramifications.

The great irony was, today he had *not* succumbed to desire, despite the temptation of a certain redhead. But he'd struggled with it. He'd tried to be strong and he knew that Guruji knew, yet still Guruji was on his case... It was an exercise in futility trying to understand his guru, whose Tantrik ways had always remained an enigma. So it was now with mixed feelings – both remorse and relief – that Crowe contemplated his future.

Crowe debarked at Kew Gardens and walked up Wheeler Street. His old Saab was parked in front of 18 Wheeler, front wheels angled into the curb to keep from rolling down the steep hill. Once red, twenty years of sun had faded it to the color of rust, conveniently disguising the decay under the rocker panels and the wheel wells.

Crowe unlocked the door and climbed the stairs to the second floor. The house was divided into two apartments, one for him and one for a tenant whose rent paid the mortgage. It was a pricey neighborhood, but reasonable when compared to the section south of Queen Street that lay within a stone's throw of the lake.

The apartment had a spacious feel. A large living room doubled as his office. In the middle was a single bedroom with an adjoining bathroom. In back was a kitchen with a walkout to a large deck. Large windows at either end of the apartment provided direct sunlight early morning and late afternoon.

Crowe dropped his knapsack and went out onto the deck. He looked westward to Toronto's downtown skyline – the CN Tower and the office skyscrapers clustered around Front and Bay Streets. To the south, Lake Ontario was a flat plane of darkness sparkled here and there by the lights of boats.

A cat meowed and jumped down from a patio chair. "Hey, Kosmo, how's my buddy?" Crowe stroked the large grey cat that belonged to his tenant downstairs.

He went inside. The light on his phone was blinking. He checked his messages. A request for a consultation from a local client. Confirmation from another client in New York that she'd pick him up at the airport tomorrow morning. Another consultation request from a client in Vancouver.

He went to his bedroom and checked his overnight bag. Packed and ready to go, his passport lying on top. He went to his desk, logged onto the Air Canada site and printed his boarding pass. He checked his email and found more queries from potential clients. A Dallas businessman negotiating a lucrative government contract. A British diplomat facing a bitter divorce. A natural healer in Chicago contemplating study with a shaman in Peru.

Ten years ago, Crowe had been doing readings for students trying to choose a career, and New Age housewives seeking purpose in life. Thanks to Guruji his skills had improved and his reputation spread by word of mouth to three continents, such that a steady queue of clients now awaited his counsel. Not that he was perfect, not by a long shot. He couldn't hold a candle to Guruji's 99% accuracy. Maybe if he'd remained celibate the rest of his life...

Crowe picked up his acoustic guitar, a Gibson he'd bought in university. He went out on the deck and played a few blues ballads for Kosmo. As usual, the cat made a lousy audience, twisting and turning in his chair like he couldn't get comfortable, rubbing his paws over his ears, finally retreating down the fire escape to the relative silence of the back yard. Crowe hung up his guitar. Obviously his singing left something to be desired.

13

Washington, DC

A light rain fell on the District of Columbia, rendering the streets as slick as many of the politicians and professional bureaucrats who'd staked out Washington as their turf. Dimly seen through the drizzle, the navigation lights of a low-flying helicopter blinked as it clattered across the sky toward Capitol Hill. The weather forecast called for heavy thunderstorms overnight and traffic on Pennsylvania Avenue was thin. Tuesday night was not a social night in Washington and most mandarins were in bed with their wives or concubines. In the J. Edgar Hoover FBI Building, however, the office lights were still on.

In his office overlooking Pennsylvania Avenue, FBI Director Robert Bueller sat at a semi-circular mahogany desk that supported a tall stack of files at one end and, moving clockwise along the curve, five other stacks of descending height, his own little mountain range of information. As he scanned one of the day's active files, overshadowed by the familiar vista of hundreds more to read, he realized his Sisyphean workload was costing him both his marriage and his stomach lining. Although visits to the best restaurants in Georgetown and gifts of jewelry temporarily assuaged the former, the only relief for the latter came from bottles of pink liquid stored in his desk drawer.

His phone rang. He glanced at the number and saw it was

a call he'd been expecting. "Evening, George."

Eight miles away in Langley, Director George Gann of the CIA sat in his own office behind a granite-topped desk the size of a snooker table. Lined up on it like fighters on the deck of an aircraft carrier were several briefing files, each with color-coded flaps identifying them as urgent reading and/or handling by the Director. "Hey, Bobby. I've got Mack Horton, Los Alamos security chief, on the line."

"Go ahead," Bueller said.

Eighteen hundred miles and two time zones away, Mack Horton sat alone in his Los Alamos office. Horton was a veteran of two wars, in one of which he'd caught shrapnel in his left knee. Although the VA surgeons had given him a titanium-and-ceramic replacement joint, the wound had ended his military career. Luckily he'd done a stint in Army Intelligence which, aided by a good buddy network, had got him into the National Laboratory five years ago.

"Tell us what you've got," Gann prompted.

Horton cleared his throat. "Twenty-eighteen hours Mountain Daylight Time, a car bomb went off in the parking lot of Site Twenty-seven. Sole casualty was Dr. Walter Cassidy. He was a team leader for several interrelated projects combating internet-based terrorism. A mathematics genius who also had management skills, he was a rarity in these parts. It's a major loss to the projects he was engaged in."

"Anything of significance in the way he was killed?" Bueller asked.

"Our technical guys are still sifting through the wreckage. They found fragments of an MP3 player and an ignition circuit wired to his vehicle's cigarette lighter. Pretty low-tech, but simple and effective. We've seen hits like this in Baghdad, Beirut, Jakarta..."

"An MP3 player?" Gann said.

"One of Cassidy's team members was only thirty feet away when this happened. He heard a loud blast of Arab music just before Cassidy's vehicle went off in all directions."

"Anything on the origins of the explosive?"

"Too soon to say. We've got a hundred pounds of debris now undergoing chemical analysis. We'll know more tomorrow."

"So no suspects?"

"Too soon to do more than speculate."

"Anything compromised?" Bueller said.

"I don't think so," Horton said. "I got State Police to secure Cassidy's house in Santa Fe till my guys got there. In the meantime I've put all our facilities on Red Alert. Until we know what's happening, we need to play it safe for the sake of the projects."

"Can't be too prudent," Bueller agreed. "Anything else?"

"Not tonight."

"Thanks, Mack," Gann said. "Keep us posted, will you?"

"Yes, sir. Good night."

Horton hung up. Bueller and Gann stayed on the line.

"What the hell is this, George? Some new counter-offensive in the war against terror? Is *al-Qaeda* going after our people the same way you've been targeting theirs? And taunting us with their music?"

"If so, it's a double twist. Number one, it's rare to see anything like this on domestic soil. Number two, it's not a typical target. They like to hit politicians and military. This would be a first for scientific personnel. But Cassidy's too low profile to merit that kind of attention."

"Too low? Your man in Los Alamos called him a genius. Is that hyperbole, or is he really an Einstein?"

"I don't know." Gann referred to a three-page resume before him. "He's got degrees up the yin-yang but so do lots of our people and no one's blown up their cars... yet."

"Maybe they're just trying to get at us any way they can, poke their fingers in our eyes, show us they can come right into our back yard like we've done in theirs?"

"I don't know."

"Your people never caught any wind of this?"

"Nothing that merited a report. But I'll kick some butt tonight and see what's what."

"You'll call me in the morning?"

"Sure."

"Who's going to tell the White House?"

"I'll do it." Gann looked at his watch. "They're always up till midnight anyway, watching Letterman."

14

Santa Fe, New Mexico

In an upper-middle-class subdivision of the city's north side, local residents coming home after an evening out found the entrance to the Piños Verdes cul-de-sac blocked by a New Mexico State Police cruiser. Two officers checked for ID and asked the residents to go straight home and not linger on the street. Even if they did dawdle a moment in their driveways to gawk, there was little to see.

Two black Ford Explorers were parked at the end of the street, blocking the view of both the carport and the front door of the ranch house. Even if a curious neighbor walked down for a closer look, another State Police car was parked crosswise in front of the two Explorers where a pair of state troopers served notice that the scene was off limits.

Inside the three-bedroom ranch house, built in the seventies and extensively remodeled, four Los Alamos security officers searched the place with all the zeal of DEA agents looking for an elusive ounce of banned substance to justify a property invasion. But these agents didn't need a warrant because the fine print in Dr. Walter Cassidy's employment contract stated that such incursions "to retrieve intellectual property in the interests of national security" were warranted on the say-so of the Security Office of the Los Alamos National Laboratory, under the command of Mack Horton.

In the living room, Agent Black used a cell phone to make an encrypted call to Horton back in Los Alamos. As the phone rang at the other end, Agent Black stepped aside to let Agent Green pass, carrying two cardboard file boxes to one of the Explorers parked out front. In Cassidy's office Agent Blue disconnected the cables from a desktop computer.

"Speak to me," Horton answered.

"We're almost finished," Agent Black told his commander. "We've purged his filing cabinet. He seems to have been pretty upright. Most of it's personal stuff, him and the wife. Damned little here that's work-related and what we've seen isn't sensitive, more like stuff you could get off the net or a good library if you knew where to look."

"You're sure he hasn't squirreled anything away?" Horton said. Some of these guys, and the brainier they were, the more they had that anti-establishment rogue gene in their systems, liked to 'archive' vital elements of their projects. It was a perverse job-security gambit, like taking a boss's kid for hostage as insurance against getting fired.

"We've been here for hours and found nothing." While Agents Black and Blue had tackled the obvious stuff – computer and paper files – Red and Green had gone through the house infrastructure, tapping walls, tugging loose carpet, shining flashlights into crawl spaces. They'd emptied cabinets, poked holes in box springs, checked toolboxes and suitcases and a hundred little hiding places where clever people thought they could hide something from Uncle Sam. And all Uncle Sam had found was a little stash of weed, a licensed handgun and a knobby battery-powered marital aid called The Throbber.

"How's his wife taking this?"

"I don't know," Black said. "We haven't seen her. You tried to contact her, right?"

"I phoned the house as soon as it happened and tried her cell phone several times too," Horton said. "Never got an answer so all I could do was leave messages."

"You think maybe somebody got to her same time as

him?"

"I don't know what to think at this point. I'll call the Santa Fe Police, get them to canvass the neighbors, see if anyone knows her whereabouts."

"What about the State troopers here?"

"Tell them to stand down. We'll let the city cops handle the canvass. Once you're finished there, wrap it up and bring it on home."

"Out of here in an hour, I reckon. You'll still be in the office when we get back?"

"Are you kidding me?" Horton told Black about his conference call with Bueller and Gann. "I'll be sleeping under my desk until this is all wrapped up in a pretty little package and delivered to Washington."

15

New York

Shift change at Manhattan's Mid-Town North precinct on 42nd Street was in full swing at midnight. Patrol officers horsed around in the locker room, the bachelors planning to decompress in local cop hangouts, the married ones anxious to head for the Lincoln Tunnel and home to Jersey. In the squad rooms, watch commanders briefed incoming shift officers on the state of affairs in their precinct, bounded by Lexington Avenue and the Hudson River in one direction, Park Avenue South to 43rd Street in the other.

Most everyone who worked out of the MTN precinct relished the jurisdiction, even if only because they didn't have to deal with the Times Square and Port Authority scumbags of their neighboring precinct, Mid-Town South. Still, although the genteel theatre district was smack in the middle of their territory, even drama queens occasionally killed someone in a hissy-fit, so it wasn't like the Homicide squad had nothing better to do than sit around solving crossword and *sudoku* puzzles.

Detective Jake Levinson hunched over a desk with several active case files, one of which he'd opened just minutes ago. Thirty-six years old, Levinson was at a typical crossroads in life, divorced two years ago but now with a steady girlfriend whose regular hints of marriage and mommy-hood were a test of his wavering commitment. Personal stuff aside, he was doing okay, had never been shot, had only once been obliged to kill a perp, and had accumulated an excellent track record for solving cases that fell to him. With luck and maybe another five to ten years, he might make lieutenant.

Separated by the widths of their two desks, his partner Arnie Rossimoff rooted like a truffle pig through the remains of some Chinese take-out. Rossimoff was a walking cliché from the wrong end of the neat-cop/sloppy-cop paradigm, for which the brass had an uncanny ability to construct odd pairings. Whereas Levinson prided himself in being clean-shaven, wearing polished shoes and showing up for work in a clean shirt and a tie that didn't need to be paisley to disguise food stains, Rossimoff was a haberdasher's nightmare.

Arnie looked like he'd slept in his clothes and just woken up, not necessarily in a bed. He wore dark teal pants, the sort favored by utility repairmen, heavily creased at the knees and crotch. His footwear were scuffed black Adidas walking shoes, his shirt a faded plaid, his too-wide-to-be-stylish tie a catch-all for soy and Szechuan hot sauce. Rossimoff had never been married and it wasn't hard to figure out why. If doubts lingered, a visit to his book-cluttered studio apartment on 53rd, where the tiny bed-sit, the mini-galley kitchen and the peeling bathroom stall, all denied daylight at the bottom of an eight-storey air shaft, reminded one of life on a submarine, bereft of luxury or female association.

"Want some more before I polish it off?" Rossimoff offered Levinson a carton in which remained several nuggets of General Tao chicken.

"Thanks." Levinson speared a piece of chicken with a chopstick. It was pretty good. Rossimoff had picked it up at Foo King Chinese Kitchen on 10th Avenue on his way into work. Levinson generally preferred Lucky Wok or Panda Restaurant, but was happy so long as no dishes featured Wild Deer, generally suspected to be a euphemism for garbage-fattened rodent, of which New York had many.

"Foo-king good, right?" Rossimoff grinned, revealing a piece of no-longer-crispy spinach stuck in his teeth.

Levinson turned his attention back to the file that lay before him, which at this point included only the patrol officers' initial report, his own brief field notes and a few photos of the victim and the general crime scene.

Lieutenant Pickett approached their desks. "What's the situation on Fifty-first?"

"Victim is Janis Stockwell, age thirty-six," Levinson said. "Discovered by a passerby at eleven-ten. No purse or wallet on the scene, but we got an ID from a medical bracelet she wore. Broadway ticket stub in her coat pocket. Looks like she got mugged on her way home."

"And resisted? Most locals know better."

"Most crackheads are on a short fuse," Rossimoff said. "You don't give it up on the count of five, they're all over you like hyenas on a sick antelope."

"We found her pepper spray on the scene," Levinson said. "Not that it seems to have done her any good."

"Might have set the perp off," Rossimoff speculated.

"Cause of death?" the Lieutenant asked.

Levinson shook his head. "Not sure. Looked like she was strangled. Visible trauma to the neck." He handed a crime scene photo to Pickett. In the color closeup, bruising ran from windpipe to beneath her right ear. "But she's with the ME. We should know pretty soon."

"You notify next-of-kin?"

Rossimoff nodded. "Her husband was on business in Frisco, but he's on his way home now."

"How'd he sound?"

"All broken up." Rossimoff sucked his teeth. "Over the top, if you ask me." A lifelong bachelor, Rossimoff had apparently never shed a tear for a lost companion.

"You guys worked the scene? Anything else I should know?"

"She was found lying between two parked cars," Levinson said. "We got the CSU to dust the adjacent vehicles for prints. They're now running them through AFIS."

Rossimoff swallowed the last bit of moo-shoo pork. "We canvassed the street, couldn't find anyone that saw anything, but we've put it out to the media with a request for info. Maybe some good citizen will pick up the phone."

"And we flagged her credit cards," Levinson said. "Soon as they get used, we'll pick up the trail."

"Okay. Keep me posted." The Lieutenant headed back to his office.

Levinson's phone rang. He glanced at the call display as he answered. "Levinson. What's up?"

Rossimoff struck bottom in the last take-out carton, extracting limp remains of formerly crispy spinach. He tossed the cartons into his waste basket, opened a package of wipettes and swabbed his chin and hands. He was inspecting his tie for collateral damage when Levinson hung up.

"That was the ME," Levinson said. "Time of death now fixed at roughly ten-forty-five, give or take ten minutes. Turns out Mrs. Stockwell did indeed suffer severe neck trauma, but apparently that wasn't what killed her."

"Concussion?" Rossimoff speculated. "Heart failure?"

"Anaphylactic shock."

"An allergic reaction? Like shellfish or something...?"

"Something very hot and spicy," Levinson hinted.

"The pepper spray!?"

"Seems the perp emptied the canister down her throat."

Rossimoff coughed heavily, as if the news had left a bad taste in his own mouth.

16

Wednesday

New York

Wednesday morning, Air Canada flight 702 from Toronto arrived at LaGuardia on schedule. Among the travelers was Axel Crowe. Wearing black jeans and a charcoal-colored leather jacket, Crowe carried a single overnight bag slung over his shoulder.

As he passed a news-stand, he saw the headlines of *The New York Times*, which read *'Security Tightens for Terror Alert'*. Fifty feet down the concourse, where it opened into the baggage claim area, two guards with bullet-proof vests and pistols on their hips were giving passersby a more-than-casual scrutiny.

Bypassing the baggage carousels, he entered the Arrivals lounge, where a uniformed chauffeur was holding a sign that said 'Axel Crowe'. Crowe identified himself.

"May I take your bag?" the chauffeur said, reaching for it.

Crowe followed him to the exit. At the curb, an airport security officer stood next to a white Lincoln Town Car. Crowe glanced at its vanity plates. *LISA C*. Every letter of the alphabet had its numerological counterpart. L and S were both 3s, I and A both 1s, and the C was a 2. Add them up and you got a 10, which reduced to 1, the number of power and royalty.

The chauffeur pressed a folded bill into the security officer's palm. He opened the rear door and, after Crowe had seated himself inside, put his bag in the trunk and sat behind the wheel.

"Good morning, Mr. Crowe," said the silver-haired and elegant woman from the other side of the plush leather rear seat. "I'm Lisa Carmichael." She offered her hand and Crowe took it, feeling in her grip the heat and strength he'd come to associate with successful entrepreneurs. He glanced at her thumb whose upper phalange was larger than normal and graced by a broadly rounded nail. Lacquered of course in a high-quality polish, but it was the form rather than the substance of the nail that interested him, indicating she was headstrong and determined.

"Did you have a good flight?" Carmichael asked as the Lincoln slid away from the terminal.

"Yes, thanks. I hope it wasn't an inconvenience, your picking me up this way."

"Not at all. I live in Long Beach so it's not much out of the way."

Crowe had a closer look at Carmichael. He guessed her to be about fifty years old, although with the cosmetic surgery she'd had on her eyelids, she probably passed for forty among those who didn't know better. She was otherwise a lovely specimen of a woman, the age bracket for which Crowe reserved a special fondness because they formed a significant portion of his clientele demographic. Mature, successful, smart enough to know that not everything in life could be interpreted by lawyers, accountants or trusted girlfriends.

"Would you like some coffee or juice?" She indicated a service unit that included a steel carafe on a burner and a mini-fridge.

After a quick survey of what was available, Crowe accepted a bottle of mango juice. Rich in anti-oxidants and glutamine acid, an important protein for concentration and memory.

The Lincoln moved at highway speed along the Brooklyn Queens Expressway. Carmichael poured herself a coffee and turned in her seat to face her fellow passenger. She wore a dark blue business suit whose pants were belted with a silver buckle. Aside from a pair of silver-and-emerald earrings and a matching band with a larger stone on her ring finger, she showed little sign of ostentation despite her apparent wealth. Crowe had studied her birth chart a week ago when she'd called to make this appointment. He assumed correctly that she was a self-made woman who'd enjoyed great success in the fashion industry over the past seven years.

"Kevin Blaikie spoke very highly of you, Mr. Crowe, but he never told me exactly what you do for him."

"For Kevin? Typically I find witnesses who've gone missing, whose testimony is crucial to cases he's handling." Although born into wealth, Blaikie had been trained as a corporate lawyer and ran a large management consultancy that specialized in corporate malfeasance, typically involving accounting fraud and major pension irregularities. Usually there was some guilty little gnome who'd skimmed a fortune, or a whistle-blower who could identify executives in the know and on the take.

"And convince them that testifying is worth their while?"

"No, I'm just a finder. Kevin has persuaders to handle that other part."

"He can be pretty persuasive himself," she said.

Crowe knew what she was hinting at but said only, "I haven't been the focus of his charm. Or maybe I'm just impervious to it."

"You do have an impenetrable look about you, if you don't mind my saying so."

Crowe shrugged. "Some people accuse me of being too business-like, but I keep my private and professional lives separate. That's not to say I don't occasionally develop a personal relationship with a client. It's just not something that happens very often."

"I'm sure you have your reasons."

"It all boils down to objectivity," Crowe said. "The kind of work I do, it's all about making subtle judgments. It's hard enough to make the right call based on a complex set of factors without having bias thrown in. You get too friendly with a client, next thing you know you're subconsciously trying to put a positive spin on things when what the client really needs is the truth. Would you want your doctor, after viewing your medical test results and seeing something that made her suspect cancer, say it's probably nothing, just a shadow, because she likes you and doesn't want to worry you?"

"Of course not. I want the truth, not a varnished facsimile."

"I'd soon be out of business if I couldn't consistently deliver that to my clients."

"I appreciate that." She sipped her coffee. "From what Kevin told me, I should think of you as a private investigator that uses – what's the diplomatic term – esoteric techniques?"

"Think of me as a personal advisor. And to put it bluntly, I use palmistry and astrology, but other things too depending on the situation."

"And most important, he says you produce results."

"Most of the time."

"Not one hundred percent?"

"Only God gets a perfect score. The rest of us are just playing at His feet."

"Hmm. You're quite a philosopher." She checked his hands for a wedding band but saw only an odd ring that seemed to be made of bone, with several small deeply-set stones around its circumference. "Are you married, Mr. Crowe?"

"Only to my guru." Trial separation notwithstanding, Crowe reflected.

"You don't enjoy the company of women?" After a hesitation, she added, "Or men, perhaps? I have many lonely but attractive friends."

"It's a mixed blessing, but I enjoy solitude."

"Wasn't it Nabokov who said that solitude is Satan's playground?"

"There's also an African proverb," Crowe said. "*Better to travel alone than with a bad companion.*"

"Are you always this cynical?"

"Only about my personal relationships."

Carmichael's phone rang. She looked at the display. "I'm sorry, I've got to take this call."

Crowe turned his gaze out the window, tuning out her conversation with some business associate, a small matter of five thousand blouses from Hong Kong being held hostage by an over-zealous customs broker in Los Angeles. The Lincoln followed the expressway as it angled west, heading for the Williamsburg Bridge.

Fifteen minutes later, they were in SoHo. The chauffeur parked the Lincoln in front of a five-storey building just as Carmichael finished her phone call. The chauffeur opened the door for his employer. Crowe let himself out and joined Carmichael on the sidewalk.

Crowe saw a black kid in a basketball jersey, number eight, on the stoop of a convenience store a few doors down, tossing popcorn to pigeons milling on the corner. One of the pigeons dragged a broken wing, the tips of its feathers frayed ragged, like a broom drearily sweeping the sidewalk.

Crowe looked at the number over the building entrance. 845. He combined the numbers and reduced them to a single digit, eight, a routine that was second nature to him. Eight was associated with Saturn. Today was Wednesday, ruled by Mercury. The idea of foreign commerce popped into his mind. Try explaining that to a client, it made as much sense as cricket did to a Super Bowl fan, so he never bothered. But one man's tablet of meaningless hieroglyphics was another man's Rosetta Stone.

The world is gross, the signs are subtle, Guruji used to say.

Carmichael looked at her watch. She barely had a moment to sigh in exasperation when a blue Lexus pulled up to the curb behind the Lincoln. A mid-forties blonde in a pinstripe pant suit scampered onto the curb.

"Hi Lisa, sorry I'm a few minutes late."

"We just got here. This is Axel Crowe. Pamela Ritt."

"Please. Call me Pam." She gave Crowe a brisk handshake and turned to a lockbox fastened to the front railing of the building. She worked the combination and extracted a set of keys.

The chauffeur stayed with the Lincoln. Crowe followed Carmichael and the real estate agent through the marble-floored foyer and into an elevator to the top floor. Pamela unlocked the door and let them into a large bright loft decorated with expensive furniture and bold art on exposed brick walls.

"Many of my clients are big names in sports and entertainment, people with eight-figure incomes," Pamela told Crowe. "One of them bought this place for six mil, then spent another million on design and renovations. He's lived here only a year and now he's put it up for sale."

"Asking...?" Crowe said.

"Seven-five."

"Not exactly a fire sale price, but interesting enough to consider." Carmichael looked at Crowe. "What do you think? Should I buy it?"

He looked at his watch. "I'll need a few minutes."

"I'll leave you two alone," Pamela said. "I'm going across the street to pick up a coffee and make a few phone calls."

"Take your time," Carmichael told Crowe. "I'll read my email." She strolled into the living room and seated herself in what appeared to be the most comfortable leather chair. She took a BlackBerry from her purse and went to work.

Crowe glanced at the windows at one end of the loft, noted the shadows falling across the hardwood floor and established a sense of compass direction. He paced off the breadth and span of the loft. Pausing at the windows overlooking the street, he saw the ledge outside was fouled with pigeon shit. Nothing remarkable in that but he was still thinking about the pigeon with the broken wing.

He climbed the stairs, counting seventeen steps, to a large sleeping area above the kitchen. In itself this violated principles common to *vaastu shastra*, the Vedic precursor to *feng shui*. Kitchens contained fire and knives, incompatible with bedrooms. As if that wasn't bad enough, a Japanese sword was mounted above the headboard of the king-size bed.

From the railing of the sleeping area, Crowe looked into the living area where Carmichael sat reading her BlackBerry. Mentally, he divided the loft's floor plan into nine zones and noted Carmichael's position within one of them.

He took his iPhone out and started his astrology app. Entering the current time, date and location, he created a horary chart, a snapshot view of the planets for this time and place. He sat on the bed, studying the chart a few minutes before descending into the living area.

In his mind it was clear. Gemini rising indicated his client, whose ruling planet Mercury was in the eleventh house of profit with an exalted Sun in Aries indicating accomplished desires. The seller was seen through the seventh house, whose lord Jupiter was debilitated in Capricorn and in the eighth house of misfortune. If that wasn't the signature of a bankruptcy case, he didn't know what was.

Carmichael returned her BlackBerry to her purse. "What's the verdict?"

"The owner's a professional athlete?"

"That's right. He plays for the Knicks."

"Has he suffered an injury?"

"He sprained his ankle in the New Year and was benched for most of the season."

"Aside from that, he's lost a bundle in the stock market and his marriage is probably on the rocks."

Carmichael tugged an earlobe. "What's that tell me? This place has bad karma?"

"Yes," Crowe said, "but only for him."

"What about me?"

"What sticks to him slides off you."

She smiled at the analogy. "What do I do about this place?"

"Offer six-nine."

"Isn't that a bit low ball? Pamela suggested seven-three, seven-two at worst. It's a decent market."

Crowe knew there was no point trying to explain his logic. "Offer six-nine and hang tough. You'll get it. And as much as your basketball player lost here, you'll gain."

"Really?" Carmichael's eyebrows arched.

"Don't let anyone live here. Just rent a few pieces of office furniture – a small oval conference table with five chairs right around here, and over there...," pointing to a spot near the brick wall, "a desk with a phone and a computer."

"Then what?"

"You're going to flip it."

"How long will that take? You know what I could rent this place for?"

Crowe consulted the chart on his phone. "I expect you'll get an offer within the month."

"You're kidding!"

His phone played a Rolling Stones ring tone. *Gimme Shelter.* Crowe answered.

Carmichael stood and walked around the living room area, gently chewing on a thumbnail, giving his recommendation some serious consideration.

On the phone, Crowe was saying, "Kevin? Slow down a bit. Say again? Your sister...?" He listened. "Okay, take it easy. Yes, I understand, but I'm sure they're giving it all their attention. Yes, of course. I'll be there in half an hour." He pocketed the phone and stood. "I'm sorry, Ms. Carmichael. I've got to go."

17

Washington

FBI Director Bueller had been in the office until midnight the night before. If it weren't for the fragile state of his marriage he might have slept on the sofa bed, but these days that wasn't a sensible option, for neither his marriage nor his health. His marriage was now a perpetual question mark the frenetic activity of his workday pushed to the back of his mind, but his ulcer was ever-present. From the first briefings of the day through meetings and conference calls to the chauffeured drive home, reading one last report before he fell exhausted into bed beside his disenchanted wife, his ulcer gnawed at him like a wolverine trapped in a wooden crate. He couldn't stomach this much longer.

Just before nine, CIA Director Gann arrived with a rap-a-tap-tap at the office door. Bueller looked up from the report he was reading, and beckoned Gann in. "Grab a seat. Ridgeway's scheduled to call any minute."

"Where's Tom this morning?"

"Miami, giving a pep talk to the Coast Guard."

The phone rang. Bueller answered it and hit the button on his speaker-phone to include Gann in the conversation.

A thousand miles away, Secretary of the Department of Home Security Tom Ridgeway sat in the office of the Rear Admiral, Commander of the Seventh Coast Guard District in Miami, whose territory included Florida, Georgia and South Carolina. From the window overlooking a slip, Ridgeway saw half a dozen naval cutters with Old Glory flapping at their masts. It was a blustery day in Miami and in an hour he'd add a little bluster of his own, lecturing a hundred new Guard recruits, along with two hundred existing staff, on their vital role in defending America's maritime perimeters.

Bueller sipped pink liquid from his coffee cup and got things started. "Morning, Tom. I've got George here."

"Hi, Tom," Gann said. "Having nice weather there?"

"Better'n your little shit-storm, I reckon. How's that situation in Los Alamos?"

"They secured Dr. Cassidy's Santa Fe home last night," Bueller said. "Nothing out of order there but just to be safe they removed everything even vaguely work-related. We were a little concerned at first because we thought his wife had disappeared too. But according to an agenda we found in her office, turns out she's in New York."

"She in the service too?" Ridgeway asked.

"No. She's a freelance writer, does project proposals for different branches of government."

"Including the National Laboratory?" Gann interjected.

"No," Bueller said. "Mostly state level. Departments of Agriculture, Economic Development, Indian Affairs, Transportation..."

"Any possibility Dr. Cassidy's death isn't what it seems?" Ridgeway asked. "Something personal, and nothing to do with national security?"

"That seems highly unlikely," Gann said, "what with him getting blown up in the parking lot where he works, to the accompaniment of Arab music."

"I agree with George," Bueller said. "And although it's a coincidence his wife being out of town, no reason to suspect her. We'll talk to her anyway when she gets back home but I don't imagine much will come of it."

"Anything on the bomb that was used?" Gann asked.

Bueller consulted the file. "C4 military grade plastic explosive. No surprise there, with so much stuff having gone missing over the years. And they identified an MP3 player that was part of the package, a cheap model from Wal-Mart."

"Any suspects?" Ridgeway asked.

"I've contacted our Albuquerque office," Bueller said. "A few local Islamists on their radar screen merit questioning. They're conducting pickups today."

"Anything further that concerns DHS?" Ridgeway said. "Anything you need from me?"

"Far as George and I can see, no need to alarm the public." As far as Bueller and Gann were concerned, they had to be prudent with DHS. The relatively new organization, however well-funded in its mandate, was populated with less-than-stellar personnel – retirees from national security and military organizations providing direction to a cadre of still-wet-behind-the-ears recruits who hadn't made the grade for the FBI or CIA.

"So no change recommended to the Threat Advisory level?" Ridgeway referred to the five-color code that reflected the risk of terrorist attacks on an unsuspecting but otherwise apprehensive American public.

"Roger that," Gann said. "No change."

"At our end," Bueller said, "the FBI has issued an internal directive for an Orange Alert that applies only to national security clearance projects and personnel, pending further notice. And you, George?"

"The CIA has advised likewise for consulates and off-shore scientific installations. Not much else we can do for now until those suspects are interrogated."

"We should know more by end of day," Bueller said.

"We'll keep you posted, Tom."

"Okay, I'll leave you guys to it," Ridgeway said. "I've got to go inject some inspiration into a hundred new recruits."

Bueller hung up, and looked at the pink residue in the bottom of his coffee cup. To each his own medicine.

18

New York

The Lincoln pulled up to the curb in front of a high-rise on Central Park South. Lisa Carmichael signed a check with a flourish of her Mont Blanc pen and handed it to Crowe. "Please give my condolences to Kevin. I'll try to give him a call sometime this evening."

"Thank you." Crowe reached for the latch but the chauffeur already had the door open. Crowe climbed out and the chauffeur handed him his overnight bag.

After being greeted by a doorman who was expecting him, Crowe rode the elevator to the 19th floor penthouse condo of his wealthy client, Kevin Blaikie.

They'd known each other three years. Blaikie had been in town one year for TIFF – the Toronto International Film Festival – and on the suggestion of a Hollywood friend had booked a consultation. A year later he'd asked Crowe to help find a witness who'd gone missing, a corporate accountant in a big pension-plundering case that was going to court. Every now and again he performed similar services for Blaikie.

Along the way they'd become friends, but their social activity mostly consisted of Blaikie buying lunch or dinner in the most expensive restaurants in Manhattan, and Crowe telling anecdotes about his numerous pilgrimages to India, for which Blaikie seemed to have a bottomless appetite.

There were only two apartments on the penthouse level, one facing the park and the other looking at a distant Jersey. Emerging from the elevator, Crowe barely had time to glance at his dim reflection in the polished marble walls of the foyer before a door opened and Blaikie beckoned him in.

Despite his natural good looks, Blaikie was a wreck – red eyes, unshaven whiskers, wrinkled clothes he might have slept in. Crowe caught a scent of coffee, Scotch and anxiety. Blaikie closed the door behind him. Crowe set down his overnight bag and gave Blaikie a strong embrace. Blaikie looked like Humpty-Dumpty after the fall, the cracks in his shell radiating from the hole in his heart.

"Have you slept at all?" Crowe said.

Blaikie shook his head. "I had to go to the morgue to identify her. Then I was with the police for an hour answering questions. By the time I got home it was almost four, and there was no way I could sleep after that. I decided to stay up until seven so I could phone my parents, be the first to tell them before they heard it through the media. In fact, I need to go over to their place soon. My mother's out of her mind with grief…"

Blaikie led the way into the large living room, whose art collection was the envy of any serious aficionado. Blaikie was a major fan of the Surrealists and their Dadaist predecessors, and he'd accumulated works by Dali, Magritte and many others. The paintings and a handful of sculptures were scattered throughout the apartment, rendering a museum-like quality to the otherwise minimalist decor.

They sat on facing leather sofas near wall-length windows overlooking Central Park. From where he sat, Crowe could see a kite flying over the park. Blaikie took a carafe from an end table and poured himself coffee. He raised an eyebrow at Crowe, who shook his head. Blaikie sipped coffee, grimaced and regarded Crowe with woeful eyes.

"It's a shame you never met Janis. You would've loved her. Everyone else did. Never mind she was my sister, I never knew anyone as good as her. Born to money, but never let it go to her head, never took it for granted. While her friends competed to throw lavish parties or build spectacular houses, Janis was the classic altruist. She was active in dozens of charities, raised millions in funding. She changed the lives of so many people – single mothers, inner-city kids, the homeless..."

Voice cracking, Blaikie paused to wipe his eyes with his sleeve. "It doesn't make sense her dying that way. Whatever cash she carried would have meant nothing to her. If a mugger had demanded money, she'd have handed over her wallet and walked away. If the guy had presented a good enough sob story, she'd have helped him."

"What do the police think?"

"They get dozens of muggings a week in the theatre district. Most people walk away scared but unharmed. They said it was just bad luck she encountered someone violent."

"You don't agree?"

"Janis was wealthy but she was streetwise. If she could talk a millionaire into making a major charity contribution, she could talk a mugger into taking her money and leaving her unharmed. A simple mugging gone bad? It has to be something else. Can you shed any light on this?"

Crowe took out his phone. He didn't need to create a horary chart, since the disposition of the planets was still pictured in his mind from when he'd studied them in Soho an hour ago. He was now more interested in Janis Stockwell's natal chart.

Blaikie knew his sister's birth date and place – November 20th, 1971, in New York – but didn't know her time of birth, which Crowe needed to determine her ascendant. He considered his options. In lieu of a birth time, he sometimes used the current time of day. Other occasions, different techniques... Out in Central Park, the blue kite wheeled high in the air. Blue was the color of Venus. Libra was an air sign ruled by Venus. On the wall behind Blaikie was an Ernst lithograph, *Portrait Bleu*, featuring a bird-like figure. More corroboration. Perhaps Janis Stockwell had a Libra ascendant.

"With their mugging theory, I'm concerned whether the police will develop any alternative leads." Blaikie picked up a decanter and added Scotch to his coffee.

"It's a little early to play armchair detective. Give them a chance to work with what they've got. In the meantime, if you want to be present for your parents, go easy on the booze..."

Blaikie nodded and put the coffee cup down. "You're right, I'm not thinking clearly." He rubbed his face and ran his fingers through his hair. "I've got to get my act together, not fall to pieces. I know how my father will react. He'll pull his head into his turtle shell and go numb. He won't be much help to my mother. And her health is already fragile. If they don't catch whoever did this, she'll go off the deep end."

Crowe studied Janis Stockwell's chart. It was unusual in that five planets occupied her second house. With all of the benefic planets there, it was a signature of family prestige and wealth. But two of those planets were less than a degree apart, what Vedic astrologers called a planetary war. It implied an irritant – a person or a situation – that made life hell for the individual. Crowe suspected it had something to do with an unhappy sex life but he wasn't about to tell her brother that.

Coincidentally, aside from Janis Stockwell's chart, at this moment another planetary war was being waged between two different planets. This wasn't the first time Crowe had noted a synchronicity of circumstances. He recalled a weekend several years ago in Chicago where he'd given readings for several clients. A solar eclipse had been visible across the northern USA that weekend. Amazingly, out of a dozen clients whose birthdays spanned thirty years, seven had been born within days of an eclipse. What were the odds?

Guruji had told him many years ago: *It will never make sense to someone who hasn't embraced this life we lead but, once you really start to work with the planets, they start to work with you. Make friends with them and they will be your companions for life. When you are lost they will show you the way, and when you are in despair they will give you hope. Astrology is a language and once you learn this language, the planets will speak to you.*

Crowe stared at Janis Stockwell's birth chart. In his mind's eye, he superimposed the current planetary positions, what astrologers called transits, upon the natal chart. Today's planetary war involved Venus and Mars, rulers of Janis Stockwell's first and seventh houses. This implied a war between husband and wife. The two planets were in Janis's sixth house ruling competitors. This often spelled legal proceedings as a prelude to divorce, but under aggravated circumstances, warfare could take more extreme form.

"Did your sister have a solid marriage?"

"She seemed happy."

"How about her husband?"

"What about him?"

"He's been going through a difficult time?"

Blaikie shrugged. "Hard to know. We put on a face for the public but inside we could be suffering. Why do you ask? What's Jeb got to do with this?"

In Janis's chart, Jeb was represented by Mars in an antagonistic relationship with its natural enemy Saturn. Mars indicated violence, while Saturn reflected suppression. Crowe had seen instances of this in marriage where the spouse was abusive. But abuse could be imaginative and take many forms...

"He may have been seeing someone else."

Blaikie shook his head. "I can't imagine it. Jeb's a good guy."

"It's a balancing act millions of men juggle every day. As you said, it's impossible to know what's going on inside a person's mind."

"Are you really such a cynic?"

"People call us cynics when they don't share our ability to perceive reality. I prefer to think of myself as a realist, but bear with me. I'm sure there's a third party..."

"What are you suggesting? A girlfriend who got tired of waiting? Someone capable of murder?"

Crowe proceeded cautiously. "Money and lust make the world go round. Your family has a lot of money. Maybe someone else supplied the lust."

Blaikie reached for his coffee cup. He took a drink and set it back down. He ran his fingers through his hair again and hunched forward, elbows on knees, chin resting on his balled fists.

"Now that you mention it, I felt Janis turning inward this past year. She wasn't herself. I even mentioned it to her once but she blew it off, said she was suffering a recurring migraine. I wasn't really convinced but I didn't push it. Looking back, maybe there was something going on behind the scenes."

There always is, Crowe reflected. He was reminded of a famous woodcut from a Medieval astrological text, in which a seeker of truth in the real world pokes his head through a veil to discover another world with multiple layers of existence, and wheels within wheels within wheels...

"Can you work with the police?" Blaikie said. "I can pull some strings to give you access."

"I could try, but consider this. Once I start turning over rocks, strange things may crawl out from under. What if I find something you don't like?"

"Like what? You think she or Jeb was mixed up in something unsavory?"

"All I'm saying is, it might be more complicated than it appears. The police investigation itself may turn up something unpleasant. Whatever I do may uncover other things of which you weren't aware."

"All I know is, Janis was good and decent. I'll take my chances with the outcome. I give you *carte blanche* to dig up whatever you can. And however unlikely I think it is, if it turns out that Jeb's implicated, I need to know that."

Crowe looked out the window at the kite rising and falling on the wind above Central Park. What was that line? A butterfly flaps its wings in one part of the world, and a typhoon destroys another part...

Blaikie misinterpreted Crowe's hesitation. "At triple your usual fee, and don't spare any expense. Go where you must and buy whatever or whomever you need to get it done. I'll foot the bill."

Crowe thought of his bank account and the thoroughbreds galloping through the holes in it. Truth was, he needed money as much as Blaikie needed help. He looked at Blaikie, saw grief etched in the shadows beneath his eyes, and read the plea in his gaze. Crowe nodded. More than anything else, he felt sympathy for a client who was also a friend, whose violent loss of a sister demanded resolution and justice.

19

Albuquerque

By seven-thirty, most guests had departed the Roughrider Motor Inn, a few slinking home with cheating hearts tucked up their sleeves, the rest gone for breakfast before their round of sales visits to local businesses. A block east, traffic on the I-25 revved up as people headed in for work. Up in a cloudless sky, two turkey buzzards rode a light southeast wind, working their way down the Rio Grande.

Unit 12 opened and Zeke Zabriskie stepped off the curb, letting the aluminum screen door bang against the frame. With an unlit cigarette stuck between his lips, a tan rawhide vest over a white shirt, and a crumpled black cowboy hat pulled low over his eyes, he had the hard lean look of a Marlboro Man, except harder, leaner, and possibly meaner. Thirty-five years old, he was an unemployed jack of all trades, almost none of which constituted grounds for legal employment. He lit his cigarette, coughed once and spat a bullet of phlegm far out into the parking lot. He took keys from his pocket, climbed into a mud-spattered black Dodge Ram pickup and drove off.

Half an hour later, a young Mexican woman in a green uniform emerged with a linen trolley and a vacuum cleaner from the motel office to began her morning round of cleaning up after everyone else's mess.

A few minutes later, Unit 12 opened again and Dave Munson emerged with a bowling ball in a tote bag. He was a good-looking blond with a mustache, wearing a blue nylon windbreaker that said *Bay Area Ballbreakers* across the shoulders. Also thirty-five years old, Munson was an unemployed musician whose dreams had lost their fizz over the years, like a beer left standing at room temperature. He still had the looks that could have graced a CD cover but that was all he had, and even it wouldn't make a difference this late in the game. Once upon a time he'd had aspirations of a rock star lifestyle but fate had kept him on a blues budget.

He locked the motel door behind him and climbed into the white Cavalier rental from Alamo. A couple of minutes later he was headed up I-25 toward Rio Rancho, a north end community on the other side of the river, to which many of Albuquerque's professionals had migrated in response to new homes in new subdivisions in close proximity to new shopping malls.

Having driven this route four times already, Munson no longer referred to the complimentary map provided by Alamo. He took the Paseo del Norte exit, crossed the river and turned onto Coors Boulevard. He entered a huge parking lot that was filling up fast. He locked the car and walked toward the big pink stucco building whose marquee read *Rolling Thunder Bowl-a-Drome.*

He showed his player's pass at the gate and entered a bowling complex the size of a Boeing hangar, twenty-four lanes of gleaming hardwood as far as the eye could see. His ears tingled at the joyous thunder of dozens of balls rumbling down the alleys, players warming up for the day's competition. In the galleries were team players, friends, family and assorted fans to cheer on their favorite teams.

Munson checked the schedule board to see which lane his team was playing in the opening time slot. One of the organizers hustled up to him, peered at his nametag and waved a message note in his face.

"Dave Munson? You got a call from the San Rafael Police. They want you to phone them right away." He handed Munson the message slip, a name with a 415-area-code number. "You want some quiet, you can use my office."

Munson followed him to an office with a window looking out on lanes 18 and 19. He closed the door and sat at the organizer's desk, bare except for a computer, a telephone, and a picture of the man with his wife and three *bambinos*.

Munson called the number and spoke to a Detective Fred Hutchins, partner of Detective Jim Starrett, the name on the message slip. Hutchins laid it out in twenty-five words or less. Bernie Lang had been struck by a hit-and-run driver while jogging yesterday, and died on the scene. They were notifying family or friends and Munson's was the first name that came up.

"Why didn't you call me yesterday?" Munson said with rehearsed annoyance.

"We tried your cell phone number last night."

"I'd turned it off. I was bushed, made an early night of it."

"My partner left a message."

"I hadn't even turned it on this morning. I was going to call Bernie this evening."

"What's your relationship with Mr. Lang?"

"We lived together. We're… we were a couple."

Hutchins, no stranger to Bay Area mores, didn't skip a beat. "Does Mr. Lang have any blood relatives?"

"He's got some family in Philly. A couple of sisters, what I recall, and at least one nephew."

"You got names, so we can contact them?"

"They never came out to visit or anything and Bernie only ever referred to them by their first names. Probably he's got their numbers somewhere on his computer but I'd have to look for them."

"Anyone else we should notify?"

"There's no one else to handle arrangements but me. Where is he now?"

"County morgue till the coroner's done with him."

"And then?"

"Funeral home of your choice."

Munson looked at his watch. "Okay, I gotta make a phone call, see how soon I can get a flight back home. Anything else you need to tell me?"

"Just give us a call soon as you're back in town. Either my partner or I need to have a little chat with you."

"About what?"

"Bernie's social circle."

"I don't get it. What for?"

"This is where I say, we'll ask the questions, right?"

"I don't think that's funny, under the circumstances. My best friend's dead and you're being a smartass?"

"I'm sorry for your loss." Hutchins sounded genuinely apologetic. "Please give us a call when you return."

"Sure."

Munson sat there a minute looking at the picture of the organizer and his brood. Happy little family portrait. Easy for you to smile, *hombré*, all you ever wanted was a steady job and enough money to buy a car and a TV and a washing machine, and already you'd be ahead of your old man. But for some of us, life didn't boil down to such simplicity.

Munson went to find his team. They were down at lane 22, stretching their hamstrings, checking out the balls on the opposition, a team from Florida called the Pensacola Pindroppers. Munson told them about his situation. After a flurry of condolences, his captain hugged him and said do what you got to do, beckoning for their second-stringer

Wartman to get his shoes on, he would bowl today.

"Sorry, man, that's a bummer," Wartman told Munson. But you could tell, he was so happy to play, if Munson didn't know better, he'd have suspected Wartman of having put the contract on Bernie himself.

20

New York

Carrie Cassidy had breakfast with another prospective literary agent, Sarah Diamant, at a place called Moe's on West 57th. The place was packed but Diamant spoke to the hostess and they were soon seated in a booth for two in the back.

A steady banter among waitresses and customers made it hard for Carrie to concentrate on her pitch but, once she had a shot of coffee, she was off and running with her tale of love gone wild in the Southwest. Diamant, God bless her, appeared to have no cell phone, and gave Carrie her full attention even as she wolfed her eggs and lox. Before the bill arrived, Diamant told Carrie she'd read her first five chapters and was eager to read more. Assuming the rest of the novel was as well written, she'd represent her.

Parting with an agreement to send the full manuscript as soon as she got home, Carrie danced back up Fifth Avenue to 58th Street where she checked out of her hotel and caught the shuttle to LaGuardia. En route, she turned on her cell phone for the first time today and found a message waiting for her.

The message was from Mack Horton, security officer at the Los Alamos National Laboratory, asking her to phone him as soon as possible. She'd expected something like this. When Walt failed to show up for work, they'd wonder where he was. Then she thought about it some more and decided something was wonky. It was ten o'clock here, only eight in Santa Fe.

Some days Walt pulled an all-nighter and wouldn't even check back into work until noon the next day. This was way too early in the day for them to send up a flare.

She checked the time of the message. It had been left last night at 11:57 PM local, 9:57 PM in New Mexico. She was perplexed. In one respect the time made a little sense, but only by coincidence, because she knew what should have gone down at that time. But at home, not Walt's place of work. She got a queasy feeling that whatever had happened was not what she'd planned.

She debated returning Horton's call while she had time on the shuttle but decided against it. This wasn't a conversation to share with passengers all around her. She needed to be alone and composed, tucked away in some corner of the airport terminal. She phoned her mother instead and shared the good news.

Frances was thrilled. "Oh my goodness, Carrie, that's wonderful. When will they publish it? Will it be out in time for Christmas?"

"Mom, I got an agent, not a publisher. This is a big step for me but it might take months to sell the book. Then another nine months before it appears in print."

"Nine months! Christ, it's just paper, ink and binding, not a human being." The excitement in her mother's voice collapsed like a circus tent being rolled up at the end of a summer tour.

As the terminal hove into sight, Carrie told her mother she had to go, she was at the airport, and she'd give her a call once she was home. Bye-bye, kiss-kiss, love you, talk to you later.

Carrie checked in, passed through security and went to the washroom to splash water on her face and apply fresh lipstick. Did she look like a new woman? Maybe not quite yet but things were happening. She didn't kid herself that the novel would get an advance of more than a few thousand dollars. She'd spent three years working on it, put it through so many drafts it was like an old car, repaired so many times it was more replacement parts than original vehicle. Frankly, she was sick to death of the thing and, although she'd pitched it with enthusiasm, she felt like a used car dealer moving some clunker off the lot to make way for something new.

She just wanted to get the damn thing published, get her foot on that first rung of the ladder, then find a real agent to replace Diamant whom she suspected was a second-stringer at the tail end of a career that had never seen a bestseller. Then she'd write a really good book, one of many she felt bubbling up inside her. All she needed was the freedom to be herself. And that was just around the corner...

She bought a copy of *Harper's* at a news kiosk. Her cell phone rang as she was looking for a seat in the boarding lounge. She looked at the call display but the number was blocked.

"Hello. Yes, speaking." She paused. "Oh my God, you're not serious?" She listened as Mack Horton told her what had happened to her husband. Her voice grew genuinely incredulous. "A what...!?" she said in a shrill pitch.

Some nearby passengers turned to look at her. She made a pacifying motion with her hands. It's all right, nothing I can't handle, just an unexpected *bomb* someone's dropped on me...

"Yes, I'm in New York now, but my flight's leaving within the hour." She paused as Horton told her that federal investigators were assigned to her husband's case and needed to speak with her as soon as she returned. "Why are they involved?" Another pause. "All right, I understand. I'll see them there."

She closed her phone. She rolled the *Harper's* in a tight tube and drummed her knee with it. As a teenager, she'd played drums for a few bands. That, along with screwing her brains out, had been her only relief for the enormous tensions she'd felt when her mother started getting serious about the first man to replace Carrie's father. Maybe she should buy another set of drums, she reflected, although that prospect paled in comparison to the pleasures of the other alternative.

She looked around her. The other passengers were back

to minding their business, her brief outburst on the phone forgotten. But inside she reeled with confusion and anger, not what she wanted to be feeling right now. Something had gone haywire. She silently mouthed *Fuck!* to herself. Ironic she thought, thinking of something else that began with 'F'. Something she hadn't counted on dealing with. The FBI.

Yes, her husband worked in a sensitive government job and he'd died suddenly. But he was supposed to have died at home during a burglary gone bad, in the jurisdiction of the Santa Fe Police Department. Why had he been blown up with a bomb on government property?

21

San Rafael

The San Rafael Police Department, with a complement of eighty officers, occupied the lower level of the City Hall building at 1400 Fifth Avenue, housing offices for the Chief and his staff, a Dispatch center, an armory, holding cells and interview rooms. Eight detectives worked out of another building two blocks east, at 1210 Fifth Avenue, shared with the Circle C Bank. Inside that office, accessed via keypad lock on the street level door, were half a dozen rooms on two levels for the detectives and some technical personnel.

When Detective Jim Starrett returned from a 4th Street coffee shop a block downhill, carrying coffees and pastries, his partner Fred Hutchins was just hanging up the phone.

"I caught up with Lang's boyfriend at the bowling tournament. He's going to grab the next flight home."

"How'd he take it?"

"Kind of a pissy mood, you ask me."

"Well, his main squeeze being dead could spoil his day."

"Call me insensitive, I just didn't get that vibe off him."

"Well, you saw Lang's place. Nice digs. Maybe the boy's not happy to be out on the street. When's the last time you had to look for an apartment in Marin?"

Starrett gave Hutchins his coffee and Danish and returned to his desk beneath a three-by-six-foot poster of a racing sloop in full sail. He sat in a swivel chair, put his heels on his desk and ate his muffin in four bites, washing each down with large swallows of coffee to which he'd added some half-and-half.

"You eat like a dog," Hutchins said. "Didn't your mother ever teach you to chew?"

Starrett called up his worst redneck accent. "You callin' my mama a bitch?"

Hutchins took a knife from his desk drawer, cut his Danish into slices, put butter on each and ate as slowly as if he had a toothache.

"I need to brief the Lieutenant in ten," Starrett said, getting back in character. He pulled a six-foot length of nylon rope from his desk drawer and began to tie a complicated knot in it. "What am I going to tell him?"

Hutchins looked at the file. "Lang's broken watch gives exact time of death at six-fifty-five. Seven-forty, someone reports a 1995 Jeep Cherokee stolen from Larkspur ferry terminal. Eight fifty-three, a patrol unit finds the damaged Cherokee a few blocks from San Rafael bus depot."

"And we got a definite match between the Jeep and the broken glass left at the scene," Starrett said, still concentrating on his knot.

"Coroner's report said Lang died within minutes of impact, severe multiple hemorrhaging. Basically, drowned in his own blood." Hutchins paused for a sip of coffee. "That'll happen when you get your ribs driven through your lungs."

"Tox scan?"

"Sober. Trace amounts of cannabis, recreational level, nothing else."

"So our theory thus far is...?"

"...Some joyriding teenagers swiped the Jeep from the

ferry terminal, accidentally struck Lang, panicked and fled the scene."

Starrett tossed one end of the rope across Hutchins' desk and held onto his own end. "Give us a pull there, mate."

Hutchins grabbed the rope and pulled. The knot slipped apart. "It doesn't hold."

"Right," Starrett said. "Neither does your theory."

Hutchins ate another buttered slice of Danish. "Got a better one?"

"Skid marks do."

"Yeah, how so? There were none."

"Exactly."

"So, the kid at the wheel was just driving too fast. You know kids, they're always horsing around. Maybe the driver got distracted at the wrong moment. The Stephen King scenario."

"Way over on the opposite shoulder like that?" Starrett worked on another knot.

"What're you thinking?"

"Something more than a hit-and-run. Maybe it wasn't an accident."

"Intentional?" Hutchins paused mid-Danish. "Lang was a semi-retired computer nerd. Who'd hurt a guy like that?"

"That's what I'd like to know." Starrett swung a crude knot at the end of his short piece of rope – a hangman's noose.

22

Albuquerque

The FBI field office on Luecking Park Avenue was only five miles from the University of New Mexico. Driving at posted speeds on the I-25 and city streets, the ride took nine minutes. Special-Agent-in-Charge (SAIC) Liam Cobb was accompanied by three agents, all carrying standard issue side arms. In the back of their Ford Explorer, they had additional ordnance: shotgun, rifle with scope, sub-machinegun and tear gas launcher, all occasionally used in taking down some of New Mexico's many meth labs, but weren't expecting to deploy today.

SAIC Cobb was thirty-one years old, a tall and rugged blond who'd played three years of varsity football for University of Maryland. Before assuming leadership of the Albuquerque field office and thereby the senior FBI role in New Mexico, he'd served one year in the Albuquerque office working with the DEA. The previous two years had been in Las Cruces intercepting illegal immigrants from Mexico and fugitives from American justice en route to Mexico, in which post he'd distinguished himself.

Concerned about the illegal entry of potential terrorists, Cobb had developed a profiling checklist for distribution to every car rental agency within fifty miles of the Mexican border. Based on physical appearances and English accents, it was designed to help rental agency staff distinguish Middle Eastern from Hispanic immigrants. Among the distinguishing characteristics were hands.

Mexicans attempting illegal entry had typically done physical labor, whereas Middle Eastern illegals tended to have come from better-off backgrounds. Their hands were often well-tended and the nail of the pinkie finger worn long as a mark of pride to indicate its owner did no manual work. Pride goes before a fall, Cobb had reasoned, and this simple logic had helped identify and arrest four Saudi nationals.

The Arabs had been led across the Chihuahuan Desert by a 'coyote' whose lucrative trade consisted of guiding illegal immigrants across the border. The coyote's state-side accomplice had then trucked the four from Columbus to Las Cruces where the Saudis rented a car to drive to Boulder City. There they had a vague but unrealistic plan to blow up the Hoover Dam. But at the National rental agency, a clerk had run through Cobb's checklist in his mind, noted a long pinkie nail on the man filling out the rental form. As soon as the guy had driven away with his three friends, the clerk had called the FBI. An hour later, they were all in custody. Cobb had received a letter of commendation from the Director himself.

The Ford Explorer entered the south side of the campus via Yale Boulevard. On the university gates was a banner that read 'Go, Lobos, Go,' an exhortation to the UNM basketball team that was the pride of the state, and whose games drew capacity crowds. The FBI team's destination was the Mechanical Engineering building. The campus police had been alerted, but there was little for them to do except ensure that no students got in the way of the FBI. The timing was such that they arrived on campus right in the middle of scheduled class periods.

The Explorer pulled into a faculty parking area. Cobb and his men got out. "Okay, guys, nice and cool." He checked his gun. "Let's not hurt any students."

While one agent remained outside, Cobb and two others entered the building and climbed the stairs to the second floor. The halls were largely deserted. A few students hunkered in a small lounge, poring over class notes. Cobb found Room 206 and took a quick peek through the door's window.

In the classroom a professor named Dr. Rashid Hassan diagrammed typical force vectors applying to a hydraulic turbine, the kind employed by hydroelectric generating plants. The adjacent whiteboard was a maze of formulae. Two dozen students in their twenties took notes.

Cobb glanced over his shoulder. One agent stood a few

feet behind him, the other in position down the hall at the classroom's rear door. Both had hands on the butts of their service pistols. Cobb opened the door and rapped on the window to get the professor's attention.

"Excuse me, Dr. Hassan, I need to speak to you."

Hassan paused in mid-diagram, capped his marker and came to the door. Cobb held it open. Hassan stepped into the hall, glancing from Cobb to his agent nearby.

"What is it, please?"

"I'm with the FBI." Cobb showed his badge. "I'd like you to come with us."

"But I'm in the middle of a class."

Cobb grabbed Hassan's arm and swung him against the wall. In a moment, his agent had cuffs on the professor.

"Am I being arrested?" Hassan demanded. "On what grounds?"

"On authority of the US Patriot Act."

"What have I done?" Hassan said as he was led by one agent down the hall, the other agent going on ahead, checking doorways and stairwell.

Cobb stepped into the classroom. The students looked at him expectantly. "Class dismissed," he said. They stared at him like he was joking. He didn't bother to explain. He hurried down the hall to catch up with his agents.

The Explorer headed east on Central, passing through a neighborhood of bars and boutiques, restaurants and coffee shops. After a few minutes of noisy protest during his extraction from the Mechanical Engineering Building, Dr. Hassan was now silent. As they drove east, the storefronts became grungier, boutiques giving way to second-hand outlets, trendy restaurants surrendering to greasy spoons. They crossed San Mateo Boulevard and turned into the yard of a Speedy Muffler shop.

Cobb and two agents climbed out, one of them circling around to the back of the shop. Cobb walked into the nearest service bay. A man in blue coveralls stood beneath a hydraulic lift, bolting a muffler onto a Pontiac Grand Am. His profile revealed an aquiline nose and an olive complexion.

"Achmed Sharif," Cobb called out.

The mechanic turned at the sound of his name. His polite smile faded abruptly when he saw two men standing there, one with badge in hand, the other with handcuffs.

23

New York

Axel Crowe walked from Blaikie's condo to Broadway. Late morning, the streets were dense with shoppers and workers. On Seventh Avenue, delivery trucks double-parked as men unloaded racks of clothes from the garment district and wheeled them into retail stores. People bustled along the crowded sidewalks, cell phones in one hand, coffee in the other, weaving around the panhandlers that bedeviled every unwary pedestrian. On 55th, four Hare Krishna devotees in orange robes trudged silently, absent the characteristic chanting, perhaps worn down after a morning of disregard from fellow Manhattanites.

At the corner of Broadway and 51st, Crowe looked around. In the immediate vicinity were an electronics store, a deli, a bookstore and several boutiques. Diagonally across the street a theatre marquee displayed the title of a current production: *The Bermuda Love Triangle – a romantic comedy.*

The title vaguely echoed what Crowe had suggested to Blaikie – that infidelity provided the backdrop for his sister's death. No guarantee this line of reasoning would pan out, but years of observing subtle signs of the environment gave Crowe confidence to follow his intuition. He walked east on 51st, following the same route Janis Stockwell would have taken from Broadway last night.

Crowe crossed Seventh and entered the long block leading to Avenue of the Americas. On the other side of the street several sheets of plywood were nailed over a storefront renovation. He crossed the street to have a closer look at the graffiti scrawled on the plywood. The dominant visual was a bold graphic of three cartoon figures: two men and a woman in a three-way. Around the figures were dozens of signatures in undecipherable characters.

Crowe thought of the theatre marquee – the love triangle – and now this – another love triangle – and recalled what Guruji had often told him.

Signs are everywhere – in the horoscope, in the hand, in omens. To see one sign is interesting but means nothing. To see two signs is thought-provoking and suggests you might be onto something. But only after you've seen three signs do you know you're being offered a message. And then the real work begins – to understand what it means.

Crowe continued up the street, eyes sweeping the sidewalk. Fifty feet further he saw it – the chalk outline of a body between two parked cars. The bright yellow chalk had been partially erased by overnight rain.

Crowe crouched at the curb. The pavement appeared swept clean of debris, perhaps by the CSU in gathering evidence. No way to know whether these same cars had been here last night, or new cars taken their place. The chalk outline showed a body on its side, legs partially bent, arm flung to one side. Someone on the CSU team had even outlined the hand, showing thumb separate from the grouped fingers.

Within the hand was a spider's-web of fine cracks in the asphalt, seemingly random. But when Crowe squinted a little to create a visual filter, he saw three lines bolder than the rest. These formed a triangular pattern similar to that formed by three of the major palmistry lines – the life line, head line and fate line.

Guruji's Rule of Three came to mind. Another triangle. Crowe was looking at a cryptic clue. But what did it mean?

He crouched to examine more closely the patch of asphalt outlined by the ghost hand. Inside the triangle was another figure defined by three short lines intersecting at a common point – an asterisk with six points. Although subtle, no reason to disregard it. Sub-atomic particles were subtle too, but once quantum physicists understood them, new theories had revealed a universe of subsequent applications.

Crowe stood and checked his watch. It was noon so the sun was due south. His shadow established the compass direction. He looked again at the chalk outline. The out-flung arm, whose hand held both a triangle and a six-pointed star, was pointed southwest.

Dr. Edmond Locard, a pioneer of forensic science who became known as the Sherlock Holmes of France, had stated that "every contact leaves a trace." In other words, every criminal brought something to the crime scene, and took something from it. Of course, Locard had referred only to physical evidence.

This was the metaphysical equivalent of Locard's exchange principle, more like a Zen *koan* than anything else. If the victim was walking east when attacked, but fell with one accusing hand pointed to the southwest, who was the killer? If the various signs at the crime scene, intangible as well as tangible, gave a clue to the criminal, what kind of person might that be?

Yellow chalk outline. Arm pointed southwest. Triangle in the hand. Asterisk inside the triangle. Crowe played word association, an exercise Guruji had drilled into him over many years in many contexts.

Yellow was the color of the sun, astrologically linked to government and people in power. The southwest was associated with rebels, foreigners and drug addicts. A triangle had three sides, the number of Jupiter, invoking priests, lawyers and publishers. The asterisk had six points, the number of Venus, suggesting models, artists, ladies of leisure…

Put it all together, what did he get? A renegade

government agent? A crack whore? A corporate lawyer? A foreign journalist?

His phone rang. Blaikie had pulled strings with the Mayor. With any luck, the Police Commissioner would allow Crowe to speak to the detectives handling his sister's case.

"Where's the precinct office?"

"Forty-second and Tenth. Stay in the neighborhood and I'll give you a call as soon as you get clearance."

Crowe hung up. There was an Off Track Betting outlet on West 48th, a half-hour's walk from here. He checked his watch. Almost noon. First race of the day at Aqueduct was 12:30 PM, and 1:00 PM at Belmont Park. Although he had no time to go to the track, the atmosphere of an OTB outlet, crowded with players smelling of hope and despair, was infinitely more stimulating than betting over the internet.

But the horses could be distracting. He was on the clock and Blaikie was paying the bill. He needed to stay focused on the job at hand. He reluctantly headed back toward Seventh Avenue. By coincidence, the precinct office was southwest of here, the same direction Janis Stockwell's hand had pointed. He decided to head over to Ninth and then walk down to 42nd. There were a few musical instrument stores on Ninth. Along the way he'd look for omens.

24

Denver

Carrie Cassidy had forty-five minutes to kill in Denver where her brother-in-law William lived. She debated calling him to break the news but thought better of it. They'd never got along, had in fact disliked each other from the moment Walt had introduced her as his fiancée. Besides, the National Laboratory would have William's name on file as Walt's nearest blood relative and they'd certainly have notified him by now, especially since they'd been unable to find her in the first hours after Walt's death.

She decompressed with an over-priced martini in a bar and fended off the attentions of an inebriated high roller heading home from Vegas. Meanwhile she fretted about what had gone awry in Santa Fe. It pissed her off because she'd been very clear with everyone, once they had the plan they had to stick to it.

Carrie tried to sleep on the second leg of the flight but as soon as she closed her eyes her mother popped up like a demented jack-in-the-box. That was the funny thing, Carrie could go a year without seeing her, phoning once every two weeks, and it was all quite civil, but spend a few days with Frances and it brought back ugly memories. They'd been through too much together.

When her father died, Carrie was only thirteen, and it rocked her world in the worst way. While Frances drank to numb her pain, Carrie followed in her own way. Binge drinking with girlfriends in twisted arroyos. Smoking dope and sampling prescription pills from her mother's medicine cabinet. One night, taking a trip to the hospital to get her stomach pumped.

Nobody thought of it as attempted suicide but it was like death from a thousand cuts, both for her and Frances. *You nearly killed me giving birth to you*, her mother used to scream at her, *and now you're killing me all over again.*

On the flight to Albuquerque, Carrie looked down on the San Juan mountain range. Even at this altitude she could see little towns deep in the hills. You could hunker down and get a lot of writing done in places like that, assuming you didn't go stir-crazy on Friday night. That was her problem. She needed solitude but she needed stimulation too, with a variety and frequency that was apparently unrealistic.

Her whole life she'd been searching for the elusive guy who could give it to her on a regular basis. In high school she'd scored Mensa-level on her IQ test. It was a blessing and a curse. As a teen she was attracted to jocks but they lacked the brains to be more than fuck buddies. She related more to nerds who, despite the pain of their social awkwardness, had something going on between their ears. But they lacked the balls to match her adventurousness, pushing envelopes of physical risk, morality and legality.

Briefly in junior high, she'd thought she'd found the right guy. Derek had been a swimmer for the track and field team, with dreams of Olympic medals. Brilliant in science, he wrote poetry that made her cry. He was bright and daring but, despite his Olympian dreams, didn't seem to care if he lived or died, which became obvious whenever he drank and got behind the wheel of a car. He was also confused about his sexuality and confessed to her on their last night together that he might be gay but didn't know how he could ever come out, seeing his father was a hard-ass cop and all. Next day at school, when word went around like wildfire that he'd shot himself with his father's gun, nobody understood but Carrie.

Her last year in high school, there came heavy drinking with boys, and all that went with it. A trip to the hospital for a broken arm sustained in a car accident, another time to get stitches in her scalp after a nasty catfight with tennis rackets. Arrests for underage consumption of alcohol, public indecency, shoplifting, witness to a felony, possession of a controlled substance. A weekend in a Dallas hotel with two college boys. A visit to an abortion clinic. A week in rehab. A month of useless therapy.

You could talk for a thousand years, but her father was gone and no amount of talking could bring him back.

Her mother moved on, found a second husband, kindled a new life and fanned it into flame. Illogical or not, Carrie always resented her for that. *How nice for you, now you've found a replacement, but what about me?* Her mother had tried to sustain her on a tough-love diet, but never gave her the tenderness she secretly craved.

From inside her cage of grief, she was alone with her pain. Always had been, always would be. Her mother had denied her the company of siblings. Hate your life with all your heart, you couldn't change the way it was. So she'd learned to cope the best she could. If asked what she remembered from high school, she could sum it up in two words: *Carpe diem*. Get it while you can. She should've had it tattooed on her forearm where everyone could see it.

And on the other arm, *Illegitimi non carborundum*. Don't let the bastards wear you down. God knows there were enough of them who wanted to give it a try.

25

San Rafael

Dave Munson climbed the ramp past security on his way out of the San Francisco Airport terminal, carrying only his bowling ball. He went downstairs to the baggage carousel, fetched his battered suitcase with the broken wheels and dragged it to the parking lot.

In his powder blue 1999 Nissan, he headed up Van Ness Boulevard past stucco houses crowding the sidewalk. He rolled down the windows as he drove through the Presidio, catching a whiff of sea breeze through the trees. Traffic slowed at the Golden Gate Bridge and he angled the rearview to check his face in the mirror. His skin had suffered in Albuquerque, the place drier'n a kiln oven. He was glad to be back in the Bay Area where the humidity was better for the complexion.

Thirty minutes later he parked at Bernie's house in Marin Bay Park. As he climbed out of the Nissan he paused to run his hand along the fender of Bernie's yellow Boxster. Now this was something to die for. Fortunately, someone else had done the dying...

He'd half expected to find Police tape across the front entrance but there was nothing. He dropped his luggage in the foyer and entered the kitchen. He took an opened bottle of Chardonnay from the fridge and poured himself a glass.

On the counter he found a blue memo with a San Rafael Police Department letterhead. Its message was simple: call Detectives Jim Starrett or Fred Hutchins upon arrival, at any of three phone numbers – an office number and two cell numbers. He shoved the memo into his pocket and went downstairs.

In his room he stripped off his shirt and threw it in the corner. He took his stash from his bedside table drawer and rolled a joint. He took a couple of puffs, then catapulted off the bed in a billow of smoke and went to Bernie's room, one wall of which was mirrored panels.

He slid open a panel to reveal a closet packed with clothes. Joint hanging from his lip, he flipped through the rack, selected a fuchsia silk shirt and slipped it on without buttoning it. He kicked off his running shoes and pulled on a pair of snakeskin cowboy boots that Bernie'd bought on LA's Rodeo Drive for eight hundred bucks. He stood before the mirror and struck a pose. Bernie'd had good taste in just about everything.

He went to a massive dresser adjacent the window. Lying atop it was a teak jewelry box the size of a small pirate's chest. He pawed through a mass of gold and silver jewelry, all of it expensive but some if it in questionable taste unless you were a bit of a queen. He chose a heavy silver chain from among the tangle of precious metals and looped it over his neck.

He used a remote control to power on a sound system. Cher, diva of the gay community, wailed from the Bose speakers in the ceiling.

"Half-queer, that's all you ever were..." He sang along as he danced before the panel of mirrors, getting into the groove.

After the song, he tumbled onto the bed and stubbed the half-finished joint in an ashtray Bernie kept in the night table drawer. He lay with eyes closed, listening to the next song, running his hands down his chest and over his crotch, nodding to the music.

Okay, time for some role play. He grabbed the remote and killed the music. He breathed deeply and let the silence envelop him. He closed his eyes. He was alone in the house. Bernie was gone, never to return. No, drop the euphemism. Bernie was dead. D-E-A-D. He thought about that for a while, imagining Bernie lying in a stainless steel drawer in the morgue. Naked under a sheet. No silk shirt, no snakeskin boots, no jewelry...

His mouth twitched as it curled downward at the corners. Two salty tears escaped from his eyes and ran down his cheeks into his ears. His chest trembled and then he felt it coming, rising like gorge from his gut, the remorse along with the guilt, until he was really crying, first just a sniffle as his nose started to run and then honking and wheezing, a real blubber-fest that left him curled fetal-like on his side with fists clenched between legs and the pillow under his face wet with tears.

He pulled himself upright and reached for the phone on the night table. He fished the crumpled SRPD memo from his back pocket and called the number. When he heard the phone ring at the other end, he tugged a tissue from a box in the drawer of the night table.

"Detective Starrett? It's Dave Munson. I just got home to find your note..." Sniffling, he paused to blow his nose. "Sorry, I'm a bit of a mess right now. It just hit me again when I walked in, you know, the house so quiet and Bernie not here..." He sniffled again. "He was the best friend I ever had, I loved him so much, and now he's gone and I don't know what I'm going to do..."

He paused in his soliloquy, hearing the detective trying to get a word in edge-wise. He rearranged the silver necklace on his chest and crossed his legs, angling one foot to admire the stitching on the snakeskin boots as he listened to the cop.

"That's fine. Come by whenever it's convenient," Munson said. "I won't feel like going out for quite a while."

He hung up and thumbed the remote. Music poured out of the ceiling. He reached for the remains of the joint.

26

New York

Detectives Levinson and Rossimoff drove to 59th and Fifth Avenue where the deceased Janis Stockwell had lived with her husband. The Upper East Side was a neighborhood where, if prone to fantasy, they might imagine themselves living, but only if employed as private security officers for some paranoid millionaire who needed live-in protection. Levinson parked in front of a fire hydrant on Fifth, placing an NYPD placard on the dash to prevent parking enforcement from towing them. Climbing out of the car, they paused as four young women in biking shorts and halter tops jogged along Central Park.

"Now that makes me want to take up running." Rossimoff's eyes tracked the formation of tight butts heading north.

"Only time I ever saw you run for anything, somebody'd told you there were fresh doughnuts in the lunch room."

"You're right. Broad-jumping's more my sport."

"I always thought, jumping to conclusions was what you excelled in." Levinson crossed the street to the building opposite.

"Guilty as charged." Rossimoff followed Levinson into the foyer where they flashed their IDs to the doorman and said they had business with Jeb Stockwell.

Minutes later, they were sitting under an awning on the penthouse terrace, a nice view of the park over the trees lining Fifth Avenue. Stockwell wore slacks, loafers and a cream white shirt. A Filipino maid, maybe thirty years old in a white uniform, brought a Scotch on the rocks for Stockwell, Cokes for the detectives and a plate of roasted almonds, cashews and macadamia nuts.

Levinson glanced at Rossimoff, who was unable to suppress his joy as he scooped up some cashews. Jackpot! Never in danger of shedding weight, Rossimoff was like a bear bulking up for hibernation. God forbid a few hours should pass without banking a thousand calories or more.

While Rossimoff's mouth was occupied, Levinson brought Stockwell up to speed on the results of their investigation.

"Her own pepper spray...?" Stockwell was appalled when told of how his wife had died. "My God, how bizarre! Poor Janis! She must have suffered so much."

Levinson shook his head. "The Medical Examiner thinks she was already unconscious. Her neck was badly bruised, consistent with a chokehold."

Stockwell drained his Scotch and swirled the ice in his glass, reminding Levinson of a gambler at the end of a bad night, shaking the dice for the next throw.

Rossimoff, his caloric intake now assured, wiped his hands on a napkin. "Was your wife in the habit of going to the theatre alone?"

"We had season tickets at a few theatres. It was a Tuesday night routine for us – a regular date – to see a show or a movie." Stockwell paused. "Despite several years of marriage, we worked at preserving our romance, spending time with each other doing things we both enjoyed." He raised his eyes to Levinson and his lids were rimmed with tears. "I should have been with her last night. But this week I had to attend a banking conference."

"How long were you in San Francisco?" Rossimoff said.

"I flew out Sunday. I was supposed to be there until tomorrow."

"How was your marriage?" Levinson asked.

"What?"

"You just implied that, to prevent its luster from fading, you had to buff up the romance a bit. Was it working?"

"What is this, a standard ploy to challenge the integrity of a grieving spouse?" A flush appeared in Stockwell's face, his sorrow giving way to indignation. "My marriage was solid. I think you owe me an apology."

"Thirty percent of the time," Rossimoff pitched in, "a

female victim's attacker is a spouse, boyfriend or an ex."

"Screw your statistics," Stockwell said. "Besides, I thought this was a mugging."

"We don't know that yet, and we still need to eliminate you as a suspect."

"Is that what I am?"

"Mr. Stockwell, this is difficult for everyone," Levinson said, "but we have a job to do, and that means not playing favorites with anyone. Motive alone puts you front and center. There's a lot of money involved. Her father's Abner Blaikie, am I right?"

"Listen, Detectives." Stockwell's indignation brightened his already-florid face still further. "I have a large six-figure income of my own, thank you very much, and I don't need her family's money. I can't believe this questioning. Don't you have anything better to do than needle me vague implications? Have you no tangible leads at all?" He shook a finger at both of them, like a teacher reprimanding two unruly students. "When my father-in-law hears of this, the Mayor's phone will be ringing. What the hell *are* you doing?"

"Rest assured, we're running down every lead as fast as it arises," Levinson said. "We lifted prints from several cars at the crime scene and got a hit on one set, belonged to an ex-con. But as it turns out, he's gone straight, runs a car wash over on Eighth and 43rd. Plus, he lives in Jersey and was home with his wife at the time."

"We've canvassed everyone who lives and works on the street," Rossimoff pitched in. "Nothing so far."

"But a construction worker found her cell phone and empty purse in a dumpster this morning, at the corner of 58th and Sixth," Levinson said. "A couple of hours ago, a street bum tried to use one of her credit cards at a liquor store on Eighth Avenue."

"And where was *he* last night?"

"He's a regular at a Lexington flophouse with an eleven o'clock curfew. People that run the place say he watched TV in the common room all evening."

"Then where'd he get her wallet?"

"Claims he found it in a garbage can this morning, corner of 53rd and Fifth," Levinson said.

"Since both her credit cards and cell phone were dumped," Rossimoff said, "we're assuming minor felony was not a motive."

"Maybe someone just got lucky," Stockwell suggested. "Janis often carried a couple of hundred dollars in cash."

"Still, for a mugging, it isn't typical," Rossimoff said. "Usually, a perp gets his hands on credit cards, he uses them within minutes of the crime, hoping to max them out before they're reported stolen."

"Maybe this mugger was smart, and took from her only what couldn't be traced."

"You might be right," Levinson said, "but that implies a fair degree of caution on the part of the perp. Killing someone on the street suggests otherwise. Too much risk, too little reward."

"Speaking of which," Stockwell said, "would it help if I posted a reward, asking for anyone with information to come forward?"

"It might." Levinson glanced at Rossimoff, who rolled his eyes exaggeratedly. It might hinder as much as help, they both knew. Based on past experience, the offer of a reward typically triggered an inordinate number of calls, whose usefulness typically hovered below the one percent mark. It was frightening to contemplate what might happen if Stockwell posted a large reward. The entire squad would be relegated to phone duty for weeks on end. "But let's wait for a few days."

Fortunately, Stockwell let it go at that, something to be held in reserve until the NYPD had exhausted normal procedures, which Levinson and Rossimoff promised they would devote all their waking hours to pursuing.

Back on the street Rossimoff said, "What do you think?"

"I think he's not as heartbroken as he acts," Levinson said. "All that talk about keeping the romance alive sounded pretty hollow to me."

"That doesn't prove he had anything to do with it. In the end, she might simply have been the victim of a mugger with a short fuse. As we both know, there are lots of crazies out there."

"True enough, but something about this doesn't smell right." Levinson unlocked the car and slid behind the wheel, waiting until Rossimoff had joined him in the car before finishing his thought. "You know how too much salt can ruin a dish? In this case, I think it was too much pepper."

"What do you mean?"

"It speaks of anger. Like there was something personal to it."

27

San Rafael

Detective Jim Starrett walked to the corner of 4th and B Streets where The Royal Blend served the finest cup of Kona this side of Waikiki. En route he got a call from Manny Cantata, a detective in Narcotics. Cantata was responding to a message Starrett had left him earlier. Starrett paused and sat on the edge of a giant flower pot, one of many with which the taxpayers had beautified the downtown area.

He had a one-minute conversation with Cantata and continued to the coffee shop. Some of the boutiques on 4th were having sales and there were more people than usual on the street. It was a perfect day in San Rafael, as it usually was this time of year, and everyone looked happy and beautiful and wealthy. He often wondered why none of that rubbed off on him.

As he walked back to the office, he was intercepted by a reporter from *The Marin Independent Journal*, a pain-in-the-ass whose name he never bothered to remember.

"Detective Starrett, is it true the Lang hit-and-run is now being treated as a homicide?"

"Where'd you hear that?"

"Sources close to the investigation," the reporter said with a smile that was ten percent polite and ninety percent fawning.

"You didn't hear it from me, my partner or my lieutenant so unless you crawled up the ass of the county coroner, which I wouldn't put past you, I can't imagine where you got it."

The reporter switched tack from submissive to offensive. "But is it true?"

"No comment."

Starrett shouldered his way past the guy and crossed the street. The reporter, knowing better than to dog his heels, turned toward the City Hall Building.

As Starrett entered the office, Hutchins was just hanging up his phone. Starrett set their coffees down. Hutchins popped the lid on his, added cream and sugar.

"I just got off the phone with the lawyer who handled Lang's business affairs. Our hit-and-run victim was worth almost twenty mil."

Starrett sipped the Kona, savoring the taste of the bean. This was what it was all about. He looked at Hutchins. "Don't keep me in suspense, Fred."

"Three beneficiaries. A nephew in Philadelphia. An AIDS hospice in San Francisco. And his live-in buddy Dave Munson, the latter to the tune of five million."

Starrett whistled. "Interesting..."

"Ever hear back from Manny?"

Hutchins had fed Munson's name into the computer and got a hit. Munson had been arrested fourteen years ago in Berkeley with thirty ounces of Thai sticks, possession of which had earned him a year in the Alameda County jail. Nothing else on his record, violent or otherwise. Easy to chalk it up to youthful indiscretion. Hence, their call to Cantata, see if Munson was involved in any local action that hadn't turned up on his sheet.

"Just a few minutes ago," Starrett said.

"Our boy in the game? Or did he learn his lesson?"

"Either that, or learned to fly under the radar. He's not on Manny's watch list. Nor is he listed as a known associate of those who are. As far as Manny's concerned he doesn't even exist, except perhaps as a customer whose numbers are legion."

"So maybe our boy's graduated from dope peddler to something else."

"Or maybe he just cleaned up his act and got lucky." Starrett tried to give the benefit of doubt.

"Too bad he's got an airtight alibi, being away in Albuquerque."

Starrett nodded. "Yeah, really too bad."

They looked at each other. They hated when good suspects had really good alibis. It was one of the challenges of the job, testing a foolproof alibi. But a necessary one, not unlike civil engineers who, once they'd designed a bridge, loaded their model with weights until it bent and cracked and came crashing down in a mess of debris. Looks like that's what they'd have to do with Munson. It was messy sometimes, but it was all for the public good. That's why they were paid the big bucks.

28

Albuquerque

Carrie Cassidy's flight came in on time. The plane taxied to the terminal, across the south face of which the name *Albuquerque International Sunport* stood out in big bold letters. She was intercepted just inside the Arrivals gate by a robust blond man in a tan suit.

"Mrs. Cassidy? I'm FBI Special-Agent-in-Charge Cobb.

May I have your car keys, please?"

"I can drive myself."

"It's better if you come with me. I need to ask you a few questions. One of my associates will follow with your car."

Carrie retrieved her keys from her purse as they traversed the arcade toward the baggage carousels. Cobb was in a hurry and walked ahead, scanning the crowd of travelers, occasionally glancing over his shoulder to make sure she was still with him. At the baggage carousel they waited as the first pieces of luggage came off the conveyor.

She handed him the car keys. "How did you recognize me?"

"A photo from your husband's file." He gave her an apologetic smile.

She studied him as they waited, a writer's habit she'd developed, always observing people. His diction pegged him for a New Englander and he had the coloring of someone who'd spent more time in the sun than his genetics were designed for. The back of his neck was sunburned. It was easy to burn at an altitude of five thousand feet, which was why New Mexico had the highest incidence of skin cancer in the country.

Her luggage tumbled off the conveyor. Cobb signaled another man of whom she'd been previously unaware. Once that guy had her luggage and car keys in hand, they went out into the parking lot to her car, a ten-year-old red Honda. She followed Cobb to a white Ford where he held the passenger door open for her.

Within a few minutes, they were headed north on the I-25.

"What can you tell me about my husband? How did he die, exactly?"

"Nobody told you anything?" Cobb sounded surprised.

"The security officer who phoned me, Horton, said there was an explosion in the parking lot at work. That's all he knew, or that's all he was prepared to tell me."

Cobb cleared his throat. "Someone planted a bomb in his

car. Because of the nature of his work, we suspect a connection."

"The war on terrorism."

Cobb glanced at her. "Did he discuss his work with you?"

"No more than he was allowed to."

"But you put things together."

"There's not much a man can keep truly secret from a woman. Not if she really wants to know."

"Why did you want to know?"

"I'm curious by nature." She let a moment pass. "Do you know who did it?"

"We picked up some suspects today but it's too soon to tell if they were involved."

"When will you know?"

"Impossible to say. Every investigation is different."

"These suspects are from Santa Fe? Is it somebody we would have known?"

"I can't discuss it." Cobb cleared his throat again. "But I need to ask you about your movements the last three days. What were you doing in New York?"

"A combination of business and personal affairs. My mother lives in Manhattan. I've written a novel and I'm looking for an agent. I left here early Monday. That afternoon I saw one agent and did a little shopping. That evening, took my mother to a show. Tuesday, saw five agents. Dinner that evening at my mother's. This morning, breakfast with another agent and caught my flight home."

"Who knew about your being out of town?"

"Aside from Walt, only a girlfriend I play squash with."

Cobb was silent for a few minutes. They passed one of the area's casinos, built a short distance from a dried-out river bed on a luckless stretch of land halfway between Albuquerque and Santa Fe. "Did your husband have money problems of any kind, business or gambling debts?"

"Quite the contrary. He was a very smart investor."

"Skeletons in the closet? Personal enemies of any kind?"

"Only his brother."

Cobb glanced at her. "What do you mean?"

"Just kidding. His brother hated my guts. It was an issue between them. But if push came to shove, William would sooner kill me than Walt."

"Did he ever receive any threats?"

"Not that I know of." She looked at him. "Your questions don't seem to have anything to do with his work. Does that mean you just don't know what the motive is, that it might have been personal?"

"Tell the truth, we're still exploring all possible theories."

"And what's the best among them?"

"I'm not at liberty to discuss that."

Carrie reflected on that. He could be as canny as he wanted but it wouldn't get him anywhere. And as long as he hadn't cuffed her and informed her of her rights, she had nothing to worry about yet. She took a tissue from her purse, dabbed her eyes and blew her nose. "Can you tell me what's happened to his body?"

"It's with our medical examiners."

"Do you know when he... it will be released?"

"Probably tomorrow."

"Do you know anything about his death benefits and insurance?"

"Someone from Human Resources will explain all that to you."

"Do I have to call them or is someone going to contact me?"

"They know you're coming back today. You'll probably get a call."

They were both quiet for a bit. Carrie stared out the side window watching the sagebrush go by. After a bit Cobb cleared his throat and glanced over at her.

"You'll pardon my saying this, Mrs. Cassidy, but you don't strike me as being overcome by grief."

"What do you know?" she snapped at him, giving him a taste of her righteous indignation. "Maybe I cried my eyes out all the way from New York."

"Did you?"

She turned in her seat, giving him a hard look. Was he disappointed? Had he expected her to cry on his big rugged shoulder? Maybe it was an option she should have exercised. She did like his looks, that bulked-up physique that suggested weight training and punching bags and sweaty cardio-vascular workouts. And to work for the FBI, he had to be smart...

"I'm trying to be strong. Crying won't bring him back."

Cobb nodded and said no more.

Carrie stared straight ahead, wishing they were driving twice as fast so this would be over sooner. Still she knew Cobb's suspicions had to be addressed. She decided to take a chance and throw him a bone. It was something that would eventually come out so he might as well hear it from her as from one of Walt's friends.

"Truth is, Walt and I went through a rough patch a few years ago. I moved out for six months. He begged me to come back and eventually I did. But something died between us and no amount of resuscitation ever brought it back to life. Maybe I've already done my grieving for him and our marriage."

That left him lots to read between the lines, but it was as much as she would confess to this G-man. Truth be told, her sex life with Walt had gone down the tube years ago. Although she'd accepted that he'd always be a little on the chunky side, and in the early years enjoyed his weight bearing down on her, lending momentum to the old bump and grind, there was a limit. But once Walt hit forty, he'd piled on the pounds and then there was no way she could pretend that flab was sexy. She'd tried to get him to exercise but he was an Einstein, not a Schwarzenegger, and he stayed fat.

It didn't help that in the past few years the War on Terror had placed huge strains on their marriage. The pressure to produce results was enormous, forcing him to work fifteen-hour days, frequently pulling all-nighters, after which he wasn't much good for anything but a meal together and a little TV before he crashed. A lot of wives and mothers hated the war because it had killed their husbands or children. Carrie was supposed to feel lucky because Walt was serving his country without leaving it. But what most people didn't understand, the war was like a big old twister that had come through their lives, turned their home inside out, and sucked Walt up into a maelstrom that had taken him far away.

And thus had begun her wandering phase, in which she'd successfully sought alternate partners on a catch-as-catch-can basis. But even that didn't make her happy because of all the sneaking around. After a while she just began to resent Walt, seeing him as her jailer in a sentence of monogamy she didn't want to serve. She'd moved out, gone to Alamogordo for a winter, her excuse being that she needed to break the back of the novel she'd been struggling with for over a year. The real reason was that she just needed time alone, to sleep with whomever she wanted, free as a college girl again, and not have to watch the clock.

"So you didn't love him any more?"

"It wasn't that I stopped loving him, but that I loved him in a different way. He was a great guy and we had some wonderful times together. I'm going to miss his clever repartee and his jokes. He was like a big teddy bear, and my bed's going to feel empty without him there beside me. In fact, I don't know if I can keep on living in that house. There're too many memories."

She had worked herself into an emotional state appropriate to the occasion. She took another tissue from her purse and blotted her eyes again, half surprised now that there were really tears there.

"We'll do everything we can to bring his killers to justice," Cobb reassured her.

29

New York

Axel Crowe walked west on 51st, shifting mental gears, moving his centre of gravity from left brain to right. Man was a highly evolved thinker but much of the human psyche remained pure animal, and there were techniques for accessing that primal intelligence. Guruji had taught him many things, half of which were non-rational. Astrology, palmistry and *ayurveda* all depended on one's ability to memorize hundreds of principles and invoke them when a particular configuration in the birth chart, palm print or human face triggered their recall. But for every rule of logic, Guruji had a totally intuitive wild card up his sleeve.

One night at a party thrown by a wealthy Hindu in Toronto, Guruji had set up shop in the kitchen, armed with a cleaver and a bowl of fruit. People queued up to ask him questions, and he chopped the fruit in four and gave answers based on how the quarters fell and what they looked like inside. Other occasions, Guruji strolled with Crowe through Parkdale, looking at house numbers and the shape of windows, Guruji saying whether the resident lived alone, had children, or cared for a sick person, after which Crowe knocked on doors to confirm Guruji's declarations.

Crowe felt a twinge of regret. He'd learned all the logical stuff from Guruji and, though not a master, had achieved a level of superiority over most people in the field. But as for the intuitive stuff, he'd barely wet his toes in an ocean so deep and wide it awed him to think what lay beneath the surface. With Guruji's guidance, he might have gone deep sea diving. Since that was no longer likely, he would settle for splashing around in the shallows.

At Broadway and 51st was a news stand painted turquoise. Behind the counter stood an old white-bearded guy in a jacket with a howling coyote on his left breast. Nearby, a young woman handed out flyers for an off-Broadway play called *Wicked*.

At 51st and Ninth a hot dog vendor sold cheese dogs, chili dogs, corn dogs, kosher dogs and veggie dogs from a cart. Once upon a time Crowe had enjoyed hot dogs but fourteen years of vegetarianism had pretty much ruined the allure of tube-tied mystery meat for him. The sight of the vendor, however, reminded him of a joke. *A yogi goes to a baseball game and orders a hot dog. The vendor asks him, what do you want on it? The yogi says, make me one with everything.*

Intersections were focal points of energy, which was why Crowe paid attention to what he saw on street corners. In Tantrik philosophy dawn and dusk were considered magical moments, literal transition points between day and night. For the same reason, spring and fall equinoxes represented seasonal transition points. Geophysical space had its 'power points' too – the seashore, the junction of rivers, the peaks of mountains, the entrance of caves, as well as crossroads and doorways – places where movement experienced a block or a change in direction.

A famous philosophical treatise likened the human psyche to a fisherman's net. The twine represented subliminal impressions from our previous lives. The knots in the twine were our unconscious actions bound to reality. The resulting net was the mesh that trapped us in our personal perceptions and experience of life.

Stand at the crossroads of time and space, Guruji would say, *and you will see, hear, smell, taste and touch everything. And via the portal of your subtle senses, you will experience all that is, all that was, and all that will be...*

No sooner had he recollected Guruji's words, Crowe smelled pizza. A little further down Ninth Avenue he came upon the Casanova Pizzeria. He realized he hadn't eaten anything since a bowl of cereal at six this morning. He entered the pizzeria and ordered a slice with goat cheese, black olives and sundried tomatoes. One of Guruji's favorite combos. Crowe reflected on the irony of eating pizza at Casanova's, perhaps never sharing one again with Guruji, all because he had the recessive Casanova gene...

He sat at the window counter and drank a can of Brio while he checked his astrology app for the planetary lineup at post time in Belmont Park. You could keep the punter away from the track but these days you couldn't keep the track away from the punter.

A black man walked by carrying a pre-school girl on his shoulders. She dug the heels of her sneakers into his ribs and whipped him with the ponytail of a black Barbie gripped in one hand. The black man rolled his eyes at Crowe as he passed his window, clearly having a good time. Crowe waved to the little girl, who stuck out her tongue.

He studied the online tote board and selected a few promising horses for the day's races. He tripled his usual bet for Black Daddy in the Ninth, figuring the omen he'd just seen would pay out. He made his bets online and finished his pizza.

His phone rang. It was Blaikie.

"I just got a call from the office of the Chief of Police," Blaikie said. "You're cleared to meet the detectives at Mid-Town North who're handling the case. Levinson and Rossimoff, about an hour from now."

"What did you tell them about me?"

"Only that you're a private investigator and a personal friend." Blaikie paused. "Don't worry, I didn't alienate them by revealing your true stock-in-trade. Speaking of which, when I was with my parents this morning, I asked my mother what time Janis was born. She remembers five forty-five AM."

After they hung up, Crowe put the birth time into his astrology app. Sure enough, Janis's chart came up with Libra rising, just as he'd speculated this morning. Score one for intuition.

30

Los Alamos

Several miles outside of Los Alamos, Site 8 of the National Laboratory squatted on a hillcrest commanding an impressive view of the Jemez Mountains. The building's few windows, tall and narrow as giant gun slits, were recessed into a façade whose concrete slabs contained a lot of iron, resulting in a rusty weathered look that blended into the landscape. Satellite dishes clustered at the southwest corner but the rest of the roof was clear, and at its north end was painted a huge 'H' surrounded by a circle, indicating a helicopter landing pad.

A five-seater Bell Jet Ranger descended, its prop-wash setting aflutter the American and New Mexico state flags that flew in front of the north-end entrance. Special-Agent-in-Charge Liam Cobb climbed out, ducking his head beneath the rotor as he walked to the roof entrance where Mack Horton waited for him.

They exchanged greetings and went downstairs to Horton's office where they sat at a table in front of a gun-slit window. Horton's secretary brought glasses, a selection of soft drinks and some jalapeño nachos in a bowl.

"So, any progress?" Cobb asked.

"Our analysts are finished with Dr. Cassidy's vehicle," Horton said. "Not much news beyond what we had twelve hours ago. Explosive was C4 plastic, ignited via a thermocouple wired to the cigarette lighter."

"If Cassidy was a smoker, why didn't it go off earlier in the day on his way to work?"

"Whoever did this was clever." Horton took pen and paper from his desk and drew a schematic for Cobb. "There were five components: digital timer, thermocouple, MP3 player, and a primer embedded in a pound of C4. We figure the timer was set to wake up the circuit sometime late in the working day. That's why Cassidy was able to drive his vehicle to work but nothing happened because the circuit was asleep. But then, say, around four or five PM, the timer woke up the circuit and primed the system. When Cassidy quit work shortly after eight PM, he entered the parking lot and started his vehicle. That switched on the MP3 player wired into the car's sound system and pumped out some high-decibel Arab music. The thermocouple kicked in a few seconds later and ka-boom!"

"And all this stuff was inside the car?"

"You know how big a pound of butter is. Squash it down to half the height and twice the footprint, shove it under the driver's seat. The timer, thermocouple and MP3 player combined were no bigger than a pack of cigarettes."

"You're sure it was *inside* the car? Not under the chassis or in the engine compartment?"

"No doubt about it, once we saw Cassidy's body. You want, I can show you pictures."

Cobb fluttered his hand. "I believe you. I'm just working backwards now. How did someone gain access to his car?"

"We've looked into that," Horton said. "It hasn't been serviced since the New Year, when he had it in for an oil change. He hand-washed it himself, didn't want to risk anyone scratching the finish. And his wife had her own ride."

"Yet somehow, someone got into his car."

"It didn't happen on government property. Our parking lots are all under camera surveillance. We've reviewed the video of all the installations where he worked."

"So someone got to the car offsite."

"Could have been in his own back yard. Cassidy lived at the end of a cul-de-sac. There are street lights but at three in the morning, is anyone around to observe a prowler?"

"That'd be pretty risky. What about the car's security alarm?"

"Our guys say there are ways to defeat them with magnetic fields."

"What do you think happened?"

Horton shrugged. "You know what car thieves do? They

copy the VIN from the dashboard tag visible through the windshield. Then they go to a dealership and say they've lost their key. Believe it or not, the dealership often cuts a replacement without demanding proof of registration."

"So somebody gained access to his car and wired the bomb..."

"...While his wife was out of town," Horton said. "You were going to interview her. What came of that?"

"She accounted for her whereabouts the last three days. She had receipts – flight, hotel, meals, cab fare – and everything seems to check out. She visited her mother while in New York to meet prospective literary agents. She's written a novel, trying to get it published."

"Let me guess. A high-tech counter-terrorism thriller?"

Cobb shook his head. "Some sort of Bridges-of-Madison-County love story set in Truth or Consequences, New Mexico. Incidentally, also the title of the novel."

"Truth or Consequences? Now there's a one-horse town for you. But not a bad title, I suppose, although I would have thought something more like a murder mystery. But what do I know about publishing? You get any sense of how happy their marriage was?"

"She was pretty forthcoming. They had a trial separation two years ago when she spent a winter in Alamogordo writing her novel. But she moved back in last year."

"I've heard rumors she's a bit of a wild one," Horton said. "Kind of anorexic-looking for my tastes, speaking as a happily married man, but some guys find that attractive."

"Reading between the lines, I think she and Cassidy had some problems with their sex life, probably why they split up. But he must have offered her some inducement, she didn't say what, to come back home."

"Maybe she just couldn't make it on her own. Maybe she figured she'd wait until she got her book published, then make the big leap."

"Could be."

"What'd you make of her? You think she's involved

somehow?"

"I don't know. She's smart and a bit on the tough side. But certainly didn't come off as your typical grief-stricken widow. When I took her to task on it she gave me a throwaway confession about how their better days had faded in the sunset."

"That's kind of weird, right? You'd think if she was guilty she'd act all heart-broken, try to keep suspicion at arm's length."

"Unless she's using reverse psychology on me. Make me think, an attitude like that, she might be guilty of adultery, but has nothing worse to hide."

"So what now?"

"My gut says there's something there but it's not obvious. Despite her being in New York the day her husband died, I can't bring myself to cross her name off my watch list."

"Other than the spouse is always the number one suspect, any particular reason you've got a hardon for her?"

"Given her circumstances, an aspiring writer and all, material motive looms large. You said Cassidy had a substantial life insurance policy, right?"

"Four times salary, which makes her the beneficiary of over six hundred grand," Horton said. "Not like that's a huge fortune."

"Goes a long way in the poorest state of the Union."

"Maybe in Truth or Consequences. Not in Santa Fe."

"You're probably right. But then there's his estate. She said he was a smart investor. And maybe there's a private insurance policy. Might be a few million when you add it all up." Cobb stretched. "Or maybe I'm just fishing."

"Not getting anything from your Muslim detainees?"

Cobb scowled. "Aside from threats of lawsuits for violating their civil liberties? Problem is, they're coming up clean, and we're looking stupid because we don't have a clue who's behind this."

31

San Rafael

While Hutchins stayed in town to work another current case, an apparent murder-suicide stemming from an adultery that had spiraled out of control, Detective Jim Starrett drove out to Marin Bay Park to see Dave Munson. After being buzzed through the entrance gate, he drove up the hill to Lang's house. The yellow Boxster had been joined in the driveway by a faded blue Nissan and a gleaming black Mercedes E500. He peered through the tinted windows of the Mercedes, admiring the leather upholstery and burl walnut wood interior trim. It was tough being a working stiff in Marin County where so much wealth was evident.

He rang the doorbell. A blond guy, late thirties, good-looking in a soft kind of way, answered the door. Starrett introduced himself, confirmed Munson's identity, and was invited inside. As he entered the living room he encountered a tall slim Vietnamese man in cream-colored slacks and a brightly-patterned silk shirt.

"Um, this is Dr. Tranh," Munson said. "Detective Starbuck."

"I believe it's Starrett," Tranh corrected Munson.

"Still making house calls, Doc?" Starrett said.

Tranh said nothing. Starrett looked at Munson, whose face in this light now looked flushed.

"I was having an anxiety attack," Munson said. "Dr. Tranh was kind enough to deliver some medication."

Starrett looked at the Vietnamese, recalling a case in which he'd been involved, a fatal overdose that had almost led to conviction for malpractice-and-manslaughter, but had crumbled for lack of evidence. "What kind of dope you pushing these days, Doc?"

Tranh smiled and said smoothly, "You know, I could construe that as slander, Detective."

"Are you finished here?"

"I was just leaving."

Munson accompanied Tranh to the door. They exchanged a few words. Tranh departed. Munson returned to the living room.

"Just so you know," Starrett said, "Dr. Tranh's had more than one patient end up on a slab. He's a little careless with his prescriptions."

Munson shrugged. "Do you want a drink? I was just going to pour myself a glass of wine."

"Thanks, but I'm on the clock."

"It's just wine, Detective." Munson went to the fridge. "A really fine Sauvignon Blanc, probably the best you've ever had."

"I'll have to take your word for it."

Munson poured himself a glass, lit a cigarette from a pack on the kitchen counter and joined Starrett in the living room. Starrett sat in an angular chair of chrome and brown leather, Munson sinking into the yellow sectional sofa.

"I need to know more about Bernie," Starrett said. "His daily routine. Who he hung out with. Any problems he was having."

Munson drew on his cigarette, blew smoke toward the ceiling. "What's that got to do with a hit-and-run?"

"Dave, let me spell something out for you." Starrett leaned forward in the chair. "If a guy gets dinged for a felony offense, say, possession with intent to traffic and does a year in County, that's like a piece of stinky shit that sticks to him the rest of his life. And if you think something that happened fourteen years ago is forgotten, you're dead wrong. It's a scent any cop can pick up at will, like a bloodhound introduced to a suspect's dirty underwear. And if you think that an association, however innocent, with a guy like Dr. Tranh might not awaken a little curiosity on the part of our narc squad, you are also wrong. The weed we discovered in your room yesterday while investigating Bernie's death could justify a warrant to turn this house inside out. If we found anything else, say, coke of dealing weight or a large quantity of unprescribed drugs, proving to a judge that you're still up to your ears in it, you could be looking at jail time all over again."

It was so quiet in the room, Starrett could hear Munson swallow hard. Munson reached for an ashtray on the end table. "Okay, you've got my attention."

"Good." Starrett took out his pen and notebook and leaned back in the chair. Ugly as it was, it was pretty comfortable with excellent back support. "Now, I'll ask questions and you'll give answers without hesitation or fabrication, and if everything seems to make sense, I won't have to take out my big stick and stir up the shit that's settled at the bottom of your hot tub. Okay?"

Munson nodded.

"Give me a rundown on a typical day for your friend. And don't spare the details."

Munson took a long drag and thought a moment. "Bernie was a late sleeper, stayed in bed until eleven in the morning. He usually made a few calls during the lunch hour, caught up on news with friends, made plans for the evening. He talked to his stockbroker almost every day, diddling with his portfolio. Afternoons he usually watched a movie. He was a big movie buff, had pay-per-view and all the movie channels on cable. End of day he always went for a run up the China Camp road a couple of miles and back."

"Always at the same time?"

"Pretty much like clockwork."

"And afterwards?"

"He'd have a soak in the hot tub, maybe a glass of wine and a smoke, listen to some music."

"And his evenings?"

"He'd take a nap early on. Then it was social time. Sometimes we'd have friends over for the evening. Other times he'd go into the city for dinner, then hit a few clubs for some late-night cruising."

"*He'd* go..? What about you?"

"Sometimes I went, but not always," Munson shrugged. "Depends on whether I was invited."

"I thought you were a couple."

"We loved each other, but we had an open-ended arrangement."

Starrett said nothing but waited for more.

"After he made a killing in the stock market," Munson continued, "Bernie realized he had a lot of time and money on his hands. He needed to get out more, take advantage of what life had to offer."

"Even if that didn't include you?"

"It was his money, not mine. It wasn't like I helped him pick the stocks. He didn't owe me anything."

"I'm not talking about the money. I'm talking about his seeing other people. Didn't that bother you?"

"We were best friends and part of that friendship was based on a mutual understanding that sometimes you meet someone else who turns your crank. They're good for a spin around the track but you don't necessarily want to wake up and see their face on the pillow next to you every morning."

"That why you have separate bedrooms?"

Munson shook his head. "He didn't bring them home. He was good that way. Usually he didn't even stay out all night."

"Among his acquaintances, anyone you might regard as questionable?"

"Not the ones I met. When we'd go out together, it was a genteel crowd. Just regular guys."

"And when he went out alone?"

"He used to tell me stories…" Munson rolled his eyes. "I think he was getting into rough trade toward the end."

"Can you give me names?"

"No. But I know some of his favorite clubs." Munson raised one finger after the other. "Big Dick's. The Back Door. XTC. Man 2 Man. They're all in the Castro District."

Starrett took notes.

"Was he ever threatened by anyone – for personal or business reasons?"

"No. And I'm pretty sure he would have told me if he had. He certainly shared all his other anxieties with me."

"Such as...?"

"AIDS, the environment, politics, the economy. He worried a lot."

"At least he didn't have to worry about money."

"No."

"And now, neither do you, right?"

"His lawyer hasn't shared the specifics with me but apparently I'm one of his beneficiaries. Is that a crime?"

"Not that I'm aware of... yet."

They sat there a moment, looking at each other. Starrett was almost reluctant to get up and leave. It was serene here. No phones ringing, no loud music from the next door neighbor, no sound of traffic from the street. He looked outside at the redwood deck, the hot tub, the view of the bay over the treetops. It was an oasis.

"Is there anything else, Detective?" Munson said, interrupting Starrett's reverie. "If not, I'd like to lie down a bit. I'm somewhat sensitive to medication."

Starrett stood and pocketed his notes. En route to the door he asked, "Did you guys have a housekeeper, a gardener, anyone with access to the house on a regular basis?"

"No."

"Then who does that work?"

"Me."

"That part of the arrangement?"

Munson shrugged. "It was a fair tradeoff."

Starrett nodded. "You're a very agreeable guy, Dave. I'm beginning to see why Bernie liked to have you around."

Munson smiled. "I liked to pull my weight."

32

New York

Axel Crowe arrived at the Mid-Town North precinct on 42nd Street at one o'clock. When he presented himself at the front desk, the desk sergeant made a brief phone call upstairs, signed him in and gave him a visitor's badge.

A few minutes later, Crowe was shaking hands with Detective-Sergeant Jake Levinson. In thirty seconds he formed a quick assessment. Levinson had a dry complexion and chapped lips. His brown hair was graying at the temples, his blue eyes red-rimmed. In *ayurveda*, a *vata*-type constitution suggested restlessness, insomnia, emotional instability and often difficulty in relationships. Crowe glanced at Levinson's hands and saw nails bitten to the quick, but a long index finger which implied self-confidence, leadership and a strong sense of justice.

Levinson sat in a swivel chair behind his desk and waved Crowe into a fixed chair opposite. "Kevin Blaikie said you're a private investigator? May I see some ID?"

Crowe took two laminated cards from his wallet and placed them on the desk. Levinson studied them.

"A private investigator's license issued by New York State, but an Ontario driver's license?"

"I'm a dual citizen."

"So you live in Canada and work in the US?"

"It's one big free-trade continent," Crowe said with a disarming smile.

Levinson returned his cards. "We agreed to meet you out of courtesy to the family of the deceased, Mr. Crowe, but I'm not clear on what you're looking for."

"Neither am I. Could you start by bringing me up to speed on Janis Stockwell's death?"

Levinson frowned. "This is still an active investigation."

"And I have no desire to compromise any element of it.

Anything you share with me will be kept in strictest confidence."

Levinson regarded him warily. "Kevin Blaikie's hired you?"

"We have an ongoing business relationship. I'm on a retainer." Crowe cleared his throat. "But my interest in this case is different, since it's a matter of great personal importance to the Blaikie family in general. You know Janis Stockwell was the daughter of Abner Blaikie?"

Crowe watched the detective. Levinson had probably been made aware of Janis Stockwell's family connections. Any career-limiting decisions would have to be considered in light of Abner Blaikie's influence with the Mayor and, therefore, the Commissioner of Police. At this very moment, he was probably thinking it wouldn't hurt to cut Crowe a little slack in the name of public relations.

"Okay, let me show you what we've got." Levinson stood and went to a wall-mounted map of Manhattan. The perimeters of the Mid-Town North precinct were marked in red – from the Hudson to Lexington, and 59th to 43rd Streets. He indicated three blue stickpins, each tagged with the initials 'JS', planted on the map. "Her body was discovered on 51st between Sixth and Seventh, by a passerby at eleven-ten last night."

Crowe took out his iPhone. "Estimated time of death?"

"Ten forty-five, give or take."

Crowe entered data into his astrology app. An event chart for Janis Stockwell's death appeared on the screen.

To his trained eye, the disposition of the planets provided Crowe clues to the circumstances surrounding her death, including a partial profile of the murderer. Ironically, the rules of interpretation had been cognized by some *maharishi* in the Himalayas thousands of years ago, absent any first-hand experience of man's nefarious affairs. Like any rule-based system it sometimes generated contradictions, but if the astrologer had enough intuition, he could usually arrive at a workable hypothesis.

With Scorpio rising, a fixed sign suggested murder connected with a family member. The seventh house was Taurus, a female sign, and its ruler was Venus, a female planet. Together, they indicated a female killer. Venus in dual sign Pisces implied more than one person involved. An exalted Venus in planetary war with Mars described an aggressive professional who was into sports or martial arts. Other clues suggested a criminal in transit. Rules for determining the killer's weapons gave blunt force, strangulation, smoke or a poisonous gas. The challenge for Crowe was to synthesize this disparate information in a way a layman could understand.

Levinson pointed to the remaining stickpins. "A homeless guy found her wallet in a garbage can at 53rd and Fifth this morning. Her purse and cell phone were discovered by a construction worker in a dumpster at 58th and Sixth."

"Any useful prints on her things?"

"Aside from those of the vagrant and construction worker, no."

Crowe studied the event chart. Running through the third and ninth houses was an axis that astrologers called the Moon's nodes, inflection points in the lunar orbit that were key in timing eclipses. Vedic astrologers called them Rahu and Ketu, a pair of polar opposites – sensuality versus spirituality, ego versus selflessness, domination versus surrender. In Vedic myth, Rahu was associated with serpents, their sudden striking power and venom…

"But you found a weapon at the scene?"

Levinson hesitated a beat. "No. She was strangled."

"Some kind of poison?"

"No."

Crowe persisted. "An aerosol? Something like Mace?"

Levinson and Crowe locked eyes. Levinson blinked first and his glance shifted briefly to a case file on his desk, as if to confirm it was still closed. His eyes betrayed his obvious confusion, probably wondering how Crowe had known about something so specific at the crime scene.

"Mrs. Stockwell had a pepper spray," Levinson admitted. "Her attacker turned it against her. That's a critical piece of information we've kept as our hole card. Only reason I'm sharing it, you already seem to have insider information, courtesy of the family. But if it leaks to the media, I'm holding you responsible."

"The family hasn't told me anything about how she died. But don't worry, I'm accustomed to keeping secrets," Crowe assured him. "Any prints on the dispenser?"

"One, but too smudged to be useful."

"Could I see her stuff, including that fingerprint?"

"It's all with Forensics."

"Where's that?"

"Downstairs."

"I might be able to tell you something they can't."

Levinson considered this a moment, then picked up his phone. "Tracey, it's Jake. Can you bring up the Stockwell evidence?" As he hung up, he looked at Crowe through fresh eyes – part suspicion, but maybe also a grudging respect.

Crowe walked over to the precinct map for a closer look.

"You want a coffee?" Levinson offered. "A soft drink?"

"No, I'm good, thanks," Crowe said. "How's the husband look?"

"No criminal record. Only thing on his file is a 15-year-old DUI from California. No criminal associates and no bad habits that we can find. He's a VP of Media Relations at Centurion Bank, been there over seven years, chairs a community service organization that coordinates charitable donations from the Manhattan banking community. Near as we can tell, he's a boy scout in a corporate pinstripe."

"You sound frustrated."

"Try desperate," Levinson confessed. "His father-in-law has a lot of clout with the Mayor. And the Commissioner takes a special interest in the Mid-Town North, which is home to many of his well-heeled supporters. So I've got my ass on the front burner and my boss is cranking up the heat."

An attractive early-thirties brunette entered the office

with a file folder and an evidence box containing several items. Crowe acknowledged her with a polite nod. Levinson took the file folder from her and dumped on his desk the box contents, all of it in plastic evidence bags. The effects included a black leather purse with a broken shoulder strap, a dark green wallet, a silver-colored cell phone, a red plastic pepper spray dispenser, something tiny and white in a small see-through plastic canister, and something indeterminate in another canister.

The brunette stuck out her hand. "Hi, I'm Tracey Lovegrove." She wore a stylish pair of red glasses and her hair was tied in a thick ponytail.

"Axel Crowe." Crowe shook hands, noting the pliable warmth of her grip. In an instant, he'd pegged her as a *pitta* type in the *ayurvedic* system. Athletic build, springy gait, alert eyes, slightly curly hair, lightly flushed complexion. A tendency to move fast, and keep moving – physically, mentally, emotionally. Same type as him.

"Where are we at with fingerprints?" Levinson asked her.

"After eliminating those of Mrs. Stockwell and the homeless guy who found her wallet, I was able to lift two partial prints, index finger and thumb," Tracey said. "Same process of elimination for the construction worker who found her purse and cell phone. The phone had no other prints on it, but the purse had partials of a thumb, index and middle fingers."

"What about the pepper spray?"

Tracey picked up the bag containing the red dispenser and pointed. "Like the other items, the surface seems to have been quickly wiped. But here on the button where it's recessed, there's a partial print of what I assume to be an index finger."

"That's all we've got – three partials?" Levinson said.

Crowe turned as another detective in a black overcoat, unshaven with a thick shock of unkempt black hair, entered the office. Crowe sized him up – overweight with a pale and oily complexion, someone who needed regular jolts of caffeine to jumpstart a body made sluggish from over-indulgence in a high-carb diet. In *ayurvedic* terms, a *kapha* type. But behind those dark brown eyes was an alert intelligence, like that of a hungry reptile.

Levinson said to Crowe, "My partner, Arnie Rossimoff." And to Rossimoff, "Axel Crowe, private investigator retained by the Blaikies."

"To get in our way?" Rossimoff sniffed.

"Right now," Levinson chided his partner, "we'll take all the help we can get."

Rossimoff stared at Crowe, a toothpick moving from one side of his mouth to the other, like a snake's tongue taking a sample of the environment, trying to decide whether this was predator, prey or just part of the scenery.

Crowe offered his hand. Rossimoff shook with apparent disdain. Crowe felt a cool and oily grip, like handling a fresh eel. He noticed Tracey shifting a bit to one side, giving Rossimoff a wider berth. Had those oily hands strayed her way or was she just trying to get upwind of an overcoat that looked like it had slept on the Bowery?

"May I have a look at those prints?" Crowe said.

Levinson opened the folder that Tracey had brought and removed a sheet with a blowup of three fingerprints. He handed it to Crowe.

Crowe studied it and observed, "Despite the partials, the fingertips all have a spatulate shape. Fingerprints have arch patterns on both the index and middle fingers. Thumb has a whorl with a forked line that penetrates the center." He closed his eyes a moment, factoring in the event chart of Janis Stockwell's death, a map that bore the signatures of both victim and perpetrator. When he opened his eyes he said, "This is a woman who works as a writer, editor or critic of some kind."

Rossimoff snorted. "You can't read sex or occupation from fingerprints."

"She's also athletic," Crowe said.

Rossimoff was about to object again when Levinson

signaled to hold his tongue.

"...and has no moral boundaries when it comes to getting what she wants."

"Sounds like a Tonya Harding," Rossimoff quipped.

"Not a professional athlete," Crowe said. "Foremost, this woman's a thinker."

"Shit," said Rossimoff. "A man's worst nightmare."

Tracey gave him a wicked look. Rossimoff turned away, shaking his head like a fighter who'd just taken a solid punch.

Levinson said to Crowe, "Not to dispute your ideas, but this seems very speculative. Even if it were true, I don't see how useful it's going to be."

"Useful or not," Tracey spoke up, "he just mentioned something that conforms to the crime scene evidence." She held up one of the evidence bags containing a see-through plastic canister.

The others closed in to take turns handling the evidence bag. Inside the canister was a tiny piece of white fabric or leather, about half the size of a pinkie fingernail.

"What is that?" Levinson said.

"Cabretta leather. A high-end leather advertised as 'second-skin-thin' typically used for driving, shooting or golf gloves, but also for police service because of the combined protection, dexterity and sensitivity it allows."

"No shit!" Rossimoff said. "Where'd this come from?"

"It was stuck in Mrs. Stockwell's front teeth," Tracey said. "I'm speculating that the assailant clapped a hand over her mouth while trying to break her neck. I think Stockwell bit her assailant's hand and got a piece of leather in the process."

Levinson and Rossimoff nodded. It made sense.

"If you look closely," Tracey said, "the fragment has a small perforation, just like the ventilation holes in gloves."

"Probably a golf glove," Crowe said, "typically white, no matter the sex of the player."

"So much for it definitely being a woman," Rossimoff said.

"Still a possibility," Levinson conceded, "and it supports

his idea of an athletic killer."

"Anybody can buy a pair of golf gloves," Rossimoff countered.

"You've got to admit, Arnie, it's a critical piece in the profile," Levinson said. "We're not looking at some crackhead in a mugging that went sour. We're looking for a murderer who gave some thought to how this would go down."

Rossimoff shook his head, reluctant to admit defeat.

"Another reason I agree with Mr. Crowe about the killer being athletic," Tracey said, "is the way she tried to kill Mrs. Stockwell. It takes strength and skill to snap someone's neck. I'm thinking someone with military service, police training or expertise in martial arts."

"Martial arts," Crowe agreed.

"Why do you say that?" Levinson said.

"Just something that came to me." Crowe didn't want to defend his use of astrology. "Besides, a killer with a military or police background would have launched a more aggressive and violent attack. A piece of pipe struck at the base of the skull could have killed her on the spot and been disposed of down the nearest storm drain. But the actual attack suggests someone who's a bit naïve about what it takes to kill another person. Martial artists are trained to fight and disable, less likely to kill. That makes me feel this person was slightly out of her depth."

"*Her* again?" Rossimoff said.

Crowe turned to Tracey. "What else did you find of the victim's?"

Tracey held up the other see-through canister, the one in which there appeared to be nothing, but with a closer look revealed a few strands of fiber. "In the clasp of the purse I found a tuft of wool and polyester that didn't match clothing worn by the victim."

"Anything identifiable?"

"You want my educated guess, it's from a jacket lining, typical of stuff sold by L.L. Bean and other sportswear manufacturers. Worthless as a clue to search for a suspect, but might be useful as a sample to match against a suspect."

"Anything else?"

"No."

Crowe picked up the evidence bag containing the purse. "May I open this?"

Levinson produced latex gloves from a box in his desk drawer. Crowe donned the gloves and removed the purse from its bag. He turned it in his hands, brought it to his nose and sniffed. He wet a fingertip with spittle, rubbed it on a patch of leather and sniffed again. He closed his eyes.

The three police staff watched him with varying degrees of interest, Rossimoff with cynicism, Tracey with fascination and Levinson with curiosity as to where this would lead next.

"*Piñon*," Crowe pronounced.

"Say what?" Levinson said.

"A small pine indigenous to the American Southwest," Tracey said.

"One with a very distinctive scent," Crowe nodded. "The person who handled this has been around burning *piñon*, probably a campfire, maybe a fireplace."

"Come on," Rossimoff said. "Her purse was found in a dumpster full of other crap."

"That only reinforces my opinion. There're no *piñon* in Manhattan."

"I don't buy it," Rossimoff said. "A dog's got a nose that subtle but I doubt you do."

Crowe smiled. "So the dog and I are the only ones who know that for lunch today you had pasta *arrabiata* with a glass of red wine?"

Rossimoff checked his loosely-knotted necktie for the telltale sign of pasta sauce that had betrayed him.

"Not on your tie – on your breath."

Rossimoff flushed a deep red, embarrassed at having been sniffed out.

After relishing Rossimoff's awkward moment, Tracey said, "We don't have the equipment here but the FBI could do a spectrographic analysis, confirm your theory about the *piñon.*"

"Let's say it's true," Levinson said. "What does it tell us anyway?"

"The killer left the crime scene with Stockwell's purse under her jacket," Crowe said. "Given body heat and humidity, the scent transferred from jacket lining to purse."

"Muggers don't do that," Rossimoff said. "They take the money and plastic and ditch the other crap the first chance they get."

"I agree," Crowe said, "which is why we know this *wasn't* a mugging."

Crowe looked at the map on the wall. In his mind's eye, he was still thinking of the two graphic patterns he'd observed at the crime scene – the triangle of cracks in the asphalt where Janis Stockwell's hand had lain, and the more subtle junction of finer cracks that formed a six-pointed asterisk.

As in all things, Guruji had taught him, one first had to paint a picture with broad brush strokes using the grosser elements. The trend is your friend, as the market traders said, their challenge to weed out signal from noise, sifting through a mountain of financial data to find the nuggets of information that would guide their million-dollar decisions. First you figured out whether you were bull or bear, then the stock-picking followed. Guruji could have made millions on the stock market but his life was uncomplicated by lust for money or anything else.

Staring at the map, Crowe projected the triangle in his mind's eye onto the precinct grid of streets and avenues. Keeping its proportions in mind he played with the size of the triangle, comparing it to the three blue stickpins marking the locations of Stockwell's body and her disposed possessions. After a long pause, he turned to face the others. They all seemed to be holding their breath, waiting for him to speak.

"If I were you," Crowe told Levinson, "I'd canvass every hotel within a three-block radius of Sixth and 58th. You're looking for a woman from the Southwest who checked out in the last twenty-four hours."

33

Larkspur, California

It was another beautiful day in Marin County, except for the felonious residents of San Quentin, because even though the maximum security prison occupied prime real estate on San Francisco Bay, the inmates didn't have rooms with bay views. From down in the yard, all they could see was blue sky, and smell salt air, and hear distant traffic on the Richmond Bridge, a daily taunt of the senses that only served to remind them of freedom lost. On the other hand, the security officers manning the guard towers could watch the distant traffic of oil tankers, container ships or Navy frigates navigating the channels to and from the docks and naval shipyards on the east side of the San Francisco peninsula. Even closer, there were sailboats coming and going from San Pablo Bay, plus the regular-as-clockwork ferries in and out of Larkspur.

Over at the ferry terminal, at the mouth of Corte Madera Creek, commuters were in full transit mode. Cars spilled off the freeway and into the huge terminal parking lot, while a steady flow of buses discharged passengers in front of the terminal building. The commuters flashed their transit passes at the entrance and crossed the dock to a waiting ferry.

In the administration building office overlooking the dock, Detective Jim Starrett had a chair pulled up next to that of Delray Perkins, a black man in his early fifties whose desk placard read *Terminal Superintendent, Bay Area Transit*. Perkins was working his computer and Starrett was looking over his shoulder.

"Thank God, no more videotape to mess with," Perkins was saying. "Couple of years ago, we went digital. Used to be, this was mostly for insurance purposes, 'cause we do get our share of fender benders, but since 9/11, it's a whole new operation. Thank Homeland Security for all this new equipment. Way it works now, everything from four different surveillance cameras, 24/7, is saved on hard disk. Once a week we archive that, and then the camera feed re-writes the hard disk. So, here you go, my man."

Starrett peered at the flat-screen monitor. It showed a high shot of the parking lot on the west side of the terminal. In the corner of the screen a block of text gave the day, Tuesday, the calendar date, and the time, *19H00*.

Starrett unfolded the Larkspur & Sausalito Ferry Service schedule Perkins had given him, and looked at the ferry times. "The Jeep was reported stolen at seven-forty. According to this schedule, there's a ferry arrival at seven-thirty-five, which is probably when the owner showed up." He took a folded page from his shirt pocket and glanced at the police report. "Owner said he'd parked in his usual spot, right beside post number four."

Perkins tapped the screen, whose resolution was good enough to clearly read the number '4' painted on one of the tall pylons whose floodlights illuminated the parking lot at night. "Not there at seven."

"That figures," Starrett said, "because I know it was busy running down my hit-and-run victim at six-fifty-five. Back up an hour."

Perkins typed in *18H00*. The screen refreshed and Starrett saw blank spaces in the parking lot suddenly filled by vehicles that hadn't been there in the previous view. There was now a blue Jeep Cherokee parked next to pylon Number 4.

"So it's there at six," Perkins said. "Now what?"

"When'd the next ferry arrive?"

"Six-oh-five," Perkins said.

"Give us the view at six-oh-seven," Starrett said.

Perkins hit the fast-forward button. The screen blinked at one-second intervals. A number of vehicles disappeared from the screen as their owners, arriving at six-oh-five, drove away. The Jeep didn't budge. Perkins froze the screen at *18H15*.

"Next arrival's six-twenty," Perkins said.

"Go ahead."

Perkins typed in *18H20* and they watched the screen in

real time. At *18H22* dozens of people appeared at the bottom of the screen, spreading across the parking lot. Cars began pulling out of their parking slots and heading for the exit. They watched a man in a cap and a windbreaker approach the Jeep. He paused for a moment on the far side of the Jeep, where it was impossible to see what he was doing, but in a moment the door opened and he was inside the vehicle. After another brief pause, he drove away.

"Bingo!" Perkins said.

"Any way to get a closer look at him?" Starrett asked.

"Not with this technology." Perkins shook his head. "I could copy this segment, maybe you got somebody can enhance it, like they do on TV cop shows."

"You got a camera on the other side of the lot?"

Perkins worked his computer and they had a look at the Jeep from the far side of the parking lot. In this clip, the guy in the windbreaker pulled a shim from his sleeve and used it to work the driver's side door. Once inside the car, the guy was bent under the dash for all of thirty seconds before the Jeep was on its way.

"Not the first time I've seen that," Perkins said. "Some of these guys are amazing, into a car and gone in less than a minute, even with an alarm. 'Cept what this guy wanted with a ten-year-old Cherokee, I can't imagine."

"Car theft was only the means, not the end." Starrett leaned back in the chair to stretch. "So, help me here, Delroy. Do you know the Peacock Gap Golf and Country Club, Biscayne Drive?"

"From the inside, no. When it comes down to choosing between membership fees and mortgage payments, the choice has been pretty clear so far."

"But you know where it is?"

"Sure, I've driven by."

"How long you think to drive from here to there?"

"Rush hour? Say, six-thirty on a weeknight?"

"Yeah."

Perkins scratched his head. "It's only about six miles, but

that time of day, the freeway's like a parking lot. I'd call it twenty minutes, give or take."

"Sounds reasonable," said Starrett. "So our car thief drove away at six-twenty-five, add twenty, we're now at six-forty-five. That leaves ten minutes to spare before the hit-and-run."

"*This* guy did that?" said Perkins.

"It's possible," said Starrett. "Now let's consider the return leg. From Biscayne Drive back into San Rafael, no freeway, that's ten minutes easy, and our car thief dumps the Jeep near the bus depot, say seven-oh-five or shortly thereafter."

"That time of day," Perkins said, "buses from the San Rafael depot run to Larkspur every twenty minutes. He could've caught the seven-twenty, which would take at least a half-hour ride. Earliest he'd be back here would be, let's say, seven-fifty."

"In time for a ferry?"

"He would've missed the seven-forty."

"I can't see him standing around fifteen minutes in San Rafael waiting for a bus, not after what he'd done. What if he took a cab?"

"Going against the traffic, he could be back here in fifteen, twenty minutes, say seven-thirty at the latest."

"Let's have a look."

Perkins typed *19H20* into the computer. They stared at the monitor, viewing the largely-vacant parking lot from a camera on a pole on the west side.

"Hang on, wrong camera," Perkins said. "Let me get the one for the ticket entrance."

He selected a different camera. The screen changed to a view from just inside the terminal that covered both the ticket booth and the turnstile entrance. There were no passengers in the frame. Perkins fast-forwarded the playback.

They watched as a gaggle of passengers, obviously a disembarking busload, suddenly appeared at *19H31*. Perkins switched from fast forward to real time. They watched passengers surge through the turnstile. Then nothing for two minutes. But then at 19H33, they saw the guy they'd viewed earlier, a lone man in a black windbreaker, jeans and running shoes, and a cap pulled low over his eyes. Perkins froze the frame.

"Not the best angle," he said, "but as good as it gets."

"Make me a copy of both sequences," Starrett said, "the one in the parking lot where he jimmies the Jeep door, and this one here." He took a card from his wallet and slid it onto Perkins' desk. "Email them to me, and I'll take it from there."

"That it for today?"

"I owe you one, man." Starrett stood and clapped a hand on Perkins' broad shoulders. "You ever get a traffic violation, you give me a call." He turned toward the door.

"Don't go away empty-handed," said Perkins, pulling open one of his desk drawers. "I got three right here."

"Are you shittin' me?"

"No, sir." Perkins handed Starrett the three tickets.

Starrett looked at them. They were three to nine months old, nothing serious, just parking violations, and all issued in Novato, about fifteen miles up US-101. That was a bit out of his jurisdiction, but what the hell, a promise was a promise.

"Guess it's your lucky day, man."

Perkins didn't say anything, only nodded with a big-toothed grin, like he'd just won the lottery.

34

New York

Axel Crowe thanked Detectives Levinson and Rossimoff for sharing their information, and left the Homicide office. Tracey Lovegrove departed at the same time and followed him to the elevator, the fingerprint folder and evidence box tucked under her arm.

"Where's your office?" he said.

"Two floors down."

"You don't use the stairs?"

"I'm lazy," she shrugged.

"I don't think so. When you first arrived, you were slightly out of breath. Didn't you take the stairs to come up?"

She made a face. "What are you, some kind of cop?"

"I'll bet that line gets a lot of use around here."

She laughed. It sounded good on her, like she'd had some practice.

He studied her. "You're an attractive woman. No wedding ring. You must get a lot of attention."

"From lots of married guys who don't interest me."

Crowe didn't ask who she was interested in. The elevator doors opened on a crowded compartment. Crowe stood next to a patrol officer and a woman wearing a vinyl miniskirt and a very full tube top who bore an uncanny resemblance to a well-known actress. Tracey squeezed in next to him. They rode down to the main floor. It seemed to Crowe that she was pressed up against him more closely than was dictated by the available space in the elevator.

"Did you miss your stop?" he said.

"I need to go out for a coffee," she said. "Join me?"

"You can't leave the station with case evidence under your arm."

"Duh."

They disembarked at the ground floor. Crowe returned his visitor's badge to the desk sergeant. Tracey handed her file folder and evidence box to the sergeant, asking him to mind it for a few minutes, and followed Crowe outside.

"Come on," she hooked her arm in his. "I'm buying."

They went to a coffee shop called New World Bean where Tracey got a latte and Crowe a *chai*.

"Where are you staying?" she asked.

"Washington Square Hotel."

"No kidding! We're practically neighbors. I live in the East Village."

"I stay there every time I come to town."

"Got any plans this evening?"

"No."

"What do you like to eat?"

"I'm partial to Indian food." Fourteen years with Guruji had etched deep grooves in his dietary patterns.

"Do you know Dharma Dosa over on 7th Street near Bowery?"

"No. Are they good?"

"The best. Are you up for a little adventure?"

"Twist my arm."

Jokingly he held his hand out. Taking him seriously, she gripped his fingers in one hand, thumb in another, and applied an opposing leverage that made him wince before she released the pressure.

"What is that, some kind of cops' hand grip?"

"You'd be surprised, the things I know," she smiled.

Crowe caught a cab to the OTB on West 48th. En route, he called Blaikie and brought him up to speed. Blaikie was surprised to hear about the pepper spray. The cops hadn't even told him that.

"Did your sister have any connection with the Southwest?" Crowe asked. "Business deals, investors, competitors…?"

"Not that I know. Maybe my brother-in-law could tell you."

"I'd like to meet him. I know it's only the day after, but do you suppose he'd talk to me?"

"I'll give him a call."

At the OTB, Crowe bought a program for today's races at Santa Anita. He pored over the fact sheets, circling today's prospects with a red pen. After he'd identified a few horses that looked like contenders, he checked his astrology app for the planetary lineup at post time. He readjusted his estimation of which horses had the best shot at win, place or show, and went to a betting wicket.

Once that was done, he checked the results for the first three races at Belmont that had run today. As it turned out, he'd picked a couple of money-makers. It was a good sign and the day's program had only just begun. He'd noticed over the years that if he got the first race of the day right, he often did well in the balance of the races. The tough part was learning to walk away when the first race bore no fruit. We were conditioned, he reflected, by old adages like, *If at first you don't succeed, try and try again*, when in fact his experience at the racetrack seemed to suggest it was more like, *Well begun is well done*.

His phone rang. Blaikie had spoken to his brother-in-law Jeb, who'd reluctantly agreed to meet with Crowe. But it had to be soon, and it had to be brief.

Crowe arrived at Jeb Stockwell's co-op fifteen minutes later. An attractive Filipino maid ushered him into a very large apartment with a living room that boasted a grand piano, several works of art and a wall of windows overlooking Central Park.

Adjoining the living room was a study paneled with bookcases. Jeb Stockwell was seated behind a desk with a laptop and some scattered papers. He stood when Crowe entered and came around the desk to shake hands. He was a little over six feet tall and had the look of a retired athlete, someone who'd once been in shape but had been overtaken by the good life, whose taste for good food and drink had got the better of him.

Crowe encountered a large soft hand whose grip promptly slackened as Stockwell broke off the handshake. Crowe glanced at Stockwell's hand and saw long fingers, buffed nails and a tapered thumb that, as soon its hand was free of Crowe's, tucked reflexively under the first two fingers, like a turtle withdrawing its head into its shell.

Crowe raised his eyes to Stockwell's face and gave him a

sympathetic look. "My condolences, Mr. Stockwell. You must be devastated. Were you married long?"

"Seven years."

In that brief look at Stockwell's face, more analytic than sympathetic, Crowe saw many things. Stockwell had a flushed complexion and a deep crease in the forehead that indicated a distressed liver, probably accompanied by the bilious emotions that went with it. His eyes, whose green irises were heavily flecked with gold, spoke of substance abuse, while a slight tremor of the lips signaled a thirst provoked by dehydration. The man was in a state of nervous exhaustion, probably held together by regular infusions of alcohol.

According to *ayurveda*, Crowe labeled him a composite *pitta-kapha* type, the kind of guy who'd work hard and play hard while indulging in more than his body was equipped to handle, until some day he'd blow a gasket – an aneurysm, a heart attack, a liver failure. With too much heat and pressure inside a congested system, eventually something had to give.

"Please, have a seat." Stockwell gestured to a pair of leather chairs in front of the desk. As Crowe seated himself, Stockwell returned to his chair behind the imposing desk. "Kevin tells me you're trying to make sense of this tragedy."

"I doubt I can do that. But if I can help the police find the killer, at least you and your in-laws will have the satisfaction of seeing justice done."

"You don't think the police are up to the job?"

"I have the greatest respect for the police. But sometimes they get trapped in their own perspectives."

"And you're going to enlighten them?"

Crowe caught the whiff of sarcasm but let it go. Sometimes it helped to think like a tennis player: when the other player's ball was headed out of bounds, no point in swinging at it. Stockwell was either in mourning, or he wasn't. Either way, his emotions were raw and Crowe wasn't going to get flustered over a little cynicism. In his line of work he dealt with it on a regular basis.

After a moment of silence, during which Stockwell fussed

with some papers on his desk, Crowe took out his phone and started his astrology app.

"Did your wife have any enemies?"

"No. She was a classic altruist. Everyone loved her."

"Aside from her charity work, did she have any business dealings?"

"She owned several large properties. But she left the day-to-day business to her property manager."

"Is there anyone who might have wanted to hurt you through her?"

"That's ridiculous."

"Why?"

"Because I don't have any enemies."

"Do either of you have any connection with people or businesses in the Southwest?"

Stockwell hesitated a moment and straightened the pile of papers on his desk. "No."

Crowe was looking at his astrology app. In the right hands, it was the next best thing to a bullshit detector. Close inspection of the third house usually revealed whether reports were true or false. Right now, he believed Stockwell was blowing smoke.

"Never been there on vacation?"

"Once or twice, I guess."

"Together or alone?"

"We've been to Canyon Ranch a couple of times."

"What's that?"

"An exclusive spa hotel in Tucson."

"No old friends, college buddies or business associates in the Southwest?"

"Janis? None I can recall."

"And you?"

"No." Stockwell couldn't conceal his growing impatience. "What's all this about the Southwest anyway?"

"There's a tentative connection."

Stockwell laid a hand atop his papers, as if he were afraid they might fly away. "With all due respect, Mr. Crowe, this seems like a monumental waste of time – both mine and yours. Why don't you just leave the investigation to the police, and go back to tracking down corporate whistle-blowers, or whatever you do for Kevin." He made a show of looking at his watch. "I'm expecting a call any minute regarding the unpleasant business of my wife's funeral arrangements. Can we wrap this up?"

Crowe put his phone away. He was being given the bum's rush but he took it gracefully. The maid appeared out of nowhere, apparently summoned by a buzzer to show him the door. In lieu of a farewell handshake, Stockwell gave him a curt nod as she led Crowe away.

In the foyer Crowe paused at the door she'd opened and asked the maid, "What's your name?"

"May Lee."

"You're from the Philippines, May?"

"Yes."

"Buddhist, Catholic or Muslim?"

"Catholic."

"How long have you worked for the Stockwells?"

"Two years."

"Are you a legal immigrant?"

"Yes."

"Does Mr. Stockwell have a girlfriend?"

The confusion in May's face was almost painful to witness. Her eyes dropped quickly to one side. She began to close the door on him. "I'm sorry. I don't know anything about that."

Crowe headed for the elevator, reflecting on this brief but meaningful exchange. It was just like operating a lie detector – a couple of innocent questions to establish a baseline of facial expressions, then a slight escalation of inquiry to test her response before hitting her with the loaded question.

Crowe knew it as surely as if May had signed an affidavit to the effect: there was another woman.

Stockwell's grief, shallow as it was, would be short-lived.

35

San Rafael

When Detective Jim Starrett returned to the office, the video clips from the Larkspur Terminal surveillance were in his email. He went looking for Myke Brane, the detective unit's computer geek. Starrett explained what he needed. Brane assured Starrett he'd get right on it. Starrett returned to his desk and forwarded the emails to Brane.

He phoned the Novato police, spoke to the woman in charge of traffic violations and got Perkins' three tickets purged from the system. It could never have been done for anything serious like a DUI but for chicken shit like this it was all in the name of the higher good to reward cooperative citizens.

He returned to his two other active case files, tidying up the paperwork for the domestic murder-suicide, now resolved to everyone's satisfaction. He also made a few phone calls related to a double murder involving the Merguez brothers, who'd become a bit too entrepreneurial selling ecstasy in Terra Linda, a territory controlled by Los Diablos del Norte. In this case he was working with Manny Cantata whose Narcotics portfolio obliged him to stay abreast of every drug dealer in Marin County with an illicit annual income of a hundred grand or more, a task as futile as shoveling back the tide on Stinson Beach.

Starrett took a break from his phone calls and put his feet on his desk. He took his rope from his desk drawer and played with it a few minutes. He was in the middle of a complicated knot when Hutchins walked in.

"This what you do all day when I'm not here, lie around on the poop deck?" Hutchins placed a pair of coffees on the corner of Starrett's desk.

"Some people do their best thinking in the shower. I like to tie knots."

"Captain'll tie a knot in your dick one of these days." Hutchins sat with a quiet groan. He'd hurt his left knee five years ago trying to catch a fleeing perp, and ever since then it'd been his Achilles heel, aching after a few hours on his feet.

Starrett blew on his coffee and took a sip. "How'd you make out at the bank?"

"Most of Lang's money was in T-bills or mutual funds except for two small apartment buildings, one here in San Rafael, one in Tiburon. Between one thing and the next, he had a steady income of roughly eighty grand a month."

Starrett whistled.

"Before taxes," Hutchins added, as if that mattered.

"So he was living in a style to which neither of us will ever be accustomed."

"Spending about ten grand a month."

"On...?"

"Restaurants, shows, hotels, trips, personal stuff."

"Anything out of the ordinary?"

"Three months ago he withdrew sixty grand in cash."

"Given his income, not a huge sum."

"Still quite a chunk of change for a guy who put everything else on credit cards."

"Gambling?"

"Doesn't fit the profile. After I went through his Visa and MasterCard statements, I found out who his travel agent was. I checked his travel history. In the past five years, he's only been to Vegas a couple of times, and the last was over two years ago."

"You don't have to go to Vegas to gamble."

"I also talked to Vice, who talked to a few key bookies. Lang's not a player."

"Internet gambling?"

"Not with cash. It's all credit cards."

Starrett began to tie a different knot. Hutchins glanced through the message notes on his desk. Starrett's phone rang and he spent a few minutes in conversation, mostly listening, but towards the end, giving some directives.

"What's up?" Hutchins said after Starrett was finished. "Any luck in Larkspur?"

"That was Brane, just giving me an update." Starrett brought his partner up to speed on the ferry terminal surveillance. "Brane went through the video clips, isolated half a dozen best shots and sent off JPEGs to the FBI. Guy over there had a quick look, said he'd do what he could. But given the camera angle and resolution, it's one-in-a-million getting a hit with face recognition software. Assuming our mystery man's even in the database."

Hutchins shook his head. "Gotta love those odds."

"Brane also sent the best face shot off to TRAK. Evening shift, it'll be out there with every cop in the Bay Area, with a request to bring this guy in for questioning."

"Maybe we'll get lucky," Hutchins said doubtfully.

"Speaking of which, one of us needs to cruise Castro tonight, see if there's any truth to what Munson said about Lang and rough trade."

"Don't look at me, man, my knee is killing me."

"You don't have to walk. Just wear a dress and high heels, sit at the bar showing some leg and they'll swarm around you like flies on a fresh pile of shit." Starrett tried to keep a straight face.

Hutchins caressed his beer belly. "You think anyone's going to hit on a pregnant cross-dresser?"

"You got a purty mouth. Someone bound to take a shine to you, boy."

"You sound like one of those hillbillies in *Deliverance*."

Starrett twirled some rope between his legs. "Y'all git on down here and show me what you can do."

Hutchins had to laugh. "If anyone's right for this, it's you. At least you look like you've been to a gym."

"I'll flip you for it."

"I'm not going."

Starrett tossed a quarter, caught it and slapped it onto the back of his hand. "Call it."

"You call it."

"Give me head or give me tail," Starrett insisted.

Hutchins showed him the finger.

"We'll call that a tail." Starrett lifted his hand to reveal the eagle. He showed it to Hutchins. "You won the call. Guess it's your lucky day."

Hutchins relaxed with a smirk. "My lucky day, maybe your lucky night."

36

New York

Axel Crowe left Stockwell's co-op and took the subway to Greenwich Village. He bought some cashews and a fresh carrot juice with a shot of wheat grass at a health food store. He walked over to Washington Square, sat on a bench facing the late afternoon sun and listened to a black kid play some Delta blues on a beat-up acoustic guitar.

Crowe loved cashews even though Guruji had warned him that the human constitution was barely capable of eating nine a day without adverse effect. The nut, shaped like the tusk of an elephant, was a common offering in India to *Ganesha*, the elephant-headed patron deity of astrologers.

Crowe checked the end-of-day results for Belmont. Yes! Black Daddy in the Ninth had placed, paying off 36-to-1 on a $10 bet. He'd picked a few other winners and was up a little over $500. Not bad for a day's work, and the horses were still running on the west coast. He'd wait until later to check the race results for Santa Anita.

The guitarist finished his set and circulated with a hat, seeking donations from locals and tourists. Many turned their backs and walked away, but at least half of them dug some change out of their pockets. Crowe dropped a ten in the kid's hat. The guitarist did a double-take, like he expected Crowe to ask for change, but Crowe just gave him a thumb's up sign.

He walked back to Waverley Place and the Washington Square Hotel. His room had an Art Deco theme, with accents of dark wood, marble-topped night tables and art on the walls. He stripped to his underwear, did half an hour of yoga and took a shower. After toweling off, he spread a spare blanket on the floor and sat naked facing east to meditate for half an hour.

Axel Crowe looked forward to dinner with Tracey Lovegrove but wasn't sure what he expected after that. She was spunky and it gave him a charge to talk to her, to be in her presence. But she occupied borderline territory, the exact limits of which he hadn't yet determined.

Because of his training under Guruji, Crowe often sorted people into categories. Although it had no status in western sociology, the Hindu caste system was a useful model. Intellectuals and spiritual people like Guruji were *Brahmin*. Police and other wielders of power were *kshatriya*. Businessmen like Blaikie and Stockwell were *vaishya*. Trades and service personnel like Stockwell's maid were *shudra*. The outcasts of society were *mlechcha*: derelicts sitting on street corners with hands out, lying on a park bench with empty bottle or spent needle.

Women could be classed via the same model, but other categories were both descriptive and useful. Women were mothers, sisters, lovers, angels and rarely, but possibly, demons. You might have the bad luck to meet a *Kali*, the Hindu goddess of time and change, death and destruction, and she would add your head to her collection of skulls.

Crowe had resolved many years ago never to fraternize too closely with clients. He wouldn't allow himself to become intimate with a female client, no matter how attractive or available. In his line of work there were inevitable opportunities, and his knowledge of a client's birth chart made any vulnerability all too transparent. For that reason alone it was unethical.

Peers and associates were different but even there he was circumspect. There was no telling if or when a relationship would change and he might be left in an awkward situation, needing help perhaps, and the bitter end of an affair might preclude rational cooperation. He recalled one of Guruji's remarks, about how certain people were sexually attracted to each other by virtue of their unresolved karma. *If it is necessary, it will happen and give joy,* he said, *and if it isn't necessary, it won't happen, or it will bring pain.*

At seven o'clock Crowe walked over to Cooper Square, where 4th Avenue turned into the Bowery at 7th Street. Tracey was standing next to the big cube sculpture in the square. She wasn't wearing her glasses this evening but was dressed in a red silk shirt over a tight pair of jeans tucked into cowboy boots. Surrounded by somber New Yorkers in black, she stuck out like a long-horned steer in a herd of Jerseys.

"Waiting for the stagecoach?" he said.

"What's the matter, you don't like cowgirls?"

"Based on your accent, I had you pegged for a Georgia peach, not a Texan."

"Good ear. But I do love the Southwest."

"Me too." He kissed her on both cheeks, a habit acquired during his early years in francophone Quebec.

They walked a few blocks to the restaurant. Along the way, they engaged in one of those get-acquainted conversations so typical of first dates.

"So, are you married?" she asked.

"Never. What about you?"

"I gave it a try. It lasted seven years."

"Lots of people hit that bump in the road. The seven-year itch."

"Never been married, and you're how old?"

"Forty."

"Peter Pan syndrome?"

"I don't think so. I just know myself."

"You think the rest of us are fools?"

"It works for most, just not for me," Crowe shrugged. "I lived with someone for a couple of years but that was a decade ago and it ended amicably."

"What happened?"

"She said I never had any time for her. She gave me an ultimatum, not a hostile one, just a request to clarify my choices. But I'd already passed the fork in the road and I couldn't turn back."

"And she accepted that with grace?"

"Grace under fire. She understood me. She was good that way."

"You don't get lonely?"

He shrugged. "Every now and again, even the anvil misses the hammer."

"Is that why you're having dinner with me?"

"Don't New York women have a reputation for being ball-busters?"

"Relax, I won't hurt you." She took his hand and led him toward the restaurant.

Crowe caught a whiff of curry and turmeric. The front door of Dharma Dosa was flanked by two green ceramic elephants, each supporting a flowerpot into whose soil were thrust sticks of burning incense. Inside were a dozen tables, most of them occupied, but as they entered, another couple vacated a window table. A waiter cleared the table and brought them menus.

"There's only one thing to order here," Tracey said, "and that's the *dosa*."

Crowe looked around. It seemed everyone was eating rolled-up crepes stuffed with meat or vegetable. They ordered vegetarian *dosa* and *lassi*, a drink comprising water, yogurt and fresh mango. They ate with their fingers, dipping pieces of *dosa* in the condiment bowls.

"You have a slight accent," Tracey said. "Where are you from?"

"I was born here but I grew up in Montreal."

"Born here in New York City?"

"Upstate. My father was Boston Irish, my mother a French-Canadian from Montreal."

"How'd they meet?"

"In the sixties, my mother was a devotee of Swami Muktananda who had an ashram in upper New York State. My father was a peace activist, giving lectures all over the state. They met at the ashram and fell in love. They commuted back and forth to be together but never married. I was their love child."

"Where are they now?"

"My mother runs a halfway house for juvenile girls in Montreal. My father has a software firm in Boston."

"Do you see them often?"

"I try to check in regularly."

"Any other family?"

"No. What about you?"

"My parents had tried but almost given up on having kids by the time I came along, so I've got no siblings either. My dad was a civil engineer for Georgia's Department of Transportation. He's retired now, lives in Daytona Beach. I go down every three months to spend time with him. My mom died a few years ago of breast cancer. I worry about that now, thinking it might happen to me. I have anxiety attacks sometimes, but I work out a lot and try to eat well."

"Where'd you go to school?"

"Georgia Tech for my bachelor's in chemistry, then University of Florida for a master's in digital forensics."

"What brought you to New York?"

"My ex got a transfer here. So I applied to the NYPD and got a job just like that." She snapped her fingers.

They finished their meal and sat content, just looking at each other and savoring the moment. The waiter cleared their plates and they ordered a pot of tea.

Crowe asked her about her job. She told him about some of the cases she was working on – a grade school white boy dumped in the Hudson with his wrists wired to his ankles, a black man in his late twenties shot at close range by four different weapons on Central Park South, a gay playwright found hanging from the chandelier in his Bryant Park condo.

"Not exactly dinner conversation," she apologized. But she'd made no mention of the Stockwell case. However curious Crowe might have been, it was unethical for her to discuss it without clearance from Levinson.

"Think of me as a doctor," he said. "I have a morbid curiosity for the human condition."

"I can relate to that. In my line of work I've become all too familiar with the human condition, especially its decaying process."

"What got you into forensics? Is there a cop somewhere in the family tree?"

"Two of my uncles were detectives in Atlanta. I loved hearing them talk about cases they'd worked. I liked the idea of catching criminals with science. Police culture I could do without. Hanging around cops is a lousy lifestyle. Most of them have way too much stress in their lives but they think they can drink their way out of it. Not a good combination."

"So what do you want to be when you grow up?"

"I've been with the NYPD five years. Lab work is a total snore, so technical and repetitive it's like a clerical job with scientific equipment. Field work is more interesting, so I enjoy getting out of the office to process a crime scene. But you know what really turns me on?"

The *double-entendre* sparked a little something in Crowe. He found her very attractive in a way he couldn't put a finger on, although he wouldn't mind feeling around for it. He resisted the temptation to flirt, knowing it was a slippery slope. He reminded himself not to get personally involved. Maybe when this case was over...

"An Aries always enjoys a chase," he said.

"How'd you know I was an Aries?"

"Intuition."

"You're good." She looked into her tea cup, as if she was going to read her tea leaves. "Now I've lost my train of thought..."

"What turns you on... professionally?"

"Yes, thank you." She raised her eyes. "I'd really like to get into researching new technology, finding new applications in forensic science. Forensic profiling, for instance, is a relatively new science and we've barely scratched the surface of what's possible. It could have a greater impact on crime resolution than anything else I'm doing."

Crowe nodded. A kindred spirit.

Tracey leaned back and stretched her legs. "Ready for a walk? Maybe we can find a drink in this part of town."

"There's a blues bar on Bleecker that I visit every time I'm in town," Crowe said. "Are you up for that?"

Tracey raised one of her boots from beneath the table. "Even cowgirls dig the blues."

37

Santa Fe

In the late afternoon quiet of the north-end suburb, Piños Verdes seemed like a dead-end street to nowhere. Stucco houses with red tile roofs lay baking under the sun. Vehicles were parked in the shade of car ports, draped with covers or left victim to the sun from whose glare the stunted pine trees of the street offered no protection.

At the house at the end of Piños Verdes, a red Honda Accord sat under a car port. Beneath the car, a small grey lizard crouched in its oasis of shadow, tiny tongue lapping water that had dripped from the Honda's air-conditioning system.

Inside the house, the drawn curtains produced a midday gloom. A large fireplace was framed by bookcases, shelves groaning with books on science, art, and travel. Above the fireplace hung the head of a long-horn steer, horns coated in chrome, skull cloaked in leather, like a mask Georgia O'Keefe might have designed for a Mardi Gras costume ball. A brown leather sofa and two easy chairs flanked the fireplace area. A Mexican throw rug lay on the wide-planked floor.

Alone in the living room, wearing only camisole and panties, Carrie Cassidy danced and whirled, clapping her hands and stomping her feet to the nouveau flamenco of local guitarist Ottmar Liebert thundering from the sound system.

Carrie loved music. During high school her favorite bands had been Aerosmith, Bon Jovi and Tom Petty, but for sheer emotional power, she'd related most to Alanis Morissette whose angst and anger came through loud and clear via her unique lyrics and phrasing.

At her mother's urging, Carrie had taken piano lessons but never liked it. At age sixteen she'd unearthed the four-piece drum kit her father had stored in the garage but rarely played because Frances said it disturbed the neighbors. From the outset, when she kicked the bass pedal and beat the sticks across the tom-tom, snare and high-hat, she knew she'd found the perfect medium to pound out her frustrations and defy her mother at the same time. Every day after school she was in there for an hour or two, ghetto blaster cranked to the max, playing along with the music, learning the licks. Within a year she began sitting in with local garage bands.

Guitarists were a dime a dozen but drummers were rare, and she'd liked the way it felt to be a desired commodity. And even though she sat behind the rest of the band, she knew she was in charge, because she who controlled the beat delivered the song.

Los Alamos

Twenty-five miles away as the helicopter flies, a satellite dish on the roof of National Laboratory Site 8 was receiving a signal routed via the communications system to a monitoring station.

Mack Horton exited the elevator, turned down a hallway and entered an office. Agent Green sat at a desk watching a live video feed on his flat-panel display. At his side was a telephone with multiple speed-dial buttons, a clipboard with a pale green form, and a half-eaten burrito. He nodded in acknowledgement but said nothing as Horton looked over his shoulder.

On the screen, Carrie Cassidy was dancing like a dervish in her living room.

"Is she alone?" Horton asked.

"Just her and her dancing muse," Green said.

They watched her for a minute. At one point she skidded on the Mexican rug, almost lost her balance, but recovered nicely to continue her clapping twirls around the furniture.

"And the subtext is?"

"Psychologists say exercise produces anti-depression endorphins. Perhaps she was advised it was a good way to combat grief. You're familiar with the five stages defined by Kubler-Ross? Instead of 'Denial', maybe she's simply chosen to substitute 'Dance'."

Horton looked at the back of Green's head. Had he been equipped with X-ray vision, perhaps he could have looked right into Green's brain, and determined whether Green was (a) infected by the New Age virus rampant in the Santa Fe area, (b) so well read he had to be a Democrat, or (c) a wiseacre. But from his vantage point, all he could see was that Green had a bad case of dandruff – a social liability but nothing to merit a reprimand.

Horton turned his attention back to the video feed. Mrs. Cassidy's performance had turned erotic. As he watched her spirited bump-and-grind, the like of which he hadn't seen since one blurry night in a Singapore bar two decades ago, parts of his body warmed to the sight.

"Does this strike you as suspicious?" Horton asked.

"Just because she's happy doesn't mean she's guilty," Green said. "What if your spouse died and left you a fortune?"

"No amount of money could replace my wife." Horton's

unsullied marriage of seventeen years was the one thing in his life he was most proud of, eclipsing anything he'd done in his country's service, and the devotion to which paid emotional dividends he hoped to enjoy till death did them part. "But I get your point."

"Maybe Dr. Cassidy was a rotten husband. A cheater or a beater..."

"Still, it's kind of weird. What about phone and internet activity?"

"Nothing of consequence." Green checked his log. "Her brother-in-law called her from Denver to discuss funeral arrangements but it turned pretty nasty. You'd think they'd have had the decency to set aside their differences during a time of mourning."

"One man's mourning is another woman's new beginning."

"What do you mean?"

Horton told Green that, given material motive, the FBI hadn't ruled out Mrs. Cassidy as a potential suspect.

"And you don't agree?"

"I don't buy the money angle. There were easier ways to do him in. With all the speed freaks in New Mexico, breaks-ins are common. One of them could have turned ugly, got a resident killed."

"So you're still thinking, national security angle."

Horton stared at the monitor. "Guilty until proven innocent."

"Do we share this with the FBI?"

"Let's just keep it between the two of us." Horton patted Green on the shoulder. "It's completely illegal, after all."

Green looked over his shoulder. "I thought nothing was illegal so long as it's vital to the national interest."

"I'm so glad we understand each other. Keep me posted." Horton took a last look at Carrie Cassidy doing the funky monkey in her underwear, and went back upstairs.

38

New York

Axel Crowe paid the cover charge at The Whammy Bar and led Tracey inside. Tonight's act was The Dirty White Boys, a four-man Dallas blues band. No tables were free so they sat at the bar. Crowe bought a club soda for himself and a Corona for Tracey.

"You don't drink?" she said.

"Not on the job."

"This is working?"

"It is for me. Isn't it working for you?"

She caught the double meaning of his words and laughed as the bartender placed their drinks before them.

Onstage, lead guitarist Little Stevie Highrider, one part Comanche and three parts Texas redneck, was doing some fancy finger work on the upper frets. Crowe gave the music his full attention for three songs, applauding at the conclusion of each, until the band finished their set and took a nature break.

The lead guitarist and bassist stepped down from the stage, the latter joining one of the stage-side tables. Highrider came up to the bar just behind Crowe and ordered a beer. He wore black jeans, snakeskin boots, a turquoise silk shirt and a red bandanna to keep his shoulder-length hair out of his eyes.

Crowe gave the guitarist a nudge with his elbow. "Hey!"

Highrider looked at Crowe. His face broke into a grin, his dark complexion accenting his fine white teeth. He gave Crowe a hug. "Damn it, Axel, what're you doing here? If I'd known you were in town, I'd have got you a pass." He looked over Crowe's shoulder. "And one for your foxy little friend here too."

"Didn't that sort of talk go out with the eighties?" Tracey shook hands with Highrider as Crowe introduced them.

"Where'd you find her?" Highrider asked Crowe.

"She found me," Crowe said.

"Well, you always led a charmed life. You still living in Toronto?"

"Yep, but now I've got a house in The Beaches."

"I might see you this summer. We're talking about a Canadian tour."

"That'd be great."

Highrider raised his bottle in salute. "I need to talk to some guys from Swamp Music who want us to switch labels. Come up and join us next set?"

Crowe shrugged.

"Don't worry about leavin' this little cutie alone a few minutes. Seein' those shit-kicker boots she's got, I wouldn't mess with her."

"No, you wouldn't," Tracey said.

Highrider laughed and went off to join his bassist at the stage-side table.

"How do you know him?" Tracey said.

"Client privilege," Crowe said.

"What, you're his drug connection?"

"Astrologer," he said with some reluctance, but only because people in the West had such a clichéd view of it. Tell someone you were an astrologer, first thing they said was, guess my sign. For most, their understanding was limited to newspaper horoscopes. Entertainment for the masses.

"I thought you were a private investigator."

"That's part of it..." In India, if you told someone you were an astrologer, they'd show you their hands, because they understood that being a 'seer' – someone with an ability to predict – involved a range of techniques wherein astrology, palmistry, *ayurveda*, numerology and omens were part of a larger continuum.

They spent the next fifteen minutes talking about astrology. Tracey had lots of questions and Crowe, having heard them all before, had the answers. Like many women, she was open-minded to the notion that astrology and other psychic arts had potential to reveal things the rational mind might overlook. As Crowe was fond of quoting from Guruji, *The subtle has the capacity to penetrate the gross, but not vice versa.*

Upon hearing Crowe had a guru, Tracey wanted to know more. But by then The Dirty White Boys had returned to the stage and plugged in their guitars. As the other players checked their tuning, Highrider came to the microphone and addressed the crowd.

"Folks, with your indulgence, I'd like to invite onstage a friend of mine from Toronto who plays a pretty mean guitar – Axel Crowe."

The crowd responded with polite applause. Crowe wove his way through the tables and bounded onstage. A roadie handed him a Stratocaster and plugged it into a Marshall amp. Crowe slipped the guitar strap over his shoulders and adjusted the controls.

The drummer used his sticks for a four-count. Highrider launched into the lead riff of a little-known number by ZZ Top called *Brown Sugar*, he and Crowe trading riffs all the way through the solo and into the back end. They slowed it down a bit for Stevie Ray Vaughan's *The Sky is Crying*, where Crowe played the lead solo. Then they were off again, tearing into Freddie King's *Palace of the King*. Crowe hung back for the first half, providing fills to Highrider's lead, then took turns on lead riffs, a bar each, and went smoking on out through the last chorus and wrap-up.

"Ladies and gents, a tip of the hat to some of the greats of Texas blues," Highrider said. "And thanks again to that extra guitar from Toronto, please give us a hand for Axel Crowe."

Half the crowd rose to their feet amid the extended applause. Crowe bowed and handed the Strat back to the roadie. He gave Highrider a hug and descended from the stage, face flushed with the excitement of performing before a live audience.

"You're full of surprises!" Tracey said. "Who taught you to play like that – your guru?"

Crowe drained his club soda. "He was more of a percussion guy. But that's it for me, nothing else up my sleeve."

A waiter beckoned for them to take a vacated table where they watched the band finish their second set. Tracey bought the next round of drinks. Highrider came over for a couple of minutes, thanked Crowe again for joining them onstage and apologized that he couldn't hang out, but had to finish his conversation with the label reps.

"We'll catch up this summer," Crowe said. "Give me a call when you know you're coming to Toronto."

Crowe and Tracey left The Whammy Bar at midnight. He took her hand to cross the street. As they walked through Washington Square Park, he felt a *frisson* that had nothing to do with the cool night air. He looked over his shoulder. Two men were following them, coming on at a brisk pace. Crowe scanned the area, looking for the nearest point of safety, an all-night convenience store a hundred yards away. At the same time he made sure the two men following weren't part of a coordinated gang attack, something that could end badly, no matter how prepared he was.

"Don't look around," he murmured to Tracey, "but we're being followed."

"How many?" she said, cool as an East Villager, as if this happened every night on the way home.

"Two. They'll come up on us in about fifteen seconds. I'm going to turn and confront them. I want you to run."

"Sure. You want me to climb a tree too?"

"Don't be a smartass."

"Don't be a hero. Let's both run."

He squeezed her hand. "I'll be right behind you."

Crowe glanced over his shoulder. The two men were only six feet away. He turned and snapped a photo of them with his phone. The brief flash startled the men, one of them raising his hand to shield his eyes or block the view of his face. The other man charged Crowe.

Crowe pivoted on his heel and shoved the phone into his

pocket. As the other man tried to tackle him from behind, Crowe snapped his arm back, driving his elbow into the man's cheek. Guruji had taught him there's a point immediately in front of the ear where the lower jaw connects to the skull. Fingertip pressure into the ligaments at the top of the mandible reveals a sensitive nerve bundle, whereas a powerful blow delivered with an elbow produces excruciating pain, loss of hearing, visual black out and nausea.

As his assailant dropped to his knees, screaming that he'd been blinded, Crowe turned to deal with the other attacker.

Tracey had run but hadn't gone far. She'd circled around the nearest tree and led her pursuer in a circular chase that left him empty-handed and panting for breath. In the meantime, she'd called 911 and taken a photo of her winded adversary.

When the guy saw Crowe coming, he made a run for it. Crowe chased him across the park to a van waiting on the south side. It squealed off down the street before he had a chance to get a look at its plates.

Crowe jogged back to Tracey, cursing himself for leaving her alone. As it turned out, she'd followed him, thinking he might need help.

"Are you okay?" she said.

"Yeah." He hugged her. "You?"

They walked back to where Crowe had felled the first attacker. The guy was gone. They heard a door slam and looked to the north side of the park. The van had circled the block to pick up their other team member. They drove away, doubtlessly cursing their ineptitude.

"Shit," Crowe said.

Tracey waved down a police car that had just entered the park. She showed some ID and talked to the cops for a few minutes. They gave her a brief salute and drove away.

"I said I'd file a report in the morning. Nobody got hurt, and there's nothing they can do without license plates."

"What about the photos?"

"Even with good pictures it could take days, even weeks. If one of us had been killed it'd be different, but shit like this happens all the time."

"Like battlefield triage? To get any attention, you've got to have a limb blown off?"

"Let's get out of this park." She beckoned. "You want to walk over to my place?"

"My hotel's closer." Crowe didn't want to go back to Tracey's place in case they were still being followed. He didn't think this attack was one of those random events, part of the essential New York experience... Or was that just self-centered paranoia?

The ego's identification with the body makes it believe that the world revolves around it, Guruji used to tell him, *when in fact the world consists of six billion egos, each thinking it's at the center.*

They headed across the park to the Washington Square Hotel, just a couple of egos seeking shelter for their bodies.

39

New York

As soon as Crowe and Tracey were in his hotel room, they took out their phones to compare snapshots of their assailants. Crowe's picture had caught both men, although one had raised his arm to cover his lower face. Crowe looked at the other. Hadn't he seen him at the Whammy Bar? Crowe and Tracey exchanged phones. He looked at the picture of the guy who'd chased her. He didn't recognize him but it was a nice clear shot.

"You know either of these guys?" he asked her.

"No, but I've got access to a database that might. Email me that picture. I'll submit it with the incident report. Maybe we'll get lucky and come up with an ID."

He asked for her email address and sent the picture.

She looked in his minibar. "Do you mind? I could use a

drink. I'm still shaking."

"Be my guest."

"Are you having something?"

"I'm not much of a drinker."

"You nursed two club sodas at the bar. What are you, a recovering alcoholic?"

"Just a moderate in all things." And grateful for it, he thought. Had he been drunk in the bar, he might not have got out of the park.

"They have Glenlivet here. Can I get you anything? Another club soda…?"

"It has been a long time since I tasted single malt." When in Manhattan…

Guruji used to say, *The road to hell is walked with hesitation and half-measures because, even though we desire oblivion, we fear it.*

She took two small bottles of Scotch from the fridge. She unwrapped the drinking glasses and inspected them. Like a forensic scientist, he thought. Was she looking for fingerprints too?

She went down the hall to get some ice. While she was gone, Crowe checked the day's results for Santa Anita. Not much cause for celebration on the west coast track. He'd barely made $100.

She came back with ice. She dropped a few cubes into each glass and poured the Scotch. She gave him a glass and they tapped rims together.

"*Santé,*" he said. "To your health."

"Mud in your eye."

The single malt went like smoky lava down his throat and into his belly. He exhaled the tension he'd been holding and leaned back against the headboard.

Tracey sat on the other side of the bed. She looked at him a moment and laid a hand on his. "Thank you."

"For what?"

"You were good out there. Those guys could have creamed us if you hadn't decked that one so fast. You know martial arts?"

"A little." Crowe had been on the varsity judo team and studied some karate with a teacher in Toronto's Koreatown. He'd also learned a few things from Guruji, not only special techniques but also states of mind, subtle things that could tip the scales between two evenly-matched opponents. Guriji had made sure he could protect himself, in more ways than one...

Crowe savored the last of the Scotch and set his glass aside. Heat radiated up through his chest to his head. He checked the time. It was after one. "What time do you have to be at work?"

She hesitated. "It's flexible."

"We should think about getting some sleep."

"Sure." She picked up her phone. "I'll take a cab home."

"Maybe it's better if you stayed here."

An eyebrow arched. "You sure that's a good idea?"

"For security reasons. We don't know what those guys in the park wanted, and whether they've called it quits or returned to wait with a gun. All I know is, rats like the dark, so I'd feel better if you stayed here tonight."

"Makes sense," she shrugged. "I just need to get up early enough to go home and change clothes before going to work."

"Six o'clock early enough?"

"Perfect."

"You can have the bed. I'll sleep on the floor."

Crowe peeled the coverlet off the bed. He liked her a lot, but he didn't see any reason to act in haste. He folded the coverlet twice, making a thin underpad, and laid it on the carpet. It was nice to be with her no matter what the pace. He took a pillow from the bed and found an extra blanket in the closet.

The karma of sex is tricky, Guruji said. *It can tickle your nose with a peacock feather, or it can take a big bite out of your ass.*

When Tracey returned from the bathroom, Crowe turned out the lights. They each got under their respective covers.

"You sure you're okay down there?" she said in the dark.

"I've slept in worse conditions," he said.

Sex was a sacred act for Crowe. Although Guruji had cautioned him against the perils of unethical coupling, Crowe had studied the *Kama Sutra* and discussed its obvious and hidden meanings with professors, swamis, and practitioners of Tantrik sex. As in all things esoteric, there were at least two layers of meaning – the gross and the subtle.

"Like a yogi on a bed of nails?" she teased.

"Something like that."

If two people allowed themselves to be carried away by desire for physical pleasure alone, their union might give brief satisfaction but leave a bitter taste. But if they connected at a soul level dictated by their karmic need to continue something started in a previous life together, the experience was ultimately satisfying, regardless of the sexual details. No connection, no compulsion. But given that spark of recognition, an inner flame to ignite the soul's passion, anything was possible.

They were quiet for a while. Then he heard her sigh.

"Are you okay?" he said.

"I usually can't sleep unless I read a bit."

"You want me to tell you a bedtime story?" he joked.

"I would like to know what got you interested in astrology."

"It's kind of boring."

"Perfect," she said.

40

San Francisco

Shortly before midnight, Detective Jim Starrett parked his car on Market Street a few blocks northeast of Castro. Before leaving home he'd showered and splashed on a bit of Alfred Sung. He wore faded jeans that hugged him like a second skin, and a silk shirt with the top three buttons undone, revealing a silver chain and the key to his sailboat nestled in his abundant chest hair.

He strolled up Market, glancing into the windows of antique stores that lined the street. By the time he reached Castro Street, he was seeing men to women in a 20:1 ratio, and even the women were gay. Castro was a sloping street along which all the action gravitated to the block between 18th and 19th. Although it was Wednesday night, the sidewalk was thronged with guys who'd converged on the neighborhood to check out the scene. Men clustered at the corner of Castro and 18th, debating which of many clubs to hit. Starrett had the same problem, but for different reasons. Instead of a good time, all he wanted was a good lead. At least he wasn't going in blind, having in hand the list of bars Munson had given him.

In the next hour, he worked his way through Man 2 Man, The Back Door, Moby Dick and Rock Hard. In each, he mentioned Bernie Lang's name to the bouncer at the door and showed a photo from *The Marin Independent Journal*, Lang looking smart and prosperous in a leisure suit. Three times out of four, the photo jogged a vague recall in the bouncer's mind but no tangible information. Starrett repeated the process inside with bartenders and waiters. As his search elicited doubts or sympathies, Starrett was occasionally offered consolation by a number of willing substitutes. He didn't know whether to credit this attraction to his appearance or the scent of Alfred Sung, but wrote it off to the latter, sparing himself the deeper issue of confronting the former.

Starrett visited another three clubs – Daddy's, Pendulum and Midnight Son. It was after one o'clock and he was tired, ready to call it quits as he approached the last place on his list, a club called No Woman No Cry. Beneath the marquee stood a bouncer in his mid-twenties, a black guy with about two hundred pounds hard-packed on a six-foot frame, bare-chested and nipple-ringed, wearing white leather pants with rhinestone-studded suspenders and a white leather bill cap.

"I'm lookin' for someone," Starrett told the bouncer.

"Ain't we all." The bouncer ran a feral eye up and down Starrett, getting a noseful of his cologne.

"Name Bernie Lang ring a bell? Fifty or so, dot-com nouveau riche, likes to party, maybe into rough trade."

"Sounds like a lot of people. I can't do nothin' with that."

"Can you do something with this?" Starrett showed Lang's photo.

"I know him. But he ain't into rough trade. Trannies more his thing."

"Yeah, that too," said Starrett, keeping up with the pace.

"You look like a cop. What's your angle?"

"I am a cop. Lang was killed yesterday in a hit-and-run. I'm investigating his death. I need to talk to anyone with whom he had a relationship."

The bouncer held out his hand. Starrett gave him twenty bucks. The bouncer jerked his head toward the entrance. "Bobbi Chang. Slant-eyed cutie in red at the bar."

Starrett went inside where a very big man, possibly a lesser cousin of Jabba-da-Hut, filled a cashier's booth to overflowing with pale tattooed flesh. Starrett paid the cover, ignoring the pursed lips making kissy-faces like a blowfish in mating season, and entered the club.

The long bar up front was packed shoulder-to-shoulder with what looked to be both men and women. Beyond that, through an arched doorway whose steps descended into an urban Dante's Inferno, was a maelstrom of bodies, stripped to the waist, squirming and heaving like a school of fish on a tsunami of techno-beat. Lights flickered and flashed like heat lightning, the smell of testosterone welling up from the dance floor like the wind that blows ahead of a heavy summer storm. Starrett hoped he wouldn't have to go down there to look for Bobbi Chang.

He walked along the bar, running his eyes over the crowd, and saw that what he'd first taken for women were actually transvestites. Many were more beautiful than any woman he'd dated, their hair and makeup flawless, their hourglass figures sheathed in revealing dresses, their feet in expensive high heels. When he saw the oriental in a red dress being nuzzled by a fifty-year-old businessman, he said a silent prayer of thanks that he didn't have to go dancing with the mob down under.

Starrett sidled next to Bobbi and gave her a closer look – jet-black page-boy haircut, curves swelling a red silk dress with a side slit almost up to her ass, matching red heels on rather petite feet. He wedged himself between Bobbi and the businessman to catch the bartender's attention.

"Excuse me," the businessman whined with irritation.

Starrett flipped his wallet open for the businessman to see his badge. The scowl on the guy's face evaporated like spilt milk on a hot sidewalk, quickly replaced by resignation. He looked at his watch, downed his drink and vacated his stool. Starrett eased himself onto the seat and looked at Bobbi face-to-face. Damn, she was cute. He kept his gaze on her almond-shaped eyes, avoiding the distraction of her décolletage.

"Is that a gun in your pocket, officer," Bobbi said, "or are you just happy to see me?"

"Both." Starrett was dismayed he'd been made so readily but it simplified things. "Apparently you're friendly with a guy named Bernie Lang?"

"Why are you asking? Has he done something naughty?"

"I'm not sure what he's done, but he's getting buried in a day or two."

"No shit!" Bobbi raised her hand to her mouth. "I mean, oh dear...!"

Starrett waited to see what other reaction the news might provoke. But all Bobbi did was stare at her empty glass.

"What're you drinking?" Starrett said.

"I'm partial to Sex on the Beach. What about you?"

Starrett took a twenty from his wallet and waved it at the bartender.

"How did it happen?" Bobbi asked.

"Car accident."

The bartender came over. "What can I get you?"

"Bud Light for me. And whatever my little China doll needs to stay lubricated."

"They don't sell K-Y at the bar," Bobbi said in a mock whisper, "but I have a tube in my purse..."

"Give it a break. This is business."

The bartender delivered their drinks. Starrett drained half his Bud in one swallow. Bobbi took a sip from her SOB. Starrett looked down at Bobbi's cleavage. Her nipples pushed against the thin fabric.

Bobbi batted her lashes. "Ever mix business with pleasure?"

"Whenever I can." Starrett seized a nipple and gave it a twist.

Bobbi yelped and swatted his hand away. "Fuck, man, that hurts!"

"Enough foreplay. Now let's get serious. Tell me everything you know about Bernie Lang and don't spare the details."

Bobbi folded her arms across her chest and looked sullen. Starrett regretted his strong-arm tactic. How many times had he cautioned his own understudies, a carrot works as well as a stick.

As if reading his mind, Bobbi said, "I'll tell you what I know, but be nice."

"Let me buy you another drink."

Bobbi drained her SOB. "Let's go somewhere else. It's so fucking loud in here I can hardly think straight."

"I thought maybe that was part of the attraction."

* * *

Bobbi insisted on going back to her place, a one-bedroom apartment in a house hanging off the hillside a few blocks from Castro. It was furnished in neo-Oriental style, black lacquered furniture and Chinese art on the walls. Starrett had a quick look around, making sure there was no roommate with a loaded gun and a head full of meth to set it off. Less wary cops had been surprised with worse.

Bobbi made herself a drink. Starrett selected a Bud from the fridge and twisted the cap off. Last thing he wanted was a mixed drink and to wake up next morning in a dumpster without his clothes. A few years ago an Oakland detective had been doped with a loaded drink in an after-hours bar and woke up with a bloody machete and a dead hooker in a motel bed. Get too close and sometimes they feed you to your own keepers.

Starrett sat on the sofa. Bobbi put Sade on the sound system and sat beside him.

"Are you married, detective?"

"Only to my job." Starrett drank from his bottle. "Tell me about Lang. How long have you known him?"

"It would have been our first year anniversary next month."

"I'm sorry to hear that."

"He was nice. He treated me well. We went out a lot. He loved to dance. Do you like to dance, detective?"

"I have two left feet."

"I love to dance." Bobbi stood and made a few turns around the floor. Starrett had to admit she was pretty smooth on her high heels. Bobbi beckoned. "Come on. Show me what you've got. You don't have to do anything. You can just lean up against me and I'll do all the moving."

"This isn't my social night out. This is a criminal investigation."

Bobbi pouted and made a few more turns around the floor before returning to the sofa. She laid her hand on

Starrett's thigh. He left it there, trying to be nice. If he didn't think about it too much, it wasn't hard to imagine she was a real woman. God knows she looked better than some he'd slept with.

"You know what Bernie told me last time we were together?"

"That you were hotter'n a Szechuan chicken?"

Bobbi made a face. "He was going to pull the plug on his terminal relationship and make a fresh start."

"When was this?"

"Just last week. But he'd been thinking of it for months."

"Had he discussed it with his boyfriend?"

"No, but he was working up the nerve. They'd been together a long time and Bernie'd put him in his will and everything. But things weren't that great between them any more."

"Ever since you came into the picture?"

"You must admit, I have a lot to offer." Bobbi leaned forward, giving him an eyeful of her generous cleavage.

"You do have a point."

"You know what else Bernie told me last time we were together?" Without waiting for him to reply, Bobbi pressed her mouth against his ear and whispered. As she leaned against him, her hand slid up his thigh to cup his crotch. Maybe she was searching for a concealed weapon, but Starrett didn't think so.

41

New York

In the Washington Square Hotel, Axel Crowe lay on the floor staring up into the darkness, wondering where to start the story of his life in astrology.

"When I was fifteen I answered a magazine ad to get a computerized astrological report on my chart. It was pretty basic but detailed enough to differentiate me from my friends, and it got me hooked. I bought books, taught myself how to calculate and interpret a chart. Pretty soon all the kids at school were calling me Zodiac the Weirdo."

"There's a Japanese saying," Tracey said from above. "*The nail that stands up gets pounded down.*"

"I had an epiphany in high school, where I saw the world split in two – those who believed, and those who didn't. *For the man of faith, no proof is necessary, but for the man of no faith, no proof is possible.* But I didn't care. I already knew I was different."

"What do you mean?"

"When I was little I used to see things. Shadows, auras, things that weren't there..."

"Did you tell your parents?"

"My mother called it the Irish gift of second sight. One night I woke up to see a yogi, naked and cross-legged, floating in the corner of my bedroom. But when I told her that, she feared I was mental. That's when I stopped sharing my visions with her."

"Were either of your parents interested in astrology?"

"No. My father could do math in his head like a human computer, and was an amateur astronomer with a telescope. My mother wrote poetry and short stories for literary magazines. When she got something published she'd buy champagne and celebrate with friends as if she'd just made the New York Times bestseller list."

"If you're half Irish, shouldn't you have been working with Celtic runes or something?"

"Been there, done that. Over the years I tried it all – tarot, I Ching, crystal balls, dowsing... I can work with just about anything, but astrology and palmistry work best for me."

"So you're a New Age kind of guy."

"Please. Some of that stuff is too flakey. Indigo children are the savants of the new world? Most critical studies say they're more likely to be diagnosed with ADHD. *The Secret*? Norman Vincent Peale wrote *The Power of Positive Thinking* fifty years ago. Nobody ever went broke by over-estimating the public's taste for old wine in new bottles."

"My ex was a follower of *Master of Money*, these motivational seminars that were supposed to make him a millionaire. He wasted tens of thousands of dollars. If he'd put it into property like I wanted, he'd have been further ahead. It was one of the reasons we broke up."

"Most of these money-and-success gurus sell the same false promise – that if you just want it badly enough, it'll come to you. So many people blame themselves for their failures, when in fact it's just a natural consequence of karma. We can't all be millionaires, married to perfect spouses, with two talented children."

"Speaking of gurus, can you tell me how you met yours?"

Crowe hesitated. It was a personal story he'd told to only a few close friends. But there was something about Tracey, his sense of having known her before, that made him feel she was already part of his life. It was like picking up a thread that had been dropped, two high school sweethearts rediscovering each other at their 30-year reunion, realizing they'd never stopped thinking about each other.

So he told her the story, or at least part of it.

Sanjay was a well-known astrologer in Calcutta when his guru told him to leave India and move to Canada. Sanjay knew Canadians were polite people who played hockey and walked to work in sub-zero temperatures but he didn't think Canada was the place for him. He was a warm-blooded Bengali and didn't own anything heavier than a sweater. But his guru said he had karma to fulfill, to find in Canada a worthy student who would become a detective, using knowledge of the Vedas to solve crimes.

Sanjay said goodbye to family and friends and left for Canada, leaving thousands of clients mourning his departure. He barely spoke the language but within a week of arriving in Toronto he found a job as a night watchman and enrolled in English classes. After meeting people at a local temple he began taking on clients from Toronto's large Indian community. Soon he was invited to dinner everywhere and his astrological practice became so successful he quit his security job.

Meanwhile he kept an eye out for this special student his guru had sent him to find. At first he thought he'd find his student within the Hindu community but all the bright young people were intent on becoming doctors, lawyers, engineers and computer programmers. Their parents had immigrated to give them a better life and the last thing they wanted for their sons and daughters was to spend years cross-legged on a mat, chanting mantra and memorizing verses from *Brihat Parasara Hora Sastra*, the bible of Vedic astrology.

Winter came and overstayed its welcome. Sanjay questioned a karma condemning him to exile in this icebox of a country. He watched the snow fall on his patience while he imagined his own guru back in Calcutta, drinking *chai* under a mango tree within a circle of rapt students, telling stories about sticky karma that could bind you to your fate like a wet tongue on a frozen iron gate. Life wasn't fair but Sanjay refused to be discouraged. He threw a very ripe mango at his kitchen wall and interpreted from the way the juice ran down the baseboard that his special student would appear in three days time.

At that moment, a 23-year-old Axel Crowe was just getting off a Voyageur bus from Owen Sound, where he'd spent fourteen days in an off-season cottage on Georgian Bay, fasting and praying for the appearance of a guru.

He'd sought a teacher ever since high school. For five years he'd stopped every Indian he met on the street, asking if they knew anyone who could teach him *jyotish*, Vedic astrology. If his mother hadn't been sick, he might have gone to India. In lieu, he'd been to Montreal, Boston, New York, Philadelphia and Chicago, all in vain. Now and again he'd meet someone, but within a day, a week or a month, he'd exhausted them of what little they knew, and the search was on again.

Faint with hunger, he caught a streetcar back to his one-bedroom apartment in the Annex, ate and crashed into a deep sleep of exhaustion. When he woke up he felt rested but depressed. His faith had been shaken. The chorus line from *Born Under a Bad Sign* came to mind – "*If it wasn't for bad luck, I wouldn't have no luck at all.*"

For two days he moped around the apartment, staring out the window and wondering what to make of his dreams. He wanted to learn *jyotish* but he couldn't penetrate the books written in quirky English, never mind Sanskrit. He was doomed to return on Monday to his low-level job as a court records analyst, pushing paper for the legal system. Where was the justice in that?

He played his guitar and broke two strings.

Saturday evening he got a call from his buddy Dave inviting him to a party in Parkdale. Crowe said he wasn't feeling up to it. Too bad, Dave said, because my friends are having an Indian theme with all kinds of curry and stuff, and a couple of musicians playing *tablah* and harmonium. Hearing the call of the *raga*, Crowe perked up and said he'd go.

As soon as he walked into the house, Crowe saw an Indian man with very close-cropped hair sitting in one corner of the living room. Crowe went over and introduced himself. After a few minutes of polite talk, Crowe asked the man, whose name was Sanjay, if he knew any *jyotish*.

Whereupon Sanjay said something in Sanskrit and then

told Crowe in halting English exactly where he'd been and what he'd done the last two weeks – the town, the cottage on the lake, the mantra he'd chanted, the color of the blanket on his bed, the book he'd read on the bus, what he'd eaten when he got home. And the wine-red bear paw of a birth mark on his right shoulder.

Crowe fell to his knees, clasped Sanjay's hand and cried like a lost child who'd just found his father. And Sanjay patted him on the back and said, it's going to be all right now, we've found each other.

"Are you all right?" Tracey whispered in the dark. "I heard your voice crack."

"Memories," Crowe said. "What they can do to you..."

Crowe knuckled his eyes, wiping his tears away. He should have known better. It had been a long time since he'd told his story. He'd forgotten how even its retelling could bring so much to the surface. But what lay beneath was more profound than what floated to the top. The beauty of his story was that it wasn't really about him, but about a *parampara* – a lineage enlivened by the genius of Sanjay's own guru, who'd seen across time to know the intertwined destinies of both his student and his student's student.

Crowe turned and lay on his side, suddenly weary of talking. Tracey must have felt it. In a few moments he heard her breath fall into the rhythm of a sleeper. And in a few more minutes, he went where she had gone.

42

Thursday

New York

Axel Crowe awoke at five o'clock. Despite the makeshift bed on the floor he'd slept well. He sat up. Tracey lay curled on the nearby bed, knees drawn up, face turned toward him. He watched for a moment as she slept, admiring her beauty, taking comfort in the serenity of the dawn. They'd made a late night of it and an extra hour in bed would do him no harm. He lay back down, closed his eyes and drifted back to sleep.

He got up at six, folding his blankets into a tidy pile. He woke Tracey and went for a shower. As he toweled off, he glanced at himself in the mirror. Forty years old and he still had the body of a thirty-year-old. He weighed the same as when he'd graduated from high school. Although he couldn't do as many push-ups or sit-ups, he did yoga and swam and could run a 100-yard dash if he had to catch a streetcar.

When he came back into the room, Tracey was still in bed but awake. Crowe clapped his hands. "Let's go. Don't you have criminals to catch and justice to serve?"

"Right. If we can't catch the many who are guilty, how can we save the few who are innocent?" She sat up with her back to him and pulled on her shirt.

"You're cynical. I like that in a woman."

"Guilty as charged." She punched him in the shoulder as she passed.

While she took a shower, Crowe ordered room service: coffee and toast for her, juice and a muffin for him. They ate together and he walked her to Cooper Square, where she said she'd continue alone to her condo at First Avenue and 9th Street.

"Busy day ahead?" he asked.

"The Stockwell case? The Commissioner's taking an

interest."

"Say no more. Maybe we can catch up end of day, compare notes?"

"I'd like to, but no promises."

"Same for me. I'm on the clock and I've got to start earning my keep." He gave her a hug and she waved goodbye as she headed off.

Crowe walked back to Sheridan Square, stretching his legs as he took in a few sights. A couple of guys, mid-thirties in business suits, went by holding hands. An older man dressed in a powder blue leisure suit walked a Pomeranian with a matching blue collar. On a billboard above the square the Marlboro Man looked down on the street from astride his horse, a pack of cigarettes in his tanned hand.

Crowe sat on the terrace of a café and ordered an espresso. After reviewing and responding to some email, he browsed a copy of *The Village Voice* someone had left on an adjacent table. One of the Sex columns featured an article: '*Threesomes, a Navigational Guide.*'

He read the article, not because it interested him, but resonated with what he'd seen yesterday near the crime scene: The Bermuda Love Triangle playing on Broadway, the cartoon graffiti of a three-way on a construction siding, the triangle in the hand of the victim outline.

It reaffirmed Crowe's suspicion of a love triangle in this case. But with whom? Assuming Jeb Stockwell and his wife were two sides of the triangle, who was the third? The Filipino maid? When he'd asked May Lee if Stockwell had a girlfriend, she'd shut down immediately. Discretion or guilt?

If not May Lee, who else? The mystery woman from the Southwest? Someone in San Francisco? Crowe took a mental trip across the continent and back – northeast, southwest, west coast – that left him with the visual of a big triangle and much emptiness in between, which pretty much described his situation, not knowing which way to turn.

When in doubt, walk it out, Guruji used to say.

Crowe walked back to Washington Square Park. In the

southwest corner of the park, near Macdougal and West 4th Street, a half-circle of chess tables were permanently installed beneath some trees. It was a hangout for chess aficionados and hustlers, some looking to play the game of kings, others looking to hustle a few bucks. A microcosm of life in general.

Even at this early hour, several people had gathered to do battle. Crowe strolled among the tables, looking over players' shoulders, and paused to watch a teenage boy playing simultaneous games with three other people. Crowe had played chess in high school and studied the game well enough to understand the classic strategies, so he appreciated what the kid was up against.

The first thing that caught his eye was the three-on-one action. Another triple play. As he watched the teenager rotate through opponents, Crowe saw more triplicity at work. The kid worked his knights hard, actively moving them through the front lines of the opposing pawns, attacking and defending as required. Knights were the commandos of the chess battlefield because they didn't need a line-of-sight, making irregular jumps over other pieces – two steps in one direction, a third step at right angles. The knight's move was itself triangular.

What was a knight? A warrior or samurai, defender of a king or emperor. Less commonly, a mercenary or soldier of fortune whose allegiance could be bought. A knight occupied the *kshatriya* class of India – a soldier, policeman or security officer – whose strength and skill in weaponry served the dictates of his superiors.

Crowe turned this idea in his mind, trying to see how it fit the rest of the picture. He could only speculate on three possibilities: Janis Stockwell's killer had not acted alone, her murder was part of something still larger, and there was a mastermind behind all this.

Within a few minutes, the teenager closed each of his three games with a checkmate that left his opponents shaking their heads in dismay and admiration. Crowe mused that, if he was up against a strategist of this caliber, his assignment was ill-fated.

But as William Blake had put it so well, *If the Sun and Moon should doubt, they would immediately go out.*

Doubt never accomplished anything, Crowe reflected, except to plant seeds of indecision and inaction. Better to have the faith of a fool and plunge on, never mind the obstacles, so long as he heeded his own compass of intuition and induction.

43

Santa Fe

Carrie Cassidy stared at her computer, trying to decide what her two characters in this scene, an aging cowboy Casanova and the magazine journalist who'd fallen under his spell, could possibly say to each other after he'd given her the orgasm of her life in the back of his 4x4 parked on a deserted road in the Cimarron foothills...

Next to her computer was last night's empty wineglass, a dirty ashtray and a pack of cigarillos. She took a cigarillo from the pack but didn't light it. It was almost as satisfying to chew on the plastic tip, inhaling the sweet musk of the cigarillo, as to fire it up and turn that aromatic humidity into dry smoke.

But today, suck as hard as she could at the well of her inspiration, she wasn't getting any good ideas. She wondered what her heroine saw in this randy old cowpoke. Was she so shallow as to compromise the objectivity of her story for a joyride in the foothills? Worse still, did Carrie recognize herself in this characterization?

That was the problem with writing. Although Carrie enjoyed its solitary nature, the plotting and word play as much as using research for an excuse to go anywhere and talk to anyone, the downside was it made her think too much about what made her tick. It was almost as invasive as therapy.

Write about what you know, the experts advised. She liked to think she knew men but who was she kidding? Men constituted the great dilemma of her life. What was that line from Mae West? *A hard man is good to find.* She had to laugh. She'd found a lot of those but they didn't stand up to scrutiny for long. Maybe she was too much of an idealist, wanting to have her beefcake and eat it too.

She loved the male body and the more sculpted it was, the more she was a sucker, literally, for its charms. But most of the jocks she knew were one-trick ponies. Problem was, she needed someone to engage her at all levels. Literature, politics, science, art – she was interested in it all. Her dream date was a guy who knew which wine to order with dinner, who could debate any topic *du jour*, and who could deliver dessert at the end of the night. Was that too much to ask?

Held up to the light of reality, apparently it was. Demand far exceeds supply, God had shrugged. Take a number.

What was it about brains and brawn? Did some perverse law of nature dictate the two couldn't coexist within the same man? She felt like she'd spent a lifetime in pursuit of *Homo Erectus Cogitus.* The critter was more elusive than Bigfoot. In the good old days Walt used to perform remarkably well for an endomorph and what he lacked in abs and pecs, he made up for in imagination. As for brains he was like a ripe Brie, oozing with intellect. Trouble was, his work had taken him far away from her, like an astronaut soldier sent to wage war with distant aliens, and when he occasionally came home on furlough, he wasn't the same Walt any more. She missed him already...

She lowered her head into her hands. She could feel a tension headache coming on, which meant she had to either have a drink or masturbate, if not both. She looked at the clock. She had her principles. It was too early in the day to start drinking.

* * *

San Antonio, New Mexico

FBI Special-Agent-in-Charge Liam Cobb was in his Ford Crown Victoria heading west on Route 380 with one of his field agents, Paul Kramer. They'd just crossed the Rio Grande and were approaching San Antonio. They'd been debating where to stop for lunch on the Bureau's tab. There was almost nothing in San Antonio so it looked like it would have to be in Socorro, another 10 miles up I-25, where there was a Taco Bell. However, mindful of the need to acquaint Kramer, a recent transfer from Wisconsin, with real Mexican food, Cobb debated a multitude of better options, such as Don Juan's Cocina, Burrito Tyme or El Sombrero Café.

It was a gorgeous day and the only thing in the sky was a cloud of cranes, maybe two hundred strong, heading for Bosque del Apache, a huge wildlife preserve a few miles to the south. When Cobb's phone rang he glanced at the display and recognized the exchange for the National Laboratory. It was Mack Horton.

"What's up?" Cobb said.

"Any luck with those guys you picked up the other day?"

"We questioned them for twenty-four hours but it seems we're wasting our time. They both have rock-solid alibis, their residences were clean and, on closer scrutiny, they don't seem to have much sympathy for, never mind connection to, the organization we suspected of being behind the bombing. We're going to cut 'em loose today."

"So that's it for suspects?"

"Unfortunately."

"What about Cassidy's wife?"

"I'm just on my way back now from Alamogordo, where one of my guys and I spent an evening making inquiries. I talked to the woman whose house she rented two winters ago. It's just a few blocks away from a bar that's popular with military personnel."

"So, what's that make her – a patriot?"

"The landlady was pretty observant, her own house being

just across the street, and she saw who came and went. Mrs. Cassidy had an active social life, sometimes going out with a different guy every week or two. But as she admitted, her marriage was on the rocks, so who am I to cast a stone?"

"If adultery was a crime, we'd have to lock up half the country."

"I also got one of my staff to dig into her past. Born and raised in Austin, very active in track and field, scored 750 on her SATs. Father was in the service, a sergeant in the Marines, but was killed in 1983 during the Beirut suicide bombing of his barracks. She went to Berkeley on an Army scholarship, got a bachelor's in literature. Despite four years in California, no hint of radical politics. If anything, she's right wing. A registered Republican, does *pro bono* PR work for the NRA. Worked for a year as a script reader in LA, then moved to New Mexico in the mid-nineties. Met Dr. Cassidy in ninety-seven and married him the following year."

"But she was out of town when he died."

"Yeah, yeah, don't remind me."

"So you've eliminated her as a suspect?"

"Not entirely. She's still got financial motive. Aside from his government life insurance, Dr. Cassidy's estate is worth almost five million. He made some good investments during the dot-com era and cashed in before it imploded."

"Wish he'd told me."

"You and me both, pardner."

"Where's that leave us for suspects?"

"Flappin' in the wind."

"Never mind she was in New York at the time, what about an accomplice? If she was dating military in Alamogordo, she could've met someone handy with explosives."

"I'm ahead of you," Cobb said. "In Alamogordo last night, we visited every bar in the vicinity of Holloman Air Force base with her photo in hand. Got a few names and visited human resources on the base this morning to look at service records for anyone she associated with. But this was two winters ago and personnel change. A lot of servicemen have transferred elsewhere in the country or shipped out to the Middle East. Unless something comes out of the woodwork, we could be at a dead end."

Los Alamos

Horton took the elevator downstairs to visit Agent Green in the monitoring room. Green had his feet up on his desk, reading an internal report with one eye on the monitor carrying the live feed from the Cassidy residence. Horton peered over his shoulder.

From the living room where the mini-camera had been planted, they could see through the patio door to a courtyard where Carrie Cassidy sat at a small table. There was a glass of white wine within reach as she smoked a cigarillo and leafed through a magazine.

"What's up?" Horton said.

"Writer's block. She's been in and out of her office all morning, can't seem to sit still. Offscreen in her bedroom for half an hour but since noon she's switched gears."

"What's she reading?"

"*Car & Driver.*"

"Any visitors?"

"None."

"Made any phone calls?"

Green referred to his log sheet. "Her mother in New York. Her brother-in-law in Denver. Her agent in New York. Locally, a few friends, a couple of funeral homes. This morning, a local BMW dealership."

"Isn't the funeral today?"

"Yep."

"Received any calls?"

"Condolence from friends but not many. It's kind of pathetic. You don't know whether to feel sorry for her or Dr. Cassidy."

"I talked to his team. He'd pretty much mastered the art of arrogance, at least at work. I don't know what he was like in private life."

Green gestured to the screen. "How long you want me to keep logging time on this?"

Horton reflected that, if the FBI were taking a hard look at her too, his illegal and unsanctioned surveillance was undoubtedly redundant. If by some freak circumstance she discovered their covert bug, her first call would be to a lawyer and there'd be total hell to pay. He was too close to pension to justify that kind of risk.

"Give it the rest of the day. If nothing develops, take the first opportunity to yank our gear out of there."

44

New York

Axel Crowe returned to his hotel and spent the rest of the morning on the phone with clients. At noon, he took the Lexington Avenue subway uptown. He was dressed now in a suit with shirt and tie, just another man on his way to a business meeting, except his business was unlike any other. From the 68th Street stop, he walked over to First Avenue to look for the Upper East Side funeral home.

He saw a marquee, *Oakes & Shannon Funeral Home*, over the entrance of a granite-faced building. A taxi stopped in front and a middle-aged couple disembarked. Crowe followed them into the chapel. Two dozen mourners were already present, circulating past the family of the deceased to view a casket flanked by floral displays.

Kevin Blaikie noticed Crowe and beckoned him over. "Axel, I assume you met my brother-in-law, Jeb Stockwell?"

Stockwell, wearing a double-breasted black Armani suit,

gave Crowe a brief nod as if he'd met him perhaps a year ago rather than just yesterday.

Blaikie and Stockwell shifted their attention to the chapel entrance. Crowe saw an elderly couple in the doorway – a robust man with a florid complexion holding the arm of a thin frail woman, both in their seventies.

"Excuse me, Axel, my folks have just arrived."

From previous discussions with Blaikie, Crowe knew a little about his family. His father Abner Blaikie was a self-made multi-millionaire who'd pioneered Trump's formula, buying distressed midtown hotels and office buildings for renovation during the last twenty years of New York's real estate renaissance. Thanks to tax breaks for the ultra-rich, he was now worth close to half a billion.

Blaikie's mother Amy, formerly a top-ranked golfer, had developed hyperthyroidism in her fifties and lost a lot of weight. Although she still attended the odd social function and twice-weekly bridge games with friends, she was now a virtual recluse.

Blaikie and Stockwell went to greet the elderly couple, leaving Crowe alone near the funeral dais. He went to the casket and viewed the deceased. Janis Stockwell was a blonde with plain but handsome features – a high brow and strong jaw line. She wore a blue long-sleeved dress and her hands were folded on her stomach. Her face was too obscured by cosmetics to read much in her features, so Crowe's attention quickly shifted to her hands.

From the back of the hand, there was little to observe, but Crowe saw her index fingers were long and slim – often the mark of altruists who pursued their calling through teaching, diplomacy, spiritual pursuits or charitable work. Her pinkie finger appeared to be quite short, implying a diminished libido.

The ring finger on her right hand bore a wedding band with five one-carat blue sapphires, and an engagement ring with a five-carat blue sapphire, both in white gold. Blue sapphire was associated with Saturn which ruled the fifth house of children for a Libra ascendant. Such a gemstone suggested denial of children, perhaps fortuitously, since otherwise they would have been without a mother.

'Crowe turned to survey the crowd of mourners whose number had doubled since his arrival. The elderly Blaikies, accompanied by their son, slowly made their way, like a glacier to the sea, toward the casket. Mrs. Blaikie was visibly shaky; her husband and son helped keep her upright and ambulatory. Crowe respectfully stood aside to allow the elderly Blaikies room to come to grips with every parent's nightmare, the viewing of a dead child.

He moved among clusters of mourners who spoke in hushed tones, their conversation alternating between the tragedy of a premature demise and the catching-up on news between people who hadn't seen each other in a while.

Crowe saw a young woman enter the chapel, her flowing platinum hair standing out from heads whose luster paled in comparison. She was tall and wore a dark blue pinstripe jacket and skirt, the business-like appearance of which only exaggerated her significant beauty. She paused at the door and signed the guest book. After scanning the crowd, she headed toward Jeb Stockwell.

The blonde gave Stockwell a brief embrace and murmured some condolence. Seemingly aware of the many eyes upon her, she broke off and moved toward the casket. There she spoke to Blaikie and his parents, and spent a few moments before the casket, her head bowed.

Crowe went to have a look at the guest book. *Katrina Korba*. The exaggerated loops of her signature suggested a woman whose ego was still a work-in-progress. The name sounded familiar. Maybe a model whose face had been on a magazine cover?

Crowe watched Stockwell. As the widower dealt with a steady flow of sympathizers, accepting condolences and exchanging words to fill the void of a situation for which language was inadequate, he looked tense, like someone who desperately needed to take a leak. No matter with whom he spoke, his eyes darted back and forth to Korba. Crowe noticed that, whenever he wasn't shaking hands, his right thumb was tightly gripped inside his fingers, like a child hiding a cherished possession from schoolyard bullies.

After a few minutes at the casket, Korba drifted back through the crowd, which parted almost choreographically as she returned to Stockwell. It was uncanny, Crowe observed, how even sophisticated New Yorkers sometimes acted like a school of fish or a flight of birds, recognizing a different creature in their midst. Korba and Stockwell exchanged a few words and a brief embrace, and then she departed. Stockwell visibly relaxed, as if he'd been holding his breath for several minutes.

Crowe left the funeral home and saw platinum hair flouncing in the afternoon sunlight as Korba walked up First Avenue. Crowe caught up with her on the other side of 70th Street.

"Miss Korba, could we talk? I'm a friend of Jeb's brother-in-law."

She gave him a startled look. "How do you know my name?"

"I recognize you from some fashion magazine," he said, playing to her vanity.

"What do you want to talk about?"

"Your relationship with Jeb."

Her eyes flickered alarm. "Jeb? We're just friends."

"More than just friends, Miss Korba. The police don't know that. But I do."

45

Washington

The directors of the FBI, CIA and DHS met in downtown Washington for a late lunch. Unfortunately, the nature of their business didn't allow dining either publicly or in one of the private rooms of the many fine and discreet restaurants catering to men of power. Instead, the FBI's concierge service arranged for lunch to be brought in to the J. Edgar Hoover Building, where the three ate in the oak-paneled and bug-free conference room adjacent the director's office.

Although his ulcer allowed him scant latitude, FBI Director Bobby Bueller ate a little of the sole that his secretary had ordered for him, its soft bland flesh acceptable to his tortured stomach, along with a modest helping of mashed potatoes.

CIA Director George Gann had a robust appetite and wolfed down three veal cutlets with a huge salad and a glass of wine. He ate veal, Bueller reflected, like a man who was going to face the firing squad. Or order one. Did he know something Bueller didn't?

Tom Ridgeway, fresh from his trip to Miami on behalf of Homeland Security, was sunburned on his face and arms. According to the overnight surveillance report, he also had a bad case of carpet burn after a night on a yacht with some enthusiastic Republican supporters. War was hell.

Bueller finished his mashed potatoes and sipped some warm water. He laid his hand on the slim report adjacent his plate. They each had a copy but since it was color coded at level three, it meant the world as they knew it wasn't ending, so neither Gann nor Ridgeway had hurried to read it when Bueller handed copies out.

"Given our joint intelligence," Bueller said, "it appears the Cassidy bombing wasn't part of a terrorist plot. It's day three and we have no new incidents, no new evidence and no real suspects. I propose we downgrade the domestic security alert from orange to yellow. Any objections?"

Gann looked at Ridgeway to see how he'd react to being told when and how to do his business. Ridgeway shrugged and wiped a smear of garlic butter from his chin. That man did love his scampi tails.

Ridgeway cleared his throat, climbed into the saddle, and lassoed control back over to his side of the table. "Much as I hate this fucking system, I prefer to maintain orange for another four days. If things remain quiet, we'll go back to yellow. People hate it when we jiggle the security alert up and down. Makes us look like fucking yo-yos."

Gann shook his head. "This is different because it's not terrorism and it's not a threat to the general public. The public doesn't even know what's going on."

"None of us know what's going on." Ridgeway turned to Bueller. "What's up with that, Bobby?"

"Sometimes things just aren't what they seem," Bueller shrugged. "We worked the terrorist angle, it just doesn't add up. What looks a whole lot better is Cassidy's wife."

"More ways than one, I hear," Ridgeway leered. "I've seen a couple of pics, but I'd like to see more."

Bueller bit his tongue. If Ridgeway wanted pictures, the FBI's surveillance library could show him a few, like the one with his bare ass humped over a brace of thousand-dollar call girls. Instead he said, "Our local team is keeping an eye on her but it may take a while. She obviously didn't do her husband on her own, being away in New York, and not being too likely a bomb handler."

"So you're waiting for an accomplice to crawl out of the woodwork?" Gann said.

Bueller shrugged. "One way or another, we may hand it off to the locals anyway."

Ridgeway slapped his hand on the insubstantial report. "We're still responsible for a large population of federal employees. Until we're sure that terrorism isn't a factor in this recent attack, I insist we stay on orange alert until next

Tuesday. I hope you'll agree that any kind of knee-jerk reaction reflects badly on the administration."

Bueller looked at Gann. They exchanged nods.

"Done," said Bueller. He smiled at Ridgeway. "Got any room for dessert?"

"Dress it up purty," Ridgeway chuckled. "I'll eat anything."

46

New York

Axel Crowe led Katrina Korba to a café on First Avenue where they took a booth in the rear. Katrina ordered a *latte*, Crowe a Perrier. They said nothing for a few moments, holding silence until the waitress had come and gone. She took out a pen and doodled on the paper placemat. She drew a capital 'K', then added two diagonals to the left side of the vertical so that it looked like two 'K's laid back-to-back. The waitress returned with their drinks and went away.

Crowe indicated her doodle. "Does that symbol mean something to you?"

"It's my brand, a Double-K for Katrina Korba." She made the lines bolder with additional pen strokes. "Two Ks joined at the hip but looking in opposite directions." She looked at Crowe. "Why? Does it mean something to you?"

Crowe recalled the same image etched in the cracked asphalt where Janis Stockwell's dead hand had been outlined by the CSU.

"It's similar to an astrological symbol. A *sextile*. An asterisk with six points."

"What does that mean?"

"Astrologically, it can represent a secret friendship. Geometrically, it connects six points on a circle, sixty degrees of separation."

Katrina sipped her *latte*. "Didn't they make a movie about that?"

"That was *six* degrees of separation."

"Is there something significant about the number six?"

"Could be... six places, six people, six events. Three pairs..." Crowe caught himself thinking aloud.

"What kind of business are you in, anyway?"

"Mostly, I find things for people."

"Really? Perhaps I should hire you. Can you find my sanity?" She gestured vaguely. "I seem to have lost it somewhere in this city."

"May I see your hands?"

Katrina held out her hands. They were long and slim and so pliable as to appear almost boneless. Crowe tested the flexibility of her thumb. It angled away from the index finger at about a hundred and twenty degrees. Its top phalange bent even further backwards from the lower, giving her thumb the look of a boomerang. Her index finger was short and all her fingertips came to a point. Her skin was soft and most lines on her hand were delicate except for a distinct fate line.

"A classic water type, you're very sensitive, emotional, artistic, intuitive. You'll bend over backwards to please other people who take advantage of you because you can't say no. You grew up in someone else's shadow. You struggle with self-doubts but you'll make lots of money, first in the fashion business, later in show business."

"I'm studying acting."

"Good. You need a profession where you get immediate feedback."

"What about my love life?"

"Things are a little more difficult there."

"Story of my life." Katrina shrugged. "What's happening this year?"

"I assume you're a Pisces. Twenty-one years old?"

"Yes. How'd you guess?"

"What day of the week did your birthday fall on this

year?"

"It was a Tuesday. March 17th."

Crowe didn't need his astrology app for this one. The only planet of interest here was Mars, which ruled Tuesday. "This year, you'll buy property and have a surgery."

Her eyebrows arched in surprise. "I just bought a condo last month."

"And you're thinking about having an abortion."

She dropped her eyes. Her hands wrestled with each other.

"Because you know it's not Jeb's."

Her eyes jerked up to meet Crowe's. "How can you know all that?"

"Tell me about you and Jeb."

Katrina sighed. "It's a story as old as the hills. Small-town mid-West girl wins state beauty competition, comes to New York to make her name. She signs with a modeling agency, shares an apartment with another model and starts looking for Mr. Right. After she's been around the block a few times and met all the worms in the Big Apple, her principles get a little frayed around the edges. So when she meets Jeb Stockwell, who treats her like a class act but eventually admits he's married, she just hopes it will sort itself out in the end."

"But you hedged your bets nonetheless..."

"This winter, it was touch-and-go between us. He told me he loved me and it was just a matter of time before he left her, but I knew he wasn't doing anything about it. Nobody needed to draw me a picture. He can't turn his back on her family wealth. As much as I wanted him I could see it was tearing him apart. He was unhappy and anxious all the time and it was spoiling what we had. I was getting depressed. We were having terrible fights, an endless cycle of breakups and makeups. That's when I started seeing this guy I'd met in acting class. Then about three months ago Jeb's mood suddenly changed and he was confident everything would work out, we just had to be patient a little longer. Trouble is, by then I was getting serious about this actor and one night we got a little careless…"

She dabbed at her eyes with the napkin.

"And now you have a decision to make," Crowe said.

"Am I going to have this baby?"

"Are you prepared to be a single mother?"

"You don't think the actor…?"

Crowe shook his head.

"Or Jeb…?"

Crowe drank some Perrier, thinking of the most diplomatic way to say this. "Katrina, I know you're looking for a substitute father figure, but Jeb's not the one."

"What do you know about my father?" Her eyes started to well with tears.

Crowe could visualize the astrological chart of the moment. The planets symbolizing the father were in a ruinous state, suggesting a trauma from the recent past. Having lost something so dear had left in Katrina a wound not yet healed…

"You were very close to him. Even though your mother favored your older sister, you were your dad's favorite. He died shortly after you moved to New York. It's what made your career here such a bittersweet experience. But you couldn't have saved him by staying. It had been in his blood for a long time."

"Leukemia." She used the napkin again. "He was only fifty-three. It was so unfair."

"It often seems that way but it sorts itself out in the end. I think he must have told you something just before he died. Do you remember?"

"He said I had to love myself first and then everything else would follow…" Katrina started to cry and her tears were full-blown now, giving vent to her emotions in a way that might have been embarrassing for anyone other than a Pisces, for whom it was a necessary catharsis.

Crowe held her hand.

47

Santa Fe

In the north end of Santa Fe, a modern chapel on a rocky slope overlooked the freeway. It had a peaked tile roof and a large wooden cross studded with nails to keep the pigeons off. A reception hall was available for various community functions and behind it was a courtyard with dozens of stone benches, some with tables, huddled in the shade of stunted trees. A stucco wall with a row of anti-trespasser spikes surrounded the compound. The sign over the wrought iron gate read *Our Lady of the Desert Fire*.

Uphill and across the street, a van with the logo of *Sierra Air Conditioning* was parked in a driveway. On the roof of that house two men were attending to its swamp cooler, an indigenous air conditioning system of Navajo invention. Because of the blistering sun the A/C men had erected a tarp to shade them while they worked. Beneath its cover they'd mounted a tripod and a camera with a telephoto lens and directional mike sighted on the chapel courtyard.

In the chapel a priest addressed a small gathering of mourners: Carrie Cassidy, a few friends, some neighbors on her street, a handful of Walt's National Laboratory co-workers, and his brother William.

"Today we honor the memory of Walter Cassidy," the priest recited in a monotone, "a man who enjoyed life to the hilt, supported his community and died in the service of his country. We wish him safe passage."

Carrie reflected that, aside from his slavish dedication to anti-terrorist technology, the only time she'd ever seen Walt up to the hilt in anything was her, and in the last few years there hadn't been much of that either.

It went off with near-military precision. No body to view, no eloquent friends to fluff out the time with eulogies. From the chapel organ's opening chords of *Born in the USA* to start the service, and *Bridge Over Troubled Waters* to end it, barely forty minutes passed.

Carrie and her brother-in-law stood at the chapel door to receive condolences as the funeral party moved from chapel to reception hall. Sorrow had a thirst and beverages were available to slake it. The Desert Fire seemed to have been designed by a Southwest libertarian, a pleasant anomaly in itself, explaining why Carrie had chosen it for the service. Any church whose reception hall had a discreet wet bar was her kind of place.

Bringing up the rear of the mourners was Walt's boss, Hank Grover, a tall man in his early sixties with a military bearing and a crew cut of thick white hair. He shook hands with William and embraced Carrie for longer than she welcomed. William headed toward the reception hall next door. Grover took Carrie's arm as they walked together.

"You going to be all right, little lady?"

"Sure. Why shouldn't I be?" She tugged her arm free.

"Well, he was your husband. You're going to miss a man around the house."

"The hours he worked, you probably saw more of him than I did."

"Well, if you need anything at all – day or night – you just give me a call. You know I live just over there on Paseo del Ombra, not a few minutes' drive away. I'd be happy..."

"Thanks, Hank, but I'm not looking for any kind of companionship these days. I just need to be left alone."

"Sure, I understand, I only meant that maybe, after you were finished grieving..."

In the reception hall Carrie turned her back on him and went to the bar. She got a glass of white wine and went into the courtyard. In its furthest corner, two stone benches flanked a stone table beneath a tree. She opened her purse and took out her cigarillos. She hadn't been there a minute before William showed up.

He was a heavy man in his fifties, wearing a suit that hadn't been pressed in a year. He had a goatee and horn-rimmed glasses that had gone out of fashion many years ago. He looked like the academic he was, a business professor at some second-tier college in Colorado. He was drinking a Coke.

"Where's your mother?" William sat on the opposite bench. "She didn't have the decency to come and see her own son-in-law laid to rest?"

"Ever since 9/11, she's afraid to take a plane. What can I do about it? Sedate her and ship her in a cage?"

Carrie lit a cigarillo and took a long sip of wine. They were silent for several minutes. She flicked ash onto the flagstones. "Something on your mind?"

He shook his head. "I got it out of my system years ago."

"You mean, at the family reunion when you told me – in front of everyone – that I was Walt's intellectual inferior, and the only thing I had to offer was a piece of well-worn pussy?"

"I don't remember quite those words."

"You remember my recommending a good surgeon to remove the stick from your ass?"

"I do remember that."

"At least now I won't have to attend any more Cassidy family functions."

"You never fit in anyway."

"I just had too much personality for you guys."

"You're pushy, that's your problem."

"If it weren't for me, Walt would still be an associate professor of computer science at the same no-name university you work for, where the highlight of your year is the annual budget review."

"At least he'd still be alive."

Carrie dropped her cigarillo and ground it under her heel. William looked at a couple of women who'd entered the courtyard. Carrie opened her purse, took out a Beretta with a silencer and aimed it from under the table. She pulled the trigger and the gun coughed. William dropped his Coke and clutched his gut as blood gushed between his fingers. He looked at her in astonishment. She put the gun in her purse and stood.

"Are you coming back?" He held out his empty can. "Can you get me another Coke?"

That was the problem with being a writer. Reality was never as sweet as fiction. She walked away without a backward look. She preferred to remember him the way she'd imagined.

48

New York

Axel Crowe hailed a taxi. Promising to keep her name out of the police investigation if possible, he dropped Katrina off at her Riverside condo and continued to the Midtown North precinct. In the Homicide squad room he found Levinson hunched at his desk, marking documents with a highlighter. A nearby fax machine cranked out incoming transmissions. At the adjacent desk, Rossimoff had a phone in one hand and a souvlaki in the other as he issued directives with his mouth full.

"That's right, your guest registry for the last forty-eight hours, preferably a spreadsheet. I need it ASAP, so here's my email..."

Levinson looked up and beckoned Crowe to take a seat. He took another fistful of paper from the busy fax machine.

"Making any progress?" Crowe said.

"We concentrated our search around Sixth and 58th." Levinson indicated the wall map on which Mid-Town North was outlined. Roughly two dozen yellow stickpins were scattered between Central Park and 51st Street. "These hotels have responded thus far. To date, we've got over six hundred guests originating from the Southwest, meaning California, Nevada, Utah, Arizona, Colorado, New Mexico and Texas. Almost fifty women registered solo."

"How many checked out yesterday?"

"About a dozen."

Rossimoff put his phone down. "What if this broad was with her husband and they registered under *his* name?"

"Let's continue to assume she was on her own," Crowe said. "At least it helps narrow your focus. If it doesn't pan out, you can always expand your search to couples."

Rossimoff's expression reflected his skepticism. "How are we supposed to know which of these women were intellectuals?"

"Check their hotel phone records. You must have access to a reverse directory. Look for calls to literary and theatrical agents, book and magazine publishers, production companies and TV studios. Even speaker's bureaus and universities."

"We can do that," Levinson said.

"I'd also suggest taking prints from every hotel room whose guest fits the profile."

"Are you nuts?" Rossimoff said. "Dust dozens of rooms on speculation? Maid service would've wiped up most prints by now anyway."

"Except for bathrooms, housekeeping isn't that meticulous," Crowe said. "There're a lot of places – like the desk, bedside tables and dresser – where so long as it isn't visibly dirty, the chambermaid may not even pass a rag over it. It's a long shot but it's only twenty-four hours since yesterday's checkout. Sooner it's done, the better."

Rossimoff looked doubtful. "That calls for more CSUs than we have available."

Crowe indicated the cluster of yellow stickpins around the south end of Central Park. "You barbecue an elephant one slab at a time. Only a dozen women from the Southwest registered under their own names and checked out yesterday? Start with them."

The two detectives exchanged looks. "It's worth a try," Levinson said.

* * *

Crowe went down two floors and found the CSU section. He asked for Tracey Lovegrove and the receptionist paged her. He flipped through a copy of *Guns & Ammo*. Tracey appeared in a white smock, a pair of safety goggles atop her head. They left the building and went around the corner to New World Bean for coffee.

"I sent last night's photos to a friend at One Police Plaza," she told him. "There's a backlog at the FBI so he ran them through the NYPD's face recognition database first. One picture couldn't generate a match but the other did. A guy called Darin Guff."

"Any criminal record?"

"Not yet. Guff was bonded by a security company but got fired six months ago for performance reasons."

"What company?"

"An outfit called Phalanx. They service the banking and insurance industry."

"Is it possible to get a list of their clients?"

"I did. One of their clients is Centurion Bank."

"Stockwell's employer."

"I know. I looked at his file."

"I don't get it. Stockwell and I just met yesterday afternoon." Crowe told Tracey about his conversation with Stockwell and his domestic. "I asked him if he and his wife had any connections in the Southwest. And I asked his domestic if he had a mistress."

"Maybe he didn't like your invading his privacy."

"Asking questions is one thing. Throwing a scare into someone for asking is like something out of a Mafia movie."

"Maybe you touched a nerve."

"Any idea as to the whereabouts of Mr. Guff?"

"A squad car visited his last known address. No longer lives there, and no forwarding address. There's an assault warrant out on him so we'll see what happens."

Crowe checked his watch. "I've got to run. I promised I'd meet my client end-of-day, give him an update."

"Will I see you tonight?"

"I don't know. This case might take me out of town. In the meantime, stay away from The Whammy Bar. If someone's put a contract on me, I don't want you becoming collateral damage."

"Is that just your oblique way of saying you like me?"

"No, *this* is my way." He leaned over and kissed her. They left the coffee shop and said goodbye with a parting hug. Crowe hailed a cab to take him uptown.

49

San Rafael

Detective Jim Starrett was driving to work when a kid on a skateboard flew through the intersection at C Street. Starrett hit the brakes and his coffee slopped all over his right leg. Cursing, he leaned on the horn as the skateboarder, middle finger held high in parting salute, disappeared around the corner. Obviously a kid who'd had too much sugar in his morning cereal.

In the office, Starrett went to the squad room's coffee machine and poured himself a cup of second-rate brew. Hutchins looked up from his paperwork.

"Late night?"

"Didn't get to bed until three."

"Home alone, or over in Castro?" Hutchins teased.

Starrett gripped his crotch. "Bite me."

"I bet that's what you tell all the guys."

"Last time I give you and your bum knee a break," Starrett scowled as he lowered himself into his swivel chair. "Situation like this comes up again, I'm all out of pity."

"I thought I won that flip fair and square."

"Using my trick nickel."

Hutchins laughed and said no more, giving Starrett time

to scan the morning sheets and message notes on his desk. Manny Cantata had a line on a new witness, someone who might have heard a couple of Diablos plotting to whack the Merguez brothers. Starrett made a quick call to set up a meeting with Manny and the snitch.

"How'd you make out last night?" Hutchins asked. "Or what happens in Castro stays in Castro?"

Starrett opened his desk drawer and took out his piece of rope. He passed one end around his left wrist and tied a one-handed bowline hitch with his right.

"Contrary to what Munson told me, Lang wasn't into rough trade at all. He was into trannies." Starrett told Hutchins about Bobbi Chang. "More to the point, Lang was pretty much stuck on Bobbi. They'd been seeing each other for almost a year."

"Exclusively?"

"Well, not from Bobbi's perspective, but apparently Lang was getting serious. He'd discussed buying Bobbi a condo or having her, him, whatever, move to San Rafael."

"Sounds like love to me."

"According to Bobbi, Lang was a romantic. Their typical date was dinner theatre, cabaret, that sort of thing. He was a great dancer, knew all the classic ballroom numbers. One reason he and Bobbi got on so well, he could take her to dance clubs and pass as a regular couple."

"A real straight arrow."

"Moderate drinker, only smoked a little pot, wasn't into heavy drugs. Far as Bobbi knew, Lang didn't gamble. All in all, nothing about the guy suggests association with anyone from the wrong side of the law."

"Except for his housemate."

"You mean Munson's fourteen-year old trafficking felony?" Starrett tied a quick slip knot, then jerked it so hard the rope twanged.

"Yeah."

"Despite that brief stint as a guest of Alameda County, Manny says Munson's got no criminal associates of that sort."

"What about that sixty grand Lang withdrew a few months ago? If it wasn't some kind of payoff, what was it?"

"I asked Bobbi if Lang ever loaned her any money. Bobbi said no."

"Back to Munson."

"He's hiding something."

"Anyone did time, they tend to develop a non-cooperative attitude."

"I still think he's got something to do with this. He had motive. Bobbi said Lang was going to talk to a lawyer about revising his will. If Munson suspected Lang was going to dump him, maybe he'd want to take the money and run. If *he* had withdrawn sixty grand, dollars to doughnuts it'd be money for a hit."

Hutchins shook his head. "We can't connect Munson to the money. And we don't know who ran down Lang. All we know, it wasn't Munson, since he was in Albuquerque that day."

"And your alternate-reality theory?"

"Maybe Bobbi and Munson knew each other. Bobbi gave Munson a heads-up as to what was coming. Munson knew Lang's routines. But because he's in the will, he had to be out of town. Bobbi hot-wired the car and ran down Lang."

"There're so many things wrong with that, I don't know where to start. First, I think Bobbi really loved Lang and, if she let things just take their course, she'd have soon been in Lang's house, if not in his will. Scratch off motive."

"Where was she at the time of the crime?"

"Up in Napa shooting hardcore in a vineyard with a crew of muscled Hispanic boys. So no opportunity either."

"You confirm that?

"Yep. Bobbi gave me the director's number. I called and it checks out."

"So maybe they only planned it together. Somehow one or the other borrowed the money from Lang and, ironically, paid for a hit man."

"Whom we still don't know either."

Hutchins shrugged. "You've met Munson. Is he the type to plan a hit like this?"

Starrett shook his head. "Sort of a low-voltage intellect, know what I mean? One of those flakes whose brain cells went up in smoke."

"You see a lot of that in Marin."

"You see a lot of that everywhere."

Hutchins was silent for a bit, sipping his coffee. "Maybe Bobbi supplied the brains."

"Maybe brains, but not the heart for something like this."

"You think you know her that well?"

"I don't think she's got a mean bone in her body. I think she's just a hopeless romantic."

"Yeah, you and me and the Governor."

Starrett stared into space and sipped from his coffee, now growing cold and bitter, somewhat like his ex-wives.

"Maybe we're all wrong on this," Hutchins said. "Sometimes, even low-lifes come into a legitimate inheritance."

"Sure," Starrett said, no more convinced than Hutchins.

"So, how do you want to work it?"

"I'll ride the desk today." Starrett twirled a lasso over his head. "Why don't you spend a little time looking over Munson's shoulder, see what he's up to?"

50

New York

At five in the afternoon, Central Park South lay in the shadow of hotels, high-rise condos and office towers ranged along 59th Street. Axel Crowe sat on a bench, the Pond at his back, Grand Army Plaza to his left. A breeze carried the scent of horses from the hansom rentals that stood in a tired line along the curb of the nearby plaza.

He took out his phone and asked himself, what next? Opening his astrology app, he studied the horary chart for answers. Mercury, lord of the Virgo ascendant, was in the last degree of Aries in the eighth house. Mercury represented him, the investigator in the house of death. It would change signs in three or four hours, implying he was about to make a move.

His quarry, the seventh lord Jupiter, was debilitated in the fifth house with Rahu, one of the eclipse-makers. Was the killer drunk, stoned, blind or delusional? Crowe recalled Jeb Stockwell's face, a portrait of stress and substance abuse. Three planets occupied the seventh house – Moon, Venus and Mars in Pisces. Three planets in a water sign, and Pisces symbolized oceans. Crowe thought of boats and sailors... but how did that connect with Stockwell?

Blaikie's midnight-blue S-Class Mercedes entered the underground garage of his condo building. Crowe stood and crossed the street.

Minutes later, they sat facing each other across the large coffee table in Blaikie's living room. Blaikie's tie was loosened, his jacket flung over the back of the sofa. Except for his red-rimmed eyes, his face had the colorless look of a bad painting in which the artist had failed to render a convincing flesh tone. With Scotch in hand, Blaikie was giving himself a transfusion of amber.

"Sorry I had to skip the funeral," Crowe said. "I had to follow up on something."

Blaikie stared at the ice in his drink, as if words were frozen there and he was waiting for them to thaw out. "I had more than enough company. There was a moment in the cemetery when I just wanted to walk off into the trees and be alone with my memories of Janis." He swirled the ice in his glass. "I guess there'll be time for that."

"How are your parents taking it?"

"They're both medicated to the gills. My father will come to terms with it in due course. My mother's going to be a mess for a while."

"I'm so sorry for your loss."

"Thank you," Blaikie said. "But your help gives me comfort we'll eventually know what happened to Janis and why." He took another drink. "Did you learn anything today?"

Crowe told him about his conversation with Katrina Korba.

Blaikie shook his head in disgust. "How long's Jeb been seeing this bimbo?"

"Almost a year. But Katrina's not a bad girl. She was vulnerable and made a bad choice. Jeb didn't even tell her he was married at first."

"What a sleazebag. I should go over there and punch his lights out. How could he do that to Janis?"

"The way most men rationalize it, so long as their wives don't know, it's a victimless crime."

"Well, it's wrong. Janis was victimized in every sense of the word. Doesn't it seem likely he had something to do with her death?"

"Aside from freeing himself to be with Katrina, I assume he gains financially."

Blaikie nodded. "When we turned thirty, Dad gave us each real estate properties worth a hundred million. Plus she had a stock portfolio... And there was no pre-nup."

"My guru says, the two things that most threaten the integrity of a man's soul are lust for money and sex."

"The universal motives."

"But in this case, no opportunity. Jeb was in San Francisco."

"He could have hired someone. There are people who'll kill for as little as a thousand bucks."

"Sure, but it's risky. First, they're not people we're comfortable with. Second, there's a chance they'll slip up, or talk about it, or roll over to make a deal against some other felony. You see Jeb dealing with that kind of character?"

"Up until today I couldn't see him as an adulterer either, so what do I know?"

"Tell me what you know about him. What's his family background and education? How'd he meet Janis?"

Blaikie poured a little more Scotch into his glass. "He grew up in Chicago where his father was a district manager for the Illinois Central Railway. His mother was a school teacher. I met them both at the wedding although that was the first and last time. His dad died a few years later, cirrhosis of the liver. I remember him knocking back the drinks at the wedding and it made me worry whether Jeb was a chip off the old block."

"You might be right." Crowe told Blaikie about his facial diagnosis of Stockwell and the telltale signs of an overworked liver.

Blaikie frowned. "Do you see that in my face?"

"Your liver's okay," Crowe assured him. "But don't take it for granted, okay?"

Blaikie resumed Jeb's biography. "Jeb was class valedictorian, got a scholarship to Northwestern where he studied Commerce. Varsity wrestling team, debating society, a well-rounded guy. But something happened in his second year, don't ask me what, and he lost his scholarship. Kept going to school, though, worked summers in the rail yards and graduated on schedule. He spent a year in Accounting at Illinois Central, then got into an MBA program at Berkeley. Janis met him in a jazz club in San Francisco while on vacation. They hit it off and had one of those whirlwind affairs. As soon as he graduated he came to New York."

"How'd all this go over with your parents?"

"Dad was skeptical at first. He's been around the block and seen every kind of hustler so he's always been wary of opportunists, especially around Janis. Maybe it's every rich man's fear that some no-account will sweep his daughter off her feet, marry into money and make off with the family jewels. Dad wanted a pre-nup but Janis wouldn't hear of it. In due course the more Dad saw of Jeb the more he liked him. He's smart, well spoken and a terrific bridge player. Mom thought he was great fun and that he'd make Janis very happy. I guess she was right for a few years."

"Did Jeb ever work for your father?"

"Dad offered, but Jeb was more interested in banking than real estate. But Dad's well connected and, once he saw Jeb was going to be in Janis's life, he lent a hand in getting him started. He made a few calls and Jeb had a job offer the next week."

"Do you know his birth date?"

"Not by heart but it's in my calendar." Blaikie checked his BlackBerry. "December 10th."

"Do you know what year?"

"He was two years older than Janis. Born in sixty-nine."

Crowe entered Jeb's birth data into his phone app, using noon for a birth time. He studied the birth chart a few moments. Having met Stockwell he was sure that, given his fair-haired complexion, fidgety hands and generally nervous temperament, he had Gemini rising. Blaikie's description of Jeb as a clever-witted card player lent further credence to it, and the fact that he'd been two-timing his wife put the nail in the coffin. The Mercurial types were notoriously restless marital partners. Crowe adjusted the birth time to give Jeb a Gemini ascendant.

First thing that caught his eye, Stockwell's Moon and ascendant ruler Mercury were both in Sagittarius in the seventh house. Since the Moon and Mercury were the fastest-moving planets, this suggested a fickle love life and a roaming eye. Being in a dual-bodied sign just aggravated Jeb's wanderlust.

"Does he travel a lot?" Crowe asked.

"He goes to San Francisco a few times a year."

Crowe recalled the horary chart he'd reviewed while awaiting Blaikie's arrival. All those planets in Pisces on the western horizon suggested more than trivial activity on the west coast. Blaikie's mention of San Francisco triggered a hunch. In Stockwell's chart, his eleventh house of friends was occupied by a debilitated Saturn, suggesting less-than-stellar acquaintances. "Does he have any old college buddies out there he stays in touch with?"

"He's never mentioned anyone in particular."

"Someone with a boat? Or a waterfront property?" The Moon, prominent in both Jeb's chart and the horary chart, ruled water.

"He leases a thirty-foot sailboat in Southampton during the summer. He's talked about buying one of his own."

"Do you know where he usually stays in San Francisco?"

"The Hyatt Regency Hotel, I think."

"Is it near a marina?"

"Close to the Embarcadero, where you can catch a ferry to the North Bay or take a boat tour of Alcatraz..." Blaikie thought for a moment. "Now that you mention it, Jeb said he'd learned to sail while he was getting his MBA at Berkeley. Apparently, several local sailing clubs operate out of Berkeley Marina in the East Bay."

The more he looked at Jeb's birth chart, the more Crowe felt Jeb was more than just a widower. "I need to go to San Francisco," he told Blaikie.

"If it helps you root out what's behind Janis's death, you have *carte blanche*. When do you want to go?"

"Tonight."

"Okay. I'll drive you to the airport."

"No, you've had a bad day and you've been drinking." Crowe stood. "You should walk over to your parents' place, get some fresh air and clear your head. However much you might need to be alone, they need you more. Think of your mother."

Blaikie rubbed his face and sighed. "You're right." He stood and walked Crowe to the door. "But give me a call if you need anything."

51

Santa Fe

As far as writing went, this wasn't one of Carrie Cassidy's best days. As far as staying sober, it wasn't her best day either. But the day was far from over. Maybe she'd sit at the computer again and pound out a really good chapter. Or maybe she'd finish the bottle of wine and pass out on the couch dreaming of Oprah's Book of the Month. So many highways, so many back roads to drive.

She reflected on something Frances had said of her years ago when they'd quarreled over her mother's decision to remarry. *You're an impatient narcissist. You think it's all about you, and you want it all now.* Carrie admitted now there was truth in that.

Writing wasn't the best career for a narcissist – too much risk, too much waiting, too little reward. Because she'd gone so far down that road she felt bitter she had so little to show for the time she'd wasted. Desperation had crept in one day at a time until she felt like a coyote caught in a trap, literally no way out, forced to chew her leg off to escape.

Distressed at this image of entrapment, she decided to leave the house for a while. She took the Honda and headed south on US-285. Santa Fe BMW was just off Cerrillos Road. Maybe she'd take a closer look at some of the cars she'd seen in this month's *Car & Driver*.

Last year's performance review, Walt had received a big bonus. He'd been so pleased with himself he'd bought a fully loaded X5. She'd hoped a little generosity might have spilled over onto a Beemer for her too, nothing big, she'd have been happy with just a 3-series. But with Walt it was all *I-me-mine* and apparently her automotive needs didn't warrant a second thought. So Walt was toast now and the X5 that should have become hers was a hulk of blackened metal and melted plastic. In due course she'd get the insurance money but she was fed up with her current ride and ready for something nicer, the sooner the better.

When she entered the BMW lot she was greeted by Sandy Bishop, the dealership's top salesman. "Howdy, ma'am. Lovely afternoon, isn't it?"

"Sure is." Carrie looked at him. In slacks, blazer and loafers, he reminded her of a young Bob Barker on *The Price is Right*. Her first thought was that she'd like to break his nose and give his flawless face some character.

"What can I interest you in today? One of our SUVs, maybe?" He glanced at the sun-faded Honda she'd arrived in. "I could give you a little something for that Accord. What is it, a ninety-nine?"

"Ninety-eight."

"So, what are you in the mood for?" He gave her a big smile to go with the *double-entendre*. He patted the fender of an X5. "You like 'em big and powerful?"

"Yes, I do," she smiled in return, "but I was thinking of something a little sportier."

"Like our Z4 Roadster...?"

He walked her down the row of demo vehicles, past the sedans to the Z4 at the end. It was red too, but a Technicolor world away from her washed-out Honda, and the white leather interior was like the skin on a high school beauty queen. He opened the door for her. She sat in the driver's seat and laid her hands on the wheel.

"Does this come in black leather too?"

"Whatever you like, so long as you like black, tan or white."

"How about a test drive?"

"Sure. I'll go get the keys."

When he returned he opened the driver side door but Carrie didn't budge. She held her hand out for the keys. He hesitated.

"Maybe I should do the driving and you could just ride along."

"Why?" Her green eyes gave off a bit of cold fire.

"I believe I smelled alcohol on your breath."

"I had a glass of wine with lunch. Is that a crime?" In fact she should have said, '*two* glasses of wine *for* lunch', but was that any of his business?

"One glass?"

"Yes." One glass, two glasses – mere details.

"Okey-dokey." He gave her the keys and went around to the other side of the car. "But let's take it slow."

They buckled up. She started the car, adjusted the rearview mirrors and drove off. They went south on Cerrillos a couple of miles, passing under the I-25 and then she looped around and got on 25 North.

"It's a three-liter engine," he told her. "Six-cylinder, two hundred and twenty-five horses. Zero to sixty in five point nine. Top speed, a hundred and fifty five. Not that you would ever want to..."

His patter faltered as she accelerated up to the speed limit. He glanced at the speedometer and saw eighty. She looked at him and smiled, the wind fluttering her hair. His right hand gripped the door handle and his left hand, too embarrassed to clutch his balls, turned into a white-knuckled fist on his knee.

Nine miles and five minutes later she took the Old Pecos Trail exit, looped around and got back on 25 South. At his urging she took it a little slower this time and they were back at the Cerrillos exit in six minutes. But instead of taking NM-14 North she headed south and within a mile they were on a two-lane undivided highway and she was passing everything in sight. Up ahead a semi-trailer was approaching and they were in its lane.

At the last possible moment Carrie jerked the Roadster back into her lane and the semi went by with air horn screaming. Carrie tossed her head back and let out a rebel yell. She shifted down, hit the brakes and skidded to a halt in the yard of an abandoned service station.

She turned to Bishop and said, "I love it. I'll take it."

He flung open his door, leaned out as far as he could and puked up his big green lunch of avocado and chicken salad.

Carrie handed him a tissue to wipe his chin. "But I want it detailed first."

Back at the Cassidy ranch house on Piños Verdes a white Econoline van with decal signage reading *Esmeralda Electrical* backed into the carport. In the driver's seat Agent Black shifted into park and picked up a walkie-talkie.

As soon as the van came to a halt Agent Blue was out of the vehicle. Screened from street view he picked the side door lock to the house. In the living room he mounted a chair, reached atop a bookcase and took down a stereo speaker cabinet. There was a one-inch porthole in the speaker enclosure that gave the bass its oomph, and stuck inside this porthole was a lithium-battery remote camera. He extracted the camera and replaced the cabinet atop the bookcase.

Out in the van Agent Black glanced at the dashboard clock. One minute and counting. The only thing moving on the street was a senior citizen on a Segway scooter going up and down the cul-de-sac in careful practice laps.

Inside the house Agent Blue entered Carrie's office, crawled under the desk where her laptop connected to a cable router and removed from one of its ports a device that had allowed a remote viewer to capture everything that appeared on her computer screen. He pocketed it too and left the house, locking the door behind him.

As Agent Blue slipped back into the passenger seat, Agent Black put the van in gear and drove away, nodding to the old guy on the Segway as they exited the cul-de-sac.

The senior citizen, with a big grin on his face like a kid who'd just learned to ride his first bike, waved both arms and called out as they passed, "Look, no hands."

52

New York

Axel Crowe took a cab from Central Park South back to Washington Square, using his phone en route to check flight schedules. There was a Delta flight out of JFK at 8:25 PM, getting into San Francisco just before midnight local. He booked it and called Tracey.

"What's up?"

He told her what was happening. He could hear the letdown in her voice. Tell the truth, he was disappointed too. "I hope to be back in a day or two. We'll see each other then."

"Send me a postcard," she joked. "*Having a terrible time. Wish you were here.*"

Crowe checked out of his hotel and took a cab to the airport. He'd been less than fifteen minutes in the departure lounge before the PA announced boarding for his flight.

As soon as they were aloft and leveled out, the flight attendants came around offering reading material and refreshments. Crowe took a *Wall Street Journal* and a Perrier with a wedge of lemon, no ice. He read a few articles and checked his stock portfolio. He wasn't obsessive about this and hadn't looked at quotes in a week, since most of his investments were mid- to long-term. So far he was up ten percent on the year. Better than the horses but not as much fun.

The passenger next to him was an attractive woman about forty years old with auburn hair and trendy aquamarine-framed glasses. Crowe noticed her hands were somewhat square-ish with short fingers but her lightly-tanned skin was as youthful as a teenager's. Her index finger was unusual – almost the same length as her middle finger. Her nails, as if compensating for her blunt-tipped fingers, were long and done in a French manicure. When the attendants came by she'd asked for a *Vogue* and a martini with extra olives. The magazine was now tucked into the net pocket before her, the martini inside her.

"Hi." She offered a dry and muscular hand. "My name's Miranda Flanagan."

"Axel Crowe."

"I am totally whacked and desperately need a nap but I'm also famished. Could you wake me up when they serve dinner?"

"No problem."

"Thanks." She put her earphones on, tipped her seat back and went to sleep.

Crowe took out a book and read for a while. When the flight attendants returned forty minutes later to serve dinner, he woke his neighbor up. Miranda glanced at the menu, interrogated the attendant about what wines were available and selected one to go with the chicken. Crowe had already chosen pasta and a tomato juice. Their meals were promptly served and Crowe set his book aside.

"I pride myself on keeping up with the latest bestsellers," Miranda said with an impish smile, "but I think I overlooked that one. What're you reading?"

Crowe glanced at the book on his armrest. Like the text within, the jacket title was in Sanskrit

"*The Yoga Sutras,* by Patanjali."

"Patanjali? Who's that, the new Deepak Chopra?"

"More like the old one. Several centuries years old."

"Are you some sort of Hinduism scholar?"

"A student of Vedic philosophy."

"Have you been to India?"

"Many times."

"To see your guru?"

"No. My guru lives in Toronto."

"So instead of sitting under a mango tree you meditate beneath a maple tree?"

"All winter long. But in the spring I get a little maple syrup to reward my diligence."

Miranda laughed. "I hung out at a spiritual commune during university – back in the late eighties – with a guru called Babaji Hanuman. He was very fond of Coca-Cola."

"Where did you go to school?"

"Stanford."

"Where you studied law?"

"Yes. How did you know?"

"I'm good at guessing things."

"And what takes you to San Francisco?"

"A little assignment for a friend."

"You make it sound rather mysterious. Has your friend lost a valuable *objet d'art* or something like the Hindu equivalent of the Maltese Falcon?"

"As they say in your business, I'm not at liberty to discuss it."

"Oh, I don't practice law anymore. I got out of that a few years ago. The legal profession in America is a pack of dogs chasing money like a bitch in heat."

"What do you do now? Something to do with publishing?"

"Say, you are good!" Miranda beamed. "I'm a film rights agent. I look for books that might make good movies and acquire the rights for my clients. So I travel a lot between New York and LA and read a lot of books."

"But you live in the Bay Area?"

"Napa. My husband owns a vineyard. Do you like wine?"

"I used to, but I don't drink much any more."

"Hmm." She studied him. "That's very disciplined or virtuous."

"I try to be both."

"What's the name of your guru?"

"Guruji."

"Isn't that just a generic salutation?"

"He's a pretty generic guru."

She made a face. "Now you're just being evasive."

"I get that from my guru."

"Come and visit us sometime. I met my husband at an ashram and he enjoys Eastern philosophy. Are you in San Francisco for long?"

"I'm not really sure. Hopefully, just for a day or two."

"Just long enough to find the Maltese Falcon?" Miranda joked.

Crowe nodded. "And the Lindbergh baby."

53

San Rafael

Detective Jim Starrett spent the morning in the office. After catching up on paperwork he called the regional FBI office in San Francisco, to whom the JPEGs of Mystery Man from the Larkspur ferry terminal had been sent yesterday.

"I talked to Quantico this morning," the technical liaison officer said. "They're not getting anywhere with those JPEGs. They ran them through their facial recognition database but got no hits. Quantico said either your guy's not in the system or the image is too poor to make a match."

"Any suggestions?"

"Submit the whole video clip. Maybe someone can find a better image to work with."

"How long will that take?"

"How important is this?"

"It's a potential homicide case."

"Potential?"

"We got this guy on video hot-wiring a vehicle involved in a fatal hit-and-run."

"Get your senior officer to endorse the request, I'll send it back to Quantico. They'll put it in the queue relative to priority and workload. You know how it works."

Starrett hooked up with Manny Cantata at lunchtime. Cantata was thirty years old, wore his hair long and had rings in both ears. Today he wore jeans, running shoes and a basketball jacket. They walked three blocks to where Manny kept his ride, a black '03 Mustang, in a private parking lot a discreet distance from the SRPD.

"Nice shoes," Starrett said as they got into the car. Cantata's Nikes had a brilliant yellow stripe along the sole and over the back of the heel.

"Air Zooms." Cantata put his foot on the transmission hump so Starrett could have a better look. The black leather upper featured a stunning yellow lasering in an intricate design. "Originally designed for Kobe Bryant but you can order your own design on the web. Boys on the street see these, they know I'm one cool *hombré*."

"Never any doubt," Starrett said.

Cantata keyed the ignition and the engine rumbled. They wheeled out of the lot and thundered up 101 a few miles, took the Terra Linda exit and entered a strip mall just off Northgate. A Safeway, Kinko's and Starbucks anchored the mall while a bunch of other little shops clung like remora to the body of the sharks.

They entered the Sonoma Taco Shop and ordered the daily special, chicken enchiladas, while commiserating over their love lives. Cantata was going out with a hot Jewish girl from Mill Valley but the prospects for being accepted by her family were poor, his being an uncircumcised spic undercover narcotics cop and all.

They were sucking back the last of their Doctor Peppers when a shifty-looking Hispanic kid in baggy pants and oversize sweatshirt, cap on sideways and shoelaces dragging tattered, came in and ordered a beef burrito and Coke to go.

Cantata and Starrett went outside and sat in the Mustang. The kid came out a minute later. Cantata popped the door and hunched his seat forward so the kid could slide in back.

The kid's name was Gato and he looked like a cat too, the homeless kind that rips open garbage bags searching for table scraps. It took only a few minutes to determine that he was a lying piece of shit who hadn't seen or heard anything except some second-hand speculation about the Diablos killing the Merguez brothers, and all he wanted was some informant cash or other considerations, like a free hand dealing weed out of the nearby Northgate Mall. Cantata got out to open the door and when Gato emerged, cuffed him in the back of the head and sent his cap flying.

"Sorry for wasting your time," Cantata told Starrett as they headed back to town. "I shoulda pumped him a little more over the phone."

"Shit happens," Starrett said. "But I had to have lunch anyway and that was a good enchilada."

That afternoon Starrett spoke on the phone to three different parole officers – in Sausalito, San Rafael and Novato – under whose jurisdiction fell certain known associates of the Diablos. He went through the roster of names, determining current addresses, whether employed and where, how regularly they checked in, whether they frequented locations habituated by other known felons…

He'd just finished his last call when Hutchins entered with two cans of iced tea. Starrett leaned back in his swivel chair and caught the can that Hutchins tossed.

"Anything new on our friend?"

Hutchins shrugged. "He visited a funeral home over at Mount Tamalpais Cemetery, spent an hour there. Had lunch with a couple of friends at that new seafood restaurant in Corte Madera. A bottle of white, a few laughs, all very light and lively. Spent the rest of the afternoon bowling."

"*Balling* with his friends? Instead of grieving?"

Hutchins laughed. "Bowling. At the local place over by Pickleweed Park."

"When's Lang's funeral?"

"Newspaper says, day after tomorrow."

"That's it, huh?"

"Yep. Didn't strike me as a guy in mourning. He's back home now, probably soakin' in the hot tub with a chilled bottle of Napa on the side." He sipped his iced tea. "Doesn't seem fair, does it?"

"You know what's not fair? Some weekend sailor with a boat bigger'n mine."

"What about a tranny with a dick bigger'n yours?"

Starrett laughed. "Unthinkable."

Hutchins lowered himself into his chair. "Anything on your end?"

"Feds called. No hits on the face recognition database." Starrett told Hutchins about resubmitting the video clip to Quantico under the Captain's signature. "And I haven't heard squat from TRAK, so I guess no one on patrol's seen our mystery man." He briefed Hutchins on the Merguez brothers case.

Hutchins wasn't much interested in it. Far as he was concerned every second Saturday should be set aside for drug dealers to meet in vacant parking lots and kill each other off. It was a dog-eat-dog world and they were welcome to gnaw on each other's bones. But the death of an upstanding citizen like Bernie Lang was something he wouldn't let go of. "What are we going to do about Munson?"

"Damned if I know," Starrett sighed. "He's got a compelling motive but he was nine hundred miles away at the time. And with no ID to make this guy on the Larkspur video, we've got a snowball's chance in hell of establishing a link to Munson. Based on evidence in hand, it looks pretty hopeless. Only thing keeps me intrigued is his obvious fabrication about Lang's sexual preferences, and that missing sixty grand."

"Maybe Lang had another friend Munson didn't know about. Maybe Lang put up the money for a sex-change operation. The dollar amount sounds about right, doesn't it?"

"But Lang's already got a tranny in Bobbi Chang."

"You can never have too many friends. Maybe he's grooming someone else for a dance partner."

"Maybe. But there's no law against footing someone's sex change. Why would Lang pay cash?"

"Maybe that's how the doctor wanted it."

"No! And cheat the IRS?"

"Hard to believe, but it happens."

Starrett reviewed his conversation last night. "Maybe I should have asked Bobbi for the name of her doctor."

"A professional lapse in interrogation technique?" Hutchins winked. "Or maybe you'd just like an excuse to go back again tonight, squeeze her a little harder...?"

Starrett grimaced. "Days like this, you start to wonder if you shouldn't transfer to someplace else where gender bending doesn't make life so complicated."

Hutchins drained his iced tea and pitched the empty into the trash can. "I'm going to pack it in for the day. Let's sleep on it and tomorrow morning we can decide whether to hold 'em or fold 'em."

54

San Francisco

Axel Crowe's flight landed at San Francisco International Airport at eleven-thirty PM. He walked through the departure lounge with Miranda Flanagan. It was many hours past his bedtime back east but he'd napped after dinner and taken a homeopathic jet-lag remedy, so he felt as good as could be expected. Crowe and Miranda said goodbye at the baggage claim area, having already exchanged business cards on the plane.

"Now I mean it," Miranda said. "If you find yourself with a few days to spare, come for a visit. Make it a working vacation if you like. I had my chart done about ten years ago but I wasn't too impressed. I'd like to see what you can do with the Vedic system. And if I endorse you, I know a dozen friends who'll want to see you too."

"I'll keep that in mind." Truth was, doing personal charts to satisfy people's curiosity didn't interest Crowe like it used to. People asked for advice in personal matters but they seldom took it. Over the years he'd discovered it was better to work with business clients. His sizable fees made clients take him seriously, and his batting average generated referrals in proportion to results.

But Miranda Flanagan was an interesting woman and Crowe had enjoyed her company on the plane, so he was gracious. He gave her a hug and a kiss on either cheek before they parted ways.

Crowe took a taxi downtown to the Hyatt Regency. At the front desk a handsome black man whose name tag said *Maxim* greeted Crowe and began the registration process.

"A friend of mine was here earlier this week, said he had a great room. Can you put me into the same one? My friend's name was Stockwell."

Maxim studied his computer screen. "That was one of our Regency Suites. And you're lucky it's not the weekend so it's available. How will you be paying?"

Crowe gave him a credit card.

The suite was on the 18th floor: bedroom with king-size bed, parlor with sofa, rooms decorated in hues of gold, blue and russet. There was a television in each room, a workstation and a 30-foot balcony with a bay view. Crowe dropped his travel bag and opened the balcony door. He looked down at the boulevard lights along the Embarcadero. Somewhere out in the fog a ship's horn blasted long and low. He inhaled deeply of the ocean air. After the dry air of the flight cabin it was tonic to his lungs.

Leaving the balcony door open, he changed from suit to

sweat pants and T-shirt. He used the complimentary iron to press his suit pants and hung them with his jacket. Then he spent fifteen minutes doing yoga.

Afterwards, as he lay resting on the carpet, he looked under the sofa. On hands and knees he went around the room, looking under tables and chairs, beneath cushions of sofa and armchairs. He looked under the bed and checked the drawers of the bedside cabinets and workstation. Among the complimentary hotel stationery and envelopes, he discovered something – a small triangular piece of paper.

He laid it on the desktop. It was an inch on each side with a serrated edge along the diagonal. On one side was printed 'Monday April 18' and on the other side, 'Tuesday April 19.' It was a rip-off corner tab from someone's daily agenda.

What interested Crowe was the date – Tuesday April 19th – the day Janis Stockwell had died in New York while her husband was in this very room. Tuesday was the day of 'Tiw', a Teutonic deity regarded by ancient mystery religions as equal to Mars the Roman god of war. In the world of astrology Mars was associated with violence, either endorsed via the police and military, or illicit in the form of criminal activities. This little scrap of paper and its implicit symbolism meant more to Crowe than anyone else who might have discovered it.

Meaning is in the eye of the beholder, Guruji used to say.

Crowe examined more closely the contents of the drawer. Setting aside the hotel's Directory of Services and its stationery printed in russet tones, itself a muted color of Mars, he examined a handful of tourist brochures.

One opened into a detailed street map of San Francisco which he spread on the desk. In the corner was a smaller map of the greater Bay Area. He placed the rip-off tab upon this smaller map, its apex on the North Beach where the hotel was, and looked to the other corners of the equilateral triangle. One touched Berkeley. Crowe was bemused by the power of an intuition enlivened by years of practice and trust. Stockwell had studied at Berkeley, sailed out of the Berkeley Marina and met Janis Blaikie there in the final year of his MBA.

The other corner of the triangle touched land near San Rafael on the North Bay. Crowe wasn't sure how this fit together but felt confident that parts of what he needed to learn about Jeb Stockwell would be found around the apices of this triangle – San Francisco, Berkeley and San Rafael.

Tonight he'd sleep on it, trusting that tomorrow his logic would pick up where his intuition had left off. Tomorrow he'd find something that made sense of a killing three thousand miles away.

55

Albuquerque

In the evening Carrie Cassidy drove her new BMW to Albuquerque. Exiting I-25 at Central Avenue, she drove up past the university to the strip of coffee shops, bars and restaurants popular with students and locals. She parked behind a place called Murphy's Law with a big terrace and a lively college crowd.

Carrie found a table on the terrace, turned her chair west to catch the setting sun and caught the attention of a waitress.

"Need a food menu?" the waitress said.

Carrie shook her head. "A pint of Kilkenny and a shot of Bushmills."

She surveyed the crowd. At the next table were four college boys built like football players. One of them, a tall blond with rippling biceps, glanced over at her. Carrie returned his stare, holding it until he shifted his glance, letting him know who was calling the shots.

The waitress brought her drinks. Carrie lit a cigarillo, downed the shot of whiskey and saluted the football players with her empty glass. They laughed and raised their mugs in return.

She sipped her Kilkenny and closed her eyes a moment, feeling the last warm rays of the sun on her eyelids.

The fullback for the University of New Mexico Lobos was twenty-four years old and had just finished writing the last of his fourth-year finals towards a degree in Kinesiology. He knew pretty much everything about the human body, including the fact that after eight mugs of beer in less than three hours, he was at 0.12% blood alcohol and very susceptible to suggestion, even if she was almost old enough to be his mother.

On the other side of Murphy's parking lot was the Route 66 Motel. Its flashing neon sign promised daily and hourly rates, an attractive proposition for those who sought horizontal comfort with a newfound friend or needed to sleep off a little booze.

Carrie and the fullback wobbled across the nearly-vacant lot to the motel office. Carrie paid for a room and led the way to the end unit, him pawing her all the way.

Once inside the room, she was on him like a cougar. The poor boy barely had a chance to get his pants down before she had her mouth all over him.

On the wall over the bed was a framed movie poster, *Route 66 Runaway*, depicting a teenage girl hitching a ride from two cowboys in a pickup.

Carrie straddled the fullback and got down to business.

Carrie awoke in the middle of the night hearing someone whistling outside. She pulled on the fullback's football jersey and opened the door. Two men stood ten yards away, leaning against a pickup truck. One came forward until she recognized him.

It was Zeke Zabriskie dressed in military camouflage, field cap tipped low on his forehead. He held out his hand.

"Spare change for a veteran?"

"Who's your friend?"

The fat man came stumbling forward, ragged clothes flapping, face and hands as blackened as if he'd fallen into a fire. It was Walt. "Why?" he said. "Why?"

Carrie woke from the dream with a start, shivering with the draught of the air conditioner on her wet skin. She sat up and hugged her arms around herself.

Beside her, the fullback lay sprawled and snoring. She'd originally planned on doing him again in the morning but, now that she was awake and disturbed by the dream that had woken her, she couldn't stay.

She dressed by the intermittent flashes of light from the motel sign outside. She took a last look at sleeping beauty. He had a great ass, even with the claw marks she'd left on it. She opened the door and stepped outside.

56

Friday

San Francisco

Axel Crowe awoke at three AM, a dream still flickering in the shadows of his consciousness. A young woman in a black-pajama karate outfit stood poised on a dojo mat, ready to attack. Crowe assumed a posture of readiness. The woman held up a blood-red palm. Crowe said, *Did you hurt yourself?* The woman stuck out a black tongue and said, *It's not my blood.* Then she hurtled across the mat, never landing a blow, but circling Crowe like a demonic dancer with arms and legs in a violent flurry.

Crowe shook off the dream and got up. He went to the bathroom, drank some water and crawled back into bed. It was too early to start the day so he closed his eyes again.

The dream had caused a rush of adrenaline. Who was that woman? No one he recognized but the black tongue and the bloody hand made him think of *Kali*, the Tantrik goddess. Did she have anything to do with the Stockwell case? *Kali* was a complex figure, both maternal and malevolent, and her frenzied dance was thought capable of causing the world to unravel.

With a full day ahead Crowe wanted to sleep another hour or two. He folded his hands on his chest and focused on his breathing – in through the left nostril, out through the right. The left nostril was associated with *ida*, the lunar *nadi*, the channel of nerves that ran down the left side of the body. The right nostril governed *pingala*, the solar *nadi* running down the right side. Yogic practice dictated that, to become more alert, one should breathe though the right nostril, but to calm down, breathe though the left. After a few moments Crowe lapsed into a light sleep.

He awoke again at six and got up completely rested. He

showered and phoned room service, then meditated for half an hour. He'd just finished stretching his stiff legs when a bellboy arrived with a Japanese breakfast from the hotel menu, consisting of a small omelet, steamed rice, grilled salmon, *miso* soup with *nori* seaweed, and a pot of green tea.

Having eaten the breakfast of a samurai, he went down to the lobby and booked a rental car. The agent gave him a map and used a highlighter to mark the route to Berkeley. Within a few minutes, he was on I-80 East heading toward the Bay Bridge.

Berkeley, California

Crowe parked the car on Telegraph Avenue, a street of coffee shops, music stores, used bookstores and boutiques a short walk from the Berkeley campus. Although not sure where this would lead, he trusted the clue he'd seen in Stockwell's chart. College friends, the more disreputable the better, would lead him to the heart of the matter.

The Doe Library had a red tile roof and large columns spanning the breadth of its main entrance. He spoke to someone at the information desk and was sent to the second floor reference center where a Japanese librarian pointed him to the stacks on the opposite wall. Crowe located three Berkeley yearbooks – 1992, 1993, and 1994. He carried them into the North Reading Room, a cathedral-like space with massive skylights and rows of reading tables fitted with network connections for student laptops.

He sat at a table and flipped through the most recent of the yearbooks. It didn't take long to find the 1994 MBA Graduating Class, a group photo of a hundred students, but no caption for their names. On the following few pages, however, were headshots with names of the grads in alphabetical order. He found and studied the photo of Jeb Stockwell, blandly handsome, with his blond hair long and a ring in his left ear.

Crowe flipped through the rest of the yearbook, skimming the faculty grad sections, lingering over each group photo of the athletic teams, activity clubs and miscellaneous associations that complemented academic life on any campus. He found Stockwell's photo in two – the Berkeley Sailing Club and the Karate Club.

Crowe was chagrined to admit he hadn't anticipated this other side of the banker. Jeb had come across as a bit of a limp wrist and Crowe had difficulty reconciling his impression with a picture of Stockwell in a karate outfit. He noted, however, that Jeb wore a yellow belt, one of the lowest grades. Most of the other two dozen students wore orange or green belts, although a few wore blue and brown belts. The instructor, a Japanese man of indeterminate age, predictably wore a black belt.

Crowe opened the 1993 yearbook and found the group photo for the Karate Club. Stockwell was there again, still wearing a yellow belt. The guy next to him was the same person standing beside him in the 1994 group photo. Crowe placed the two photos side by side. The other guy, Dave Munson, was also blond but his hair was much longer and he had a mustache. Crowe noticed Munson had an orange belt in 1993 but a green belt in 1994, so he'd moved up a grade in the intervening year.

Crowe opened the 1992 yearbook and examined that year's Karate Club photo. Stockwell wasn't in the picture. Maybe that was the year he'd worked at Illinois Central, before attending Berkeley. But Munson was there, this time in a yellow belt.

Crowe scanned the rest of the group. The instructor, Ken Ataka, appeared in all of the photos. A few other students appeared in all three photos too. Of the two brown belts in 1994, one was a woman – Carrie Woods – tall and slim with short dark hair. She'd had an orange belt in 1992, a blue belt in 1993 and a brown belt in 1994, which meant that somewhere in '92-93, she'd moved up two grades. Stockwell could have learned a thing or two from her, Crowe thought.

He refocused his attention on Stockwell and Munson side-by-side in the '93 and '94 photos. Were they friends? Crowe studied the '94 picture. The photo had caught Munson with gaze turned, not toward the camera, but toward Stockwell. It wasn't much but it gave Crowe the feeling they knew each other outside the club.

He returned to the 1994 photo of the Berkeley Sailing Club. No more than a dozen members but there among them, again at Stockwell's side, was a smiling Dave Munson. Crowe checked the club photos for '92 and '93. Stockwell and Munson appeared in neither.

Crowe returned to the 1994 MBA grad section and scanned the faces for Munson but couldn't find him. He went through the other faculties and found Munson had graduated with a Fine Arts degree. While looking for Munson, he also spotted the woman from the karate club, Carrie Woods, who'd graduated with a degree in Journalism.

Crowe carried the three yearbooks back to the reference hall and photocopied every page on which Stockwell had appeared. He then went back to the Japanese librarian at the reference desk.

"Do you have an alumni directory?"

"There's a computer room just inside the north entrance. You can use any of the terminals to access our intranet."

Crowe went downstairs to the computer room and found a free terminal. After a few minutes he navigated his way through the intranet and found the alumni directory. He spread the photocopies of the Karate Club beside the keyboard and went to work.

An hour later Crowe walked back down Telegraph to his rental car. The sidewalks had sprouted dozens of street vendors selling T-shirts, CDs, jewelry and tourist mementos. Crowe added money to the parking meter and headed uphill, looking for the address he'd copied from the alumni directory.

A three-storey white brick apartment building near

Dwight and College had seen better days. Bikes chained to the second- and third-floor balconies overlooked the street. From an open window came the sound of Nirvana's *Smells Like Teen Spirit* and on the breeze was the distinctive scent of marijuana, possibly a glaucoma sufferer just having a morning eye-opener, although the odds weren't likely.

In the foyer was a directory with two dozen bell buttons, less than half of them labeled with names. Crowe deciphered the scrawl below the superintendent's bell. Jorgé Bocasucra. Crowe rang the bell three times before he was buzzed in. He followed a sign down a flight of poorly-lit stairs to a basement office that reeked of body odor.

A man in his mid-fifties, grizzled and overweight in a T-shirt, sat behind a cluttered desk. Salsa music played from a radio atop a filing cabinet. The man looked up from a folded racing sheet upon which he'd been marking his favorites for the day at Santa Anita. He swallowed something he'd been eating and sipped from a can of Tecate the size of an artillery shell.

"No vacancy," he said.

"I'm not looking for an apartment."

"I don't need no paintin', plumbin' or pest control either."

"How about interior decorating?" Crowe's gaze wandered across the cluttered desk, the stacks of cardboard boxes in the corner, the basement window with a view of untrimmed weeds outside.

"Whattya want?"

Crowe laid the photocopy of the 1994 Berkeley Karate Club on the desk. He tapped his finger on Dave Munson's face. "This guy used to live here."

Bocasucra peered at the photo, then up at Crowe. "What's the deal?"

"That's between me and Mr. Munson."

"Loan collection," Bocasucra guessed.

Crowe shrugged.

Bocasucra took another sip of beer and wiped his mouth with the back of his hand. "He doesn't live here no more."

"When did he move out?"

Bocasucra scratched his ear. "Shit, I dunno. Maybe five, seven years ago."

"Ever see him with this other guy?" Crowe pointed to Stockwell in the picture.

"Sure. They shared an apartment. Two-bedroom, top floor."

"When was this?"

"Maybe ten years ago, give or take. They was both going to college here."

"But when Stockwell moved on, Munson stayed on?"

"Till I kicked him out."

"Why was that?"

Bocasucra scowled. "A dozen fuckin' reasons. Too many wild parties, for one. He had an electric guitar, an amp the size of a fuckin' coffin, you could hear it from down here. I'd get so many tenant complaints, come midnight I'd have to throw the switch on his power. Decent musician but no respect for workin' people. Aside from that he was dealin' weed and I didn't like his faggy face. That enough reasons?"

"What about the other guy?"

"He was okay," Bocasucra shrugged. "Always paid the rent on time. Responsible type, y'know, future businessman and all. While he was here it was okay but after he moved out it was all fuckin' downhill."

"You see anyone else here that hung out with Stockwell?" Crowe showed him all of the photocopies from the yearbooks.

"Her I remember." Bocasucra jammed a fat finger down on Carrie Woods in the 1994 Karate Club photo. "She used to come around a lot. I could never figure which of them she was doin'. Shit, maybe both, for all I know. College kids, they're like fuckin' rabbits, any time day or night ..." He made a *flacka-flacka* sound with his two wet palms pumping together.

"You got a forwarding address for Munson somewhere here..." Crowe nodded toward the boxes leaning in the corner, "in your filing system?"

"You asked me five years ago I mighta said yes. You

think I give a rat's ass where he is today?"

"I hesitate to question your memory but might it be stimulated by the sight of Ulysses Grant?"

"Who?"

Crowe took a fifty-dollar bill from his pocket.

Bocasucra licked his lips. "Maybe."

"How specific is your recall?"

Bocasucra frowned. "I never had a real address. All I remember was, he was livin' on a houseboat in Sausalito."

"That's a little vague for my needs." Crowe folded the bill in his hand, ready to pocket it.

"Wait, wait, it's all comin' back to me now. He was gettin' welfare for a while and I think he was afraid someone was gonna steal his checks. So he was gettin' his mail forwarded to a place that rents airplanes."

"Airplanes?"

"Yeah, Sausalito Air Charter, somethin' like that." Bocasucra held out his hand.

Crowe gave him the money. "You want a bit of advice?"

"Get a shave and take a shower?" Bocasucra glowered. "Tell me something I haven't heard."

"Today at Santa Anita, is there a horse with a Japanese name running?"

Bocasucra ran his finger down the race lineups. "Suzuki Sue, filly in the fourth, four-to-one."

Crowe nodded. Synchronicity was in play. Japanese breakfast in the hotel. The Japanese librarian at Berkeley. The karate instructor, Ken Ataka. And now Suzuki Sue in the fourth, a number associated with foreigners.

"You want to do something productive with that fifty, there you go."

"No shit?" Bocasucra licked his lips again. "Whattya got, inside knowledge?"

"You could say that." Crowe placed his two hands together, bowed from the waist and said, "*Sayonara.*"

57

Sausalito, California

Back in the car Crowe studied the rental agency map. He took I-580 West through Richmond and its waterfront oil depots and across the bridge toward San Rafael. He took the exit for Marin City and Sausalito. After turning onto Bridge Boulevard he saw a dock with a floatplane at the water's edge.

A sign on the roof of a Quonset hut read *Marin Air Charter*. Along with a commercial outlet offering boat repair, it occupied a spit of land jutting into Richardson Bay. There were marinas on either side of it and more docks further east along the shore.

Crowe entered the office, little more than a desk, three chairs, a soft drink vending machine and a huge map of Marin County covering one wall. He walked through a door into a workshop where he saw a cluttered workbench, a pair of pontoons lying on the floor and cases of engine oil stacked against a wall. The smell of aviation fuel, hydraulic fluids and cleaning solvents brought back memories. He went through a back door and onto a dock where a man in khaki coveralls sat astraddle the rear fuselage of a Cessna 180, using a screwdriver to secure an aerial behind the cabin.

"Good morning," Crowe greeted the man.

The man looked at his watch. "You're early. Didn't we say noon?"

"Sorry, I'm not who you think I am. I'm looking for a friend of mine used to get his mail forwarded here, name of Dave Munson?"

"Dave, sure." The man dismounted from the fuselage, alighting on the starboard pontoon. "But he's long gone from these parts."

"Know where I can find him?"

"Not a clue."

"When he was getting his mail sent here, do you know

where he was living?"

The man pointed toward a marina out along the spit. "See that low-lying piece of flotsam with the satellite dish on the cabin, the one that's never been painted?"

"When'd you see him last?"

"Couple of years now." The man squinted at Crowe. "Why? He in some kind of trouble?"

"I don't know. Is he the type?"

"Not around me, he wasn't."

Crowe drove out to the end of the spit. A motley fleet of water craft was moored at the docks – sailboats, cabin cruisers and houseboats. The houseboat the man had pointed out was moored to a piling whose crown was stained white with seagull droppings. As Crowe approached he heard an electric guitar, a funk riff being played over and over again.

He crossed a gangway from dock to deck. The houseboat was about fifty feet long with a low cabin and a peeling foredeck that sported a tired-looking set of PVC patio furniture and a furled patio umbrella. A ship's bell was mounted on the corner of the cabin roof. Crowe seized the lanyard and gave it a good shake. Down below, the guitar paused.

"Come in, for Christ's sake," said a voice from below deck. "It's not like the hatch is locked."

Crowe descended a few steps into the cabin. The place was a clutter – bench seats scattered with clothes, newspapers and magazines, a TV, a sound system and a great assortment of musical gear. Standing in the middle of it with a sunburst Gibson Les Paul guitar slung over his shoulders was a guy wearing only a pair of jeans.

"Hi. My name's Axel."

"Waylon." The guy, whose long black hair was tied in a pony tail, suddenly cut loose with a muted repeat of the funk riff Crowe had heard on arrival. "What can I do for you?"

"I'm looking for Dave Munson."

"What's up?"

"I'm a friend of a friend."

"Yeah? Who's the friend?"

"Jeb Stockwell in New York."

"Never heard of him."

"They used to be roomies in Berkeley."

Waylon got a canny look in his eye, like it suddenly made sense. "He owe the guy money?"

"Not that I know. Does he have outstanding debts?"

"When he moved out a few years ago he owed me three months' rent. If you're looking to collect, take a number."

"Know where I can find him?"

"Nope."

They stared at each other. Waylon broke eye contact, picked up a pack of Winstons and shook out a cigarette. He lit up and lowered himself onto a bench seat.

Crowe nodded at the guitar Waylon cradled in his lap. "That's a real Les Paul."

"Yep."

Crowe extended a hand. "You mind?"

Waylon shrugged and handed him the guitar. Crowe sat on the amp and held out his hand for the guitar pick. Waylon dropped it into his open palm.

Crowe played a slow blues riff, *Catfish Blues* by Muddy Waters, and adjusted the tone control before he cut loose with the lead riff from John Mayall's *Little Girl*. He let the last note ring and fade away, and handed the guitar back to its owner.

Waylon let out a huge whoosh of cigarette smoke. "That's pretty sweet." He leaned the guitar against the bench seat and looked at Crowe with a newfound sense of appreciation. "Where'd you learn to play like that?"

"Self-taught."

"Good for you." Waylon offered the pack of Winstons. "You want a smoke?"

"No thanks. When'd you last see Dave?"

"He in some kind of trouble?"

"I'm not a cop. I just want to talk to him about a gig."

"A gig." Waylon gave him a doubtful look.

Crowe held his gaze. Waylon dropped his eyes and

reached for an ashtray into which he flicked some ash. Waylon took a long pull on his cigarette, let smoke trickle out his mouth as he spoke again.

"Funny thing. Yesterday he dropped in out of the blue and gave me the fifteen hundred he owed me. Said he was sorry to have made me wait so long but he just came into some money and he wanted to square things. We had a beer and a smoke and caught up on old times."

"What's he up to these days?"

"Shacked up with some sugar daddy in one of those gated communities near China Camp. Day he showed up he was driving a Porsche."

"Dave's gay?"

"More like AC/DC," Waylon shrugged. "Maybe he was always that way but I think it was something he picked up in the joint."

"He did time? For what?"

"He was dealing a little weed and one of his customers rolled on him. It was chicken shit, more'n a dozen years ago."

"You got an address or a phone number for Dave?"

"Yeah. He invited me to come over for a jam next week." Waylon moved to a cluttered desk, found a scrap of paper and handed it to Crowe, who jotted down the particulars. "Your friend Jeb's not gonna whack him or anything like that, is he?"

"Don't be silly. He just wants to talk."

"That gig you mentioned? You need a guitarist, keep me in mind, right? I could blow Dave off the stage any day."

Waylon launched into a heavy-metal power riff as Crowe climbed the stairs to the deck.

San Rafael

Using Google Maps on his phone, Crowe found San Pedro Road and the gated community of Marin Bay Park. Another car was entering the estate just as he arrived and Crowe followed it through the open gate. He drove up the hill and parked his rental on the street. A yellow Porsche and an old Nissan occupied the driveway. He rang the doorbell. The door opened to reveal a barefoot guy in aquamarine pajama pants and a Grateful Dead T-shirt. His blond hair was swept back on a skull that seemed smaller than average.

"Dave Munson?"

"Yeah. Waylon just called to say someone was looking for me. Who're you?" Beneath a neatly-trimmed mustache, his teeth bore a nicotine tint. On his breath, however, Crowe could smell he'd been smoking something other than cigarettes.

"I'm a friend of Jeb Stockwell."

Munson looked like the proverbial deer in the headlights. His already wide pupils cranked open another f-stop and his Adam's apple bobbed. Too stunned or witless to respond, he stared dumbly at Crowe.

Crowe unfolded the photocopies from his back pocket and showed him the group photo of the 1994 Berkeley Karate Club. As Munson stared at it, Crowe saw the veins in his temple pulse at an abnormal rate.

Munson thrust the page back at Crowe as if it were on fire. "Sorry, don't know anyone by that name."

"You should cut back on the dope, Dave, because it's really affecting your memory. Didn't you share an apartment with Stockwell in Berkeley?"

"What the fuck's it to you?"

"Been in touch with Jeb recently?"

"None of your business. And if you don't get off my property, I'll call the cops."

"So this is your place? I thought it belonged to someone else."

Munson said nothing more but he looked like someone who'd said too much already. He took a step back and raised his hands in a threatening gesture, the sum total of which signaled his confusion as to whether he should fight or flee.

Crowe didn't budge. He was curious to see how long this posturing would last.

"You see these hands?" Munson said. "I killed a guy

once."

Crowe looked at Munson's hands. He had the spatulate fingers of an athlete or musician but a delicate thumb, so he lacked the drive to become truly proficient at anything. Crowe looked into Munson's eyes where he saw radiant lines of gold in his washed-out blue irises and red specks in the white of his eyes. This was someone whose *prana*, or life force, had been sapped by addiction to drugs and sex.

"Karate and music don't mix, Dave. You took that fork in the road years ago. You had to protect your hands, keep those fingers limber, not stiff. All you ever wanted to be was a killer guitar player. I'll bet the only thing you've ever killed is time."

Munson thrust a kick at Crowe's knee. Crowe had already seen the shift in Munson's centre of gravity and was ready for it. He sidestepped the kick, grabbed Munson's foot with both hands and pulled it up to chest level. Munson fought to retain his balance. Crowe pressed a thumb under Munson's foot. Munson screamed like someone had shoved a hot poker up his butt. Crowe released him. Munson fell off balance and crumpled to the floor.

Crowe returned to his car and drove away. His sole purpose in confronting Munson had been to emulate a bat's shriek and see what echoed back. Based on everything Munson had said and done, Crowe had just learned a few things. Munson and Stockwell had seen each other recently and had something to hide. Combined with Munson's addictions, that got Crowe thinking about threesomes again. Did Munson's recent financial windfall have anything to do with Janis Stockwell's death?

58

New York

Jeb Stockwell was enjoying a quiet day of mourning. Since he was supposed to have been in San Francisco for the conference, there was nothing else on his schedule this week. He'd given May Lee time off. Yesterday had unfortunately demanded his attendance at the funeral and the forced show of bereavement with the in-laws. Thankfully that was now behind him. Last night he'd drunk a whole bottle of Bordeaux by himself and fallen asleep watching TV in his king-size bed.

Today he'd woken with a throbbing head but he'd taken two aspirin and now sat in his housecoat on the terrace taking some sun. The *New York Times* and *Wall Street Journal* lay on the patio table but his mind was far from the mundane world. He was thinking of Katrina's long legs and how he loved to twist her like a rubber pretzel into positions limited only by his boundlessly perverse imagination.

He got a major *frisson* just thinking about her and wondered whether this weekend was too soon to get together. He'd have to wait a respectable amount of time before he could introduce her to his world but so long as they kept a low profile, no reason he couldn't resume enjoying her once or twice a week as he had in the past year.

The house phone rang. He picked up the cordless and glanced at the call display. He saw the 415 area code but didn't make the connection until he heard the caller's voice.

"It's Dave," Munson said.

"What the fuck?" Stockwell almost dropped the phone. "You know you're not supposed to call me."

"I know, I know. But a guy showed up at the house just a few minutes ago asking about you. He had a picture from the Berkeley yearbook, the karate club."

"What?"

"He wanted to know if I'd been talking to you."

"Did you get a name?"

"He didn't say."

"What'd he look like?"

"Tall and fit, in his thirties, I guess. Dark hair and eyes that look right through you. And he knew stuff about *me*."

"What stuff?"

"My playin' guitar, doin' dope, karate…"

That part about the penetrating eyes reminded Stockwell of Blaikie's friend. Axel Crowe had visited him on Wednesday; yesterday he'd showed up at the funeral home. "What'd you tell him?"

"Nothing, I swear. You know him?"

"Could be one of my brother-in-law's associates."

"Your brother-in-law?" Munson's voice went up in pitch. "He knows about your wife? What's he doing here? Man, if he connects the dots, we're fucked."

"Relax, will you?" Stockwell said, as much to himself as Munson. "There's no way anyone can put it together, never mind prove anything."

Munson was far from reassured, and growing a little more frantic with each sentence. "I no sooner get Bernie's place to myself and next thing I know I'm lookin' at a room in San Quentin? Man, I don't like the sounds of this. I'm gonna split town for a while."

"No. Stay cool." Stockwell made calming motions with his free hand, like a faith healer trying to cure Munson's paranoia from a distance. "Don't do anything that'll make you look suspicious."

"What are we going to do?"

"Don't worry. I'll take care of it. And Dave, listen…"

"What?"

"Don't ever call me here again. You know the drill."

"Sorry."

Stockwell hung up. He could feel the blood pressure pounding in his eardrums. He covered his face with both hands, trying to hold it together.

59

Santa Fe

At the house on Piños Verdes where once a faded red Honda had rested its balding tires, a bright red BMW Z4 sat under the carport, waxed and detailed and ready to roll.

Inside, Carrie Cassidy was at her computer, fingers beating a lively tattoo on the keyboard. She was having a good day and in three hours had pounded out an average day's production. No wine today, just lots of coffee, jet fuel for her brain.

Absorbed in her fictional world, she was startled by the flutey ringtone of Skype from her computer. She usually turned off all the phones when she was writing but often forgot to mute the computer. She toggled to the Skype window and looked at the caller ID. *Green Hornet*. Stockwell's homage to Bruce Lee. She took the phone call, no video.

"It's me," Jeb said. "I'm calling from an internet café."

"I don't give a shit where you are. *Why* the fuck are you calling me?"

"Dave just phoned a few minutes ago. Some guy showed up at his door this afternoon. I think it's a psychic my brother-in-law knows..."

"A psychic? Are you kidding me?"

"He helps Kevin track down reluctant witnesses to testify in class action suits."

"How'd he find Dave?"

"Damned if I know. But he sure as hell threw a scare into him."

"You too by the sounds of it."

"He's ready to cut and run. I warned him to stay cool but, tell the truth, I don't like it either. This shouldn't be happening."

"There's no way to connect you and Dave."

"Tell this guy. Apparently he already knows we were

roommates. He even had a picture of the Berkeley Karate Club."

"Did he mention me?"

"You'd have to ask Dave."

"I'm not calling Dave. We're not even supposed to be calling each other."

"We're not supposed to be having this problem either. What're we going to do?"

"I'll take care of it."

"How?"

"You don't want to know."

"You're right. I don't."

She hung up and looked for the number of her troubleshooter.

Jemez Springs, New Mexico

Zeke Zabriskie sat on the front porch of his single-storey house overlooking a clearing in the trees where his Dodge Ram pickup was parked. He wore a tattered T-shirt, cut-off jean shorts and a pair of *huaraches* that looked like they'd walked all the way up from Mexico. He used a cleaning rod to push an oiled swab down the barrel of his 12-gauge pump shotgun. As he worked, he took alternate pulls on a Marlboro and a can of Coors.

When his cell phone rang, he grabbed it off the porch railing and said, "Yeah?"

"Hey," Carrie said. "You're up and about?"

"For you, darlin', I'm always up."

"Are you busy?"

"Never too busy for you." Zeke fed Polymag see-through cartridges into the magazine.

"I can do without the stroking, okay."

"Well, it's just so darned nice to hear from you too. It's been quite a while."

"Listen. I need you to do something for me."

"Sure. All you gotta do's ask." Zeke pumped a shell into the chamber and sighted on a ground squirrel digging a hole near his shed twenty yards away.

"I'm not asking for a favor. It's a job."

"That's the problem with you. All business and no pleasure."

"Just shut up and listen, okay?"

Because he had both a soft spot and a woodie for her, Zeke did as he was told. It didn't take long to hear her out. He went to the kitchen to get a ballpoint and wrote an address on the back of an envelope.

"Any questions?"

"No, ma'am."

"Then saddle up and get moving."

"Yes, ma'am."

She hung up.

He returned to the front porch. Out by the shed, the squirrel had finished digging a hole and was looking at it like he'd forgotten whether he was going to put something into it or take something out. Zeke picked up the shotgun, took a bead on the critter and clucked his tongue. The squirrel looked in his direction. Zeke's finger tightened on the trigger until it was just a pussy hair short of firing a load of number four shot that would shred the target into itty bitty pieces. He took a deep breath, then relaxed his finger and raised the barrel. The squirrel scurried off into the underbrush.

Zeke laid the shotgun over his shoulder. Within his heart, which had experienced every kind of pain and sorrow known to man, he had only a small reserve of pity for the innocent, and he'd just used up his daily quota. Anyone else crossed his path today, they'd better have God on their side.

He went inside and got ready to go hunting.

60

San Rafael

Axel Crowe waited in his rental car a hundred yards down the road from Marin Bay Park. He'd been here half an hour. The downside risk was some local citizen might get suspicious and call the police; upside, he didn't expect to wait much longer. As soon as he'd left Munson, Crowe had noted the exact time and used his astrology app to produce another horary chart. Question was, when will Munson leave the house? According to an esoteric technique, Munson should do so after forty-three minutes.

Crowe checked his watch. A few more minutes to wait. Mentally he connected the dots in a possible scenario. Janis Stockwell was killed while her husband was in San Francisco. Jeb Stockwell stood to inherit millions. Years ago Jeb shared an apartment in Berkeley with Dave Munson. Could Munson have killed Janis Stockwell on behalf of his old roommate?

Crowe used a Yogic technique to test this question. With a finger he closed each nostril in turn and breathed through the other. Guruji said the dominant flow in the nostrils alternates between left and right throughout the day and night, reflecting the shifting balance of *prana* within the body's *nadi*, or nerve channels. Currently his right nostril was flowing stronger. Rule was, if the right nostril was dominant when a question was asked on a Tuesday, Saturday or Sunday, the answer was positive. But since today was Friday, the answer was negative.

So if Munson didn't kill Janis Stockwell, why had he been so unnerved when Crowe mentioned Stockwell's name?

A yellow Porsche roared out of the gated community. Crowe trailed it west on San Pedro Road and through downtown San Rafael. They crossed the freeway and followed Francisco Boulevard East past a marina before turning into the Country Club Bowling Lanes. Crowe idled past as Munson exited the car with a tote bag for a bowling ball.

Crowe went inside a few minutes later. The place had a dozen lanes and an elevated lounge area where people could have a snack and watch the action. Crowe spotted Munson in a blue polo shirt about five lanes away, tying on his shoes. Another guy in the same lane was hurling a ball at the pins. This time of day only three other lanes were occupied and the collective rumble of balls was subdued.

Crowe entered the lounge which was deserted except for an elderly couple playing video poker and a girl behind the food counter. He looked at the menu display. The clerk, a redhead in her twenties, wore a name tag that said *Tammy*.

"Help you?" she said.

"I'll take a lemonade. No ice."

She held a drink container under a spigot. "Something to eat with that?"

"Is that popcorn fresh?" Crowe said, looking at the popper.

"Just made it this afternoon. You want butter, salt?"

"Plain, thanks."

Crowe took a table near the railing and watched Munson and his friend. He ate his popcorn and sipped lemonade. Munson was good, usually downing a set of pins with one or two balls.

The redhead appeared with a couple of napkins. "You might need these."

"Thanks." Crowe wiped his fingers even though they didn't need it.

Tammy was still standing there. "You lost?"

"No more than the average person. Why do you say that?"

"You're not here to bowl."

"You know that line from *Being There*? Maybe I just like to watch."

"I'll bet you do." She had freckles and something of a tomboy manner, the way she stood there with a hand on her cocked hip, giving him a hint of her attitude.

"No law against that."

"You look like a cop. Or a suspicious husband." She scanned the lanes. "Is that your wife down there, the one who laughs?"

Six lanes away a blonde was bowling with a muscled guy a few years older than her. Each time she knocked down a few pins she whinnied like a horse.

"Thankfully, no," Crowe said. "You want some popcorn?"

She sat in the opposite chair, took a single kernel and munched it thoughtfully as she studied him. "Are you an Aries?"

"No, but it's not a bad guess. Why do you say that?"

"That scar on your forehead. Lots of Aries get a knock in the head."

"Lucky for me I've got a hard head."

"Yeah?" She licked her fingers and wiped them on a napkin. "How hard is it?"

Crowe looked at her and shook his head. *I'm not goin' there.* She blushed. On a redhead it looked like she was about to spontaneously combust.

He pretended not to notice. "That guy in the blue polo shirt." Crowe pointed at Munson. "Is he a pro?"

She turned to look. "Dave? He's what you'd call semi-pro. Plays a lot of tournaments. He was in New Mexico for nationals earlier this week but his boyfriend got killed in a hit-and-run and he had to come home."

"Really? What day was that?"

"Tuesday. It was in the paper. Everybody around here was talking about it."

"Doesn't look like a guy in mourning."

"Dave's not completely all together. He's had his share of uppers and downers, if you know what I mean..." She angled her head back and sang a plaintive Mick Jagger, "Goodbye, Doobie Tuesday..."

"Thing like that could set a guy back, make him revert to bad habits."

"I think he's got it under control. Hope so. Be a shame to blow his inheritance."

"The boyfriend left him a bundle?"

"According to the rumor, a coupla mil."

Behind them a video poker machine whooped like a police siren as a torrent of coins clattered down a metal chute. The elderly couple embraced and began a lively waltz among the tables.

Tammy nodded toward them. "Ain't love grand?"

Crowe didn't wait around for Munson to finish his game. He returned to his car and used his phone to locate the San Rafael Public Library on E Street. Fifteen minutes later, he was seated in its reading room with all the local newspapers. He hit pay dirt with the Wednesday edition of *The Marin Independent Journal*. The headline for the story read '*Hit-and-Run Claims Local Venture Capitalist*'.

The article said Bernard Lang had died instantly after being struck at 6:55 PM Tuesday evening by a Jeep Cherokee while jogging on San Pedro Road. The Jeep reported stolen from Larkspur terminal was later discovered at San Rafael bus station.

The article described 50-year-old Lang as a flamboyant entrepreneur who'd got his start in the used foreign car parts business. He'd got in on the ground floor of the Silicon Valley boom and exited with his fortunes intact just before the Nasdaq imploded.

He was survived by two sisters in Philadelphia. In lieu of flowers, donations were suggested for the San Francisco AIDS Hospice.

The police were still investigating Lang's death. Anyone with relevant information should call Detectives Starrett or Hutchins at the SRPD.

Crowe stared out the nearest window. Bernie Lang had died at 6:55 PM Pacific. According to the NYPD, Janis Stockwell had died at 10:45 PM Eastern. The time zones were three hours apart, which meant Lang had died at 9:55 PM Eastern, less than an hour before Stockwell.

What were the odds? Jeb Stockwell and Dave Munson had been roommates in Berkeley a decade ago; their respective partners had died the same night. It looked like more than a coincidence.

Crowe opened his astrology app and produced an event chart for the hit-and-run. With Virgo rising, a dual sign suggested the perpetrator was a visitor, not a local. Seventh lord Jupiter was debilitated on the axis of the moon's nodes, so the person may have been an alcoholic or drug user in a disguise. The seventh house contained an ordinary Mars but exalted Venus, so the perp was successful in life, but unhappy.

Crowe wasn't entirely satisfied with this analysis but sometimes that's the way it went. Perhaps in Guruji's hands this chart might have revealed more. For now he'd be content with what he'd learned and take it to the next level another way.

61

San Rafael

Crowe walked to the San Rafael Police Department at 1400 Fifth Avenue. He told the duty officer he had information regarding the Lang investigation. The duty officer made a quick phone call and sent Crowe back out onto the street.

"Detectives are in another building, one block east. Twelve-ten. Detective Starrett will meet you there."

When Crowe arrived at the address, a tall man with a wind-burned complexion stood just inside a door with a keypad lock. He opened it and Crowe entered.

"Detective Starrett? I'm Axel Crowe." He showed identification, including his New York State investigator's license.

They went upstairs to Starrett's shared office. As Starrett studied his ID, Crowe noted the cop's receding hairline, blue eyes and long-fingered hands with cracked nails. A *vata-pitta* type, physically restless with a heated temperament but cerebral too, quick to form concepts and organize facts. A guy incapable of relaxation but desperately needed it via meditation or deep sleep before he burned out.

"You're working a case in California?"

"It originated in New York."

Starrett handed his ID back. "How's Bernie Lang figure into it?"

Crowe laid it out in brief: Janis Stockwell's death, allegedly a mugging; her family's wealth and the inheritance motive; Jeb Stockwell's mistress and the passion play; the Berkeley connection to Stockwell's former roommate Dave Munson. Crowe showed Starrett photocopies from the Berkeley yearbooks.

"Stockwell was in San Francisco Tuesday night. Lang was run down at six-fifty-five Pacific, Stockwell's wife killed around ten-forty-five Eastern. Within an hour of each other."

"Some coincidence."

"Not if they were coordinated."

Starrett looked skeptical. "You think Munson reciprocated?"

"It's possible."

"Not unless he can be in two places at once." Starrett told Crowe about Munson's bowling tournament in Albuquerque, and that Starrett's partner had spoken to Munson on his cell early Wednesday.

Crowe was momentarily deflated but considered the scenario from a different perspective. "Maybe he flew into New York Tuesday evening, killed Janis Stockwell and flew back the same night. For that matter, how do you know he was actually in Albuquerque when he phoned your partner?"

Starrett looked uncertain. "Excuse me a minute." He left the office and returned a minute later. "One of my guys will see if your theory holds water."

"I heard Munson has a record. Do you have his date of birth on file?"

Starrett flipped through his file, looked up Munson's DOB and read it off to Crowe. July 25th, 1973.

Crowe entered it into his astrology app, using San Francisco as a tentative birth place. Since birth time was unknown he used physiognomy and color to guess the ascendant, factoring in Munson's small head, protuberant eyes and aquamarine pajama pants. Pisces rising fit with what he knew of Munson – artistic temperament, drug abuse, sexual ambivalence, incarceration... That settled, he studied the chart.

Munson's ruling planet was a debilitated Jupiter opposite the Sun. A daydreamer who couldn't put the pedal to the metal. Seventh lord Mercury was retrograde at the edge of a sign, implying confused sexuality or unstable partners, maybe both. Four malefic planets in angular houses indicated trouble. Natural enemies Mars and Saturn were in mutual conflict, amped up by the poisonous Rahu/Ketu axis. It suggested a tough life, self-destructive ways and exposure to violence, but more likely as a victim than a perpetrator.

Starrett picked up the photocopies Crowe had brought. He took a magnifying glass from his desk and studied the people in the Berkeley karate and sailing clubs.

"Recognize anyone?"

"This guy looks like a suspect we caught on security video." Starrett told Crowe how the Lang investigation had led him to the Larkspur ferry terminal. He was now waiting to hear back from the FBI regarding a facial recognition scan.

"Can I see what you've got?"

Starrett took the two pictures from the Lang file, the guy who'd jacked the Jeep.

Crowe studied the two pictures, a midrange shot of a man beside a Jeep, a closer shot of the same guy entering a turnstile. Crowe turned the latter around and used a pencil to point out a detail for Starrett.

"This looks like Stockwell. See the way his thumb tucks

inside his fingers? It's a classic sign of insecurity, like waving a flag that says, I'm in way over my head. I saw him do this when his girlfriend showed up at his wife's funeral."

"Interesting, but no grounds for a warrant," Starrett sniffed.

"But if it's him, doesn't this get your attention?"

A tall guy with curly hair and glasses stuck his head in the office. Starrett looked up. "What've you got, Brane?"

Brane shot an enquiring look at Crowe. Starrett nodded, it was okay to speak in front of him. Brane handed a schedule printout to Starrett.

"No direct flights between Albuquerque and New York. With connections, average transit time is six hours. American Airlines, Delta and Northwest have flights departing ABQ between one-ten and one-thirty in the afternoon, arriving LaGuardia or JFK between nine-fifteen and nine-twenty at night. Driving time from LaGuardia to Times Square is about twenty minutes, half an hour from JFK. Assuming flights ran on schedule and street traffic was normal, it's technically possible for a perp to get on site and execute a hit by ten-thirty. But it'd be so tight, odds are it couldn't be done."

"What about the return leg?"

"Last flight out of New York connecting to Albuquerque is with America West, departing eight-twenty-five."

"So he could have got in that night, but couldn't get back. What about early the next morning?"

"American Airlines, Delta and Northwest depart from five-thirty to six-oh-five, arriving ABQ around ten-thirty local."

Starrett checked the case file notes. "Hutchins received a call from Munson at the bowling tournament a few minutes before eight o'clock Pacific. That's nine o'clock Mountain, at which time Munson was either in the air or had never left Albuquerque…"

"I talked to Verizon. Munson's phone was active only in the Albuquerque area from Saturday through Wednesday. Since then, it's been back in Marin County."

"Thanks, Myke. Good work."

Brane nodded and left.

"So much for your theory of two coordinated murders," Starrett said to Crowe.

"Maybe it's just more complicated than we think."

"What do you mean?"

Crowe told Starrett about some clues at the scene of Janis Stockwell's murder, suggesting a woman from the Southwest was involved.

"Based on a scent of *piñon* and three incomplete fingerprints?" Starrett shook his head. "Give me a break!"

"Laugh all you want, but my logic's led me here and now you have Stockwell for the Lang hit-and-run."

Starrett was momentarily at a loss for words. "Say it is Stockwell and the terminal surveillance connects him to the Jeep that killed Lang. Maybe that's enough to bring him in for questioning. But Munson was in Albuquerque on Tuesday, not in New York. There's still no evidence of a conspiracy."

"Unless there's a third person."

"Who?"

"Beats me. But I don't like the look of Munson's prospects these days." Crowe stared at his chart. The current planetary war between Venus and Mars was dissipating, but it could still affect Munson. As a trigger, the Moon was at the end of its cycle, just six degrees from the Sun. "His life could be at risk. Got a valid reason to arrest and place him under protective custody?"

"Where's Stockwell?"

"In New York, far as I know."

"Then Munson's safe."

"I don't think he's in danger from Stockwell."

"Then who?"

"Maybe that woman from the Southwest." Crowe reviewed the recurring symbolism that had turned up along the way here. This whole set-up was like a three-legged table but he'd only found two legs. "Any way to find out if someone was killed in Albuquerque on Tuesday?"

"Maybe. But why?"

"Because that's where Munson was when Janis Stockwell died."

Starrett shook his head. "Now you're thinking a three-way murder conspiracy?"

"Just following my hunch. Doesn't this seem a bit odd?"

Starrett swiveled around to his computer and connected to the internet. A sign-on screen came up and he entered a password.

"What site is this?"

"National Institute of Justice, a branch of the Justice Department promoting R&D for national crime resolution. They recently added something allowing us to examine deaths by criminal causes in any state."

Crowe pulled his chair closer. Starrett clicked through several screens to access a state-by-state statistical overview.

"According to the stats, New Mexico averages about thirteen a month. But it was busy last week. Tuesday, there were three – a homicide in Albuquerque, a suicide in Las Cruces, and a car fire in Los Alamos."

Crowe referred to the Berkeley karate club with more than a dozen members. "Name of the homicide victim?"

"Enrico Bollitas. Drug-related killing at two in the morning, three witnesses, cops have the shooter in custody. Open-and-shut case."

"What about the suicide?"

"Brian Gimball, quadraplegic. Ate a bottle of pills, left a note saying he couldn't take it any more, body discovered at noon. His brother said he'd been depressed for some time."

"That leaves only the car fire."

"System says it's an FBI case pending. Unspecified address in Los Alamos. Victim's name was a Dr. Walter Cassidy."

"Time of death?"

"Eight-eighteen PM Mountain."

"That'd make it ten-eighteen Eastern. Plotted on an absolute time line, that's practically the midpoint between

Lang's hit-and-run and Stockwell's fatal mugging."

Starrett stared at the computer screen.

"Three deaths in less than an hour. Stockwell's wife and Munson's sugar daddy... And those two guys were roommates... Still think this is just a coincidence?" Crowe said.

Starrett swiveled around. "Anyone named Cassidy in the Berkeley karate club?"

They both examined the photocopies of the 1992, 1993 and 1994 group photos. No Cassidy. They checked the sailing club and MBA group photos as well.

"Zip," said Starrett.

"That was more than a decade ago," Crowe reasoned, "and there are several women in these photos. Any one of them could have married and changed her name."

He told Starrett about the apartment building where Stockwell and Munson used to live, how the super had fingered one of the karate club women as a frequent visitor. Crowe used a pencil to circle Carrie Woods in the 1994 karate club photo.

Crowe referred to his notes. "Alumni directory lists her address as 210 Tulane Drive SE, Albuquerque, New Mexico."

Starrett referred to the NIJ website. "Wrong city. The case profile lists Dr. Cassidy's address as 400 Piños Verdes Street, Santa Fe."

"Lots of people don't keep their alumni office advised of address changes."

"I could call the FBI, see if Dr. Cassidy had a surviving spouse named Carrie."

"Let's call the NYPD first. I have a feeling something's about to break."

"You got a number?"

Levinson wasn't at his desk but someone else answered his phone. Starrett identified himself and the reason for his call. The guy at the other end asked him to stay on the line while someone fetched Levinson. Starrett switched the phone from handset to speaker. As they waited for Levinson, Starrett returned to his computer screen.

"What now?" Crowe asked.

"Checking New Mexico criminal records, see if I get a hit on Carrie Woods." Starrett typed in her name. "Nothing."

"Try Cassidy."

Starrett repeated the process. "Bingo!"

"What'd you find?"

"DUI. Two years ago."

"Got an address?"

"1200 Mescalero Avenue, Alamogordo, New Mexico. But that's a different address, not to mention a different family name, from your Berkeley alumnus."

"Maybe she got married between the time she lived in Albuquerque and the time she moved to Alamogordo. You have her date of birth?"

Starrett read it off Cassidy's driver's license. "DOB, April 11th, 1969."

Levinson came on the line. Starrett introduced himself and told the NYPD detective Axel Crowe had just handed him a lead in a hit-and-run case and that he might have new information on the Stockwell killing. Levinson said he was all ears.

"Hello, Detective," Crowe said. "How's it going?"

"You're going to love this," Levinson said. "We checked the hotel phone records of every woman who fit your profile and got a hit. One made several calls to literary agents. She checked in on Sunday, checked out early Wednesday morning. Her hotel is less than fifteen minutes' walk from where Janis Stockwell was killed."

"What's the name?"

"Carrie Cassidy."

"Cassidy?" said Starrett. "Do you have an address?"

"Hotel registration gave 400 Piños Verdes in Santa Fe."

Crowe and Starrett looked at each other. Same address as the victim of the Los Alamos car fire.

"Looks like we've got a multiple homicide conspiracy, Detective." Starrett briefed Levinson on what they knew. "Soon as I get off the phone I'll produce a warrant to have you arrest Stockwell in connection with my hit-and-run. Meanwhile, better issue one of your own for Santa Fe PD to arrest Carrie Cassidy."

"What about the third guy?" Levinson said.

"I'll give the Feds a quick heads-up," said Starrett, "and pick him up myself."

62

Santa Fe

Carrie Cassidy sat on the terrace nursing her second drink of the day. At the end of the yard the ground sloped into an arroyo bordered by *piñon*. From one of the trees a crow had been cawing for several minutes and she found it disturbing, like a warning of some predator approaching.

Stockwell's call had rattled her. They'd spent enough time planning this, there weren't supposed to be any problems. But if there was one thing she'd learned in life, you didn't ignore a problem. You fixed it before it fixed you.

She looked at her watch. Zeke would almost be there by now. There was another problem but she hadn't got into it over the phone with him. Put out the big fires first and you could piss on the little ones when you had time.

Down in the arroyo the crow uttered another stricken cry and flew off. Carrie wasn't superstitious but the crow's abrupt departure made her uneasy, like being watched through a telescopic gun sight. She refused to be a sitting duck.

She started packing. During university she'd gone to Seoul one summer, following a married professor who'd said he loved her, and she'd taken only one suitcase. She stayed three months, living in a one-room flat and teaching English to Korean housewives by day, screwing the prof every evening he was free until it turned sour and she'd come back home.

She was adaptable, could get by on her wits and a shoestring. Please, God, just give me enough time to get away.

She got down on her knees, not to pray, but to pull a plastic case from under the bed. The Glock 19C was registered in Walt's name but she'd fired it hundreds of times, emptying its 17-round clip into targets. There were two boxes of ammunition, more than enough to protect her from the bad guys, no matter which side of the law they were on.

The briefcase also held five thick wads of $100 bills she'd withdrawn from the bank yesterday, cleaning out the joint account Walt had set up two years ago when she'd come home from her wild winter in Alamogordo. Fifty grand, her working capital.

The real money was still in the pipeline – six hundred grand from his government life insurance, half a mil in private life insurance, plus IRAs and a stock portfolio that added up to four million plus. In a month or two the paperwork would be done and she'd shop for a house somewhere in the Caribbean – Aruba, Belize, Cayman Islands – wherever it was warm and there was a little companionship to keep her amused.

She stuffed the gun and cash in a shoulder bag, carried the suitcase to the car. As she drove away, a crow sailed by overhead, its shadow passing over the car. She didn't know if it was the same crow she'd seen earlier but it was headed south and so was she.

Down at the BMW dealership on Camino Entrada it'd been a busy Friday afternoon and even the sales manager had pitched in to handle customers. Sandy Bishop had called in sick that morning complaining of a nasty gastro. Usually a hung-over Monday was what prompted such a call and it wasn't like Sandy to miss a Friday, traditionally a brisk sales day.

In fact he was indeed home alone and sick as a dog. After Thursday's wild ride with Carrie Cassidy had prompted him to unload his chicken-and-avocado salad, he'd felt shitty the rest of the day. As soon as he'd switched her tags and completed the forms for transfer of vehicle registration and plates, he'd gone home but in his haste had forgotten to fax the appropriate forms to the Department of Motor Vehicles.

Friday morning when the office secretary distributed the daily mail, she'd inadvertently buried the DMV forms under a couple of trade magazines where they remained undiscovered. Meanwhile, the Honda sat on the back lot waiting for a local auto jobber to tow it away for parts.

Had Bishop's manager known about this lapse in paperwork, he'd have gone straight over to Sandy's place and ripped him a fresh asshole. If a new owner, driving a car still legally registered to them, was involved in an accident that caused serious property damage or loss of life, the dealership would be liable.

Five minutes after Carrie Cassidy had hit the road, the Santa Fe Police Department got a call from New York. The Chief of the SFPD listened as Detective Levinson briefed him on the situation. Before they'd even finished their call, his secretary delivered to his desk the warrant Levinson had already faxed. As soon as he hung up, the Chief walked the warrant down the hall and the dispatcher put it out on the system.

Minutes later, two SFPD officers patrolling the Old Taos Highway accepted the call. When they arrived at 400 Piños Verdes, the place was locked and no one responded to the doorbell. One of the officers called it in while the other punched Cassidy's name into their onboard computer, coming up with only a DUI from two years ago.

"Dispatch, this is Unit Seventeen at the Cassidy residence. There's nobody home. You may want to issue an alert. Please confirm what you have on DMV. We can cruise the neighboring commercial strips, maybe spot her car."

"Roger, Unit Seventeen," the dispatcher said. "DMV registration says you're looking for a 1998 two-door Honda Accord, color red, license number eight-four-nine, Bravo Whiskey Tango."

63

San Rafael

Zeke Zabriskie made his America West flight out of Albuquerque by the skin of his teeth, sprinting through the small terminal to board just before they closed the doors. The flight connected in Phoenix where he had forty-five minutes to kill but en route the captain announced the connecting flight to San Francisco would be delayed half an hour.

Zeke slung his knapsack over his shoulder and wandered around Skyport International until he found the serviceman's hospitality lounge. He drank an overpriced Coors and shot the breeze with a couple of baby-faced marines from Camp Pendleton on their way home to Tulsa for a week's leave.

He landed in San Francisco at three-thirty, rented a car and got onto US-101 just in time for the end-of-week rush hour. It took an hour and a half to get to Marin Bay Park. The entrance gate was closed but ironically, the exit gate was open. He drove up into the gated community.

At the address he parked in the driveway beside a yellow Porsche and rang the doorbell. He was so pissed off from sitting in airplanes and being stuck in traffic that, when no one responded to the doorbell, he pounded the door with his fist. A few seconds later the door opened to reveal Dave Munson standing there with only a yellow towel wrapped around his waist, his wet hair slicked back.

"Howdy, stranger." Zeke stepped inside without waiting to be invited, his boots just missing Munson's bare toes.

Munson closed the door and followed Zeke into the living room. His unannounced visitor tossed his knapsack on the sofa and windmilled his arms to take the kinks out of his shoulders. "What're you doing here? How'd you find me?"

Zeke took in the view – big bare-assed painting on the wall, plush leather furniture, high-tech entertainment system, cabinet of antique coins. Whoever'd decorated this place had money to burn. He turned to face Munson. "What's the matter? You don't seem happy to see me. Am I interruptin' somethin'?"

"No, it's just that the cops have been sniffing around and then..."

"Cops?" Zeke went into high alert. "What did they want?"

"They were just asking questions... about a hit-and-run that happened near here."

"Oh yeah, when was that?"

"Couple of days ago."

Zeke came closer. "What do you have to do with a hit-and-run?"

"I just happened to know the guy that was killed."

"Really? I'm sorry to hear that."

Munson shrugged. "We weren't all that close."

Zeke hooked his right hand behind Munson's neck, pulled him close and bit him none too gently on the earlobe. Munson gasped and sagged against him. Zeke caught the flap of Munson's towel, jerked it away and looked down at his gear.

"Nasty-lookin' trouser snake you got there. Does it bite?" Zeke reached down and got a grip on it.

Munson's eyes fluttered as he allowed himself to be led by a short leash downstairs to the nearest bedroom.

64

San Rafael

Detective Jim Starrett called the San Francisco FBI office to bring them up to speed – how his local hit-and-run investigation had turned up a possible suspect for the FBI's case in Los Alamos, New Mexico. The FBI was grateful for the tip but their Marin County field agents were tied up all day taking down a child pornography network. Could Starrett arrest Munson on suspicion and hold him for questioning until they could take charge? The FBI agent promised to alert his New Mexico counterparts regarding this recent development.

Starrett clipped his holster to the back of his belt. He grabbed his jacket and felt to make sure his car keys were in the pocket.

"Can I tag along?" Crowe said. "I know it's not procedure but I have reason to be present. It's my case too."

Starrett admitted he owed Crowe one. "You can follow in your own car."

They went outside. While Crowe fetched his rental, Starrett made two quick calls – to Dispatch and his partner.

"Fred. Where are you?"

Hutchins was half an hour away in Tiburon, running down the whereabouts of a parolee named Nico Chorizo, acquaintance of the late Merguez brothers, cousin to a member of the Diablos del Norte. Theory was, in a deal brokered by the cousin, Chorizo might have done the Merguez hit as a way to join the Diablos.

"New development in the Lang case," Starrett told him. "Munson's into something bigger than suspected. I'm going to pick him up now. Meet me back at the office in an hour?"

"You want a hand in arresting Munson?"

"I've called a patrol car for backup. Hopefully he won't lawyer up right away and we'll have time to question him. See you back at the office."

Crowe pulled up and tapped his horn to let Starrett know he was ready. Starrett twirled his finger in the air and took off with Crowe following.

On the way out San Pedro Road, Crowe saw a dead cat on the shoulder. He didn't need to stop for a look at its entrails. The carcass alone was an omen. He had a feeling they'd find Munson too late.

His phone rang. It was Tracey.

"Just thought you'd like to know, those guys who attacked us in the park...? Last night our boys pulled Darin Guff over for drunk driving. When they punched in his name they found the assault warrant and booked him."

"What about his buddy?"

"Benny Logue. Small-time Jersey City hood. Guff was driving Logue's car, holed up at his place. Both in custody now."

"They admit to the attack?"

"Guff said he was approached by Stockwell to give you a good beating, not to kill you, just enough for a few days' hospital rest."

"Considerate."

"You know we've arrested Stockwell on a separate warrant?"

"Yeah, but it's a related case. Things are happening here. But thanks for the update. And Tracey..."

"Yeah?"

"I'm sorry I had to leave town so fast. I didn't tell you last night but I would have preferred to stay. It's just that..."

"You don't need to explain. Crime scenes have a short shelf life. You've got to follow the trail while it's still warm."

"Speaking of which, I'm just arriving at another scene now..."

"Okay. See you."

Crowe followed Starrett through the gates of Marin Bay

Park and up to the hillcrest. The detective exited his parked vehicle and walked back to Crowe's.

"Stay put," he said.

"I think we're too late."

"What do you mean?" Starrett gestured to the Porsche and Nissan in the driveway. "Looks like someone's home."

"One way or the other, he's gone."

A San Rafael patrol car came up the street and blocked the driveway. Two officers got out with hands on their pistol butts.

Starrett beckoned to the patrol cops. "Not him, he's with me. One of you, cover the back door in case Munson tries to make a run for it."

Crowe sat and waited. He didn't think there'd be any flight of suspect today. As Winston Churchill had once quipped when someone had warned him the fly of his trousers was unbuttoned, *A dead bird doesn't leave the nest.*

With the patrol cops in position, Starrett rang the bell. No answer. He tried the front door and found it unlocked. He and one officer went inside, checked out the ground floor and, finding no one, went downstairs to check the bedrooms, where they found Munson.

He lay naked on the master suite's king-size bed. The yellow sheets were covered with blood. His body was so wounded it looked like he'd been run over by a threshing machine. At a quick glance Starrett guessed more than two dozen stab wounds, sparing no major organ, internal or external.

An eight-inch chef's knife lay on one of the night tables. Made from one piece of stainless steel, a modern design running seamlessly from blade to handle, it reminded Starrett of a samurai sword, razor-sharp and lethal.

Body, bed and bloody knife were common features of many a murder scene that Starrett or any seasoned homicide cop had seen. But the bowling ball with its smoky red-and-blue swirls was something foreign. It appeared to have descended with all the force of a meteorite striking the earth, forming a crater between chin and hairline in what had once been Dave Munson's face.

Starrett felt like he'd stumbled into the lair of the Cyclops right after Ulysses had sealed his fate. In the doorway behind him one of the patrol cops breathed in an irregular pattern. In the bathroom down the hall the second patrol cop was retching.

Starrett called his partner. "Fred? Better come straight to the Lang house. Someone's whacked Munson." He paused. "No, I'll call CSU." Another pause. "Couple of dozen stab wounds, plus something for the books. You'll see when you get here."

Waiting outside, Axel Crowe used his iPhone to calculate an event chart for the Los Alamos car fire. With Libra rising, a movable sign said the criminal was a stranger to the victim. Seventh house Aries was a male sign, its lord Mars a male planet, so the killer was a man. With Mars in the sixth house ruling employees, the killer may have been hired, but in dual sign Pisces, more than one person was involved. An exalted Sun occupied the seventh. Sun and Mars were both *kshatriya* caste, suggesting the perp's connection with government, military or police. Weapons were indicated by Mercury, using trickery and subterfuge, in association with the Sun, involving fire or bombs. One last factor, based on an esoteric technique, indicated a criminal with a troubled mind close to home.

Crowe sat on the fender of his rental car, watching two crows fight over something in a tree behind the Lang property. One of the crows made a stricken cry and fluttered to another branch, giving up the struggle. The other crow launched itself into the air and flew away. Noting the direction in which it went, Crowe checked his watch and the air flow in each nostril.

A crime scene tech in white coveralls carried a garbage

bag to a van across the street and went back into the house. Starrett came out a few minutes later, lighting a cigarette as soon as he hit the street.

"The CSU's going to be there a while yet," he said.

"Can I get a look before they take him to the coroner's office?" Crowe said.

"You really want to? It's... messy."

"Believe me, I'm above morbid curiosity. Maybe I can see something you can't."

Starrett hesitated. Allowing a civilian onto a crime scene was definitely out of order, but once the CSU was finished, where was the harm?

"You sure it's Munson?" Crowe said.

"Why do you say that?"

"Is he recognizable?"

"Barely." Starrett looked at Crowe, trying to fathom the origin of these questions.

"Let me see."

Starrett shrugged. Twelve hours ago he wouldn't have given Crowe the time of day. But if Crowe hadn't come forward they'd still be in the dark with Lang's death. "When they're done."

"Thanks."

Hutchins emerged from a neighboring house and joined Starrett on the sidewalk. He'd been canvassing door-to-door for potential witnesses. He beckoned to Starrett and they crossed the street out of Crowe's earshot.

"Neighbor at number thirty-nine saw another car late afternoon," Hutchins said. "Pretty sure it was a current year white Pontiac Sunfire but never got a good look at the driver. All he saw was a guy, mid-thirties, in khaki flop hat and sunglasses. Didn't notice the plates."

"A guy. He sure about that?"

"Yeah. And he knows Lang was gay. He's never seen a woman visit the house."

"Shit."

"What's the matter?"

Starrett brought Hutchins up to speed on Crowe's theory of a three-way murder conspiracy. "Up until now, looked like this New Mexico woman might be a key figure. Find her, I figure, we pull it all together. Now we're looking at a new player, with barely two clues to rub together."

"So what now?"

Starrett nodded toward Crowe leaning against his car, seemingly oblivious to them, studying something on his phone. "For starters, let's be nice to him."

Hutchins tipped his sunglasses on his nose and studied Crowe from across the street. "What's the deal?"

"He's been helpful. And we need help."

It took the Crime Scene Unit two hours to complete their work. Starrett told them to take a break before they removed the body, weapons and bedding. The techs and patrol cops convened on the redwood deck overlooking the garden. Crowe and the two detectives donned disposable paper slippers and went downstairs to the master bedroom.

Crowe had seen a few dead bodies in his time but was shocked to see the violence wreaked upon Munson's body. He looked beyond the multiple stab wounds, the blood and the dramatically-placed bowling ball for other details that might tell a story. He recalled one of Guruji's observations:

Maya is revealed in the gross. Truth is hidden in the subtle.

"You've seen a lot of crime scenes," Crowe said to Starrett. "What do you make of this?"

Starrett cleared his throat. "First impression, this is some kind of psycho. On second thought, it looks overdone. The bowling ball's a bit much..."

"Any prints on it?"

"Only finger smudges. The CSU thinks the perp wore latex gloves. So obviously it was planned. But because of the multiple stabbing and the crushing of the face, we assume it was personal."

"Unless it was meant to look that way. Did you find the gloves?"

"No. He must have taken them away."

Crowe looked at the bed. "All this blood. The killer must have got spattered."

"The shower stall was wet. He probably showered right after."

Crowe looked in the ensuite bathroom. It had a Jacuzzi and a separate shower stall. He looked at the floor tile. "How many people have been in here?"

"Only one tech. We contained the scene to search for body hairs. Looks like the perp might have taken the drain screen after he showered but we managed to retrieve some hairs from the drain itself. We don't know who they belong to but they might prove useful to make a DNA match."

"Did they print the floor?"

"For fingerprints, I doubt it."

"That tile's a perfect surface. See if they can find a footprint."

Starrett left the room to speak to the CSU. A minute later, one of them entered the bathroom with his equipment.

Crowe walked around the bed and studied a bloody handprint on the sheet. It was a right hand. "Can you tell from the stab wounds whether the killer was right- or left-handed?" Crowe asked Hutchins.

"Right," Hutchins said. He pointed at the wall spattered with fine drops of blood. "Each time the knife exited, it threw a bit of spray onto the wall. You can tell by the way it angles, he had to be right-handed."

"This handprint is interesting. Thumb's very low-set on the hand and has a club-like upper phalange. A common feature among people prone to violence."

"Tell me something that isn't obvious."

"I'll give you a synopsis when I'm finished." Crowe decided to keep his thoughts to himself until he'd seen everything.

The index finger was very short, its upper phalange bent toward the middle finger which seemed inordinately thick. The index finger reflected identity, self-confidence and ethics, while the middle finger symbolized authority, discipline and social order. In his estimation the killer had been severely disciplined in his youth, probably by an abusive father. Betrayal by an authority figure might have paved the way for subsequent transgressions of the law.

The little finger was long but also crooked, even more so than the index finger. Reflecting both intellect and sexuality, this twisted little finger suggested a victim of sexual abuse at an early age who'd learned to lie to protect himself, thus developing a persona of fabrication and subterfuge.

Within a few minutes the CSU tech found one complete footprint and a partial of another, both left feet, on the bathroom floor. He showed the acetates to Starrett and Hutchins, who in turn let Crowe examine them.

Crowe rarely worked with footprints but the principles were the same as palmistry. He looked for deviations from the norm. In this foot the big toe was bulbous and club-like, indicating a potentially violent will. The third toe was twisted, echoing the hand's theme of a struggle with authority. A long line descended in a serpentine path from that toe to the callus of the heel, suggesting a crooked path in life. On either side of the line were several arrow-like formations, suggesting familiarity with weapons. A deep horizontal score near the heel was in the position of the classic poison line of palmistry, usually indicating substance abuse.

"So, what do you say, *Kemo Sabe*?" Hutchins chuckled.

"He comes from a family with a history of alcoholism or drug abuse. Probably physically or sexually abused. He's anti-authoritarian, never been married, but probably had military service. And he may have a tattoo of a snake somewhere on his body."

Starrett and Hutchins looked at each other with deadpan expressions. Hutchins shook his head in doubt. Starrett jotted a few things in his notepad.

Hutchins went into the hall and called for the CSU guys to take the body away. As Crowe climbed the stairs to the main floor, he met them on the way down, unfurling a body bag.

65

Bernalillo, New Mexico

On his way to the airport, Zeke Zabriskie paused to heave a garbage bag into a dumpster off Van Ness Boulevard. The bag contained bloody latex gloves, a bath towel and a drain filter from a shower stall. He returned his rental to the Alamo desk and cleared security just in time to make his flight at 6:30 PM. As the acceleration on takeoff pressed him back into his seat, he closed his eyes and reflected that, except for a few glitches, the job had gone off with military precision.

At cruising altitude he grabbed the arm of a stewardess to order a Jack Daniels and a beer. Downing the whisky, a sense of profound relief all but overwhelmed him, like taking a leak after a very long drive. He inspected his hands, especially under the nails and around the cuticles. They were clean and so was his getaway.

The flight touched down briefly in Phoenix where they exchanged passengers and then they were back in the air. Back in Albuquerque at 11 PM, he drove his truck north on I-25, twenty miles up the road to Bernalillo and his usual exit. This time, however, he turned onto South Camino del Pueblo and entered the parking lot of a Mexican restaurant called *Los Gatos Locos*.

Zeke looked for a red Honda Accord but saw it nowhere. There was a time when the mere sight of it would have given him a boner although he had to admit the effect, lacking positive reinforcement in the past year, was sadly on the wane.

He saw a few other vehicles – two pickups, an old Trans Am and a bright red BMW sports car – but nothing he recognized as her ride. He parked his truck next to the BMW and went inside.

The restaurant was dimly-lit with seating for about sixty but there were only a handful of customers. Booths ran along the front windows and down the side wall, the rest of the place occupied by tables. There were *serape*-style tablecloths, posters of Mexico on the walls, and *piñatas* hanging from the ceiling. Four Hispanics sat in a booth near the entrance. Zeke saw a short-haired brunette in the last booth along the side wall.

His pulse quickening, he walked to where she was seated. Only when he stood next to her did she look at him. She was nursing a coffee and, to judge by her expression, maybe a grudge. Zeke motioned for her to slide over on the bench so he could sit next to her. When she didn't budge, he sat on the bench opposite.

A waitress so young she looked like it was past her bedtime brought a cup and a carafe of coffee. She wore a blouse and skirt and had braces on her upper teeth.

Zeke looked at her. "Gimme a Corona, will you, darlin'?"

The waitress gestured to Carrie. "*Mas café?*"

"*Si, por favor.*" Carrie nudged her cup in the girl's direction.

Zeke waited until the girl had left, then turned his most charming smile on the woman facing him. She wore blue jeans and a black sweater that hugged her B-cups in a friendly way. She'd changed her hairstyle since he'd seen her last. It was a nice cut that framed her face, accentuating her eyes.

"You're lookin' real good, Hopalong."

"I'd prefer you didn't call me that," she said.

Not easily deflected, Zeke was determined not to be pussy-whipped. He gave her a little leer and pushed on defiantly. "Hopalong Cassidy used to be quite the little buckin' bronco."

Her icy tone headed him off at the pass. "I retired from

the rodeo, Zeke."

The waitress brought a glass and a Corona with a plug of lime jammed in the neck of the bottle. Zeke squeezed the lime into the glass, poured the bottle and drank while the lime was still fizzing the beer. He tugged his Marlboros from his shirt and offered her one. She shook her head. He flicked his lighter and drew smoke.

"You used to like it. Liked it a lot."

"I used to like cheap wine too but my tastes have changed."

"I figured that. I didn't see your car outside. What're you drivin' these days?"

"Beemer."

He nodded again, seeing the red sports car in his mind. Funny how he'd picked the parking spot next to hers. Like a homing pigeon, he thought, although the analogy troubled him. He wasn't anyone's pigeon. Chicken hawk maybe, but nothing domestic.

"Things must be goin' well for you."

"You're doing all right too." She kept her voice low. "Don't get greedy."

"Greedy? We ain't even square yet."

Carrie glanced over her shoulder, opened her purse and took something out. She reached under the table and nodded for him to meet her halfway. He put his hand under the table and received two wads of money. He jammed one between his legs and thumbed through the other, checking they were all hundreds. Lips moving as he counted the bills, he looked at the ceiling a moment to do the math, figuring it was all right. He sucked in his gut and shoved both wads down there next to his power tool, thinking he should have worn a looser pair of jeans.

He took another pull on his beer and cleared his throat. "I spent a lot of time on planes today, nothin' to do but watch the clouds go by and catch up on my thinkin'." He tapped his cigarette in the ashtray. "Month ago you give my name to a friend of yours wants to buy a gun. Turns out he needs a whole lot more'n a gun. He needs a job done. One thing leads to another and after mixin' business with pleasure I get it done. All this time I don't hear boo from you. All of a sudden today you call to say he ain't your friend no more and you want him stomped on like a cockroach. What gives? His friendship warranty expire or what?"

"You shouldn't think so much, you'll give yourself a hernia."

"I'm gonna pretend you didn't say that." He shrugged off her backhander. "You never thought I'd put it together – him needin' wet work done in Santa Fe, you pullin' strings from behind the scenes?"

"I assumed he could handle it like a man and keep his mouth shut. Turned out I was wrong."

Zeke nodded. "They don't all have your balls."

"What's your point?"

"I did you a big favor doin' his dirty work for him. I never asked no embarrassin' questions, just did it professional. Least you could do is show a little gratitude."

"Gratitude?" she hissed. "It was supposed to be a simple burglary gone bad. That's what we'd agreed on, what he asked you to do. But you had to get fucking creative with the terrorist angle and next thing I know the Feds are taking my life apart."

"I thought it would distance you," Zeke explained. "Your husband works for a top-level government installation and these *al-Qaeda* bastards are everywhere…"

She held up a hand. "Only thing needs distance is you and me. If we're seen together it could be dangerous for us both. I'm taking a big risk just being here."

"So what, I'm supposed to kiss your ass and say thanks?"

"I know you'd probably like that but why don't you just take the money and run?"

"When do I get the rest of it?"

"Soon as I read about it in the papers."

"You will." Zeke took out his cell phone and tapped a key. "I took a few pictures for you." He handed the phone to her.

To her credit, she didn't flinch. After looking she shook her head, in dismay or grudging admiration, and slid the phone back. "You are one sick fuck."

"Thank you." He returned the phone to his pocket.

She picked up her purse. "I've got to go."

Zeke reached across the table and took one of her hands in his, real gentle-like. When she tried to pull away his grip tightened like a pipefitter's wrench.

"Aside from what you owe me, I'm gonna need another fifty grand," he told her, ignoring the surprise in her face. "To keep my silence, you know, about the bigger picture that's been developin' before my eyes. And to console my hurt feelin's, especially after endurin' all these insults you been hurlin' my way."

She shook her head. "I don't like blackmail."

"Didn't your mother ever teach you to share your toys with the other kids?"

He released her wrist, picked up the Marlboros and offered her one again. She took one this time. He flicked his lighter and passed the flame under each of their cigarettes.

"I'll have to go back to Santa Fe to get the balance of what I owe you," she said.

"How about we meet right back here, say eleven tomorrow morning?"

She shook her head. "We shouldn't be seen together. I'll bring it to your place." She blew smoke at him. "But just what I owe you for today. The other fifty grand will have to wait a week or two."

"You remember how to get to my place?"

"I've driven by there once or twice."

"You shoulda dropped in for old time's sake."

"I haven't been feeling very nostalgic this year."

"Maybe we'll have time for a little stroll down memory lane tomorrow." He gave her an affectionate smile. "Did I mention my hurt feelin's are a big factor in all this?"

"I think your dick's a big factor is all."

"It's a sore spot all right."

She granted him her first smile of the night. "Let me sleep on it, see how I feel tomorrow."

His pulse quickened with anticipation, from adult to freakin' adolescent in the blink of an eye. "I'll try to remember and have a shower in the mornin'." He failed to suppress the leer on his face. "Or do you still like it dirty?"

"Take a shower. And wash your mouth out while you're at it." She got up and left.

66

San Rafael

Axel Crowe accompanied Starrett and Hutchins back to their office where they mobilized all available staff to work the first crucial hours of the Munson murder case. Crowe wasn't invited to stay but he wasn't told to go away either, so he hung around, thinking he might be able to offer some input.

The physical evidence was now at the CSU lab where knife and bowling ball were examined for latent prints. Other prints, taken from bedroom, ensuite bathroom and elsewhere in the house, were fed into the National Fingerprint File database.

Body hairs from the bed, shower drain and bedroom carpet were sorted and processed. Useless for the moment to identify a suspect, they might later be recalled if DNA comparison was required to confirm a suspect's presence at the scene of the crime.

Starrett brought Hutchins up to speed on the bigger picture. "Bernie Lang died within an hour of two other victims, Janis Stockwell in New York and Walter Cassidy in Los Alamos. That same day, Munson was in Albuquerque, Jeb Stockwell in San Francisco, and Cassidy's wife in New York.

Crowe thinks they might have done each other a favor. We need to establish a connection."

"I'll start with phone records." As part of the investigation into Lang's death, Hutchins had already subpoenaed phone records for Bernie Lang's mobile and land line, and Dave Munson's mobile, and examined them for calls to known bookies, drug dealers and felons. "Can we get phone numbers for Stockwell and the Cassidy woman?"

Starrett phoned Levinson in New York to explain what they needed. Levinson had already acquired similar records for Jeb Stockwell's home and office, his mobile and his wife's mobile. They exchanged key telephone numbers from their respective cases and promised to report back if they got a hit.

Starrett called the Albuquerque FBI office and requested telephone numbers for Walter Cassidy and his wife. The agent on the phone refused to give out any information, and asked Starrett to leave a number so the Special-Agent-in-Charge could phone him back tomorrow.

Starrett left a number and then tried Directory Assistance for Santa Fe, where he got numbers for Cassidy's home phone and his wife's mobile. Dr. Cassidy's mobile was unlisted.

Armed with these key phone numbers, Hutchins searched for a connection between Munson and Stockwell or Cassidy. Within minutes he found a call from Lang's home to Stockwell's home this morning.

"Munson probably thought he was in the clear until I showed up at his door asking about Stockwell," Crowe said. "It probably freaked him out and prompted a panic call to Stockwell."

"We should talk to New York again," Hutchins said. "If Stockwell feared Munson might crack under pressure, his next call might have been to someone who could take care of the problem."

Starrett called Levinson, who had by now scoured his own telephone histories and found the call from Lang's house to Stockwell's this morning. "Right after that incoming call," Starrett asked, "any outgoing calls to New Mexico or

California?"

"No," Levinson said. "But if he had to make a call that left no trace he could have used Skype, preferably from an internet café."

"Any way to trace the call over the internet?" Starrett said.

"Assuming you could trace a Skype account to him, best you'd get is proof one computer talked to another. You couldn't prove who was there at the time. And given the small transactions at internet cafés, they're almost always in cash."

"Any luck at your end? Did you get a warrant issued for Carrie Cassidy?"

"Yeah, but she's gone missing. The New Mexico State Police have got a bulletin out on her now."

"Shit! We don't have a clue who this new player is."

"Wish I could help you," Levinson said, "but it's been a long day at my end. I've got to go home and catch a few hours of sleep."

"Okay, thanks for your help. We'll talk tomorrow."

Starrett looked at Hutchins. They both looked at Crowe. They couldn't seem to say it, but their expressions were asking for help.

"What about the car?" Crowe said.

"What about it? Without tag numbers, we're nowhere."

"Based on Munson's chart," Crowe said, "I don't think he was capable of killing Cassidy. You met him, what do you think?"

"I have to agree," Starrett said. "He doesn't have the *cojones.*"

"So where's that leave us?" Hutchins said.

"Even if Munson was in New Mexico when Dr. Cassidy was killed, he probably didn't do it himself," Crowe said. "What if he hired someone to do the dirty work?"

Starrett nudged Hutchins. "The sixty grand."

"What sixty grand?" Crowe said.

"Bernie Lang withdrew sixty thousand dollars a few months ago," Hutchins said. "We were never able to figure out where it went."

"Munson could have borrowed it from Lang and used it to pay for the hit on Dr. Cassidy," Starrett said.

"And you said he didn't have balls," Hutchins said.

"If he paid someone to do a job in New Mexico," Crowe said, "it was probably someone from the area."

"So...?"

"If Munson came unglued the killer would be put at risk. If arrested, Munson might roll over on him in a plea bargain. So the killer came here to shut him up. You see where I'm going with this?"

"Out of town killer," Starrett said. "Flies in, rents a car at the airport, does the job and flies home."

"That white Sunfire Lang's neighbor saw," Hutchins said. "Sunfire's a popular rental model."

"Let's check it out," Starrett said. "I'll call the airlines and get passenger lists of every flight from New Mexico in the last twenty-four. Fred, you call the airport rentals and get them to pull the files on every white Sunfire rented out in the same period."

With nothing else to contribute, Crowe went outside for a walk. It was a beautiful spring evening and he smelled honeysuckle on the air. He walked down to 4th Street where a number of people milled on the sidewalk outside a movie theatre. Among them was a Japanese man with two children. Crowe was reminded of the Berkeley karate instructor Ken Ataka. He'd meant to call him earlier, but it had slipped his mind.

Crowe got Ataka's number from Directory Assistance. Despite working in Berkeley, Ataka lived in San Francisco. He agreed to meet Crowe early tomorrow morning in a park near Chinatown.

Crowe bought six large coffees and a dozen cookies at a coffee shop to take back to the detectives' office. Starrett rewarded his gesture with some news.

After 90 million print comparisons via the NFF database, the fingerprint technician had nothing to show for the effort.

Other than Munson's, there were no matches to the fingerprints gathered from the Lang house. This meant that, even if they'd captured the prints of the killer, he'd never been arrested and wasn't in the system.

"So now what?"

"Data from the airlines and car rentals should start coming in the next hour or so."

"Anything I can help with?"

"It's going to be a long night for us." Starrett glanced at his watch. "You might as well go back to your hotel. I'll give you a ring in the morning, let you know if we've found anything."

Crowe headed back to San Francisco on the 101 where a steady stream of traffic – wine aficionados returning from Napa Valley, weekend hikers returning from camping trips – accompanied him across the Golden Gate Bridge.

Crowe thought about Carrie Cassidy. Although Starrett had pulled her date of birth from the DMV file, Crowe hadn't had time to look at her chart. He wondered what her next move might be. She'd come and gone from New York with stealth and swiftness, leaving little in her tracks. Would she sit waiting for the police to appear at her door? He reminded himself to look at her chart back in the hotel, although he'd have to guess her rising sign, having never laid eyes on her, knowing nothing other than she was a writer.

Back at the hotel he returned his car to the rental agency. On a whim he asked the clerk if he had any maps of New Mexico. The clerk obliged with a map of the entire Southwest.

"I'm looking for someone. Can you give me a number too?"

"A phone number?" the clerk said.

"No, just any number between one and twelve."

The clerk shrugged. Weirdo, you could hear him thinking. He said, "Six."

In his room, Crowe calculated Cassidy's birth chart, using

Santa Fe as a tentative birth place. He chose a Virgo ascendant because it was the sixth sign in the zodiac, the number the rental clerk had given him.

The chart made immediate sense. Mars was in its own sign Scorpio in the third house, associated with powerful desire, athleticism and the arts. Venus was exalted in the seventh house and, since it ruled the second house of vocabulary and ninth house of publishing, gave evidence of a writing career. Moon in the fifth house of authorship nailed it.

But the rest of it? Ascendant lord Mercury was in the eighth house of trauma with a debilitated Saturn, hinting at a twisted mind. Moon in Capricorn was also influenced by Saturn, more evidence of a dark mind. Although exalted, Venus combust in the seventh house with Rahu indicated marital problems, a bias for multiple relationships ranging from eccentric geniuses to renegades. Was she capable of violence? The malefic planets all exerted influences on her ascendant, its lord Mercury, the Sun and Moon.

Knowing the variables of karma, Crowe hesitated to call it deterministic but it was almost as if the woman had no choice in the matter. He recalled an infamous quote from Hitler: *"I go the way Providence dictates for me, with all the assurance of a sleepwalker."*

Where would Cassidy go? Crowe checked the transits against her chart. Her ruling planet Mercury had just entered Taurus in the ninth house. The ninth ruled long-distance travel but Taurus was a fixed sign and Mercury was under the influence of Saturn, which was always a drag. He figured she would run but wouldn't get far.

He unfolded the map of the Southwest to have a closer look at New Mexico. Thus far his investigation into Janis Stockwell's murder had centered on three areas: New York, San Francisco and Santa Fe. But he might just as well substitute Albuquerque for Santa Fe since that's where Munson was when all three deaths occurred.

Crowe drew three lines connecting Albuquerque, Santa Fe and Los Alamos. In his mind's eye he compared it to a larger triangle connecting New York, San Francisco and Santa Fe. Both were roughly the same triangle he'd seen in the cracked pavement where the NYPD had outlined Janis Stockwell's outflung hand. Crowe studied the area around Los Alamos where Dr. Cassidy had died in a car fire, possibly caused by a bomb. The map's topographic features caught his eye. In the mountains west of Los Alamos was the crater of an ancient volcano, a *caldera* ten miles wide. Crowe thought of the hole in Dave Munson's face caused by the bowling ball. He reflected on Dr. Locard's exchange principle – every killer left a little piece of himself at the crime scene and took a little piece away. Although Locard had referred to material evidence, in Crowe's worldview that was only the grossest element on a broader spectrum of manifestation.

A gory image floated into his mind's eye: Munson's face with the bowling ball driven into his forehead. Blood from his right eye socket had run down his cheek. Crowe superimposed this image onto the map of the Jemez Mountains. From the volcanic caldera, a rift descended from its southwest quadrant and ran down a valley through a place called Jemez Springs.

It wasn't much to go on but it was a piece of the puzzle. Even if it didn't make sense, that could change overnight. Starrett and Hutchins were now running down leads, assembling information. This was like a jigsaw puzzle. Sometimes you had a piece in your hands but you didn't know what to do with it until you recognized the pattern in the surrounding pieces and then everything fell into place.

67

Saturday

San Francisco

Axel Crowe awoke at four in the morning. It was seven back in Toronto and if it hadn't been for the late hour he'd gone to bed last night he'd have accused himself of sleeping in. He showered, put on a bathrobe and meditated for half an hour. Afterwards he went out onto the balcony to inhale the dawn air. He could barely see the street through the fog that had crept like dense smoke between the sleeping buildings. From out in the bay came the sound of a distant foghorn.

He dressed and left the hotel. On Sacramento Street a homeless man sang to himself as he pushed a shopping cart of belongings along the sidewalk. Aside from a street-sweeping vehicle, a few taxis and a police car, there was no traffic at this hour. As Crowe walked, store signs in English gave way to Chinese. At Grant Avenue, the spine of the famous Chinatown strip, he turned south a few blocks, then east on California, looking for a small street ran parallel to Grant.

He found the entrance to a small park. It contained several benches and children's swings, with a street lamp at either end. On a plot of grass a man in a track suit practiced moves involving chops and kicks. Crowe recognized Ken Ataka, the Berkeley Karate Club instructor. Having finished the last move of his sequence, Ataka bowed to Crowe and beckoned him with a sweep of a hand.

Crowe approached. Ataka didn't offer to shake hands. Crowe placed his palms together at chest level and bowed briefly from the waist. Ataka's hair had turned salt-and-pepper since his Berkeley days but his face was as ageless as the Buddha heads Crowe had seen in the windows of antique shops on Grant.

"Thank you for meeting me, Ataka-san. I am grateful for

your assistance."

Ataka nodded. "I have a sympathetic ear for anyone willing to trade the comfort of a warm bed for the chill of the dawn."

"I'm accustomed to it. Four to six in the morning is what the Hindus call *brahmamuhurta*, the hours for meditation."

Ataka moved toward a nearby bench beneath a tree. Crowe followed and they sat together. Ataka crossed one leg over the other and placed his hands in his lap. He closed his eyes and inhaled deeply, releasing his breath in an extended sigh. He turned to look at Crowe.

"So you sit in *zazen*?"

"In the manner of my Hindu guru."

"I admire the Indian traditions even though they seem to lack a martial art."

"Actually there are several – some with weapons, some without. They are largely unknown because Hindu philosophy holds non-violence to be a prime virtue."

"But you know these arts?"

"Yes."

"And you have fought?"

"To my regret, yes."

"Regret?" Ataka looked puzzled. "Is it not honorable to defend a noble cause or protect the innocent?"

"My regret lies with my failure to resolve a situation through logic or diplomacy."

Ataka extended an open-palmed hand. "Those who can't learn from this must be taught with something firmer." His forearm curled back with a serpentine fluidity until his hand, thumb and fingers now bunched together like the hooded head of a cobra, cocked at shoulder height and ready to strike.

"My guru taught me to familiarize myself with the way of snakes but not to sleep with them."

Ataka lowered his hand back into his lap. "Was he a man of the world or a recluse?"

"A wrestler in his youth, lawyer in his middle years, teacher in his maturity. The Bengal Tiger, they called him in

Calcutta. He said his life had been built on one struggle after another – pinning opponents to the mat, winning courtroom cases, dispelling ignorance. He said the biggest challenge was to transfer the arena of combat from the gross to the subtle. Ultimately, our greatest enemy is our own desire."

Ataka inhaled deeply and released an audible sigh. "You're fortunate to have found a worthy teacher."

"I am grateful he found me a worthy student."

Ataka studied Crowe. "So tell me. What's this puzzle you're trying to solve?"

Crowe gave Ataka the Karate Club photocopy from the Berkeley yearbook. He pointed to Stockwell in the picture. "Do you remember this man? He was a student of yours fourteen or fifteen years ago."

Ataka peered at the picture, his thumb and finger feeling the paper, as if its texture were a stimulus to his memory. He nodded as it came back to him. "He was nimble on his feet but had no stamina. If you kept pressing him he crumbled."

Crowe pointed to Dave Munson. "What about this one?"

"No concentration, no discipline. Drugs, I believe. And he was afraid of being hurt."

Crowe pointed to Carrie Woods. "And her?"

Ataka squinted a moment. "Ah, yes. Our little *kamikaze*."

"What do you mean?"

"That's what the other students nicknamed her."

"Why?"

"She was fearless. She'd pursue the most aggressive attack no matter what risk of injury. Compared to these other two she was from another world. She could take a blow and come back even stronger. And she wouldn't quit. She was like a snake with its head cut off but still thrashing."

"Did she attain a black belt?"

Ataka shook his head. "We encountered an obstacle. I couldn't take her beyond the brown."

"What kind of obstacle?"

"Anger," Ataka said. "If you can't control your basic emotions, you can't master the higher disciplines."

"More a question of your refusal, rather than her ability to continue?"

"It would have been like giving an angry child a sword to play with her friends. Someone would have lost their head. It was my responsibility to prevent that happening."

"Everyone has their limits. Many things my guru never taught me. At one time, I resented his withholding them. Later I understood it was only my insatiable ego he was attempting to restrict."

"Even in matters of honesty, your guru taught you well."

Crowe bowed his head. His eyes filled with tears, reflecting upon the years it had taken him to achieve even a shadow of the humility that was second nature to Guruji. His heart brimmed with love for the man who'd shown him the path through a bramble thicket of ignorance and misperception. As he blinked back his tears he saw the first rays of the rising sun illuminating the wall of a neighboring building upon which someone had painted a red Chinese dragon.

Ataka gave him back the photocopy of the Berkeley Karate Club. "Why are you interested in these people?"

"They've been playing with swords of their own. Innocent people have been killed."

"Why is that your affair?"

"One of the victims was the sister of a friend, a good woman who used her wealth and influence to help those in need. Her death leaves a void in the lives of many."

"And now you're a vigilante?"

Crowe shook his head. "More like a bloodhound. The police will follow up on whatever I find and do what must be done. I want to keep my hands clean but I can't close my eyes in the face of injustice."

"You're a good man too. I wish you success."

"Thank you, Ataka-san." Crowe stood and bowed to the older man.

Ataka uncoiled from his seated position and stood. "Won't you stay a while and fight me? I'd like to see what your guru taught you."

"Perhaps another time. I have a plane to catch."

Before Crowe turned to go, Ataka extended his hand. Crowe shook hands with him. Ataka's grip was gentle but Crowe felt strength like a coiled spring within the older man's palm. In the brief seconds during which they were thus bonded, Crowe felt the electric current of two ancient traditions intertwine like the coils of mating serpents.

Ataka nodded as he released him, placed his palms together and bowed.

68

San Francisco

Axel Crowe returned to the hotel where he found his express checkout bill and today's *San Francisco Chronicle*. He glanced at the newspaper headlines. A front-page story read '*Pentagon Awards Fort Hunter Liggett $50 million.*' The article recounted how the largest Army Reserve Command Post in the country had received funds to upgrade its training facilities.

Crowe packed his bag. Last night he'd checked the flight schedules out of San Francisco International airport. There was an America West departure at 7:05 AM this morning, connecting in Phoenix, arriving in Albuquerque at noon.

He caught a taxi to the airport. En route he called Detective Starrett, thinking to leave him a message, but Starrett picked up on the first ring. His voice was gnarly, like someone who'd stayed up all night drinking coffee and smoking cigarettes. He and Hutchins had pulled an all-nighter.

"Any luck?" Crowe took out his phone and started his astrology app. Across the bay, a pink sky outlined the San Leandro Hills.

"Yes and no," Starrett said. "Three hundred passengers traveled from New Mexico to the Bay Area yesterday. Twenty-one rented white Sunfires. We phoned them all. Since we woke them up in the middle of the night, it was rather unpleasant."

"Any passengers you couldn't locate?"

"Yeah, and for lack of a better reason, he's our suspect. A guy named Brian Hunter flew out of Albuquerque, connecting in Phoenix. But the contact number he gave the airline was out of service."

"Hunter?" Crowe recalled the front-page lead about Fort Hunter Liggett in this morning's newspaper. "What area code?"

"New Mexico, Alamogordo area."

Crowe studied the chart on his phone. The ascendant, Sun and Moon were all in Aries at this moment, giving the archetypal fire sign a singular importance. This drew his attention to Mars, the warrior planet that ruled Aries.

"Any military bases near there?"

There was a pause at Starrett's end. "I think the F-117 Stealth squadrons are based in southern New Mexico. Why?"

"He's connected with the armed forces."

"How do you know?"

Crowe looked out the taxi's left window. Mars was in the 12th house of the horary chart. He could see it at this very moment, about thirty degrees above the horizon. It was still within a few degrees arc from Venus, brighter and more elevated. In Vedic myth, Mars was *Kartikeya*, the god of war; Venus was *Shukra*, the guru of the *Asuras*, a demonic class of deities. This was a war the warrior couldn't win.

Crowe didn't answer Starrett directly. "Don't most airports have a designated serviceman's lounge? If he's military, Hunter might have used the one in Phoenix while waiting for his connecting flight. Maybe someone remembers him."

"That's a bit of a long shot."

"Got any better ideas?"

Starrett cleared his throat but said nothing, reluctant to admit it.

"Any news from New York?"

"NYPD took Stockwell into custody last night. So far he denies any wrongdoing but we'll get someone to ID him on the Larkspur surveillance and then we'll see."

"Tell Levinson to lean heavily on him."

"He's probably lawyered up by now."

"What about Carrie Cassidy?"

"Santa Fe called me back last night. She's disappeared but they've got the airports and borders covered. Hopefully it's just a matter of time."

"Speaking of airports, don't forget what I said about the serviceman's lounge."

"I'll check it out," Starrett said.

At the airport, Crowe queued at the security gate. The line was long but moving briskly. Another Orange Alert day. He marveled at how the flying public had become dulled to the omnipresent security threat. He dumped his things into trays and placed them on the conveyor belt. He was on the other side of the scanner when his phone rang.

"I checked with Sky Harbor Airport," Starrett said. "Hunter did use the serviceman's lounge in Phoenix. But he's got no record so he's not in our system. And I can't access military files."

"What about DMV?"

"An address on Mesquite Road, Holloman Air Force Base."

"Where's that?"

"Alamogordo."

"So now what?" Crowe took his bag and headed for the departure gate.

"I spoke to the New Mexico State Police. They'll exercise my warrant to pick Hunter up for questioning."

"You going down there?"

"No. Our budget's tight and my Chief watches the bottom line like most women watch their waist lines."

"What? You don't watch yours?"

"Don't bust my balls."

"What about the FBI?"

"I contacted their Albuquerque office and gave them a heads-up. With Dr. Cassidy dead and his wife a bona fide suspect in a three-way conspiracy, Hunter looks like the missing link between Cassidy and Munson."

"Will they act on it?"

"They're very tight-lipped. Between me and you, I get the idea the Cassidy case was being treated as a national security matter. I think originally they had it pegged as some kind of terrorist thing but couldn't get beyond the theory. With a lead on Hunter, maybe now the pieces will fall into place. At least they can gain access to his military records."

"Can you give me the coordinates for the agent you spoke to?"

"No," Starrett said. "You're not even supposed to know what I just told you. And if it ever comes up, you never heard me mention national security. But I'm very grateful for how you helped us with the Lang and Munson cases. If you need to reach the FBI, just go on their website and look up the New Mexico office."

Crowe arrived at his departure gate just as they announced boarding for his flight. As the other passengers presented their boarding passes, Crowe called his client in New York.

Blaikie answered. "Hi, Axel. What's up?"

"I don't have time to share details but things are developing quickly. Seems I stirred up a hornet's nest with my visit here."

"No kidding! The police arrested Jeb but they won't tell me anything other than he's wanted for questioning out there. What about that woman from Santa Fe?"

"We're pretty certain she had something to do with your

sister's death. There's a warrant for her arrest but she's disappeared. I'm leaving for Albuquerque now."

"Disappeared? How will you find her if the police can't?"

"Kevin, I need you to pull some strings for me but legally, it's a bit murky. You might be putting someone at risk."

"I've got a few favors in reserve. What is it?"

"Do you know anyone in New Mexico who works for the military? I need someone with Department of Defense security clearance."

Blaikie sucked in his breath. "You like to play in the big leagues, don't you?"

"If we're going to take a swing at it, let's put it out of the park."

"Let me see what I can do."

Crowe had just put his phone back in his pocket when it rang. It was Tracey.

"How's your weekend going?" he said.

"I'm in the office," she said.

"You need to get a life."

"Tell me about it," she said. "But we just got a break. You know we fingerprinted the vehicles adjacent Janis Stockwell's body. We matched one print on file but as it turned out the felon in question was miles away with an airtight alibi at the time. But after we followed your lead and identified Carrie Cassidy as the woman from the Southwest, we dusted her hotel room and ran every print lifted against prints from the crime scene. We got a hit!"

"A match between hotel and crime scene doesn't prove anything. If she's got no record, you don't have her prints."

"We do now. Soon as we had her name I went looking. Turns out she had a small contract with the Department of Defense five years ago. And ever since 9/11 all contractors must be fingerprinted. It took a call from our Captain to get DOD to let us have a peek but they gave it up this morning. All we've got is one finger but that's all it takes."

"Nice work! Take the rest of the weekend off."

"I think I will. Want to join me?"

"Wish I could. I'm about to get on a plane for New Mexico."

"To get your kicks on Route 66?"

"We'll see."

"Remember that line from *Hill Street Blues*?" Her tone turned serious. "Be careful out there."

69

Albuquerque

When Axel Crowe disembarked in Albuquerque, a man in military cap and jacket stood waiting in the arrivals lounge. As Crowe approached, he saw Military Police insignia. The officer fell into step beside him but not for a moment did Crowe think this might be Brian Hunter closing in for another kill. Crowe had spent some flight time studying the chart he'd produced this morning. He believed Hunter was no longer in active service.

"Mr. Crowe? I'm Captain Mack Loomis, Kevin's friend. Please follow me."

They left the main terminal concourse and entered a short corridor where Loomis keyed open a door marked *Authorized Personnel Only*. On the other side was a longer corridor whose walls and ceiling were a uniform pale blue. A security camera tracked them all the way to the end where Loomis used his key on another door.

They stepped outside. Loomis took from his pocket a security badge with a number and a bar code, and clipped it to Crowe's lapel. They descended some stairs and walked to a nearby military Jeep. Loomis opened one of its cargo bins and Crowe slung his bag inside. They climbed into the Jeep. Loomis shot off along a service lane paralleling the north side of the airport terminal.

"How do you know Kevin?" Loomis asked.

"I do some work for him." Crowe liked to keep it simple. "I'm a one-man lost-and-found agency."

Loomis glanced at him. "He said if it weren't for you the police still wouldn't have a clue what happened to his sister."

"He's just being generous."

"That is his nature," Loomis agreed.

"And you? Known him long?"

"Since grade school."

"That's a longstanding friendship."

"He's a really good guy. We got into some trouble during university. I would have ended up in jail if not for him."

Crowe remembered Blaikie having told him this story. "Way I heard it, you saved his life from a crack addict with a knife, paralyzed the guy with one punch to the neck."

Loomis was silent for a moment. "I guess that part's true. But when the guy got out of hospital he tried to get me arrested for assault. If I'd been jailed, it would've been bad news. My parents had no money for a lawyer and the arrest would have ended any hope of a law enforcement career. But Kevin insisted *he* threw the punch in self-defense so the police arrested him. He called his dad in New York and two hours later he was out on bail. The case was dismissed a week later."

"Lucky break."

"Goes beyond luck. I owe him big time."

They arrived at a security gate where two soldiers in combat gear flanked the gate with machineguns. A sign above the security hut read *Kirtland Air Force Base – Security Clearance Only.*

An officer emerged from the security hut and tugged his cap snug on a close-cropped skull. He pointed an electronic gun at Crowe's security badge. A red line flickered across the barcode and the gun beeped. The officer checked the readout and gave a thumbs-up to someone inside the hut. The gate swung open.

"Go ahead, Captain Loomis."

After parking the Jeep and passing through another

security desk at the main entrance, Loomis led Crowe down a broad corridor. Crowe saw lots of Air Force personnel but almost as many civilians, everyone wearing security badges.

Once inside Loomis' office and behind a closed door, Crowe said, "I was surprised to see so many civilians in here." He looked out the window. On the tarmac a hundred yards away were four Lockheed F-22 Raptor fighter jets.

"Twenty thousand people work on the base. Defense company contractors, government people, our own civilian support staff..."

"On a Saturday?"

"Defense is a twenty-four-seven operation." Loomis turned on his computer. "Kevin said you're looking for information on someone in the service..."

"Used to be in the service. I'm pretty sure he's no longer active."

"Why are you interested?"

Crowe told Loomis about the three almost-simultaneous murders in New York, San Francisco and Los Alamos, and how one of the main beneficiaries was brutally snuffed out yesterday in San Rafael.

"You think the guy behind that was ex-military?"

"That's my thesis."

"Based on...?"

Crowe hesitated. "If I told you, you might not be convinced."

"Let me be the judge." Loomis had a wry look on his face. "Kevin said you were an astrologer...?"

"You find that amusing?"

"No. My aunt read palms. She was so good it was scary. She told me I'd end up in the military, get married twice, and have three kids. All true."

"What made me think this guy was ex-military was something I saw in a footprint."

Loomis nodded. "What's the guy's name?"

"Brian Hunter." Crowe approached the desk. "Mind if I look over your shoulder?"

"After I put in my password." Loomis tapped the keyboard. "Okay, pull up a chair. I'm now in the Military Police system. We have an offense reporting system, a vehicle registration system and a correctional reporting system. We maintain files on sensitive geographic areas, unlawful activities, specific individuals and criminal investigations. We also cooperate with other law enforcement agencies, especially the FBI and the DEA, and have access to the National Crime Information Center."

"But if this guy *never* ran afoul of Military Police...?"

"I can access his general personnel file, which includes service history, performance ratings, promotion/demotion events, location of assignments and payroll data."

"Do you have fingerprints on file?"

"Yes, along with blood type and DNA."

"What do you have on Hunter?"

Loomis worked the computer. Turns out there were three Brian Hunters in the system. One was age 68 and retired; one was age 22 and currently active in the Middle East; the other was age 32.

"Let's see what we have on this last guy." Loomis browsed the online file. "Three years National Guard, joined the Army in ninety-eight, made Private First Class, assigned to 32nd Battalion... Uh-oh, wait a minute. This guy's dead."

"Since when?"

"Drowned two years ago in a boating accident on the Colorado River." Loomis turned to Crowe. "How'd you get this name?"

Crowe told Loomis how the San Rafael Police had cross-referenced flights originating in New Mexico against white Sunfire rentals in San Francisco. Plus, Brian Hunter's use of the serviceman's lounge in Skyport International.

"Might be a case of identity theft," Loomis said.

Crowe took out his phone. "Can we look at the other guys in his unit, particularly during his last year of service?"

"What level of service?"

"How big's a platoon?"

"About forty."

"Let's start there."

"Give me a minute." Loomis worked the computer. "Now what?"

Crowe referred to the chart of Dr. Cassidy's car bombing. "If my reasoning is correct, the guy we want is dysfunctional in some way. Anyone in Hunter's platoon discharged for medical, psychological or criminal reasons?"

Loomis brought up a new screen. "Out of forty, only six guys meet your criteria. Seems low in the law of averages but that could be lucky for us. Three discharged for medical reasons. First guy developed diabetes, hereditary causes; second contracted Hep C from a hooker; third suffered spinal injury during live fire exercises. Number four had a nervous breakdown, discharged as psychologically unfit. The fifth guy was charged with theft of ordnance. And the sixth was discharged for striking an officer."

"Tell me more about that last guy."

"Stuart Namath, age 33. Joined the Army in ninety-nine. Disciplined in oh-one and oh-two for substance abuse. Couple of DUIs. Disciplined again in oh-three for facilitating prostitution on base. Involved in a bar brawl in oh-four, both an officer and a military policeman, court-martialed and dishonorably discharged."

"Where is he now?"

Loomis took several minutes to search the military system and then the NCIC before he came up with an answer: "He was running a meth lab, got taken down by the DEA two years ago. Currently serving seven to ten in Yuma prison."

"That leaves only the thief."

Loomis searched the record of the other man from Hunter's platoon. "Ezekiel Zabriskie. Five years National Guard, joined Army in ninety-nine. Trained in demolition, served six months in Bosnia. Made corporal in oh-two. Demoted in oh-four for threatening an officer. Charged with theft of ordnance in oh-six, court-martialed, convicted and dishonorably discharged same year."

"Don't tell me he's in prison too."

Loomis worked his way from one system to another. "Looks like he's managed to stay out of trouble since then. I've got nothing on him."

"Back to Hunter a minute. Do you have an accident report for his drowning?"

Loomis checked it out. "Date, location, witnesses, brief description of circumstances, name of the coroner who wrote the death certificate."

"Witnesses?"

"Three guys from his platoon, looks like. Dunbar, Snodgrass and... Zabriskie."

"Maybe you were right about the identity theft."

"Ideal set-up," Loomis agreed. "Guy drowns, you help recover his body and when no one's looking you swipe his wallet. Things get lost in the water so no one thinks twice about it. But Zabriskie walks away with military ID, driver's license and social security card – stuff he can use later." Loomis shook his head. "Soon as we're done here I'll flag Hunter's ID in the system, classify it as stolen identity."

"Wouldn't there be a bar code or electronic strip that would register invalid when Zabriskie tried to use it in a place like an airport serviceman's lounge?"

"It's not hard to replace a photo and get a fresh lamination. Most places, they just glance at the ID card, see the right face and you're in."

"So Zabriskie could be the guy. What have you got on file for last known address?"

Loomis looked it up. "A rural route number in Jemez Springs."

Crowe wrote down the address, recalling the name of the town he'd seen last night on the map of the Jemez Mountains.

"You're not going up there to see that guy alone, are you?" Loomis said.

Crowe didn't answer. "Can you get me a number for the local FBI office?"

70

Bernalillo

Carrie Cassidy woke up alone in Unit 6 of Sandia Vista, a three-star motel on the outskirts of Bernalillo. She'd slept with the Glock at her side but hadn't slept well. Intuition had told her not to return home to Santa Fe. Intuition also said she had to do something about Zeke and it didn't involve giving him more money.

She parted the window curtain. A swath of undeveloped land sloped away toward the Rio Grande. Her Z4 was parked behind the motel, hidden from the road. She splashed water on her face, lit a cigarillo and took a sip from a pint bottle of tequila. Breakfast of champions, she thought. Every champion has her day and perhaps today was hers.

All last night, in and out of her restless sleep, she'd turned her options over in her mind until her brain felt like one of those rotating grit-filled drums in which rock-hunters polished the garnet, hematite and turquoise they found in the hills. And what did she have to show for it? A headache. Whether that was from too much drinking or thinking was a moot point, but it pissed her off she was still at an impasse. She had to make up her mind pretty soon, even if it came down to a flip of a coin.

Stockwell worried her. She'd always figured Munson for the weak link, so no surprise he'd started unraveling at the first sign of trouble. But she'd made an executive decision on that one and sent in the commandos. One flank secured. But what if the police leaned on Jeb? Scarcely tougher than Munson, he could handle no more heat than a marshmallow. He had so much to gain, fifty million or more, she'd hoped he wouldn't cave under pressure. Her security hinged on his hanging tough. Unfortunately there was only one guarantee of silence and it was lying here at her side. She touched the reassuring weight of the Glock.

But she didn't want to go to New York. Returning there with an active investigation still underway would be downright stupid. She needed to head off in the other direction, south and across the border, to disappear in some beachside village until things cooled off. In her stead there was only Zeke. A number of flights out of Sunport in the early afternoon would put him in New York late evening. He could do Jeb and that'd be the end of that. It would cost her plenty but every form of freedom had its price. Was it worth the risk?

She stubbed out her cigarillo, unzipped her suitcase and took out a change of clothes. She showered and toweled off, ran her fingers through her wet hair and dressed. She decided to wear her running shoes instead of her cowboy boots. When she looked in the mirror she knew she wasn't getting any younger or any smarter. Just more determined than ever to play the cards Fate had dealt her. Despite all their difficulties, her mother had drilled one thing into her over the years – she was special and didn't need anyone's approval to do what she had to. Just do it.

Her mind was now made up and from here on out the rest was all downhill. She stowed everything in the BMW, pulled out onto Highway 550 and headed west.

Jemez Springs

Zeke Zabriskie woke up alone as well, although he felt as rested and content as a coyote in his own burrow with a bellyful of roadkill. After Carrie left the restaurant last night, he'd had a couple of *tamales* and another Corona and flirted with the jailbait waitress until her father came out from the kitchen, a cleaver in his greasy hands, and that was the end of that. Zeke had driven back to Jemez Springs, minding the speed limit so as not to attract a state trooper in his DUI-condition. Back home he'd popped a Coors and smoked a few Marlboros as he counted the two wads of bills she'd passed him under the table. Twenty grand, present and accounted for, sir. And more where that came from. After a few years of hardscrabble work doing odd jobs on the marginal side of things, burglaries and the occasional car theft, he was finally into some serious cash.

On top of all that, this morning in his heart of hearts he sensed a fork in the road of his pitiful travels. Seeing Carrie again had triggered a flood of memories the like of which he'd been reluctant to dwell upon ever since she'd cut him loose a year ago. He was thinking, with her old man now out of the way, maybe she'd loosen up again and they'd enjoy some good old times like that winter in Alamogordo. Out there in the white sands...

At that thought, last night's dream opened up before him and he remembered now waking up halfway through the night, his joint aching with a memory of something it'd been thrusting against but unable to sink into. He recalled the dream now, just like a day they'd actually shared in real life.

They'd been drinking shooters one afternoon in a bar off base and they'd bought a bottle of José Cuervo and driven out to the White Sands National Monument. They parked the car and walked north into the sand dunes, through scattered swatches of yucca and saltbush, until they were in an unbroken white landscape of drifting gypsum. They smoked a doobie and drank, lying on the side of a dune, winter sun warm on their faces, watching white lizards hunting white mice. They kissed and fooled around and the clothes came peeling off. As daylight faded the sands turned reddish-pink and the whole landscape took on texture as shadows lengthened, filling the spaces between each little ripple of sand and in the lee of every dune.

She got a little crazy at one point, said she saw a giant white snake slithering up on them from around one of the shadowy dunes. She wanted to go back to the car but he told her it was just the loco weed and the mescal, the desert playing tricks, and the only snake coming after her was his big old trouser snake. But she went running and he had to go after her, caught her ankle as she scrambled bare-assed up the side of a dune, and took her there in the half-shaded gully of shadow, coyote-style, both of them yipping and howling like damn fools. When the sun finally dipped below the San Andres Mountains, for a few minutes everything was bathed in a mysterious light, the sand itself seeming to glow as the horizon turned dark all around and an overwhelming sense of peace and stillness descended upon them.

Maybe it was only a dream, Zeke thought, but he wished he could live in it forever and never wake up.

A few miles north of the village Carrie turned off NM-4 and onto Jemez Canyon Trail. It wandered east through scrubby pine and rocky outcrops, following a gully's course. She drove about a mile until she saw a mailbox with 'ZZ' painted on it. From there she saw the peak of a house up among the trees. She put the car into reverse and backed across the culvert and up the lane and into the pines. She parked the BMW in front of a big black Dodge Ram pickup and turned off the engine.

As she approached the house the front door opened and Zeke came out onto his porch, barefoot and bare-chested in a pair of jeans, a pump shotgun in his right hand.

He looked toward the road, listening as much as looking. "You alone?"

"Of course." She gave him a reassuring smile. "You know me, Zeke, just a regular girl. I've never been into threesomes."

"Not what I heard one night in Dutchy's," he sniffed.

"You know those guys were worse than teenagers – all lies, lies and more lies."

"Not sex, lies and videotape?"

"Maybe a little sex but never on videotape."

He chuckled, then turned and walked ahead of her through the door and she saw the big tattoo of the snake across his upper back. "You had breakfast?" he said over his shoulder.

"I had a coffee on the road." She followed him inside, looking around as she went, having forgotten how shabby his place was.

"Skinny little thing like you ought to put on a few pounds."

"I like myself the way I am, thanks."

"So do I. But I was just gonna do a few eggs for myself. Be no trouble to add a couple for you." Zeke propped the shotgun beside the stove and retrieved a burning cigarette from an ashtray on the counter.

"I'm not really hungry. Let's just get down to business."

"Which business is that?" he said, not turning around, trying not to let too much hope creep into his tone.

"Business, pleasure – it's all the same to me."

His pulse quickened as he took a carton of eggs from the fridge and laid them on the counter. Over his shoulder he said, "Gimme a minute, I could grab a quick shower."

Carrie reached behind her back and took the gun from her waistband. "Don't bother on my account."

"So you still like it dirty?" He took a last puff off his cigarette and stubbed it in the ashtray.

"Every once in a while for old time's sake."

He turned around, his grin evaporating when he saw the Glock in her double-fisted grip. He raised his hand to wave her off, like a flight deck controller seeing a plane coming in too high and fast, but there was more momentum in that terrible moment than he could deflect. This was not the dream I had, he thought, not the way it was supposed to fly…

She shot him and the sound of it, in the enclosed space without the benefit of ear guards like she was accustomed to on the shooting range, startled her. But not as much as it startled him, the impact of the slug hurtling him backwards to slam against the fridge.

There, it was done. Yes, she could have used him to kill Stockwell but then she'd have owed him forever. Given the way he felt about her, he'd never let her forget it. She'd be doling out money or sex, if not both, the rest of her life.

She waited until he fell to the floor before she walked over to where he lay gasping, both hands clutching a chest wound that burbled scarlet down his ribs and onto the cracked linoleum floor. His mouth was moving and there was a panic in his eyes that couldn't be articulated.

"Sure, I know what you're thinking," she said. "We had some fun together and, once upon a time, maybe I did love you in a sick kind of way. But that's all over now. You screwed up my perfect plan and now you're part of the mess that needs to be cleaned up."

She let him have a good close look up the barrel of the Glock. He was still shaking his head, still trying to say no, when she shot him again.

71

Jemez Springs

Sixty miles northwest of Albuquerque, Jemez Springs sat right on New Mexico Route 4, paralleling the Jemez River. Hot sulfur springs were the big attraction in the Jemez area. There was a spa in the village and several springs scattered throughout the nearby hills, some accessible only via hiking trails that became congested on weekends when nature lovers arrived by the score to get naked and soak.

Axel Crowe had to stop in the village to ask for directions because for some reason he'd lost his internet connection and couldn't access Google Maps on his iPhone to find the road Zabriskie lived on. He bought a bottle of water at a country store and asked how to find the Jemez Canyon Trail.

"Who you lookin' for up there?" said the old guy behind the counter, his creased forehead looking more like rawhide than the weathered hat he wore on the back of his head. A Colt .45 Automatic sat in plain view next to the cash register.

"Old Army buddy."

"Bullshit," the storekeeper said. "If you'da said IRS,

maybe I'da believed you, although even that's a stretch with that northern accent of yours."

"Would you believe the Treasury Department?"

"Sure. Can you prove it?"

Crowe took a piece of well-worn paper from his wallet and laid it on the counter. The old guy looked at the picture on the bill, and looked at Crowe.

"Andrew Jackson, huh? Not much of a resemblance."

"I was having a bad hair day."

The storekeeper shoved the twenty across the counter and gestured north. "Up the road, 'bout a mile 'n' a half. You watch, you're gonna cross the river twice on the way up, then you look sharp, 'cause just before you cross it a third time you'll see a dirt road about fifty yards before the bridge. It's real easy to miss."

Crowe found the turnoff the storekeeper had described. There were few mailboxes on the road and he looked closely at each as he passed, but none declared the occupant to be a Zabriskie or Hunter or any name he recognized. He came to the end of the road and saw a mailbox with 'ZZ' on its side. Bingo! He parked his rental, a Dodge Neon, on the shoulder and got out. Halfway up a wooded slope the peak of a roof protruded from the trees. Then he heard a gunshot.

He jumped the ditch and headed up through the trees. Seconds later he heard a second shot. He dropped to a crouch and waited a minute before continuing. He moved from one tree to another until he saw two vehicles – a sports car and a pickup truck – parked in the driveway before a small wooden house.

Crowe crept up to the sports car, whose view from the house was screened by the truck. He crouched beside the BMW, unscrewed the air valve cap on the driver-side front wheel and pressed his fingernail on the valve stem. The hiss of escaping air seemed a roar to his ears but it was too little noise to draw the attention of anyone in the house. The wheel rim sank onto the flaccid tire. He retreated into the trees and swung wide of the house to approach it from the rear.

Inside, Carrie Cassidy pulled on gloves and searched Zeke's place for the money she'd given him last night. In the bedroom she jerked open dresser drawers, looked in the closet and under the mattress. Then the living room where she opened a wooden chest that doubled as coffee table, finding Zeke's dope stash and *Penthouse* magazines, before tearing through a bookcase filled with porn videos and paperbacks of true crimes and war histories.

She was getting a little frantic now, knowing she shouldn't linger any longer than necessary. It wasn't about a measly twenty grand when she stood to take down a couple of million. But if the police found the money they might not theorize a drunken argument ending in a shooting, something that happened often enough in these parts. They might suspect something bigger...

She flung open the kitchen cupboards, dumping stuff all over the place, finding only cereal in cereal boxes and coffee in coffee tins, before continuing into the fridge, coming up empty again. Only the bathroom left now, where she swept the contents of the medicine cabinet onto the floor, flipped the lid off the toilet cistern and *ka-ching*, there was her twenty grand in a plastic container floating on rusty water. She stuffed the money in her jeans and went out the door at a trot.

As soon as she reached the car she saw the flat tire. What the hell? She crouched and ran a hand over the tire, expecting to find a protruding nail, but there was nothing. Shit! She'd never changed a tire in her life and she didn't want to start now. She needed just enough air to get to the nearest service station.

She popped the trunk and looked inside. No pump. She didn't even see a spare tire! She looked in the back of Zeke's truck. There was a big aluminum toolbox but it was locked. She looked inside the cab. A key dangled from a string beneath the rearview mirror. She grabbed the key and unlocked the toolbox. She found a hand pump, fitted its hose to her deflated tire and started pumping.

Crowe, having circled to the back of the house, heard the front door slam as someone left the house. He mounted the back steps and peered through the screen door. A man lay on the kitchen floor, blood pooling beneath him. A pump shotgun leaned near the stove. Crowe went inside and grabbed the shotgun. He saw car keys hanging from a wall hook and grabbed those too. He looked at the man on the floor, whose head wound made clear he was beyond help, and went back outside.

Cassidy finished inflating the tire. As she replaced the valve cap she thought she heard something from Zeke's house. She listened. All she heard was her own labored breathing. She stood and tossed the hand pump into Zeke's truck.

Crowe edged along the house to its front corner, from where he saw Carrie near the truck. He switched the safety off and pumped the shotgun to feed a cartridge into the breech.

Cassidy spun at the sound and pulled the Glock from her waistband. She saw a head protrude from the corner of the house and a shotgun barrel pointed right at her.

"Carrie Cassidy, you're wanted by the New York police. Drop your gun and raise your hands."

She fired two quick shots. The guy was no more than ten yards away but she was hurried. This wasn't the target range with all the time in the world to steady her hand and squeeze off a slow one. The bullets went wild. He ducked out of sight.

Cassidy jumped into the BMW and started it. The guy's head appeared again. She fired another quick three shots, blowing off a few shingles as he ducked out of sight again. She threw the car into gear and gunned the engine.

Crowe ran out from behind the house, kneeled and aimed at one of the BMW's rear tires. The shotgun boomed. Before he could pump a second round, the car was out of range at the bottom of the driveway but he saw its rear end slump as it turned from view.

Cassidy swung the BMW onto the road, narrowly missing a blue Neon parked near the entrance. She stopped, leaned out

the window and fired three shots into its gas tank. She hit the
jackpot and the tail end of the Neon exploded. She matted the
gas and shot off in a trail of dust down the Jemez Canyon
Trail.

Crowe climbed into the Ram Charger, laid the shotgun
across the seat and started the engine. He hadn't driven a
manual transmission in a while but it was like riding a bike,
once you'd mastered it, you never forgot. He put the truck in
gear and descended the driveway. Swinging wide of his
burning Neon, he turned onto the dirt road and shifted into
second. Ahead, a cloud of dust drifted off the road and into
the trees. He kept the truck in second gear as he skidded
through the downhill turns, struggling to keep it in the middle
of the road, hoping he wouldn't meet another car. Just as he
rounded the last corner, he saw the BMW turn south onto
Highway 4.

San Ysidro, New Mexico

Seventeen miles of twisting river road lay between Jemez
Springs and San Ysidro. After that it was open country to
Bernalillo and the I-25 South to El Paso and the Mexican
border three hundred miles away. Observing the speed limit
entailed a six-hour drive, but Cassidy was intent on doing it in
far less. She went through the village of Jemez Springs at 60
mph, smoke roiling off a flat rear tire, scaring the shit out of
motorists and pedestrians alike. People were barely over their
outrage when a black pickup barreled down the road in
pursuit.

Odds-makers would have had a challenge on their hands.
Although the curve-hugging Z4 was made for roads like these,
its flat tire made it hard to control, never mind hit top speed.
And with its 345-horsepower V-8 engine, the Ram was
powerful but its high center of gravity made it a liability on
curvaceous Highway 4.

As Cassidy raced down the serpentine road she could

smell over-heated rubber and hear the rear tire flapping. Behind her, Crowe maintained the pressure, matting the gas on the straight-aways, fighting to make it through the curves, always keeping the BMW in sight.

Cassidy roared through San Ysidro, barely slowing for the Highway 550 intersection where she ignored a stop sign to slide around the turn, and then she was on a straight stretch toward Bernalillo. She looked in her rearview and saw the pickup a hundred yards behind.

Damn it, who was that guy? If she didn't lose him by the time she got onto the I-25, the smoke pouring off her rear wheel would attract someone's attention. Before long, highway patrol would pull up next to her, asking where the fire was. Then it would be all over except for the crying. She had to ditch her pursuer before he became a bigger liability.

A mile ahead on the right, Cassidy saw a ridge of hills that defined the edge of a mesa. Between her and the ridge was open land too barren for pasture, too far from civilization to be developed. Across that open expanse ran a dirt track worn down by hunters or prospectors, something that wasn't on the maps. She slowed the car, angled into the ditch and climbed the other side to follow the dirt track toward the hills.

Moments later, Crowe braked on the shoulder, watching the sports car tear across the open ground, churning dust in its wake. He crossed the ditch and gunned the pickup in pursuit of the BMW.

Cassidy drove as fast as she could although the sound of the undercarriage striking rough ground beneath her was a reminder she wasn't on friendly terrain. Up ahead was a V-shaped notch in the rocky ridge.

As soon as she passed though the notch, she swung the car hard left and into the entrance of an arroyo. She hit the brakes just short of getting hung up on a jumble of rocks and climbed out of the car. She hurried back twenty yards and crouched behind a rocky outcropping.

A hundred yards back, Crowe approached the notch in the ridge where the BMW had disappeared. He had a feeling of *déja-vu* like some old cowboy movie where the cavalry is lured into a box canyon, from the upper walls of which the Apaches let loose a hailstorm of arrows and gunfire. When he was half-way through the notch his premonition came true.

From the corner of his left eye he saw Cassidy emerge from behind some rocks. His door window blew open, showering him with glass. He swung the wheel hard left and matted the gas, hurtling the Ram straight at the rocks where he'd seen her.

Cassidy fired twice more into the Ram's windshield as it barreled up the arroyo at her. Its big square grille loomed above her as the truck lurched over the rocks. She fled.

Slouching below the dashboard, Crowe stomped the gas, thinking that with the high undercarriage he could climb the rocks, but the engine screamed as the wheels tore uselessly at gravel. The truck was hung up on the rocks. He grabbed the shotgun and went out the passenger door, moving to the rear of the pickup, trying to see where Cassidy had gone.

Fifty feet away on the other side of the arroyo, Cassidy aimed her pistol, wondering if she could hit him at that distance. Before she could decide, his shotgun boomed and a hail of pellets buzzed over her head. Shit, there was no walking into that hornet's nest. She turned and ran from the arroyo, exiting on the west side of the notch. She looked back. The guy was following her. Worse still, he was between her and the highway.

She broke into a trot. She was west of a low ridge of hills. Two miles south was the mesa plateau. If she could make that ridge, she could leave her pursuer completely behind or ambush him from higher ground. She looked back and saw him following her. Well, she was in good shape and wearing running shoes. She'd leave him in the dust. She accelerated her pace and headed for the mesa.

Crowe jogged after her wondering, where was the cavalry when he needed them most? He tugged his phone out and called the number for the regional FBI office.

72

Albuquerque

The first call came into the FBI's Albuquerque office just after noon, a man claiming to have information regarding a fatal car fire in Los Alamos earlier this week. The dispatcher took the caller's name and phone number and transferred him to the regional officer's weekend designate. Special Agent Paul Kramer listened skeptically to Axel Crowe's account of how he'd uncovered a three-way murder conspiracy involving victims in New York, San Francisco and Los Alamos.

Crank calls were all too frequent ever since 9/11 and the subsequent Homeland Security alerts that had raised the average citizen's paranoia to a level rivaling that of a Soviet-era dissident living next door to a *gulag*. Kramer probed for more details but Crowe wouldn't reveal how he knew about the death of Dr. Cassidy, only that he knew it was an open FBI case and that he'd acquired information suggesting that Zeke Zabriskie, former soldier and current resident of Jemez Springs, was a logical suspect. Crowe urged Kramer to dispatch officers to Jemez Springs immediately. When Kramer provided no assurance this could happen on such scant evidence, Crowe requested the regional officer call him directly, and hung up.

Kramer dithered a minute. Special-Agent-in-Charge Liam Cobb was visiting friends in Santa Fe and was loath to be disturbed on one of his rare days off. So Kramer spent ten minutes with the National Crime Information Center's database to confirm Zabriskie's existence, noting that his Army conviction for theft of ordnance had earned him both a dishonorable discharge and an entry in the NCIC records. When he saw that Zabriskie had received demolitions training while in service, the light went on.

He picked up the phone and called Cobb's number.

* * *

After getting Cobb's go-ahead, Kramer mustered a six-man SWAT team and scrambled a chopper. The Bell Jet Ranger that landed on the roof of the FBI field office had a five-seat capacity. It departed Albuquerque with pilot and three SWAT officers, leaving one seat vacant as it headed north to pick up Cobb in Santa Fe.

Kramer and three other SWAT officers drove a Ford Explorer north to Bernalillo, preceded by a New Mexico State Police cruiser to clear the way for their high-speed run to Jemez Springs. They overshot the Jemez Canyon Trail by one bridge too many. By the time they realized they'd missed their turnoff and doubled back, five minutes passed, during which a smoking BMW Z4 pursued by a Dodge Ram Charger hit the NM-4 south of them and fled the scene.

Apologizing to his Santa Fe hosts, Cobb got his wife to drive him to nearby Franklin Miles Park on the south side of the city where he rendezvoused with the chopper. His wife was left with the car and a suggestion that their hosts shouldn't delay dinner on his account, there was no telling when he'd return.

From Santa Fe to Jemez Springs it was forty-three miles as the crow flies, which the Jet Ranger covered in twenty minutes. As soon as they'd arrived over the area, the pilot checked out a dirty plume of smoke rising from a dirt road north of the village. As the chopper came in over the trees, Cobb saw a state patrol car and Ford Explorer parked on the dirt road downhill of the car in flames.

The pilot set them down at the top of the road, fifty yards from the burning car. As soon as the chopper touched ground, Cobb and the SWAT officers spilled out to check for occupants of the burning Neon and, finding none, moved into the woods toward the house.

* * *

Jemez Springs

Within fifteen minutes, the ten men from the FBI and New Mexico State Police had secured the site. Cobb spent a few minutes crouched behind the shed with Kramer before the SWAT team leader emerged from the house, weapon slung over his shoulder, helmet tipped to the back of his head.

"All clear," he called out. "One occupant, dead of gunshot."

While the SWAT team fanned out to check the surrounding woods, Cobb and Kramer went inside for a look. The victim had been shot twice, chest and head. Kramer had brought a photo he'd printed off the NCIC but there was no easy comparison between Zabriskie's mug shot and the blood-covered face of the dead man. Fingerprints would confirm if it was really Zabriskie. Cobb phoned for a CSU from Albuquerque to come up here and process the crime scene.

Someone outside called for Cobb. He closed his phone and went out onto the porch, where one of the New Mexico State Police officers said, "Sir, we need to head out. We just got a call to respond, someone reporting a high-speed chase through the village."

"Go for it."

"And one of your SWAT boys wants to talk. I think they found something." The officer and his partner ran toward their cruiser down on the road.

The SWAT team leader beckoned from the door of a shed. Cobb walked over. The SWAT leader stood aside to let him look, but barred the entrance with his arm.

"I wouldn't go in there without full body armor."

Inside the shed, lighted by a bare bulb hanging over a workbench, a SWAT officer was carefully removing items from boxes and ranging them on the workbench whose wall rack displayed screwdrivers, pliers and soldering guns. Cobb saw three different kinds of electronic alarm clock, several sizes of batteries, a bunch of primer charges on wire leads, and what looked like a dozen one-pound bags of putty.

The SWAT officer held up a bag for Cobb to see. "C4 plastic explosive."

Kramer looked over Cobb's shoulder. "What do you bet Forensics matches this stuff to the residue in Dr. Cassidy's vehicle?"

"Good work, guys." Cobb clapped the SWAT team leader on the shoulder. He walked away from the shed to confer with Kramer. "But if Zabriskie's dead, who took him down? And what happened to the citizen who called in the tip?"

Kramer's cell phone rang. The office dispatcher had the original tipster on the line again. Kramer took the call, listened briefly and passed the phone to Cobb. Cobb listened only a moment before Crowe, clearly out of breath, broke off. Cobb closed the phone and whistled to the SWAT team leader.

"I need you and one of your guys, on the double. Let's go." Cobb motioned to Kramer. The four of them ran down the driveway toward the chopper waiting at the road.

73

Little Appaloosa Mesa, New Mexico

Carrie Cassidy had been running hard for five minutes when she paused to look behind her. She couldn't believe her eyes. The man was still following her, less than a hundred yards behind. She was dismayed. He was way too athletic for his own good. Still breathing heavily, she adopted a two-handed shooting stance and tried to steady both her breathing and her pistol. When the man was within thirty yards, she fired. Missed.

Crowe slowed to a walk. He raised the shotgun, aiming it right at Cassidy. She couldn't stand still for a spray of pellets. She took another quick shot from twenty yards away, missed again, and turned to run.

Crowe ran after her. He was drenched in sweat and struggling for breath, throat burning, field of vision collapsing, conscious of little else but the woman fifty yards ahead. But with every minute he persevered, ignoring his screaming lungs and shaky legs, he narrowed the gap a couple of yards each minute. If he could keep it up, he'd run Cassidy to ground in half an hour.

Cassidy slowed to a ragged jog. She turned, almost losing her balance, and raised the pistol. Crowe could see her arms shaking, and even with two hands supporting the gun, she couldn't keep her sights on him. He raised the shotgun. Earlier when they'd abandoned their vehicles and exchanged shots, Crowe had intentionally fired over her head. Now, even if he could keep the shotgun steady, he didn't want to shoot her. But she didn't know that.

Crowe worked his tongue, gathering just enough saliva to lubricate his words. "I called the FBI," he yelled at her. "They know about you...," he gulped air, "...and Zabriskie."

Cassidy waved the gun, her lungs a wheezing bellows, hurling back a few words at a time. "You back off..., let me go..." She massaged the stitch in her side. "...I'll give you fifty grand."

Crowe's response was a hoarse laugh. "Is that what you... promised Zabriskie...?" He swallowed hard, coughing it out. "...Before you killed him?"

Cassidy turned and ran toward Crowe, skidding to a halt at the fifteen-yard mark, knowing she had to do this right, end it now. She whipped her pistol up, scared now in a way she'd never been, because this wasn't a paper target on the shooting range, this was a man with a shotgun rising to meet her sight line, and she didn't time to take a deep breath and a slow squeeze. She banged off one quick shot as the shotgun boomed, then another as she twisted away, knowing she'd missed Crowe on both counts. She turned and ran like an old jackrabbit.

Crowe lowered the shotgun and followed. As he pursued her, he counted the number of shots she'd fired. Two for

Zabiskie, five at him in Zabriskie's yard, another three into the Neon, another three at him in the arroyo, four more since then... Was that seventeen? Did an automatic carry that many shots in its clip? He was pretty sure Cassidy must be running on empty.

Up ahead, the mesa rose from the desert floor in a steep bluff, almost vertical in places. Cassidy was so intent on outstripping her pursuer, she'd neglected to pay attention to the topography. When the horizon disappeared from her peripheral vision she saw too late that she'd entered the mouth of a canyon. She faltered, realizing she might get boxed in if she wasn't careful. She looked over her shoulder and got a jolt of panic when she saw the man only thirty yards away. No way could she angle left or right because with every step she took, her pursuer would close the gap.

A jumble of rock lay at the base of the cliff, broken and sharp-edged after tumbling from above. Cassidy jammed the Glock into her waistband and scrambled up through the rocks, using hands as well as feet to negotiate the larger boulders.

Crowe halted at the base of the cliff, trying to figure out where Cassidy thought she was going. Near as he could see, the cliff was too steep to climb, its face too eroded to offer secure handholds or footholds. He maneuvered through the boulders, picking his steps so as not to fall among the broken rock, until he was directly beneath her.

Cassidy had only got about thirty feet up the face of the cliff. If he'd wanted to use the shotgun, Crowe could have blown her off the face of the cliff.

He summoned enough wind in his lungs to call up to her, "You can't make it."

Cassidy had just come to the same conclusion. She was jammed into a crevasse that gashed the face of the cliff, almost at the top of it where an overhang blocked her further passage. No way could she get around it without rope and crampons. She'd have to retrace her steps. She looked down at her pursuer, startled to see how close they were. She was totally exposed on the cliff face. Why didn't he shoot?

Crowe finally got his breath back. "This is the end of the trail, Carrie... You're finished, and you know it."

"Back off!" she yelled. "You don't know me."

"I know more than you think. I know what started back in Berkeley as a little *ménage-à-trois*..."

Cassidy pulled the Glock from her waistband. At ten yards, she could hardly miss this shot, even if the angle presented only a diminished profile of the man below. Gripping the rock wall with her left hand, she took careful aim and pulled the trigger. The action clicked on empty. What the fuck? She worked the breech block and tried again. *Nada*. She ejected the magazine to check the load but it slipped from her hand and clattered down the cliff face. Her extra rounds were in her car and the gun was useless now. She flung it at the man, striking him on the arm.

Crowe winced and rubbed his elbow. He looked for the pistol but it had fallen into a gap among the boulders. He looked up at Cassidy wedged into the crevasse, her face a mask of fury.

Cassidy scanned the rock face above, vertically and laterally, confirming her earlier fear: she had no place to go but down.

Crowe addressed his captive audience. "I know all about the three of you, Carrie. I know Jeb married money, but fell in love with someone more beautiful than his wife. When his Wall Street career couldn't feed the appetite he had, he wondered why he shouldn't have all of his wife's money. Then he fell victim to *your* imagination."

Having hurt Crowe with the pistol she'd hurled, Cassidy got an idea. She inspected the rock face at the edges of the crevasse, looking for cracks that might reveal a loose piece, and tugged at it with her fingers.

Crowe summed up the life of her partners in crime with a brevity as insulting as it was accurate. "Your buddy Dave tried to keep his dreams alive but couldn't put together anything better than a garage band for the songs he wrote. He killed time, swinging both ways, until he found a boyfriend with an estate big enough to retire on."

Cassidy broke off a piece of rock the size of a coconut and hurled it down.

Crowe saw it coming and stepped aside, the rock missing him by a yard.

"Meanwhile, you did time in a marriage of convenience, working on the Great American Novel, doing field research on characters like Zeke Zabriskie..." Crowe watched Cassidy scrabble at another section of the rock face. He checked his footing in case he had to dodge another missile. "Until one day you all ended up with a mutual itch to scratch. And the frustrated but clever writer plotted the ultimate three-way..."

"You don't know shit."

"Dave's dead and Jeb's in police custody." Crowe let that sink in. "And you're stuck... between a rock and a hard place."

Cassidy struggled to break off another piece of rock. She pried at its edge with growing desperation, pulling as hard as she could until suddenly it cleaved away from the wall. But it was so much bigger than she'd expected – a piece the size of her torso! As the weight of it toppled against her, she couldn't get out of its way, and it pushed her off balance. In a final desperate gambit, she turned with it and rode it down in a *kamikaze* scream of fury, hoping to crush Crowe beneath it as she plummeted to earth.

Crowe jumped to another boulder just in time. Cassidy, tumbling head over heels, crashed into the boulders, the 100-pound rock landing atop her with a sickening crunch.

Crowe dropped the shotgun and scrabbled to her side. He eased the rock off her chest and cradled her head in his hands.

Her eyelids fluttered with pain as she looked up at Crowe. Blood oozed from her mouth. "Damn you."

"Don't go with a heart full of hate." Crowe gently touched Cassidy's lips with a finger. "Leave it behind. Better to think of a time when you were happy. Hold onto that."

Her hands made fists. Crowe closed his hands over hers. She fought a moment before giving up and her hands went soft inside Crowe's. He looked down on her as the muscles slackened in her face and he saw her spirit getting ready to take flight. Her eyes were filming with tears and in the middle of each pupil was a black hole into which all the light was descending.

Summer was her favorite time of the year, when she and Mom went to Vermont, leaving Dad to fend for himself. They took the train on Dad's Army pass, three days and nights from Austin to Boston, reading comics and magazines by day, scrunched together in a lower bunk at night, watching America roll by beneath the stars. Grandpa and Grandma met them in Boston for a day of shopping and then drove up to Middlebury, arriving late at night, the dogs barking as they drove up the lane. When she hugged the two dogs who never seemed to forget her, and smelled the fresh hay on the cool night air, she knew she was home, really home.

In the green mountains of New England, while Texas baked under an unforgiving sun, she and Mom spent seven weeks on Grandpa's farm, going to Burlington for the Fourth of July parade, visiting relatives, picking strawberries, swimming in Lake Champlain, some nights sleeping in Grandpa's old canvas tent. While Mom helped Grandma cook meals and make preserves, Carrie spent time with her Grandpa.

She watched him milk cows in the morning, helped him feed the chickens and pigs, rode on the tractor as he mowed hay, and lay beside him when he took a mid-afternoon nap on the front porch. She loved how he looked in denim coveralls and red plaid shirt, the way he held her tight so she wouldn't fall off the tractor seat, how he always smelled of Old Spice, how his whiskers bristled her cheek when he kissed her good night.

Most of all, she loved when he let her ride his horse. Trixie had been known to kick down a stable door or jump a fence in search of sweet grass, but Grandpa always kept a firm hand on things. With Carrie astride Trixie, arms half-wrapped around the horse's neck, face pressed against the dirty-blonde mane, Grandpa walked Trixie down the lane with one hand on the reins, one hand on Carrie's ankle. It was a short ride to the brook and back but in that half hour, Carrie knew no greater joy and security, astraddle a horse with Grandpa's reassuring hold upon her.

She loved him in a way that only a child with a daddy for a soldier could understand, and she herself didn't fully comprehend until her father was killed along with most of his company in Beirut in 1983. From that distant summer day when her Grandpa winked at her, she saw a light in his eye that was pure love, and she laid a hand on his shoulder, wishing he could always be there to keep her from falling. It was the happiest, and the last, memory of her life.

Crowe folded Cassidy's arms across her broken chest and reoriented her body with her head pointing west. He took the photocopy of the Berkeley Karate Club from his back pocket and twisted it into a fuse that he set on a boulder a few feet from her head. He found matches and lit the twist of paper. As it burned, he closed his eyes and recited a mantra to *Shiva*, an invocation for the safe passage of the dead from a battlefield.

Soon after the ashes from the twist of paper had scattered, he heard a sound.

A helicopter approached from the north, coming in low like a vulture that had located the source of its carrion spoor. Crowe stood and waved. The chopper with *FBI* painted on its belly hovered a short distance away, then settled to the floor of the canyon.

74

Sunday

Albuquerque

Special-Agent-in-Charge Liam Cobb held Axel Crowe for twenty-four hours, during which he conferred via phone with Detectives Levinson in New York and Starrett in San Rafael. Eventually he understood the three-way high-wire trapeze act that had crashed to earth on his turf. While Crowe's name and fingerprints went through the NCIC database, Cobb also called the Canadian Security Intelligence Service in Ottawa to verify Crowe's credentials as a private investigator.

Although Crowe's name and prints came back clean from NCIC, his prints were nonetheless compared to those found on the wreckage of Dr. Cassidy's BMW X5, and on the pistol found among the boulders beneath Carrie Cassidy. Forensics promptly confirmed the Glock as the weapon that had killed Zeke Zabriskie.

Satisfied of Crowe's innocence, Cobb released him with an apology and drove him to the Albuquerque airport to catch a New York flight.

"I like to think of myself as open-minded," Cobb told Crowe as he stopped in front of the terminal, "but I still find it hard to believe you cracked three murders in the space of four days, doing...," he waved his hand vaguely, unable to say the words, "...whatever it is you do."

"Maybe I was just lucky."

"Lucky in more ways than one. How many bullets did you dodge – almost a dozen?"

"I was praying so much, I lost count," Crowe said. "Probably that had something to do with it."

* * *

New York

Crowe caught an American Airlines flight out of Albuquerque mid-afternoon. He phoned Blaikie during a stopover in Denver and told him what time he'd arrive at LaGuardia. Blaikie met him there shortly after ten.

"Did they break Jeb yet?" Crowe tossed his luggage into the car.

"No, but they moved him to Riker's yesterday," Blaikie said. "They could have kept him downtown another day or two, allowing easy access to his lawyer, but Levinson said it's a psychological ploy."

"It's a wake-up call to make him realize he's one step away from entering the system, no matter what."

"I guess that could cut both ways – make him stiffen his spine, deny everything, try to ride it out."

"I don't think he's got that much spine."

"Speaking of wake-up calls, this has held a mirror up to my face and I'm not proud of what I've seen. Every time I think of Janis, I'm overwhelmed by rage. If I could have just ten minutes alone with Jeb and a baseball bat..." Blaikie shook his head. "It embarrasses me to think there's so little that separates me from a beast."

"It's a perfectly human reaction," Crowe said." Yogic philosophy says we're all constantly subject to three modes of being. *Tamas* is the animal desire to feed, couple and sleep. *Rajas* is the human desire to accumulate things and wield power over others. *Sattva* is the godly desire to know reality and our place in it. In the course of our existence we cycle through all three states. The only difference between us is the amount of time we spend in each. We should count ourselves lucky we don't get stuck at the lowest level."

Riker's Island, the New York City jail given brand-name recognition via countless television crime dramas, consisted of ten separate penal facilities. It contained its own power plant, a laundry that saw a lot of orange coveralls, a bakery that made seven kinds of bread, and convenience shops for the benefit of residents who needed soap, razors or condoms. Prisoners awaiting trial, sentencing or transfer to upstate institutions cooled their heels here, along with inmates serving sentences of less than a year. No one called it home but roughly 16,000 men and women who'd made their own beds were now forced to sleep in them there every night, reflecting upon the folly of their ways.

It was a ten-minute drive from LaGuardia to Riker's, but it took half an hour for Blaikie and Crowe to get through the security to the interview rooms where Detectives Levinson and Rossimoff were doing double duty in a tag-team interrogation that had lasted almost 36 hours.

Levinson, looking like he hadn't shaved, washed nor eaten a proper meal in days, took them to an observation room with a one-way window looking into an interrogation room. Detective Rossimoff, looking more surly than usual, sat at the observation window, silently watching the occupants next door. A toothpick shifted from one side of his mouth to the other.

On the other side of the window, a haggard Jeb Stockwell in orange coveralls sat at a metal table with a man in his mid-fifties.

"His lawyer?" Blaikie asked.

Rossimoff nodded.

"Did you tell Jeb that Carrie was dead?" Crowe asked Levinson.

"I said the FBI had caught her. I told him she had her story but we'd like to hear his before we finalized charges against them. Leave it to his imagination to fill in the rest. I said we knew everything except for a few details." Levinson looked at the clock above the observation window. "He's been with his lawyer an hour now. Maybe by midnight, he'll be ready to plead out."

Crowe watched Stockwell, whose head was scrunched between his shoulders, arms crossed over his chest, hugging himself. When he briefly tugged a hand loose to scratch his nose, Crowe saw his thumb was locked tightly inside his fist.

"Judging by his body language, he's ready now."

"Let's see." Levinson rapped on the window to get their attention. Stockwell and his lawyer looked up. Levinson pressed an intercom button. "Ready to resume talking?"

The lawyer made a beckoning motion with his hand.

Levinson flipped a switch on a control panel. "Sound's on now, you can listen in," he told Blaikie and Crowe.

The two detectives entered the interrogation room and sat at the table opposite Stockwell and his lawyer.

"So, what have you got to say?" Levinson asked Stockwell.

"What are you offering?" the lawyer said.

"We can talk to the DA but you know the drill. Twenty-five to life if we go to trial. Maybe fifteen if he confesses. Depends on his story."

Stockwell grimaced. His lawyer shrugged, it doesn't get any better. He whispered in Stockwell's ear. Stockwell clasped his hands together as if in prayer.

"From the first time I got in bed with her, I knew I was out of my league," Stockwell began. "She was a first-class manipulator, even way back then as a Berkeley sophomore. She had guys twisted around her little finger. Munson and I just became her favorites."

"It was all her idea?"

"First time I heard it was ten years ago. One of those crazy what-if scenarios she came up with one night over a few joints and a bottle of tequila. Every now and again she brought it up, each time with more details sketched in, like she'd actually been thinking about it in between."

"What about Munson?"

"Dave didn't know whether to take her seriously or not. She had lots of crazy ideas and sometimes she did crazy things. Once while she was still in Berkeley she'd fucked this rich guy and then blackmailed him under threat of ruining his marriage. She said it was all fair game, that rich people should pay for their stupid mistakes."

"Kind of a coincidence you all ended up with wealthy partners."

"More like good luck. We should have left it at that."

"Why didn't you?"

Stockwell rubbed his face and examined his hands, as if he expected to find something there. "I fell in love with an illusion." He laughed. "I thought I could have it all."

"What do you mean?"

"Get both the money and the younger woman."

"What about Munson?"

"He knew Lang was seeing someone else and suspected it was getting serious. It was just a matter of time before Lang told him to move out."

"And Carrie?"

"She'd been fed up with her husband for a long time. Their sex life was dead and she was tired of sneaking around. She'd given him a chance to save their marriage but he still spent all his time on the job."

"Under those circumstances most people just get a no-fault divorce."

"She always said, if she had to sell her freedom for marriage, she should be well paid for it. It was her way of making sure she got what she deserved."

"So things just happened to converge...?"

Stockwell shrugged. "Carrie had kept in touch with us over the years. She liked to travel. New York and San Francisco, she was back and forth all the time. She kept stoking the fires... She had a sense we'd all reached the end of our ropes and it was time to, you know..."

"...to do what?

"Kill each other's partners."

"How was that going to work?"

"She had it all figured out. We'd each have the perfect out-of-town alibi. Like Hitchcock's *Strangers on a Train*, but a three-way."

"How'd she determine the timing?"

"The banking conference came up first. That was my excuse to go to San Francisco. Then Munson found the bowling tournament in Albuquerque, close enough to Santa Fe for our purposes. Once those were in place, Carrie arranged meetings with literary agents in New York."

"After that I suppose it was simple. Your victims were all creatures of habit."

Stockwell nodded. "Janis had a ticket for a show that Tuesday night. She always walked home from Broadway. I told Carrie where to intercept her. It was even easier in San Francisco. Lang took the same run every day. And in Santa Fe Carrie knew her husband would be home alone late at night."

"What happened there? If this was supposed to be a triple play, why didn't Munson kill Dr. Cassidy?"

"Dave choked in the ninth inning. The week before it was set to go down, he told me he couldn't do it. This was after Carrie had already arranged for an acquaintance of hers to provide Dave a gun in Albuquerque. Plan was, he'd drive up to Santa Fe Tuesday night, kill Cassidy and make it look like a burglary gone bad."

"And...?"

"He freaked. The more he thought about it, he knew he couldn't shoot anyone. He wanted to call the whole thing off but he was so afraid of Carrie, he talked to me first."

"What did you say?"

"I told him it wasn't any easier for me but if we wanted to get something out of this, we each had to do our parts. But if he just couldn't do it he'd better find some help. If he bailed now there was no telling how Carrie would react. She might have killed him."

"Did you really believe that?"

"We both did. We'd been in the same karate class with her. She lost her temper a few times and it was scary. When the instructor intervened she even turned on him. There was something in her, she could go ballistic in a heartbeat."

"So you came up with Plan B for Dave?"

"No, I give Dave credit for that, he worked it out on his

own. A couple of months earlier he'd borrowed sixty thousand dollars from Lang to buy into a music store in San Rafael. Lang gave him the money but the deal fell through at the last minute. Since Dave had decided not to tell Lang about it, it left him holding a considerable wad of cash."

"Which became his working capital..."

"The toughest part was convincing Carrie. She didn't like Plan B. The way she saw it, each of us had to be directly involved so that we'd all be equally guilty. But when she realized Dave just didn't have it in him, she agreed to let Zabriskie do his dirty work. Since Dave was hiring Zabriskie, that put him neck-deep in it with the rest of us."

Levinson placed a legal pad in front of Stockwell. "Write it all down. The players, the plans and what you personally did."

Stockwell's lawyer whispered something in his ear. Stockwell picked up the pen and began writing. Levinson and Rossimoff stood and left Stockwell to his allocution.

The two detectives rejoined Blaikie and Crowe in the observation room.

"Thank you." Blaikie shook each of their hands in turn. "You did a good job."

"Speaking of good jobs," Levinson said to Crowe, "That Zabriskie was a real professional. He had the FBI chasing their tails all week."

"Except he got too clever for his own good," Crowe said. "If he'd stuck with the planned burglary it might have been all right. I think there was history between Zabriskie and Carrie, and he tried to protect her. Rather than follow Munson's plan he decided to kill Dr. Cassidy outside his home and ahead of schedule, giving it a terrorist twist. But all those things just made it stand out a little more and drew the wrong kind of attention. It was supposed to be a simple three-way. Zabriskie's involvement compromised that simplicity and screwed up the symmetry of their plan."

"Up until then, they must have thought they'd planned the perfect crime," Levinson said.

Crowe shook his head. "Perfection is God's work. He guards it jealously."

75

New York

Blaikie and Crowe drove back into Queens, late-night jazz coming in clear and sweet on the car's sound system. Crowe looked up as an airliner completed its approach over the East River, dropping down toward LaGuardia. Must be hard, he thought, for inmates to watch those planes come and go while they remained cell-bound. That was fate. Most birds were free but some spent a lifetime in cages.

Blaikie took the ramp onto Grand Central Parkway and accelerated up to speed with the traffic into Manhattan. "I got a call from Lisa Carmichael today. Remember the client I sent you last week...?"

"Uh-huh."

"No sooner had the ink dried on the deed transfer, she got an offer on Friday from a Chinese multi-media company that wanted a SoHo address. She flipped the condo for a half-million profit. She asked what kind of wine you liked so she could send you a case."

"Did you tell her I wasn't much of a drinker?"

"I explained what a health freak you were," Blaikie chuckled. "So she's giving *me* the wine as a finder's fee, and sending you a case of mango juice instead."

"My guru would certainly approve."

"It gets better."

"How so?"

"I told her to throw in ten pounds of cashews."

Crowe had to laugh. Some people got paid peanuts, but he was different...

They pulled up in front of the Washington Square Hotel. Before Crowe got out, Blaikie thanked him again for what he'd done.

"It won't bring Janis back, but knowing Jeb will pay for what he's done to our family will help us sleep at night. Thank you again. Please send me your bill and I'll arrange for a funds transfer this week."

They shook hands. Crowe took his bag and got out. The Mercedes slid away into the night, its midnight blue embraced by the darkness.

Crowe checked in and went up to his room. He shaved and took a shower. Just as he was toweling off, his phone rang. Somehow he knew it would be Tracey.

The Author

Alan Annand has worked as an underground surveyor, technical writer, HR manager, astrologer and palmist. Previous writing credits include magazine articles, children's animation, and five novels under pseudonyms. Currently, he divides his time between writing in the AM, astrology in the PM, and meditation on the OM.

For other novels, short fiction and humor by Alan Annand, see his writing website *www.sextile.com*

For information about his services as an astrologer and palmist, see his other website *www.navamsa.com*

You can also find him on Facebook or follow him on LinkedIn, Pinterest, Tumblr and Twitter.

Made in the USA
Monee, IL
09 May 2021

68142374R00184